Praise for New Yo ... **Rae...**

"[Thayne] engages th ... heart and emotions, inspiring hope and the belief that miracles *are* possible."

—#1 *New York Times* bestselling author
Debbie Macomber

"RaeAnne Thayne is quickly becoming one of my favorite authors.... Once you start reading, you aren't going to be able to stop."

—*Fresh Fiction*

"Well-developed characters, plus plenty of raw emotion—and humor—add up to one of [Thayne's] finest books."

—*RT Book Reviews* on *His Second-Chance Family*
(4½ stars, Top Pick)

**Praise for USA TODAY bestselling author
Patricia Davids**

"Patricia Davids is one of the best writers in the Amish fiction genre. She's now on my must-read list!"

—Shelley Shepard Gray,
New York Times bestselling author

"Patricia Davids pens a captivating tale....
The Color of Courage is well researched, with a heartwarming conclusion."

—*RT Book Reviews*

RaeAnne Thayne finds inspiration in the beautiful northern Utah mountains, where the *New York Times* and *USA TODAY* bestselling author lives with her husband and three children. Her books have won numerous honors, including RITA® Award nominations from Romance Writers of America and a Career Achievement Award from *RT Book Reviews*. RaeAnne loves to hear from readers and can be contacted through her website, raeannethayne.com.

After thirty-five years as a nurse, **Patricia Davids** hung up her stethoscope to become a full-time writer. She enjoys spending her free time visiting her grandchildren, doing some long-overdue yard work and traveling to research her story locations. She resides in Wichita, Kansas. Patricia always enjoys hearing from her readers. You can visit her online at patriciadavids.com.

New York Times Bestselling Author

RaeAnne
Thayne

LIGHT THE STARS

**HARLEQUIN
BESTSELLING
AUTHOR
COLLECTION**

**HARLEQUIN®
BESTSELLING
AUTHOR
COLLECTION**

Recycling programs
for this product may
not exist in your area.

ISBN-13: 978-1-335-23300-4

Light the Stars
First published in 2006. This edition published in 2020.
Copyright © 2006 by RaeAnne Thayne

The Farmer Next Door
First published in 2011. This edition published in 2020.
Copyright © 2011 by Patricia MacDonald

This edition published by arrangement with Harlequin Books S.A.

For questions and comments about the quality of this book,
please contact us at CustomerService@Harlequin.com.

Harlequin Enterprises ULC
22 Adelaide St. West, 40th Floor
Toronto, Ontario M5H 4E3, Canada
www.Harlequin.com

Printed in U.S.A.

CONTENTS

LIGHT THE STARS
RaeAnne Thayne

7

THE FARMER NEXT DOOR
Patricia Davids

255

Also by RaeAnne Thayne

Harlequin Special Edition

The Cowboys of Cold Creek

The Cowboy's Christmas Miracle
A Cold Creek Homecoming
A Cold Creek Holiday
A Cold Creek Secret
A Cold Creek Baby
Christmas in Cold Creek
A Cold Creek Reunion
A Cold Creek Noel
A Cold Creek Christmas Surprise
The Christmas Ranch
A Cold Creek Christmas Story
The Holiday Gift
The Rancher's Christmas Song

The Women of Brambleberry House

A Soldier's Secret
His Second-Chance Family
The Daddy Makeover

HQN

Haven Point

Riverbend Road
Snowfall on Haven Point
Serenity Harbor
Sugar Pine Trail
The Cottages on Silver Beach
Season of Wonder

Visit her Author Profile page at Harlequin.com
or raeannethayne.com for more titles!

LIGHT THE STARS

RaeAnne Thayne

To Gail Chasan,
for helping me reach my own dreams.
Many, many thanks.

Chapter 1

On his thirty-sixth birthday, Wade Dalton's mother ran away.

She left him a German chocolate cake on the kitchen counter, two new paperback mysteries by a couple of his favorite authors and a short but succinct note in her loopy handwriting.

Honey,
Happy birthday. I'm sorry I couldn't be there to celebrate with you but by the time you read this we'll be in Reno and I'll be the new Mrs. Quinn Montgomery. I know you'll think I should have told you but my huggy bear thought it would be better this way. More romantic. Isn't that sweet? You'll love him, I promise! He's handsome, funny, and makes me feel like I can touch my

dreams again. Tell the children I love them and
I'll see them soon.

P.S. Nat's book report is due today. Don't let
her forget it!

P.P.S. Sorry to leave you in the lurch like this
but I figured you, Seth and Nat could handle
things without me for a week. Especially you.
You can handle anything.

Don't take this wrong, son, but it doesn't hurt
for you to remember your children are more important than your blasted cattle.

Be back after the honeymoon.

Wade stared at the note for a full five minutes, the
only sound in the Cold Creek Ranch kitchen the ticking of the pig-shaped clock Andi had loved above the
stove and the refrigerator compressor kicking to life.

What the hell was he supposed to do now?

His mother and this huggy bear creature couldn't
have chosen a worse time to pull their little disappearing act. Marjorie knew it, too, blast her hide. He needed
her help! He had six hundred head of cattle to get to
market before the snow flew, a horse show and auction
in Cheyenne in a few weeks, and a national TV news
crew coming in less than a week to film a feature on
the future of the American cattle ranch.

He was supposed to be showing off the ground-
breaking innovations he'd made to the ranch in the
last few years, showing the Cold Creek in the best
possible light.

How was he supposed to make sure everything
was ready and running smoothly while he changed

Cody's diapers and chased after Tanner and packed Nat's lunch?

He read the note again, anger beginning to filter through the dismayed shock. Something about what she had written seemed to thrum through his consciousness like a distant, familiar guitar chord. He was trying to figure out what when he heard the back-porch door creak and a moment later his youngest brother stumbled into the kitchen, bleary-eyed and in need of a shave.

"Coffee. I need it hot and black and I just realized I'm out down at my place."

Wade glared at him, seizing on the most readily available target for his frustration and anger. "You look like hell."

Seth shrugged. "Got in late. It was ladies' night down at the Bandito and I couldn't leave all those sweet girls shooting pool by themselves. Where's the coffee?"

"There isn't any coffee. Or breakfast, either. I don't suppose you happened to see Mom sneaking out at two in the morning when you were dragging yourself and, no doubt, one or two of those sweet girls back to the guesthouse?"

His brother blinked a couple of times to clear the remaining cobwebs from his brain. "What?"

Wade tossed the note at him and Seth scrubbed his bleary eyes before picking it up. A range of emotions flickered across his entirely too charming features—shock and confusion, then an odd pensiveness that raised Wade's hackles.

"Did you know about this?" he asked.

Seth slumped into a kitchen chair, avoiding his gaze. "Not this, precisely."

"What *precisely* did you know about what our dear mother's been up to?" Wade bit out.

"I knew she was emailing some guy she met through that life coach she's been talking to. I didn't realize it was serious. At least not run-off-to-Reno serious."

Suddenly this whole fiasco made a grim kind of sense and Wade realized what about Marjorie's note had struck that odd, familiar chord. *By the time you read this I'll be the new Mrs. Quinn Montgomery,* she had written.

Montgomery was the surname of the crackpot his mother had shelled out a small fortune to in the last six months, all in some crazy effort to better her life.

Caroline Montgomery.

He knew the name well since he'd chewed Marjorie out plenty the last time he'd balanced her checkbook for her and had found the name written on several hefty checks.

This was all this Caroline Montgomery's fault. It had to be. She must have planted ideas in Marjorie's head about how she wasn't happy, about how she needed more out of life. Fun, excitement. Romance. Then she introduced some slick older man—a brother? An uncle?—to bring a little spice into a lonely widow's world.

What had been so wrong with Marjorie's life, anyway, that she'd needed to find some stranger to fix it?

Okay, his mother had a few odd quirks. Today was not only his birthday, it was exactly the eighteen-year anniversary of his father's death and in those years, his mother had pursued one wacky thing after another. She did yoga, she balanced her chakras instead of her checkbook, she sponsored inflammatory little book-club meetings at the Pine Gulch library where she and her cronies read every controversial feminist, male-bashing self-help book they could find.

He had tried to be understanding about it all. Marjorie's marriage to Hank Dalton hadn't exactly been a happy one. His father had treated his mother with the same cold condescension he'd wielded like a club against his children. Once his father's death had freed Marjorie from that oppressive influence, Wade couldn't blame her for taking things a little too far in the opposite direction.

Besides, when he'd needed her in those terrible, wrenching days after Andrea's death, Marjorie had come through. Without him even having to ask, she'd packed up her crystals and her yoga mat and had moved back to the ranch to help him with the kids. He would have been lost without her, a single dad with three kids under the age of six, one of them only a week old.

He knew she wasn't completely happy with her life but he'd never thought she would go this far. She wouldn't have, he thought, if it hadn't been for this scheming Caroline Montgomery and whatever male relative she was in cahoots with.

He heard a belligerent yell coming from upstairs and wanted to pound his head on the table a few times. Six-thirty in the morning and it was already starting. How the hell was he going to do this?

"Want me to get Cody?" Seth asked as the cries rose in volume. *Gramma, Gramma, Gramma.*

Wade had to admit, the offer was a tempting one, but he forced himself to refuse. They were *his* children and he was the one who would have to deal with them.

He took off his denim jacket and hung his Stetson on the hook by the door.

"I'm on it. Just go take care of the stock and then we've all got to bring in the last hay crop we cut yesterday. The weather report says rain by afternoon so we've got to get it in fast. I'll figure something out with the kids and get out there to help as soon as I can."

Seth opened his mouth to say something then must have thought better of it. He nodded. "Right. Good luck."

You're going to need it. His brother left the words unspoken but Wade heard them anyway.

He couldn't agree more.

Two hours later, Wade was rapidly coming to the grim realization that he was going to need a hell of a lot more than luck.

"Hold still," he ordered a squirmy, giggling Cody as he tried to stick on a diaper. Through the open doorway into the kitchen, he could hear Tanner and Natalie bickering.

"Daaaad," his eight-year-old daughter called out, "Tanner's flicking Cheerios at me. Make him stop! He's getting the new shirt Grandma bought me all wet and blotchy!"

"Tanner, cut it out," he hollered. "Nat, if you don't quit stalling over your breakfast, you're going to miss the bus and I don't have time to drive you today."

"You never have time for anything," he thought he heard her mutter but just then he felt an ominous warmth hit his chest. He looked down to the changing table to find Cody grinning up at him.

"Cody pee pee."

Wade ground his back teeth, looking down at the wet stain spreading across his shirt. "Yeah, kid, I kind of figured that out."

He quickly fastened the diaper and threw on the overalls and Spider-Man shirt Cody insisted on wearing, all the while aware of a gnawing sense of inadequacy in his gut.

He wasn't any good at this. He loved his kids but it had been a whole lot easier being their father when Andrea was alive.

She'd been the one keeping their family together. The one who'd scheduled immunizations and fixed Nat's hair into cute little ponytails and played Chutes and Ladders for hours at a time. His role had been the benevolent dad who showed up at bedtime and sometimes broke away from ranch chores for Sunday brunch.

The two years since her death had only reinforced how inept he was at the whole parenting gig. If it hadn't been for Marjorie coming to his rescue, he didn't know what he would have done.

Probably flounder around cluelessly, just like he was doing now, he thought.

He started to carry Cody back to the kitchen to finish his breakfast but the toddler was having none of it. "Down, Daddy. Down," he ordered, bucking and wriggling worse than a calf on his way to an appointment with the castrator.

Wade set his feet on the ground and Cody raced toward the kitchen. "Nat, can you watch Cody for a minute?" he called. "I've got to go change my shirt."

"Can't," she hollered back. "The bus is here."

"Don't forget your book report," he remembered at

the last minute, but the door slammed on his last word and he was pretty sure she hadn't heard him.

With a quick order to Tanner to please behave himself for five minutes, he carried Cody upstairs with him and grabbed his last clean shirt out of the closet. The least his mother could have done was wait until *after* laundry day to pull her disappearing act, he thought wryly. Now he was going to have to do that, too.

He grabbed Cody and headed back down the stairs. They had nearly reached the bottom when the doorbell pealed.

"I'll get it," Tanner yelled and headed for the front door, still in his pajamas.

"No, me! Me!" Not to be outdone, Cody squirmed out of Wade's arms and slid down the last few steps. Wade wasn't sure how they did it, but both boys beat him to the door, even though he'd been closer.

Tanner opened it, then turned shy at the strange woman standing before him. Wade couldn't blame him. Their visitor was lovely, he observed as he reached the door behind his sons, with warm, streaky brown hair pulled back into a smooth twisty thing, eyes the color of hot chocolate on a cold winter day and graceful, delicate features.

She wore a tailored russet jacket, tan slacks and a crisp white shirt, with a chunky bronze necklace and matching earrings, a charm bracelet on one arm and a slim gold watch on the other.

Wade had no idea who she was and she didn't seem in any hurry to introduce herself. Probably some tourist who'd taken the wrong road out of Jackson, he thought, and needed help finding her way.

Finally he spoke.

"Can I help you?"

"Oh. Yes." Color flared on those high cheekbones and she blinked a few times as if trying to compose herself. "The sign out front said the Cold Creek Ranch. Is this the right place?"

No. Not a lost tourist. As Tanner peeked around Wade's legs and Cody held his chubby little arms out to be lifted again, Wade's gaze traveled from the woman's pretty, streaky hair to her expensive leather shoes, looking for some clue as to what she might be doing on his front porch.

If she was some kind of ranch supply salesperson, she was definitely a step above the usual. He had a lowering suspicion he'd buy whatever she was selling.

"You found us."

Relief flickered across her expressive features. "Oh, I'm so glad. The directions weren't exactly clear and I stopped at two other ranches before this one. I'd like to see Marjorie Dalton, please."

Yeah, wouldn't they all like to see her right about now? "There I'm afraid you're out of luck. She's not here."

Right before his eyes, the lovely, self-assured woman on his porch seemed to fold into herself. Her shoulders sagged, her mouth drooped and she closed her eyes. When she opened them, he saw for the first time the weariness there and was uncomfortably aware of an odd urge to comfort her, to tuck her close and assure her everything would be all right.

"Can you tell me…that is, do you know where I might find her?"

He didn't want to spill his mother's whereabouts to some strange woman, no matter how she mysteriously plucked all his protective strings. "Why don't you tell me your business with her and I'll get her a message?"

"It's complicated. And personal."

"Then you'll have to come back in a week or so."

He had to hope by then Marjorie would come to her senses and be back where she belonged.

"A week?" His visitor blanched. "Oh no! I'm too late. She's not here, is she?"

"That's what I said, isn't it?"

"No, I mean she's really not here. She's not just in town shopping or something. They've run off, haven't they?"

He stared at her, wariness blooming in his gut. "Who are you and what do you want with my mother?"

The woman gave a weary sigh. "You must be Wade. I've heard a lot about you. My name is Caroline Montgomery. I've been in correspondence with Marjorie for the last six months. I don't know how to tell you this, Mr. Dalton, but I think Marjorie has run off with my father."

The big, gorgeous man standing in front of her with one cute little boy hanging off his belt loop and another in his arms didn't look at all shocked by her bombshell. No, shock definitely wasn't the emotion that hardened his mouth and tightened those stunning blue eyes into dime slots.

He brimmed with fury—toe-curling, hair-scorching anger. Caroline took an instinctive step back, until the weave of her jacket bumped against the peeled log of his porch.

"Your father!" he bit out. "I should have known.

What is it they say about apples not falling far from the tree?"

Maybe if she wasn't so blasted tired from traveling all night, she might have known what he was talking about. "I'm sorry?"

"What's the matter, lady? You weren't bilking Marjorie out of enough with your hefty life-coaching fees so you decided to go for the whole enchilada?"

She barely had time to draw a breath before he went on.

"Quite a racket you and your old man have. How many wealthy widows have you pulled this on? You drag them in, worm out all the details about their financial life, then your old man moves in for the kill."

Caroline wanted to sway from the force of the blow that hit entirely too close to home. She felt sick, hideously sick, and bitterly angry that Quinn would once more put her in this position. How else was all this supposed to look, especially given her father's shady past?

She wouldn't give this arrogant man the satisfaction of knowing he'd drawn blood, though. Instead she forced her spine to straighten, vertebra by vertebra.

"You're wrong."

"Am I?"

"Yes! I was completely shocked by this sudden romance. My father said nothing about it to me—I didn't know he and Marjorie had even met until he sent me an email last night telling me he was flying out to meet her and they were heading straight from here to Reno."

"Why should I believe you?"

"I don't care if you believe me or not! It's the truth."

How much of her life had been spent defending herself because of something Quinn had done? She had vowed she was done with it but now she wondered grimly if she ever would be.

What was Quinn up to? Just once, she wished she knew. With all her heart, she wanted to believe his sudden romance was the love match he had intimated in his email.

I never meant for this to happen. It took us both completely by surprise. But in just a few short months I've discovered I can't live without her. Marjorie is my other half—the missing piece of my life's puzzle. She knows all my mistakes, all my blemishes, but she loves me anyway. How lucky am I?

Caroline was romantic enough to hope Quinn's hearts-and-flowers email was genuine. Her mother had been dead for twenty-two years now and, as far as she knew, her father's love life was as exciting as her own—i.e., about as thrilling as watching paint dry.

But how could she trust his word, after years of his schemes and swindles? Especially when the missing piece of his life's puzzle was one of *her* clients? She couldn't. She just *couldn't.*

What if Quinn was spinning some new scam? Something involving Marjorie Dalton—and tangentially, Caroline's reputation? She would be ruined. Everything she had worked so hard for these last five years, her safe, comfortable, *respectable* life, would crumble away like a sugar castle in a hurricane.

Caroline knew what was at stake: her reputation, which in the competitive world of life coaching was everything. As soon as she'd read his email, she had been struck with a familiar cold dread and knew she would have to track him down to gauge his motives for herself—or to talk him out of this crazy scheme to marry a woman he had only corresponded with via email.

Her first self-help book was being released in five months and if her publisher caught wind of this, they would not be happy. She'd be lucky if her book wasn't yanked right off the schedule.

That's why she had traveled all night to find herself here at nine in the morning, facing down a gorgeous rancher and his two cute little boys.

But she wasn't going to accomplish anything by antagonizing Marjorie's son, she realized. She took a deep, cleansing breath and forced her expression into a pleasant smile, her voice into the low, calming tones she used with her clients.

"Look, I'm sorry. It's been a long night. I had two connector flights from Santa Cruz and an hour's drive from Idaho Falls to get here and I'm afraid I'm not at my best. May I come in so we can discuss what's to be done about our runaway parents?"

She wasn't sure how he would have answered if the cell phone clipped to his belt hadn't suddenly bleeped.

With a grim glare—at her or at the person waiting on the other end of the line or at the world in general, she didn't know—then gestured for her to come inside.

"Yeah?" he growled into the phone as the toddler in his arms wiggled and bucked to get down. Wade Dalton let the boy down, busy on the phone discussing in increasingly heated tones what sounded like a major problem with some farm machinery. She caught a few familiar words like *stalling out* and *alternator* but the rest sounded like a foreign language.

"We don't have a choice. The baler's got to be fixed today. That hay has to come in," he snapped.

While she listened to his end of the conversation about various options for fixing the recalcitrant machine, Caroline took the opportunity to study Wade Dalton's home.

Though the ranch house had soaring ceilings and gorgeous views of the back side of the Tetons, it was anything but ostentatious. The furniture looked comfortable but worn, toys were jumbled together in one corner, and the nearest coffee table was covered in magazines. An odd assortment of circulations, too, she noticed. Everything from *O*—Marjorie's, she assumed—to *Nick Jr.* to *Farm & Ranch Living.*

The room they stood in obviously served as the gathering place for the Dalton family. Cartoons flickered on a big-screen TV in one corner and that's where the little blond toddler had headed after Wade had set him down. She watched him for a moment as he picked up a miniature John Deere and started plowing the carpet, one eye on the screen.

The older boy had vanished. She only had a moment to wonder where in the big house he'd gone when Wade Dalton hung up the phone.

"Sorry. Where were we?" he said.

"Discussing what's to be done about our parents, I believe."

"As I see it, we don't have too many options. It's too late to go after them. I'm assuming they left about midnight, which means they've got a nine-hour head start on us. They'd be married long before we even made it to the Nevada state line. Beyond the fact that I can't leave the ranch right now, I wouldn't know where the hell to even start looking for them in Reno since my mother's not answering her cell phone."

"Neither is Quinn," Caroline said glumly.

"I can't believe Marjorie would do something like this, just run off and leave the kids. This is your doing."

So much for their thirty-second ceasefire. "Mine?"

"You're the one who's been telling her to reach for her dreams or whatever the hell other nonsense you spout in your sessions with her."

"You don't think reaching for dreams is important?"

"Sure I do. But not when it means walking away from your responsibilities."

"Since when are *your* children your mother's responsibility?" she snapped.

Again she had to force herself not to step back from the sudden fury in his eyes. She had to admit she deserved it this time.

"That was uncalled for. I'm sorry," Caroline said quietly. "Marjorie has been caring for Nat and Cody and Tanner for two years. She doesn't see it as a burden at all."

"Right. That's why she's been paying a small fortune to some stranger so you can tell her all the things wrong with her life and how to fix them."

"That's not what I do at all," she insisted. "I try to help my clients make their lives happier and more fulfilling by pointing out some of their own self-destructive behavior and giving them concrete steps toward changing what they're unhappy about. Marjorie was never unhappy about you and your children."

Before she could continue, his phone bleeped again. He ignored it for four rings, then muttered an oath and picked it up.

This conversation was similar to the first, only Wade Dalton seemed to grow increasingly frustrated with each passing second.

"Look," he finally said angrily, "just call the tractor supply place in Rexburg and see if they've got a replacement, then you can send Drifty over to pick it up. I'll be out as soon as I can. If we put the whole crew out there this afternoon, we might still be able to get the hay in before the rain."

He hung up and then faced her again. "I don't have time to get into this with you today, Ms. Montgomery. I'm sorry you came all this way for nothing but I think we're too late to do anything about the two lovebirds. I'll warn you, though, that if your father thinks he's going to touch a penny of the income from this ranch, you're both in for one hell of a fight."

"Warning duly noted," she said tightly, wondering how a woman as fun and bubbly as Marjorie could have such an arrogant jerk for a son, no matter how gorgeous he might be.

She should cut him some slack, Caroline thought as she headed for the door. He obviously had his hands full, a widower with three active children and a busy cattle ranch.

Just as she reached the door, an acrid scent drifted from the back of the house, stopping her in her tracks.

"Do you smell something?" she asked Wade Dalton.

"It's a working ranch. We've got all kinds of smells."

"No, this is different. It smells like something's on fire."

He sniffed the air for a second, then his eyes narrowed. He looked around the gathering room, his eyes on his youngest son still playing on the carpet and the notable absence of the older boy.

"Tanner!" he suddenly roared. "What are you doing?"

"Nothing!" came a small, frightened-sounding voice from the rear of the house. "I'm not doin' anything. Anything at all. Don't come in the kitchen, Daddy, okay?"

Wade closed his eyes for half a second then took off down a hallway at a fast run.

This wasn't any of her business, she knew, but Caroline had no choice but to follow.

Chapter 2

Hot on Wade Dalton's worn boots, Caroline had a quick impression of a large, old-fashioned kitchen painted a sunny yellow with a professional-looking six-burner stove, long breakfast bar and at least eight bow-backed chairs snugged up against a massive, scarred pine table.

She imagined under other circumstances it would be a pleasant, welcoming space, but just now the room was thick with black smoke and the acrid smell of scorched paper and something sickly sweet.

Flames shot up from the stove and she quickly realized why—a roll of paper towels was ablaze next to the gas burner and already flames were scorching up the cabinets.

Even more worrisome, the older of Wade Dalton's sons was standing on a chair he must have pulled up to the stove and his SpongeBob SquarePants pajamas were perilously close to the small fire.

"I'm sorry, Daddy," the boy sniffled.

"Get down right now!" Wade yelled in that no-argument parental tone reserved for situations like this.

Though she sensed the rancher's harshness stemmed from fear for his son's safety, his words and tone still seemed to devastate the boy into inaction. He froze on his precarious perch until his father had to lift him off the chair and set him on the floor so he could get close enough to assess the cabinets.

Wade picked up the burning mess of towels and dropped them into the sink then returned to survey the damage.

Still, the boy didn't move, standing as if he didn't quite know what was happening. He looked ill, almost shocky, and he stood directly in Wade Dalton's path.

This wasn't any of her business, Caroline reminded herself. Even as she thought it, she found herself moving toward the distraught little boy.

What was his name? Tucker? Taylor? *Tanner.* That was it. "Tanner, why don't we get out of your daddy's way and let him take care of things here, okay?"

He looked at her blankly for a moment, then slipped his hand in hers and let Caroline lead him from the room. She took him into the great room where his little brother was still busy with his trucks, unaffected by the drama playing out in the other room.

She was going to ask if he had a favorite television show she could find for him as a distraction when she noticed his left hand pressed tightly to his pajama top.

A grim suspicion seized her and she leaned down. "Tanner, can I take a look at your hand? Are you hurt?"

His chin wobbled for a moment, then he nodded slowly and pulled his hand away from his chest. He made a small sound of distress when he spread out his fingers—and no wonder.

Caroline gasped at the angry, blistering red splotch covering his palm, roughly twice the size of a quarter. "Oh, honey!"

Her reaction seemed to open the floodgates of emotion. Tears pooled in his huge blue eyes and rolled over pale cheeks. "I didn't mean to start a fire. I didn't mean to! I just wanted to roast marshmallows like me and Nat and Grandma did with Uncle Seth when we went campin'. Do you think my daddy will be mad at me?"

She thought that was a pretty good bet. Wade Dalton seemed mad at the entire world, as a matter of course. How would he treat his son, angry or not? That was the important thing.

"I'm sure he'll just be worried about you," she assured Tanner, though she wasn't at all convinced of that herself.

"He's gonna be so mad. I'm not supposed to be in the kitchen by myself." His tears were coming faster now and she knew she had to do something quick to head them off or he would soon be in hysterics. Action seemed the best antidote.

"Let's just get your hurt taken care of and then we'll worry about your dad, okay?"

He nodded and Caroline thought quickly back to her thin and purely basic knowledge of first aid.

"We need to put some cold water on that," she told Tanner, her mind trying to dredge old lessons she'd learned as a girl. "Do you think you can show me a bathroom?"

"Yeah. There's one right through those doors."

She led him there quickly and filled the sink with cold water, then grasped his wrist and immersed it in the sink, though he wasn't keen on the idea.

"I don't want to," he said, sniffling. "It hurts."

"I know, honey. I'm sorry to make you hurt more but this way we can be sure the burn stops."

"Tannoh owie?"

Caroline looked down and found the youngest one had followed them into the small bathroom. Within fifteen seconds, she wasn't sure what held more interest to him—his brother's owie or the lid of the toilet, which he repeatedly flipped up and down with a nerve-racking clatter each time.

Her repertoire of distractions was severely limited but she thought maybe she could tell him a story or something, just to keep him away from the toilet and away from his brother.

"Hey, kiddo," she began.

"His name is Cody," Tanner informed her, his sniffles momentarily subsiding. "He's two and I'm five. I just had a birthday."

"Five is a fun age," she started, but her words were cut off by a loud and angry voice from outside the room.

"Tanner Michael Dalton! Where are you? Get in here and help me clean up the mess you made!"

Caroline took an instinctive step closer to the boy. What a disagreeable man, she thought, until she remembered that he likely knew nothing about his son's injuries.

"We're in the bathroom," she called down the hall. "Do you think you could come in here for a moment?"

Silence met her request for a full five seconds, then Wade spoke in an annoyed-sounding voice. "What is it? I'm kind of in the middle of something here."

Suddenly there he was in the doorway, two hundred pounds of angry male looking extremely put-upon, as if she'd pulled him away from saving the world to ask his opinion on what shade of lipstick to use.

This was his own son and she wouldn't let him make her feel guilty for her compassion toward the boy. Caroline tilted her chin up and faced him down.

"We're in the middle of something, too. Something I think you're going to want to see."

He squeezed into a bathroom that had barely held Caroline and two young boys. Throw in a large, gorgeous, angry rancher and the room seemed to shrink to the size of a tissue box.

"What is it?" he asked.

She pointed to Tanner's soaking hand, a vivid, angry red, and watched the boy's father blanch.

He hissed an oath, something she gauged by Tanner's surprised reaction wasn't something the boy normally heard from his father.

She had to admit, the shock and concern on Wade's features went a long way toward making her more sympathetic toward him.

"Tanner!" he exclaimed. "You burned yourself?"

"It was an accident, Daddy."

"Why didn't you say something?"

Tanner shrugged his narrow shoulders. "I was trying to be a big boy, not a b-baby."

The sympathy from his father was apparently more than Tanner's remarkable composure could withstand. The boy's sniffles suddenly turned to wails.

"I'm sorry, Daddy. I'm sorry. I won't do it again. I *won't,* I promise. It hurts a lot."

Wade picked up his son and held him against his broad, denim-covered chest. "Okay, honey. Okay. We'll take care of it, I promise. We'll find your Uncle Jake and he'll fix you right up."

Cody looked from his crying brother to their father's obvious concern and started wailing, from fear or just sympathy, Caroline wasn't sure. Soon the small bathroom echoed with loud sobs.

After a moment of that, Wade's eyes started to look panicky, like he'd just found himself trapped in a cage of snakes—except she had the feeling he would have preferred the snakes to two bawling kids.

Finally Caroline took pity on him and picked up the crying toddler. He was heavier than she expected, a solid little person in a Spider-Man shirt. "You're okay, sweetie. Your brother just has an owie."

The curly blond cherub wiped his nose with his forefinger. "Tan-noh owie."

"Yep. But he'll be okay, I promise."

"Uncle Jake will make it all better," Wade said, a kind of desperate hope in his voice. "Come on, let's go find him."

He led the way out of the room. Once free of the bathroom's confining space, Caroline could finally make her brain function again. She considered the ability to once more take a breath a nice bonus.

Wade carried Tanner toward the front door and she followed with the younger boy in her arms.

"Look, you're going to have enough on your hands at the clinic," she said. "Why don't I stay here with Cody while you take care of Tanner?"

It took a second for Wade's attention to shift from his injured son to her, something she found rather touching—until she saw suspicion bloom on his features.

"No. He can come with us to the clinic."

"Are you sure? I don't mind watching him for you."

She didn't need to hear his answer—the renewed animosity in his eyes was answer enough. "Lady, I don't know you from Adam," he snapped. "I'm not leaving my son here with you."

"Would you like me to come with you and then watch him in the clinic while you're occupied with Tanner's hand?"

He frowned, obviously annoyed by her persistence. Good heavens, did he think she was going to kidnap the child?

"No. He's fine with me. I'm sure there's somebody in Jake's office who could watch Cody while we're in the exam room."

With Tanner in one arm, he scooped up the toddler in the other and carried both boys out the door, toward a huge mud-covered silver pickup truck parked in the circular driveway.

Not sure what to do next, Caroline stood on the broad porch of the ranch house and watched as he strapped both boys into the truck. Wade seemed to have forgotten her very existence. In fact, a moment later he climbed into the driver's seat and drove away without once looking back at the house.

Now that the first adrenaline surge from the fire and dealing with Tanner's burn had passed, Caroline was aware of a bone-deep exhaustion. She had almost forgotten her long night of traveling and the worry over

Quinn's whirlwind romance with one of her clients. Now, as she stood alone on the ranch house porch with a cool October wind teasing the ends of her hair, everything came rushing back.

Since she was apparently too late to stop her father from eloping with Marjorie, she should probably just drive her rental back to the airport and catch the quickest flight to California.

On the other hand, that kitchen was still a mess, she was sure. She could scrub down the smoke-damaged kitchen while Wade was gone, perhaps even fix a warm meal for their return.

It was the least she could do, really. None of this would have happened if her father hadn't run off with Marjorie.

She wasn't breaking her vow, Caroline told herself as she walked back into the house and shut the cool fall air behind her. She wasn't cleaning up after her father's messes, something she had sworn never to do again. She was only helping out a man who had his hands full.

She tried to tell herself she wasn't splitting hairs, but even as she went back into the smoke-damaged kitchen and rolled up her sleeves, she wasn't quite convinced.

"There you go, partner. Now you've got the mummy claw of death to scare Nat with when she comes home from school."

Tanner giggled at his uncle Jake and moved his gauze-wrapped hand experimentally. "It still hurts," he complained.

"Sorry, kid." Jake squeezed his shoulder. "I can give you some medicine so it won't hurt quite so bad. But when you try to put out a fire all by yourself, sometimes you get battle scars. Next time call your dad right away."

"There won't be a next time. Right, Tanner?" Wade said sternly. "You've learned your lesson about roasting marshmallows—or anything else—by yourself."

Tanner sighed. "I guess. I don't like havin' a burn."

Jake straightened. "You were really brave while I was looking at it. I was proud of you, bud. Now you have to be a big kid and make sure you take care of it right. You can't get the bandage wet and you have to try to keep it as clean as you can, okay? Listen to your dad and do what he says."

"Okay." Tanner wiggled off the exam bench. "Can I go ask Carol for my sucker now?"

"Sure. Tell her a big brave kid like you deserves two suckers."

"And a sticker?"

Jake hammed a put-upon sigh. "I guess."

Tanner raised his bandaged hand into the air with delight then rushed out of the exam room, leaving Wade alone with his younger brother.

Unlike old Doc Jorgensen who had run the clinic when they were kids—with his gnarled hands and breath that always smelled of the spearmint toothpicks he chewed—Jake didn't wear a white lab coat in the office. The stethoscope around his neck and the shirt pocket full of tongue depressors gave him away, though.

Wade watched his brother type a few things onto a slender laptop computer—notes for Tanner's chart—and wondered how the little pest in hand-me-down boots and a too-big cowboy hat who used to follow him around the ranch when they were kids had grown into this confident, competent physician.

This wasn't a life Wade would have chosen, either for himself or for his brother, but he had always known Jake hadn't been destined to stay on the ranch. His middle brother was three years younger than he was and, as long as Wade could remember, Jake had carried big dreams inside himself.

He had always read everything he could find and had rarely been without a book in his hand. Whether they'd been waiting at the end of the long drive for the school bus or taking a five minute break from fixing fence lines, Jake had filled every spare moment with learning.

Wade had powerful memories of going on roundup more than once with Jake when his brother would look for strays with one eye and keep the other on the book he'd held.

He loved him. He just never claimed to understand him.

But there was not one second when he'd been anything less than proud of Jake for his drive and determination, for the compassion and caring he showed to the people of Pine Gulch, and for coming home instead of putting his medical skills to work somewhere more lucrative.

After another few seconds of pounding the keys, Jake closed his laptop.

"Well, I'd tell you happy birthday but it sounds like it's a little too late for that."

Wade made a face. "You can say that again. It's been a hell of a day."

"And just think, it's only noon. Who knows what other fun might be in store."

Wade sighed heavily. Noon already and he hadn't done a damn thing all day. He had a million things to do and now he had a little wounded firefighter who couldn't get his bandage dirty to think about.

His mother ought to be here, blast her. He was no good at the nurturing, sympathy thing. Did she ever stop to consider one of the kids might need her to shower kisses and sympathy?

"So what do you suggest we do about Mom?" he asked.

Jake leaned a hip against the exam table, and Wade thought again how he seemed to fit here in this medical clinic, in a way he'd never managed at the Cold Creek.

"What *can* we do? Sounds like the deed is done."

"We don't have to like it, though."

"I don't know. She's been alone a long time. It's been eighteen years since Hank died and even before that, her life with our dear departed father couldn't have been all roses. If this Montgomery guy makes her happy, I think we should stand behind her."

He stared at his brother. The finest education didn't do a man much good if he lost all common sense. "What do you mean, stand behind her? She doesn't even know the guy! How can we possibly support her eloping with a man she's only corresponded with through email and clandestine phone calls? And what kind of slimy bastard runs off with a woman he's never seen in person? He's got to be working some kind of scam. He and the daughter are in it together."

"You don't know that."

"They've got to be. She trolls for unhappy older

women through this life-coaching baloney, finds a vulnerable target like Mom, and then he steps in and charms them out of everything they've got."

"You're such a romantic," Jake said dryly.

"I don't have time to be a romantic, damn it. I've got a national television crew coming to the ranch in six days. How can I possibly get ready for this video shoot when I've got three kids underfoot every second?"

"You could always cancel it."

He glowered at Jake. "You're not helping."

"Why not? It's just a video shoot."

"Just a video shoot I've been working toward for almost a year! This is huge publicity for the ranch. We're one of only a handful of cattle operations in the country using this high-tech data-collection chip on our stock. You know how much of an investment it was for us but it's all part of our strategy of moving the ranch onto the industry's cutting edge. To be recognized for that right now is a big step for the Cold Creek. I don't know why Mom couldn't have scheduled her big rendezvous *after* the news crew finished."

"So what will you do with the kids?"

"I'm still trying to figure that out. You're the smart one. Any suggestions?"

"You could hire a temporary nanny, just until after the video shoot is over. Didn't Mom's note say she'd be back in a week?"

He started to answer but stopped when he heard Cody wailing from the reception area, something about a "stick-oh."

Wade sighed and headed toward the sound, Jake right behind him.

"Right. A week. Let's hope I'm still sane by then."

* * *

Cody fell asleep on the six-mile drive from Jake's clinic in Pine Gulch to Cold Creek Ranch. Tanner, jacked up by the excitement of the morning and probably still running on adrenaline, kept up a steady stream of conversation that didn't give Wade a minute to think about what he was going to do.

Tanner didn't even stop his running commentary during the phone call Wade took on his cell from Seth, who informed him glumly that the shop in Rexburg wouldn't have the part they needed for the baler until the next day. Without it, they wouldn't be able to bring the hay in, which meant they might lose the whole damn crop to the rain.

"I'm almost home. I'll get the boys some lunch and then try to come down and see if we can jury-rig something until tomorrow."

The clouds continued to boil and churn overhead as he drove under the arch that read Cold Creek Land and Cattle Company, and Wade could feel bony fingers of tension dig into his shoulders.

Sometimes he hated the responsibility that came from being the one in charge. He hated knowing he held the livelihood of his own family and those of three other men in his hands, that his every decision could make or break the ranch.

He couldn't just take a week off and play Mr. Mom. Too much depended on him meeting his responsibilities, especially right now.

But who could he ask for help? His mind went through everyone he could think of among their neighbors and friends.

His wife's family had sold their ranch a year ago and

her parents were serving in South America as missionaries for their church.

Viviana Cruz was the next logical choice. She owned the small ranch that adjoined the Cold Creek to the west and was his mother's best friend as well as a sort of surrogate grandmother to his kids. Unfortunately, she had left the week before to spend some time with her daughter in Arizona before Maggie's national guard unit shipped off to Afghanistan.

He couldn't think of anyone else, off the top of his head. Everyone who came to mind was either busy with their own ranch or their own kids or already had a job.

Seth knew every female with a pulse in a fifty-mile radius. Maybe his brother could think of somebody in his vast network who might be suitable to help with the kids for a week. Though it didn't really have to be a woman, he supposed as he pulled up to the back door of the ranch house.

"Can I watch TV?" Tanner asked when Wade unhooked him from his booster seat.

"Sure. Just no soap operas."

He grinned at the wrinkled-up face Tanner made. "Yuck," the boy exclaimed. "I hate those shows. Grandma watches them sometimes but they're so *boring!*"

By that, Wade assumed he didn't have to worry about Tanner developing a deep and abiding love for drama in the afternoons.

His injury apparently forgotten for now, Tanner skipped up the steps and into the house, leaving Wade to carefully unhook the sleeping Cody and heft him to his shoulder, holding his breath that he could keep the boy sleep. Cody murmured something unintelligible then burrowed closer.

So far so good, Wade thought as he went inside and headed straight up the back stairs to Cody's bedroom.

This was always the tricky part, putting him into his bed without disturbing him enough to wake him. He held his breath and lowered him to the crib mattress.

Cody arched a little and slid toward the top edge, where he liked to sleep, but didn't open his eyes. After a breathless moment, Wade covered him with his Bob the Builder quilt, then returned downstairs to find Tanner and figure something out for lunch.

He found Tanner in the great room with the TV on, the volume turned low.

"Can you even hear that?" Wade asked.

Tanner answered by putting a finger to his mouth. "Quiet, Daddy. You'll wake up the lady."

Wade frowned. "What lady?"

Tanner pointed to the other couch, just out of his field of vision. Wade moved forward for a better view and stared at the sight of Caroline Montgomery curled up on his couch, her shoes off and her lovely features still and peaceful.

Looked like she had made herself right at home in his absence.

He wasn't sure why the discovery should send this hot beam of fury through him, but he couldn't stop it any more than he could control those clouds gathering outside.

Chapter 3

"Hey lady! Wake up!"

Caroline barely registered the voice, completely caught up in a perfectly lovely dream. She was riding a little paint mare up a mountain trail, the air sweet and clear, and their way shaded by fringy pines and pale quaking aspen. She'd never been on a horse in her life and might have expected the experience to be frightening, bumpy and precarious, but it wasn't. It was smooth, relaxing, moving in rhythm with a huge, powerful creature.

The mountains promised peace, a warm embrace of balance and serenity she realized she had been seeking forever.

"Lady!" the voice said louder, jerking her off the horse's back and out of the dream. "You want to tell me what you're still doing here?"

Jarred, disoriented, Caroline blinked her hazy way back to awareness. Instead of the beautiful alpine setting and the horse's smooth gait beneath her, she was in a large, open room gazing directly at a painting of a horse and rider climbing a mountain trail.

Beneath the painting stood an angry man glowering at her from beneath a black cowboy hat, and it took her sleep-numbed brain a moment to figure out who he was.

Wade Dalton.

Marjorie Dalton's oldest son. In a flash, she remembered everything—Quinn's gushing e-mail about his lady love, her shocked reaction to find his lady love was her client, then that frenzied trip to eastern Idaho in a mad effort to stop him from doing anything rash.

She'd been too late, she remembered. Instead of Marjorie and Quinn, she had found only a surly, suspicious Wade Dalton and his two darling, troublemaking boys.

Striving desperately for composure, she drew in a deep, cleansing breath to clear the rest of the cobwebs from her brain, then sat up, aware she must look an absolute mess.

She pushed a hank of hair out of her eyes, feeling at a distinct disadvantage that he had caught her this way.

"I'm sorry," she murmured. "I didn't mean to fall asleep. I sat down to wait for you and must have drifted off."

"Why?"

"Probably because I traveled all night to get here." To her embarrassment, her words ended in a giant yawn, but the man didn't seem to notice.

"I wasn't asking why you fell asleep. I was asking

why in the…" He looked over at his son and lowered his voice. "Why in the *heck* would you think you had to wait for us? As far as I'm concerned, we've said everything we needed to say."

She followed his gaze to the boy, noting the bandage on his hand. "I wanted to make sure Tanner was all right."

"He's fine," he answered. "Second-degree burn but it could have been a lot worse."

"Uncle Jake put lots of stinky stuff on it," Tanner piped up from the other couch, "and said I have to keep it wrapped up for a week 'cept at bedtime, to keep out the 'fection. This is my mummy claw of death."

He made a menacing lunge toward her with his wrapped hand and Caroline laughed, charmed by him.

"You'll have to make sure you do everything your uncle told you. You don't want to get an infection."

"I know." His sigh sounded heartfelt and put-upon. "And I can't ever roast marshmallows by myself again or Daddy will drag me behind Jupiter until my skin falls off."

"Jupiter?"

"My dad's horse. He's really big and mean, too."

Caroline winced at the image and Wade frowned at his son. "I was just kidding about the horse, kid. You know that, right? I just wanted to make sure you know your punishment for playing on the stove again will be swift and severe."

"I know. I told you I wouldn't do it again ever, ever, ever."

"Good decision," Caroline said. "Because you'd look pretty gross without all your skin."

Tanner giggled, then turned back to his television show.

Caroline shifted her attention back to the boy's father and found him watching her closely, a strange look on his features—an expression that for some reason made her wish her hair wasn't so sleep-messed.

Silence stretched between them, awkward and uncomfortable, until she finally broke it.

"I made some soup for you and the boys. It's on the stove."

He scowled. "You what?"

"I figured you would be ready for lunch when you returned from the clinic so I found some potatoes in the pantry and threw together a nice cheesy potato soup."

She wasn't quite sure why, but her announcement turned that odd expression in his eyes into one she recognized all too well. She watched storm clouds gather in those blue depths and saw his mouth tighten with irritation.

"Funny, but I don't remember saying anything about making yourself right at home." Though his voice was low to prevent Tanner from paying them any attention, it was still hot.

"You didn't. I was only trying to help."

"My mother has apparently been stupid enough to marry your father, but that sure as hell doesn't give you free rein of the Cold Creek, lady."

She inhaled deeply, working hard to keep her emotions under control. No good would come of losing her temper with him, she reminded herself. As far as he was concerned, she had invaded his territory, and his reaction was natural and not unexpected.

At the same time, she couldn't let him minimize her, not when she had only been trying to help.

"My name is Caroline," she said calmly.

"I don't care if you're the frigging queen of England. This is my ranch and right now you're trespassing."

She raised an eyebrow, trying to hang onto her temper. "Are you going to have me thrown in jail because I had the temerity to make you and your boys some soup?"

"The idea holds considerable appeal right about now, believe me!"

Though she knew he was only posturing, dread curled through her just at the possibility of going to jail again. She had a flashing image of concrete walls, hopelessness and a humiliating lack of privacy.

She couldn't bear contemplating that brief time in her life—and couldn't even begin to imagine having to go back.

She took another deep breath, focusing on pushing all the tension out of her body.

"I was only trying to help. I thought perhaps Tanner might need something comforting and warm after his ordeal."

"I don't need your help, Ms. Montgomery. I don't need anything from you. It was the *help* you gave my mother that led to this whole mess in the first place."

Oh, this man knew how to hit her where she lived. First he threatened her with her worst nightmare, then he dredged up all the guilt she'd been trying so hard to sublimate.

Before she could summon an answer, two noises started up simultaneously—his cell phone rang and strident cries started to float down the stairs as Cody awoke.

Wade let out a heavy sigh and rubbed two fingers on his temple. Deep frustration showed on his features and she reminded herself she didn't want to be fighting with him. While she had worked to clean up the sticky, smoky mess in the kitchen, her mind had been busy trying to do the same to the mess her father had created in Wade Dalton's life.

She wanted to think she had arrived at a viable solution.

"I disagree," she said. "I think you do need help. And if you can swallow your anger at me—justified or not—and listen to me, I have a proposal for you."

His glare indicated that the only kind of proposal he wanted to hear from her concerned her plans to leave his ranch, but she refused to let him intimidate her.

He answered his phone just as he headed out of the room to get Cody, now crying in earnest.

When he returned five minutes later, she had Tanner settled at the kitchen table, eating soup with his unbandaged hand and talking her ear off about his trip to the doctor and the stickers he got from his Uncle Jake and how he heard Amber, one of his Uncle Jake's nurses, talking about how his Uncle Seth was the sexiest man in the county.

This Seth person sounded like an interesting character, she thought, then she forgot all about him when Wade walked into the kitchen with Cody on his hip. The rancher looked big and powerful and intimidating, and she thought his brother would have to be something indeed if he could possibly be more gorgeous than Wade Dalton.

Not that she noticed, she reminded herself. As far as she was concerned, he was grouchy and unreasonable and determined that everything in life had to go his way or else.

Still, there was something about seeing the sleepy-eyed toddler in his arms, one little hand flung around his father's neck and the other thumb planted firmly in his mouth, that tugged at her heart.

The boy studied her warily until she smiled, then his reserve melted and he gave her a chubby smile in return, which only seemed to deepen his father's scowl.

"Would you and Cody like some soup?" she asked.

Wade would have told her no but his stomach growled at just that moment and he had to admit the soup smelled delicious—rich and creamy, with a hint of some kind of spice he didn't quite recognize.

"I didn't put rat poison in it, I promise."

He didn't like this suspicion he had that she found him amusing somehow. He plain didn't like *her*. Caroline Montgomery was everything that turned him off in a woman. She was opinionated and bossy, and he didn't trust her motives one iota.

Trouble was, he couldn't figure out what she could be after. What kind of woman travels eight hundred miles to find her father, then, when she doesn't find him, sticks around to make soup in a stranger's house?

She took the decision out of his hands by setting a steaming bowl on the table and setting another smaller bowl on the counter to cool for Cody.

He could eat, he thought grudgingly. Breakfast had been a long time ago and he'd been too shocked over that letter from his mother to pay much attention to what he'd been eating.

He set Cody in his high chair and pulled him up to the table next to Tanner, then noticed something else about the kitchen. It gleamed in the afternoon sunlight shining in through the big windows.

The place had been a mess when he'd left to take Cody to the clinic, with scorch marks on the walls and a sticky marshmallow goo on the stove. All that was gone.

"You cleaned up." The statement came out more like an accusation than he'd intended but she only smiled in response. He noticed as she smiled that one of her eyeteeth overlapped the tooth next to it just a bit. It was a silly thing but he felt a little of his irritation with her ease at the discovery of that small imperfection.

"I figured you had enough on your hands right now. It was the least I could do anyway. If you hadn't been distracted yelling at me..." her voice trailed off and she flashed that crooked little smile again. "Excuse me, if you hadn't been talking to me in a loud and forceful voice, you probably would have been able to keep a closer eye on Tanner and he might not have had the opportunity to injure himself."

"He would have found a way," Wade muttered. "That kid could find trouble in his sleep. He's a genius at it."

"He does have a lot of energy but he seems very sweet. They both do."

"Sure, while they're busy eating," Wade muttered, then felt like a heel complaining about his own kids.

"Which you should be doing," she pointed out.

Right. He didn't like bossy women, he reminded himself. Even if they had cute smiles and smelled like vanilla ice cream.

Still, he obediently tasted the potato soup his boys were enjoying with such relish, then had to swallow his moan of sheer pleasure. It was absolutely divine, thick and creamy, and flavored with an elusive spice he thought might be tarragon.

Tanner and Cody were carrying on one of their conversations, with Tanner yakking away about whatever he could think of and Cody responding with giggles and the occasional mimicry of whatever his brother said, and Wade listened to them while he savored the soup.

After he had eaten half the bowl in about a minute and a half, Caroline spoke up. "I know Marjorie helped you take care of your children. Do you have someone else to turn to now that she's gone?"

He swallowed a spoonful of soup that suddenly didn't taste as delectable. "Not yet. I'll figure something out."

Before she could answer, Tanner burped loudly and he and Cody erupted into hysterical laughter.

"Hey, that wasn't very polite," Wade chided, even as he saw that Caroline was hiding a smile behind her hand. "Apologize to Ms. Montgomery."

"Nat says that's how people in some places say thank you when their food is real good."

"Well, we're not *in* one of those places. On the Cold Creek, it's considered bad manners."

Cody suddenly burped, too, something Tanner apparently thought was the funniest thing in the world.

"See? Now look what you're teaching your little brother. Apologize to Ms. Montgomery."

"Sorry," Tanner said obediently, even though he didn't look the slightest bit sincere.

"Sowwy," Cody repeated.

"Can we go play now? We're all done."

Wade washed their faces and hands—well, Cody's

hands and Tanner's unbandaged one—— then pulled Cody down from his high chair and set him on the floor.

"Remember to be careful," he told Tanner, who nodded absently and headed out of the kitchen after his brother.

"It doesn't look like his injury is slowing him down much," Caroline observed.

He sighed. "Not much slows that kid down."

"So what will you do with them while you work?" she asked again.

"I'll figure something out," he repeated.

She folded her hands together on the table and he noticed her nails weren't very long but they were manicured and she wore a pale pink nail polish. He wasn't sure why he picked up on that detail—and the fact that he did annoyed him, for some reason.

"I'd like to volunteer," she said after a moment.

He stared at her. "Volunteer for what?"

"To help you with your children." She smiled that crooked smile again. "I'm self-employed and my schedule is very flexible. I happen to have some free time right now and I'd like to help."

What the hell was her game? he wondered. "Let me get this straight. You're offering to babysit my kids while your father and my mother are off honeymooning in Reno."

"Yes."

"Why would you possibly think I'd take you up on it?"

She slanted him a look. "Why not?"

"Because you're a stranger. Because I don't know you and I don't trust you."

"I can understand your hesitation. I wouldn't want a stranger caring for my children, if I had any. But I can give you references. I was a nanny in Boston for two years while I finished college. I've had plenty of experience with children of all ages and with cooking and cleaning a house."

Did she actually think he would consider it? "Absolutely not."

"Just like that? You won't even think about it?"

"What's to think about? If you were the parent here, would you leave your kids in the care of a total stranger?"

"Probably not," she admitted. "But if I were in great need, I might consider it after I checked out the stranger's references."

His cell phone rang again before he could answer. One of these days he was going to throw the blasted thing out the window.

He saw Seth's number on the caller ID and sighed. "Yeah?" he answered.

"Where the hell are you? You said you'd be down." Seth sounded as frustrated as Wade felt.

"I'm working on it."

"Those clouds aren't moving on. In another hour we're going to be drenched and lose the whole crop. I was thinking I ought to call Guillermo Cruz and see if we can borrow the Luna's baler."

The Rancho de la Luna was owned by their closest neighbor, Viviana Cruz. Though a much smaller operation than the Cold Creek, Guillermo Cruz kept his sister-in-law's equipment in tip-top shape.

It was a good solution, one he would have thought of if he wasn't so distracted with the kids. "Yeah, do that," he told Seth. "I'll be down as soon as I can. Maybe I can throw together something to fix the other one temporarily. If we can get two machines running out there, we might have a chance."

He hung up to find Caroline Montgomery watching him carefully.

"As I see it, you don't have too many other choices, Mr. Dalton," she said quietly. "Tanner is going to need pampering with that burn of his, at least for a few days, and it needs to be kept free of infection. You can't just lug him and Cody around the ranch with you where the two of them could get into all kinds of things without proper supervision. And by the sounds of it, your plate is pretty full right now."

"Overflowing," he agreed tersely. "Your father picked a hell of a time to take a bride."

She winced and for a moment there he thought she almost looked guilty before her features became serene once more. "I'm sorry. I understand you don't want me here but for the children's sake, at least let me help for a day or two until you come up with another arrangement. I've come all this way for nothing, I might as well make myself useful."

He rubbed the ache in his temple again, the weight of his responsibilities cumbersome and heavy.

What would be the harm in letting her help for a day or two? Her presence would take considerable pressure off him and it *would* be better for the boys to have more diligent supervision than he could provide.

She was a virtual stranger but, like it or not, she was connected to him now by virtue of their parents' hasty marriage.

Anyway, the work he had to do the next few days

was close enough to the ranch house that he could keep an eye on her.

That might not be such a bad thing, he thought. If she and her father were cooking some kind of scam together, he might have some advantage in the long run by keeping his eyes open and knowing just who he was dealing with.

Hank Dalton had had an axiom for cases just like this. *Keep your friends close and your enemies closer.*

What better way to keep her close than by having her right here in his own home?

A stiff gust suddenly rattled the kitchen windows and he watched the clouds dance across the sky as he tried to calculate how much more they would have to pay for feed during the winter if they didn't get the hay in before that storm hit.

"You're right. I don't have too many options right now. I, uh, appreciate the offer."

The words rasped out of his throat as if they were covered in burrs, and she gave him an amused look, as if she sensed how hard they were for him to say.

He really didn't like being such a ready source of amusement for her, he decided.

"Where are your reference phone numbers?" he growled.

She looked at him for a moment, then scribbled some names and phone numbers on a memo sheet off a pad by the phone. Wondering if he was crazy, he grabbed them and stalked to his ranch office off the kitchen.

Ten minutes later he returned. He'd only been able to reach someone at one of the numbers, a woman by the name of Nancy Saunders. He knew it could be a set-up, that she could be part of the con, but at this point he didn't have any choice but to trust her words. She had raved about Caroline's care for her two children a dozen years earlier, about how they'd stayed in touch over the years and she considered Caroline one of the most responsible people she'd ever met.

He didn't want to hear any of this, he thought. He wasn't buying half of it but decided he would be close enough to the house that he could keep an eye on her.

He returned to the kitchen and found her cleaning up the few lunch dishes.

"Did I pass?"

"For now," he muttered. He grabbed his hat off the hook by the back door and shrugged back into his denim work coat.

"Natalie comes home on the bus about three-thirty and she can help you with the boys and with dinner. The freezer's full of food. I don't know what time I'll be in—probably after dark. You and the kids should go ahead and eat, but my mother usually leaves a couple of plates in the fridge for me and for Seth."

"Your brother."

"Right. He's second in command on the ranch and lives in the guesthouse out back, though he usually takes his meals here at the house with the family."

"What kind of food do you like?"

"Anything edible." He headed for the door, anxious to be gone. He stopped only long enough to scribble his cell number on the pad by the phone. "You can reach me at that number if you need anything."

He hurried for his truck, trying his best to ignore the little voice in his head warning him he would regret letting Caroline Montgomery into their lives.

* * *

Through the kitchen window, Caroline watched Wade hurry to his truck as if he were being chased by an angry herd of bison.

She still couldn't quite believe he had actually agreed to her offer. She hadn't really expected him to take her up on it, not with the animosity that had crackled and hissed between them since she'd arrived at the Cold Creek.

He must, indeed, be desperate. That's the only reason he would have agreed to leave his children in her care.

The man wasn't at all what she had expected, and she wasn't sure what to think of him. So far, he had been surly and bad tempered, but she couldn't really blame him under the circumstances.

He intrigued her, she had to admit. She couldn't help wondering what he was like when he wasn't coping with an injured child, a runaway mother and various ranch crises.

She was intrigued by him *and* attracted to him, though she couldn't quite understand why. Something about his intense blue eyes and that palpable aura of power and strength thrummed some heretofore hidden chord inside her.

Big, angry men weren't at all her cup of tea. Not that she really knew what that cup of tea might be—and heaven knew, she'd been thirsty for a long time. But her few previous relationships had been with thoughtful, introspective men. An assistant professor in the history department at the university in Santa Cruz had been the last man she'd dated and she couldn't imagine any two men more different.

Still, there was something about Wade Montgomery....

What had she gotten herself into? she wondered as she set the few dishes from lunch in a sink full of soapy water and went in search of the boys. Or more precisely, what had Quinn dragged her into?

Here she was falling back into old patterns, just hours after she'd sworn that self-destructive behavior was behind her.

She had vowed she was done trying to clean up after Quinn. The only thing she'd ever gotten for her troubles was more heartache. The worst had been those four months she'd spent in jail in Washington state after Quinn had embroiled her in one of his schemes.

Even though she'd had nothing to do with any of it, had known nothing about it until she'd been arrested, she had been the one to pay the price until she had been cleared of the charges.

Even then she couldn't bring herself to sever all ties with her father. Ironic, that, since she frequently counseled her clients to let go of harmful, destructive relationships.

Quinn wasn't really destructive, at least not on purpose. He loved her and had done his best to raise her alone after her mother had died when she was eight. But she was weak when it came to him and she felt like she had spent her entire life trailing behind him with a broom and dustpan.

This time was different, she told herself. This time, three innocent children had been affected by Quinn's heedless behavior. His impulsive elopement with Marjorie had totally upset the balance and rhythm of life here at the Cold Creek.

She knew from her coaching sessions with Marjorie

that the older woman had been the primary caregiver to her three grandchildren since Wade's wife had died two years earlier.

Marjorie hadn't minded that part of her life and had loved the children, but she'd been lonely here at the ranch and hungered to find meaning beyond her duties caring for her son's children.

Though intellectually Caroline knew she wasn't responsible for Marjorie's loneliness, for Quinn's apparent flirtation that had deepened and become serious, she still felt guilty.

If not for her connection to Marjorie, the two would never have met, and Marjorie would have been home right now caring for her grandchildren.

Caroline had no choice but to help Wade in his mother's absence. It was the decent, responsible thing to do.

Chapter 4

By the time three-thirty rolled around, Caroline had no idea how Marjorie possibly kept up with these two little bundles of energy.

She was thirty years younger than her client and already felt as limp as a bowl of day-old linguine from chasing them around. Between keeping track of Cody, who never seemed to stop moving, and trying to entertain a cranky, hurting Tanner, she was quickly running out of steam and out of creative diversions to keep them occupied.

They had read dozens of stories, had built a block tower and had raced miniature cars all over the house. They'd had a contest to see who could hop on one foot the longest, they'd made a hut out of blankets stretched across the dining table and, for the last half-hour, they had been engaged in a rousing game of freeze tag.

Who needed Pilates? she thought after she'd finally caught both boys.

She had to think Tanner could use a little quiet time and, heaven knew, she could.

"Guys, why don't we make a snack for your sister when she comes home from school?"

"Can I lick the spoon?" Tanner asked.

"That depends on what we fix. How about broccoli cookies?"

Tanner made a grossed-out face that was quickly copied by his brother. They adjourned to the kitchen to study available ingredients and finally reached a unanimous agreement to make Rice Krispies squares.

They were melting the marshmallows in the microwave when the front door opened. Caroline heard a thud that sounded like a backpack being dropped, then a young girl's voice.

"Grandma. Hey Grandma! Guess what? I got the highest score in the class on my math test today! And I did my book report on *Superfudge* but I only got ninety-five out of a hundred because Ms. Brown said I talked too fast and they couldn't understand me."

That fast-talking voice drew nearer and, a moment later, a girl appeared in the doorway, her long dark hair tangled and her blue eyes narrowed suspiciously.

"Who are you? Where's my grandma?" she asked warily.

Rats. Hadn't Wade told her about Marjorie and Quinn?

"This is Care-line," Tanner announced. "She can make a block tower that's like a thousand feet high."

It was a slight exaggeration but Caroline decided to let it ride. "Hi. You must be Natalie. I'm Caroline

Montgomery. I'm helping your dad with you and your
brothers for a couple of days."

"Where's my grandma?" Natalie asked again, her
brows beetled together as if she suspected Caroline of
doing something nefarious to Marjorie so she could
take her place making Rice Krispies squares and chasing two nonstop bundles of energy until her knees
buckled.

Caroline wasn't quite sure how to answer. Why
hadn't Wade told her about her grandmother's marriage? Did he have some compelling reason to keep it
from the girl? She didn't want to go against his wishes
but she really had no idea what those wishes were.

Finally she equivocated. "Um, she went on a little
trip with a friend."

"Hey look, Nat. I have the mummy claw of death."
Tanner climbed down from his chair and shook his
arm at her.

"What did you do this time?" Nat asked.

"I burned me when I was roasting marshmallows
on the stove. I only caused a little fire, though. Uncle
Jake put yucky stuff on it and wrapped it up. Do you
want to see it?"

She made a face. "You're such a dork," the girl said.

Tanner stuck his tongue out at his big sister. "You
are."

"No, you are."

Caroline decided to step in before the conversation
degenerated further. "Would you like to help us make
these? We wanted to make a snack for you. They won't
take long."

Natalie frowned. "My grandma always fixes me a
peanut butter and jelly sandwich after school."

The truculence in her tone had Caroline gritting her teeth. "I can make you one of those if you'd prefer."

Natalie shrugged. "I'm not really hungry. Maybe later." She paused. "What friend did my grandma go on a trip with? Señora Cruz? She lives next door on the Luna Ranch and she's her best friend."

Caroline debated how to answer and finally settled on the truth. If Wade didn't want his daughter to know her grandmother had eloped, he should have taken the time to tell that to Caroline.

"No. Um, she went with my dad."

Natalie digested that. "Is your dad named Quinn?" she asked after a moment.

Okay, so Natalie apparently knew more about her grandmother's love life than her father had. "Yes. Do you know him?"

Natalie shrugged. "Grandma talked to him a lot on the phone. I got to talk to him once. He's funny."

Oh, her father could be a real charmer, no question about that.

"Where did they go?" Natalie asked.

Here, things grew a little tricky. "You'd probably better ask your dad about that."

"Will they be back by tomorrow?"

"I doubt that."

"But I have a Girl Scout meeting after school. Grandma was supposed to take me. We're making scrunchies. If she's not home by then, does that mean I can't go?"

Blast Quinn for putting her in this position, she thought again. For grabbing what he wanted without considering any of the consequences, as usual. She doubted he had spared a single thought for these motherless children and their needs when he'd charmed their grandmother into eloping with him.

"I can probably take you. We'll have to work out those details with your dad."

"I don't want to miss it," she said. "Grandma and me already bought the fabric."

"We can explain all that to your father. I'm sure there won't be a problem."

Natalie didn't look convinced but she didn't pursue the matter.

The rest of the afternoon and evening didn't go well. Tanner's pain medication started to wear off and he quickly tired of the limitations from wearing the gauze on his hand. He wanted to go play outside in the sandbox, he wanted to play with Play-Doh, he even claimed he wanted to wash the dishes, that he *loved* to wash dishes, that he would die if he couldn't wash the dishes.

Caroline did her best to distract him and calm his fractious nerves, with little success. How could she blame him for his testiness? Burns could be horribly painful, especially for a child already off balance by the absence of his grandmother, his primary caregiver.

Cody, the toddler, also seemed to feel his grandmother's absence keenly as bedtime neared. He became more clingy, more whiny. Several times he wandered to the front door with a puzzled, sad look on his face and said "Gramma home?" until Caroline thought her heart would break.

Though she did help with Cody, Natalie added to the fun and enjoyment of the evening by bickering endlessly with Tanner and by correcting everything Caroline tried to do, from the way she added pasta to boiling water to how she made the crust on the apple pie she impulsively decided to make to the shade of crayons she picked to color Elmo and Cookie Monster.

By the time dinner was finished, Caroline thought she just might have to walk outside for a little scream therapy if she heard *That's not how Grandma does it* one more time.

At the same time, Caroline couldn't help but notice the girl never said anything about the way her father did things, only her grandmother. And none of the children seemed to find it unusual that they didn't see their father all evening long.

She had to wonder if this was the norm for them. Poor little lambs, if it was, to have lost a mother so suddenly and then to have a father too busy for them.

The only reference any of them made to their father came when Caroline found a cake in the refrigerator and asked Nat about it.

"Oh! That's my dad's cake. Today is his birthday and we forgot it!"

"I made a present," Tanner exclaimed. "It's in my room."

"Present. Present," Cody echoed and followed after his brother up the stairs.

"Why don't we save the pie for your dad's birthday?" Caroline suggested.

Natalie shrugged. "Okay. But grandma made the birthday cake and she makes really good cakes. He probably won't want any pie."

Caroline sighed but set her crooked-looking pie on the countertop to cool.

Despite Natalie's bossiness, she was a huge help when it came to following the boys' usual bedtime routine. She even helped Caroline tightly wrap a plastic bag on Tanner's hand so he could have a quick bath.

Her cooperative attitude disappeared quickly once the boys were tucked in their rooms, right around the time Caroline suggested it might be Natalie's bedtime, since by then it was after eight.

"I don't have a regular bedtime." Natalie focused somewhere above Caroline's left shoulder and refused to meet her gaze, a sure sign she was stretching the truth.

"Really?" Caroline asked doubtfully.

The girl shook her head, her disheveled hair swinging. "Nope. I just go to bed when I get tired. Like maybe ten, maybe eleven."

"Hmm. Is that right?"

"Yeah. My grandma doesn't care what time I go to bed. Neither does my dad. He's usually out working anyway. Sometimes I even stay up and watch TV after he comes home and goes to bed."

Natalie said this with a such a sincere expression that Caroline had to hide a smile. She wasn't quite sure how to play this. She didn't want to call the girl a liar. Their relationship was tenuous enough right now. Natalie had made it plain she didn't like the way Caroline did anything, that she wanted her grandmother back. Caroline didn't want to damage what little rapport she'd worked so hard to build all evening.

On the other hand, she certainly couldn't allow the little girl to stay up all night for the sake of keeping the peace.

She pondered her options. "How about this?" she finally suggested. "I've got some great bath soap in my suitcase that smells delicious. You can use some while you take your bath and then I'll let you stay up and watch TV until nine. Does that sound like a deal?"

Natalie agreed so readily that Caroline realized she'd been conned. She could only hope Quinn didn't decide to take his new stepgrandaughter on as a protégé, the willing pupil he had always wanted. The partner in crime Caroline had always refused to become.

The storm that had threatened all afternoon had finally started around seven and Caroline discovered an odd kind of peace watching television with Natalie while the rain pattered against the window.

They hadn't been able to find anything good on TV so after her bath Natalie had put in an animated DVD—one of her grandma's favorites, she'd proclaimed.

If it gave the girl comfort, some connection to her grandmother, Caroline was fine with any movie. Before starting the DVD, Nat dug a couple of soft quilts out of an antique trunk in the corner.

"My mom made these," she said casually.

Caroline fingered the soft fabric, deep purples and blues and greens. "They're beautiful! She must have been very talented. Are you sure we're supposed to be using them?"

Nat nodded. "We use them all the time when we're watching TV. Grandma says it's like getting a hug from our mom every time we wrap up in them and it helps keep her a part of our family to use them instead of putting them away somewhere. That one you have is my dad's favorite."

Her chest ached a little to think of Wade Dalton finding some connection to his dead wife through one of the beautiful quilts she had made.

She pulled it over her and watched the movie and listened to the rain and wondered about this family whose lives Quinn's actions had thrust her into.

She was going to kill him.

Wade glanced at the clock glowing on the microwave in the dark kitchen and mentally groaned. Ten-thirty. He had left a stranger with his children—including a cranky five-year-old with a bad burn—for more than ten hours.

He deserved whatever wrath she poured out on him. He'd had every intention of being back at the house before the kids went to sleep. But since the rain had decided to hold out until dark, they had been able to bale the entire crop, even with their busted baler, and then had had to load it and move it to the hay sheds.

Before he'd realized it, the kids' bedtime had come and gone, and here he was creeping into his own house, tired and aching and covered in hay.

At least they had been able to take care of business before the rain had hit in earnest.

Agriculture had changed tremendously just in his lifetime, with computers and handheld stock scanners and soil sensors that took most of the guesswork out of irrigating crops.

But for all the improvements, he found it humbling that he was just as dependent on the weather as his great great grandfather had been a hundred years ago when he'd settled the Cold Creek.

Caroline probably wouldn't understand all that, though. All she knew was that he'd virtually abandoned his children with a stranger all day.

He'd be lucky if she was still here.

Now that was an odd thought. He didn't want her there. He would have vastly preferred things if she had stayed in California where she belonged. He was unnerved whenever he thought of her in his house, with her soft brown eyes and her vanilla-ice-cream scent and the unwelcome surge of his blood when he was around her.

The kitchen sparkled and smelled like apples and cinnamon, with no trace of the charred marshmallow smell Tanner had left behind. He found a small pile of birthday presents on the table along with a crooked-looking pie that looked divine.

Wade studied the pile, guilt surging through him. The day had been so crazy he hadn't given his birthday much thought at all and certainly hadn't considered that his children might want to share it with him.

They had even made him a pie. Apple, his favorite. His stomach growled—Caroline's delicious soup had been a long time ago—and he wanted to eat the entire pie by himself.

He almost grabbed a fork but stopped himself. He had to face the music first and apologize to Caroline for dumping his kids on her all day.

He actually heard music coming from the great room. That wasn't the music he needed to face but at least it gave him a clue where to find her. He followed the sound, his shoulders knotted with tension at the confrontation he expected and deserved.

In the doorway to the room, he frowned. The menu to a Disney DVD was playing its endless loop of offerings but the room was dark except for the light from the television set. At first he didn't think anyone was in the room, but once his eyes adjusted to the dim light, he saw that both couches were occupied. Nat was stretched out on one and Caroline took the other, and both of them were sound asleep.

He studied them for a moment, noting Nat had pulled out Andrea's quilts. Did she miss her mother as much as he did? he wondered.

She stirred a little but didn't wake when he scooped her up and started to carry her back to her room. She was growing up, he thought with a pang in his chest. She was heavier even than she'd been the last time he'd carried her to bed.

It seemed like only yesterday she'd been a tiny little thing, no bigger than one of the kittens out in the barn. Now she was on her way to becoming a young lady.

Another few years and she'd be a teenager. The thought sent cold chills down his spine. How the hell was he going to deal with a teenaged daughter? He had a hard enough time with an eight-year-old.

He pulled back her comforter and laid her on her bed, then studied her there in the moonlight.

She looked so much like her mother.

The thought didn't have the scorching pain he used to have whenever he thought of Andi, taken from him so unexpectedly. That raw, sucking wound had mellowed over the last year or so until now it was a kind of dull ache. He was always aware of it throbbing there, but the pain and loss hadn't knocked him over for a while.

He turned to go but Nat's voice, gritty with sleep, stopped him by the doorway.

"Daddy?"

He paused and turned around. "Yeah. I'm home now. Go on back to bed, sunshine."

"You never call me sunshine anymore."

"I just did, didn't I?"

She gave a sleepy giggle then rolled over.

He watched for a few more moments to make sure she stayed asleep. He wasn't avoiding Caroline, he assured himself.

Finally, he forced himself to walk back down the stairs to the great room.

His houseguest was also still asleep, with her knees curled up and her hands pillowing her cheek. A lock of hair had fallen across her cheek. He almost tucked it back behind her ear but managed to stop himself just in time.

What the hell was wrong with him? he thought, appalled. It seemed wrong, somehow, to stand here watching her while she slept. She wouldn't appreciate it, would probably see it as some kind of invasion of her privacy. He imagined California life coaches were probably big on things like healthy personal space and respecting others' boundaries.

He had to wake her up, though he was loathe to do it for myriad reasons.

"Ms. Montgomery? Caroline?"

Those incredibly long lashes fluttered and she opened her eyes. She gazed at him blankly for a moment then he saw recognition click in. "You're back. What time is it?"

Here we go. Lecture time. He sighed. "Quarter to eleven."

She sat up and tucked that errant strand behind her ear without any help from him. "My word, you keep long hours."

"Show me a rancher who doesn't and I'll show you

a Hollywood wannabe." He shrugged. "This is a crazy time of year, trying to bring in the last crop of hay for the season and get everything ready for snow."

"The children had a little birthday celebration planned for you. We made a pie and everything. Nat said you don't like pie as much as cake so I guess you have your choice now."

He scratched his cheek. "Did Nat happen to mention I don't like birthdays much at all? And I can't say this one is shaping up to be one of my best."

She smiled a little and he was struck by the picture she made there, with her hair messy and feet bare and her eyes all soft and sleepy.

"You've got an hour left. You should make the most of it."

He had a sudden insane image of pressing her back against that couch cushion and kissing that crooked little smile until neither of them could think straight.

Where the hell did that come from? He could feel himself color and had to hope it was too dark for her to see—and that one of her life-coaching skills didn't involve mind reading.

Wherever the thought had come from, now that he'd unleashed it, he couldn't stop wondering how she would taste, whether her skin could possibly be as soft as it looked.

He wasn't going to find out, damn it. He jerked his mind away from those forbidden waters and answered her.

"My big plans include eating most of that birthday pie and then hitting the sack."

Alone, as he'd been for the last two years.

"What about the children?"

"I guess I could save a slice or two for them."

"They were disappointed that they didn't see you before they went to bed so they could give you your presents."

Because he felt guilty, he responded more harshly than he would have otherwise. "This is a working cattle ranch. The kids understand I have responsibilities. I'll try to see them at breakfast and we can open the presents then."

She opened her mouth and he braced himself for the lecture he was sure would follow, but to his surprise, she closed it again.

"Fine."

The chill in her voice annoyed him, for some reason. He deserved it, he reminded himself, and swallowed what was left of his pride.

"I'm sorry I left you alone with them so long. I should have called or something but we had to work our tails off to get the hay in before the rain hit."

"We were fine. Tanner's hand was hurting before bed so I gave him another dose of his painkiller. I hope that's okay."

"Yeah. I, ah, appreciate your help."

"You're welcome."

"Are you sure you don't mind staying a day or two, until I figure something else out?"

"Of course not. I'm more than happy to help."

He couldn't quite understand why she was so willing to step in and help him but he was too tired and hungry now to figure it out.

"Do you have a spare room I could use while I'm here?" she asked. "I left my luggage in my car because I wasn't quite sure where to put it."

"Oh. Of course. I should have thought of that earlier. There are two guest rooms on this floor and a couple more upstairs. Of the eight bedrooms in the house, only four are being used right now since Cody and Tanner share."

"Upstairs near the children is fine," she said.

"Go ahead and pick one and I'll go get your luggage and find you."

He came back five minutes later with a single suitcase from her trunk, a laptop case and what he guessed was a makeup bag.

He found her in the room across the hall from his own and he tried not to let his imagination get too carried away with what might happen if he crossed that hall in the night.

"Thank you," she murmured and he could tell by the exhaustion in her voice that she would be asleep in minutes.

"You're welcome. Uh, good night."

He brushed past her on his way out the door and was immediately assailed with the delectable scent of vanilla ice cream and warm, sleepy woman, and it was all he could do to keep from reaching for her.

He was definitely going to have come up with another caregiver solution until Marjorie came back. He wasn't sure he was strong enough to withstand having Caroline Montgomery in his house.

Chapter 5

Caroline had no clue what time the day started on a big cattle operation like the Cold Creek so she decided to err on the side of caution. Her travel alarm woke her at 5:00 a.m. and by 5:30 she stood in the large ranch kitchen with a spatula in one hand and a pencil in the other.

With the coffee brewing, biscuits cooking in the oven and bacon sizzling and popping on the huge commercial stove, Caroline tried to organize her thoughts and make some order out of the chaos that had suddenly become her life.

Quinn's latest escapade and her inevitable efforts to clean up the mess he left behind threatened to wreak havoc with her business. She had phone coaching sessions set up with a half-dozen clients today that she would have to reschedule and a speech she was supposed to give to a woman's meditation group over the weekend would have to be canceled.

The timing was lousy, a complication she could ill afford, but it wouldn't destroy her either. One of the advantages of coaching—one of its big appeals to her when she found herself burning out physically and emotionally in her work counseling abused women at a shelter—was that her schedule could usually be flexible.

Sometimes that flexibility took a little creative time management, though, like now.

She glanced out the window over the sink and saw the sun beginning its slow rise above the mountains. She hadn't done her own meditations and affirmations yet this morning so she turned down the bacon, grabbed her sweater and slipped outside to the deck outside the kitchen.

This area must be Marjorie's handiwork, she thought with a fond smile for her client.

Fall-blooming flowers and herbs filled a variety of containers, from an old metal washtub to a rusted watering can. Several sets of whimsical wind chimes hung from an awning, their music gentle and sweet. Under the awning, protected from the cool breeze, a swing covered in green-striped fabric faced the mountains, a welcoming spot to greet the morning.

She sat on the wide, comfortable swing, enjoying the soft swaying, and looked around the Cold Creek.

She wasn't really sure what she thought of Wade Dalton yet, but one thing she could tell just by looking at his ranch—the man ran a tight ship.

The barns she could see from here were freshly painted, the fences near the house gleamed white in the predawn light and she couldn't see any old farm machinery or junk parts sitting around. Everything was neat and organized.

She watched a light flicker on in a small cedar house twenty yards away and wondered if that was the guest house where Wade's brother lived. She hoped she'd made enough bacon for two hungry men and three children.

The air was sharp with fall but sweet and clear, heavy with moisture from the storm the night before. She drew it deep into her lungs and closed her eyes, mentally taking a broom and dust-pan to all the stress cluttering up her mind.

It took some effort this morning, as she had worried for a long time before she fell asleep about Quinn and Marjorie. That negative energy still flowed through her but she breathed in the sweet mountain air until she could feel herself moving back toward center.

When at last she opened her eyes she could see the promise of day in the pale rim above the jagged Tetons.

Though she had a vague memory of seeing those stunning mountains from the more familiar Wyoming side, she didn't think she'd ever been to Idaho before. How had she and Quinn managed to miss it in their rambling life?

She thought they'd been everywhere as they moved from town to town, her father charming and scamming his way across the country, always after the next big deal.

Please, God, not this time, she prayed silently as part of her meditation. Quinn's intentions toward Marjorie had to be just what they seemed. She couldn't bear thinking he might be cooking up another of his schemes. Her father knew how hard she had worked to build Light the Stars, how very much she cherished the career she had created for herself.

Her success meant everything to her. It was her mission in life, the one thing she had discovered she excelled at.

Knowing how much she loved it and how hard she had worked for her success, would Quinn have risked it all by exploiting her connection with Marjorie for less than altruistic motives?

She couldn't bear thinking of it, not now after working so hard to find serenity this morning. But in her deepest heart, she knew she must suspect it or she wouldn't have dropped everything to come after him. She wouldn't be in a stranger's house right now, cooking his breakfast.

She would be burning his bacon, if she didn't stop woolgathering out here, she reminded herself with a grimace, and slipped back inside the warmth of the house to turn it over.

Ten minutes later, she had a tidy pile of notes and an even bigger pile of bacon strips when Wade Dalton walked into the kitchen.

He must have come right from his shower as his hair was damp, his strong, chiseled features freshly shaved. Her insides quivered a little at the sight but she forced herself to push away the instinctive reaction and offer him a friendly smile.

"Good morning."

He headed straight for the coffeemaker. "Didn't expect to see you up this early."

"I wasn't certain what time you started your day

and I wanted to be sure to have breakfast ready. How do you like your eggs?"

His eyes startled, he studied her over the rim of his cup. "Um, scrambled is fine," he said after a moment. "But you didn't have to get up so early just to do that. I'm not completely helpless. I can usually manage to toast a couple pieces of bread."

She grabbed three eggs out of the refrigerator and started cracking them in a bowl.

"I enjoy cooking," she assured him as she poured a splash of milk into the eggs and beat them vigorously. "Besides, I wanted to catch you before you left the house anyway. I have a couple of questions for you."

As she added the eggs to the frying pan, she saw Wade shift his weight and realized he looked less than thrilled at the prospect of conversing with her. "What about?"

"Yesterday was so crazy, with Tanner's burn and everything else, that we really didn't have a great deal of time to discuss your expectations."

"My...expectations?" He seemed uncomfortable with the word, though she wasn't quite sure why.

"What you want from me, as far as the children are concerned."

"Oh. Right. As far as the children are concerned." He paused. "I don't know. Whatever you did yesterday is probably fine."

The day before she'd been flying blindly and she disliked going into a situation unprepared. "Last night before I went to bed I made a list of everything I feel I need to know about the children's schedules and their preferences and daily chores. I thought perhaps we could discuss it over breakfast."

She transferred his eggs to a plate, added several strips of the crispy bacon, a couple of the warm biscuits and some strawberry jam she'd found in the refrigerator.

She set it all on the table at one of the place mats she'd found earlier, along with a pretty matching cloth napkin. Wade studied the place setting with a baffled kind of expression on his face but he finally sat down and took a bite of eggs.

Caroline contented herself with a biscuit, a peach yogurt and a glass of juice and sat across from him at a matching place setting.

"That's all you're having?" he asked. "It looks like you fixed enough bacon to feed the whole county."

She shrugged, a little embarrassed that she'd overestimated what was needed. "I'm not much of a breakfast eater."

The kitchen was quiet and she thought how intimate it was sitting with a man while he enjoyed his breakfast. She found the thought disconcerting and quickly spoke up to divert her attention from how very attractive Wade Dalton was.

"Do you mind if I ask you some questions while you eat?"

"I guess not," he said in a tone that plainly conveyed he didn't think her interrogation would improve his digestion.

She plunged forward anyway. "I suppose some kind of rough schedule is the first thing I need to nail down. What time does Nat need to be ready for the bus?"

He swallowed a mouthful of eggs. "Um, you'll have to ask her when she gets up. I think it's about eight or so but she can be more specific."

Caroline wrote a question mark next to bus pick-up.

"And what time does the bus usually bring her home?"

"About three-thirty or so. You're probably going to want to ask her that for more specifics. I'm usually not around when she comes back."

Next to bus drop-off, she wrote 3:30 and then another question mark.

"Natalie told me she has Brownies after school today. I need to know what time she is supposed to be there, how long it lasts and directions to her troop meeting."

"I hate to sound like a broken record but you'll have to ask Nat. She'll know all that."

What do *you* know about your daughter? she wanted to ask but held her tongue. So far she wasn't very impressed by Wade's parenting skills. He had ignored his children completely the day before and now he seemed oblivious to the small routines that made up their lives.

Something of her thoughts must have showed on her face because his expression turned defensive.

"Sorry, but my mother took care of those kind of details."

"All right. I'll ask Natalie. She most likely at least has the name of the troop leader I can call."

She studied her list and wondered whether she'd be able to get *any* information from Wade at all. "I suppose that leaves the boys. It would help me to have some idea of their usual routine. Does Tanner go to preschool?"

"He goes a few days a week but, uh, right off the top of my head I'm not sure what days those are. Nat might be able to tell you that too. Or maybe Marjorie wrote it on the calendar or something."

"I checked there. No luck."

"Well, with his burn and all, he probably ought to just stay home for a while anyway."

"You're probably right."

Wade rose from the table, deciding even if she was a great cook, the fluffy biscuits and crisp bacon weren't worth the price of this awkward conversation. "Thanks for the breakfast but I should be on my way."

"I'm not quite finished. That still leaves Cody. Can you tell me what kind of schedule Cody might be on as far as nap time? Does he nap in the morning or afternoon?"

"Um, afternoon." It was a total guess, judging by what had happened the day before, but Wade decided she didn't have to know that.

How could one small, delicate woman make him feel like such an idiot? he wondered. He didn't much like the feeling that he knew nothing about his own children.

It wasn't true anyway. He might not be up on every single detail but he knew Nat adored horses and Tanner liked helping him fix farm machinery and asked a million questions while they were doing it and Cody enjoyed snuggling with his daddy at the end of the day.

"My mother is the one who kept things running around here." Wade's guilt at his own ignorance made him testy. "She would still be keeping them running if not for you and your Don Juan of a father."

Heat flashed in those huge brown eyes but it was gone so quickly he wondered if he'd imagined it.

"We're all trying to make the best of a less-than-perfect situation, Mr. Dalton."

"You don't need to call me Mr. Dalton in that prissy, annoyed voice. You can call me Wade."

"Wade, then. I've known your children less than twenty-four hours. I know nothing of their likes and dislikes, their routines, their favorite activities. You're asking me, a total stranger, to jump right in and take care of all these details that you don't know and you're their father!"

He stared her down. "I didn't ask you to do anything. You insisted on staying."

She folded her hands together. "You didn't exactly throw me off the ranch when I offered to help."

Just because something was true didn't make it any easier to swallow. Yeah, he'd taken her help and agreed to let her stay. He hadn't had a whole lot of options. He still didn't.

"I've known *you* less than twenty-four hours but already I know you well enough to doubt you would have gone. You're like a cocklebur, lady. You stick to something and don't let go."

She opened her mouth to respond but before she could, the back door opened and Seth came inside—in search of coffee, no doubt.

He was grateful for the interruption, Wade told himself as he watched Seth spy Caroline. Seth instantly shed his typical morning grouchiness to offer her that slow smile of his that seemed to make every female within a hundred-mile radius sit up and purr.

From the cradle, it seemed as if Seth could charm any female into doing anything he wanted. Wade didn't know how he did it, he had just seen it hundreds of times. From the checker at the grocery store to the eighty-year-old church organist, every woman in Pine Gulch adored Seth, probably because he adored them right back.

Usually he found his brother's fascination with the opposite sex—and their inevitable response—mostly amusing. He wasn't sure why but today it bugged the hell out of him.

"Morning. You must be Caroline." Seth aimed the full force of that killer grin in her direction.

"Yes. Hello."

Just because Wade was annoyed didn't mean he could ignore the manners Marjorie had drilled in them. "This is my brother Seth," he said stiffly. "He lives in the guesthouse out back and is the second in command on the ranch. Seth, this is Caroline Montgomery."

Seth smiled at her again. "I always wanted a baby sister. I just never expected to get a full-grown stepsister as pretty as a columbine. Welcome to the family."

Caroline blinked several times but seemed to soak in the whole load of baloney. "My goodness. Stepsister. I hadn't thought of that."

She slanted a quick look at Wade and he wondered why color was suddenly creeping across her cheeks.

He wasn't sure what annoyed him more—her blush at Seth's teasing or the idea that she might be related to him in any way, shape or form.

"What a crock of sh…sunshine. She's not a step-anything."

"Her dad married our mother. Seems to me that's clear enough."

Seth poured coffee and took a sip, then made an exaggerated sigh of delight. "That is one fine cup of coffee. Somebody who can make coffee like that is just what this family needs."

She shook her head. "It's just coffee. Nothing fancy."

"Not just coffee, trust me. I'm something of an expert and this is delicious."

"Would you like some breakfast?" Caroline asked. "I'm afraid I overdid it a little on the bacon so you can have as much as you want. There are fresh biscuits, too and I'd be happy to scramble some eggs or make an omelet to go along with it."

Seth grinned. "Beautiful, and she cooks, too. I'd have tried to marry Marjorie off a long time ago if I'd known about all the fringe benefits that would come from having a stepsister."

Her laugh sounded like music and Wade decided he needed to leave before he lost his breakfast.

He stomped up from the table and shoved on his Stetson. "I've got work to do," he growled.

Caroline looked startled. "But what about the rest of my questions about the children?"

"Why don't you ask Seth?" he snapped on his way out the door. "Apparently he's got nothing better to do this morning than sit around flirting with anything that moves."

He slammed the door after him, knowing they were both probably watching him like he'd lost his marbles.

The bitch of it was, he wasn't so sure they'd be wrong.

Chapter 6

Caroline's day improved considerably from its inauspicious beginning, though not at first.

Natalie nearly missed the bus since she insisted it didn't come until 8:05 and instead it showed up ten minutes earlier. She managed to make it, just barely, leaving Caroline with a cranky Tanner, who was hurting and mad at the world for it.

Cody slept in until about nine and woke with soaking wet sheets. She couldn't find anything clean to replace them, so the three of them spent the morning tackling mountains of laundry.

She didn't mind the work—it might have been pleasant except for Tanner's crankiness. He whined when she wouldn't let him have leftover pie for breakfast. He wrapped about half a roll of toilet paper around his other unburned hand so both hands would match. He threw a tantrum when she refused to let him take off his bandages to help her wash dishes.

It was all she could do to remember he was a little boy in pain and in need of comfort.

Cody was a sweetheart but he stuck to her like fly-paper and didn't seem to want to let her out of his sight. That was fine since she could always keep an eye on him, but he also managed to find something to make a mess with wherever they were—unmatched socks in the laundry room, flour and sugar in the kitchen, the rest of Tanner's roll of toilet paper that ended up stretched all the way down the stairs.

Worn out by lunchtime, she finally promised the boys a walk after they ate if Tanner agreed to wear a sock over his bandage to protect his hand and keep it clean.

Both boys were thrilled at the prospect of showing her around the ranch, so they ate their peanut-butter sandwiches quickly and even helped her straighten up the Cody mess.

Outside, they found a perfect October afternoon— sunny and pleasant, with just a hint of autumn in the cool breeze and the dusting of bronze on the trees. The storm of the day before seemed to have blown away, leaving everything fresh and clean.

Keeping close watch on Tanner racing eagerly ahead of them, she held Cody's hand and let the toddler's short legs set the pace as she enjoyed the fresh air and the beautiful mountain views.

Up close, the ranch was even more impressive than it had been in the pale early morning light. Everything she saw pointed to a well-run, well-organized operation.

Wade Dalton hadn't sacrificed aesthetics, either. Instead of what she assumed would be more efficient and inexpensive barbed-wire fences, the ranch had gray-weathered split-rail fence that looked like something out of an old Western movie.

They walked along the fence line down the long gravel driveway toward the main road, stopping to admire a small grazing herd of horses.

"Horse, horse!" Cody exclaimed with glee.

She smiled down at him, charmed by his enthusiasm. "They're pretty, aren't they?"

"See that yellow one?" Tanner leaned on the middle slat of the fence and pointed to a small buckskin pony. "Her name is Sunshine and she used to be Nat's but now she's mine 'cause Nat has a new horse named Chance. I can ride her all by myself. Want to see?"

He started to slip through the rails but Caroline grabbed him by his belt loops. "Not a good idea, bud. At least not until your uncle Jake clears it, okay?"

"But she's my horse! Grandma taught me how to take care of her. She comes when I call her, except she's too big for me to put the saddle and bridle on. Grandma helps me with that part. We ride just about every day."

"Do you go with your dad, too?"

Tanner shrugged. "He's usually too busy."

Too busy to take his son riding? She frowned but before she could say anything, Cody pulled away from her and headed off as fast as his little legs could go. "Hi, Daddy! Hi, Daddy!" he shrieked.

She turned and found Wade coming out of the nearby barn, carrying a bale of hay in each arm like they were feather pillows. He had his jacket off and his sleeves rolled up and she saw those powerful muscles in his arms barely flex at the weight.

Caroline didn't like the realization that her mouth had completely dried up, like an Arizona streambed in the middle of the summer.

Cody collided with his father's legs at a fast run but Wade managed to stay upright. "Hey there, partner. Watch where you're going."

He dropped the bales to the ground as Cody hugged one long leg. Tanner hurried over to his father, too, and hugged the other leg. She was pleased to see he didn't look annoyed at his sons, just distracted.

"Hey Dad, guess what? We're showin' Caroline around," Tanner announced. "I showed her Sunshine and told her she's my very own horse. She is, huh, Dad, 'cause Nat rides Chance now. She says Sunshine is a baby's horse but that's not true 'cause I'm not a baby, am I, Dad?"

He opened his mouth to answer but before he could, Cody tugged on Wade's jeans and held his arms out.

"Daddy, Cody up!"

Wade picked him up and immediately Cody started trying to yank off his hat. Wade held onto his hat with one hand and the wriggling toddler with the other. "I didn't expect to see you guys outside today."

"Caroline says we all needed fresh air and she wanted to see the ranch so we're givin' her a tour. She made me wear a sock on my hand so I won't get a 'fection. That's stupid, huh Dad?"

He looked at the sock then raised an eyebrow. She knew she shouldn't feel defensive but she couldn't seem to help it.

That instinctive reaction gave way to surprise when

he shook his head. "Doesn't sound stupid to me, cowboy. I think it's a good idea. Remember what Uncle Jake said—you have to keep it clean."

"I wanted to play in the sandbox but she wouldn't let me do that either," he complained.

"Tough, kiddo. Right now you need to listen to what she tells you. I know it's hard but it would be a whole lot harder if you don't do everything you can to keep your hand clean. If you got an infection, you might even have to have shots and stuff. Caroline is just trying to help you do what Uncle Jake told you. Instead of giving her a hard time, you ought to be thanking her for looking out for you."

She knew it was ridiculous but she still felt a soft, warm glow spread through her at his support of her, and she couldn't contain a pleased smile. He studied her for several seconds and she could almost swear he was staring at her mouth.

Color spread across her cheekbones and she was relieved when Tanner spoke up.

"Hey Dad! Can we show Caroline the kittens?"

"If you promise not to touch them. You'll have to just look today because they might have germs."

"I promise." Tanner took off running. The minute Wade set Cody down, the little boy raced after his brother and the two of them went inside the barn. Caroline followed and was surprised and pleased when Wade accompanied them.

The kittens were right inside the door, in a small pile of hay that looked warm and cozy. She had expected newborns, for some reason, and was surprised to see the half-dozen or so gray and black kittens looked at least a few weeks old.

They wriggled and mewed and climbed all over each other.

"Can Caroline hold one, Dad?" Tanner asked. "She doesn't have a sore hand."

"If she wants to."

"I do," Caroline declared, picking up a soft gray kitten with big blue eyes. "You are darling!" she exclaimed.

"She'll be a good mouser like her mother in a few months."

She made a face at Wade. "I'd prefer to enjoy her like this for now, all cute and furry, instead of imagining her with a dead mouse in her mouth, thanks."

"Whatever helps you sleep at night, I guess."

She laughed and met his gaze over the kitten. He was looking at her mouth again. She could swear it and she didn't quite know what to read into that.

"Any word from the newlyweds?" he asked.

Any glow she might have been foolish enough to briefly enjoy in his company, warm or otherwise, disappeared at his abrupt question and the sudden hard look.

"Nothing," she said. "You?"

"No. I expected them to check in by now. This isn't like Marjorie. Your father doesn't appear to be the best influence on her."

She had to bite back a sharp retort that maybe *Marjorie* was the bad influence on *Quinn*. But since she knew that was highly unlikely—that Wade was likely in the right since Quinn had spent his whole life perfecting the art of being a bad influence—she kept her mouth shut.

"I've tried to call my mother's cell phone at least a half-dozen times this morning. No answer."

"Same goes for Quinn. I guess they've turned them off."

"Probably because they know they've been selfish and irresponsible to run off in the middle of the night."

"Or maybe because they're on their honeymoon and in love and don't want to be disturbed by lecturing children."

She could only hope.

"Right." The skepticism in his voice was plain. "I've got to get back to work."

"Thank you for showing us the kittens." She set the little gray one back with its siblings. "Come on, guys. We'd better head back to the house so we can meet Natalie's bus and get her to Girl Scouts on time."

Both boys were reluctant to leave the fascinating kittens but they obediently walked out into the afternoon sunshine.

"Bye-bye, Daddy," Cody said.

"We're havin' cake and ice cream for your birthday tonight, Daddy, since we missed it yesterday," Tanner chimed in. "Don't forget, okay? We have presents and everything."

Wade looked about as thrilled by that prospect as the boys had been at leaving the kittens. "Is that really necessary?"

"Yep," Tanner said.

"See you at dinner," Caroline said, forcing a smile, then herded her small charges back toward the house.

Wade watched them go, Cody's little hand tucked in Caroline's and Tanner skipping ahead. Why did he suddenly feel so itchy and uncomfortable, like he'd broken open those hay bales and rolled around in them?

He wasn't sure he liked seeing her with his kids. After less than a day, Tanner and Cody both already seemed crazy about her. They sure didn't obey *him* so immediately.

A hundred feet away or so, she stopped abruptly and the three of them bent down to look at something in the dirt—a bug, he'd wager, since the ranch had plenty and Tanner was fascinated with them all.

He looked at those three heads all bent together: Caroline's soft sun-streaked hair, Cody's curly blond locks several shades lighter and Tanner's darker. His chest suddenly felt tight, his insides all jumbled together.

He wanted her. The grim knowledge sat on him about as comfortably as a new pair of boots.

How could he be stupid enough to hunger for a completely inappropriate woman like Caroline Montgomery? He didn't like her, he didn't trust her, but for the first time in two years he felt that undeniable surge of physical attraction to a woman.

Two years. He hadn't been with a woman since Andrea had died—before that, really, since she'd been pregnant with Cody and hadn't felt great the last trimester.

He hadn't even considered it until now, until Caroline had shown up on his doorstep.

Even thinking about this woman he barely knew in the same breath as Andi seemed terribly disloyal and he suddenly missed his wife with a deep, painful yearning.

In the two years since she'd been gone, the first wild

shock of unbelievable pain had dulled to a steady, hollow ache except for moments when it flared up again like a forest fire that had never quite been extinguished.

Andi should be the one out there showing bugs to the boys and walking with Cody's little hand tucked in hers and kissing Tanner's owies all better. For a moment, the gross unfairness of it cut at him like he'd landed on a coil of barbed wire.

She'd loved being a mother and she'd been great at it. It was all she'd wanted. She used to talk about it even when they were in high school, about all the kids she would like and how she planned to get a teaching degree first, then wanted to be able to stay home and raise her children.

She'd been two years behind him in school, Andrea Simon, the prettiest girl in the sophomore class. She'd been barely sixteen when they'd gone on their first date and, from that moment, he'd known she was it for him.

He picked up the hay bales and headed for the pens, remembering how sweetly innocent she'd looked at his senior prom. They'd dated on and off while she'd finished high school, though he'd been so busy after his father had died, with all his new ranch responsibilities, he hadn't had much time for girls.

Still, he'd known he loved her from the beginning and he'd asked her to marry him when she was only twenty, on the condition that she finish her education first.

The day after her college graduation, they'd been married in a quiet ceremony in her parents' garden. Marjorie and his brothers had still been living in the ranch house, so Wade had brought his bride home to the little guesthouse out back where Seth lived now.

He could still see Andi's delight in fixing up the place that summer before she'd started teaching at the elementary school in town—sewing curtains, painting, refinishing the floors. While he'd been consumed with the ranch, she'd been building a nest for them.

He cut the twine on the bales and tossed them into the trough, then went back to the barn for a couple more, his motions abrupt as he remembered the heady joy of those early days.

His wife had been his first and only love—and his first and only lover.

Something like that would probably make him look pretty pathetic in the eyes of someone sophisticated like Caroline Montgomery, but he didn't care.

He had loved his wife and would never have dreamed of straying. Their relationship had been easy and comfortable. They had always been able to turn to each other even when hard times had come—the trio of miscarriages she'd suffered in quick succession, the surgery to correct a congenital irregularity in her uterus, then the eighteen months they'd tried without success to become pregnant.

He had lived through the most helpless feeling in the world watching the roller-coaster ride of hope and heartache she'd gone through each month when she realized she hadn't conceived.

And then, three years after they'd married, Andi had become pregnant with Natalie. They hadn't told anyone for nearly half the pregnancy, until well into the fourth month when they'd finally allowed themselves to hope this pregnancy wouldn't end in heartbreak.

Andi had never been happier than she was after Natalie had come along—though with complications—

and then Tanner. She'd quit teaching, just as she had dreamed, and had spent her days coloring and singing and looking for bugs on the sidewalk.

He'd been happy because *she* had been happy and they slipped into a comfortable, hectic routine of raising cattle and raising kids.

And then fate had taken her from him and for the last two years he'd done his best to figure a decent way to do both by himself.

He sighed. Why was he putting himself through this today, walking back down a memory lane covered with vicious thorns on every side?

Because of Caroline. Because even though it was crazy and seemed disloyal to Andi somehow, he was attracted to her.

It was only his glands, he told himself, just a normal male reaction to a beautiful woman brought on by his last two years of celibacy.

She was the first woman in two years to even tempt him. He found that vaguely terrifying. He'd had offers at cattle shows and the like, but had always declined the not-so-subtle overtures, feeling not even a spark of interest in any of those women.

Something about their heavy makeup and the wild, hungry light in their eyes turned him off, cheapened something that had always seemed beautiful and natural with his wife.

He had wondered if that part of him was frozen forever. Things had been easier when it had been. But now Caroline had him wondering what it would be like to kiss her, to touch that soft skin. To remember once more the sweet and compelling curves of a woman.

He wasn't going to find out. His mother would be

back soon and everything would get back to normal, to the way it should be without strange women showing up to complicate an already stressful life.

Until then, he would just do his best to get Caroline out of his mind. Hard, relentless work had helped him survive these last two painfully lonely years.

It could certainly help him get through a few more days.

Caroline wasn't sure what to think of a man who was forty-five minutes late for his own birthday party.

"He's not coming, is he?" The resignation in Natalie's voice just about broke her heart.

"He'll be here," Caroline promised, though even as she said the words she questioned the wisdom of raising potentially false hope in the girl.

"No he won't. He's probably too busy. He's *always* too busy."

She shrugged like it meant nothing to her but Caroline only had to look at all Nat had done since her Girl Scout meeting to know her nonchalance was a facade—the festively decorated table, the cake with its bright, crooked frosting and the coned party hats Natalie had made out of construction paper, markers and glitter all told a far different story.

Caroline wanted to find Wade Dalton wherever he was hiding out on his ranch and give the man a good, hard shake.

"I'm hungry," Natalie announced after a moment. "I don't think we should wait for my dad. We should just go ahead and eat since he's not coming."

"I'm hungry, too," Tanner announced.

"Hungry, too," Cody echoed, but whether he meant

it or was just parroting his siblings, she didn't know. It didn't much matter anyway. She had three children here who needed their dinner.

"We can wait a few more minutes and then I'll call him to see how much longer he's going to be."

And maybe add a few choice words about fathers who neglect their children, while I'm at it.

The thought had barely registered when they heard the thud of boots on the steps outside and, a moment later, the door opened and a dark head poked through the opening.

A dark head that did not belong to Wade Dalton.

Caroline let out a frustrated breath but her annoyance at finding another man there instead of their father didn't seem to be shared by the children.

"Uncle Jake!"

Pique at her father apparently forgotten for the moment, Natalie shrieked and launched herself at the man. He picked her up with an affectionate hug.

This must be Marjorie's middle son, the family physician, Caroline realized. She studied him as he greeted the children with hugs all around. Jake Dalton was about the same height as Wade but perhaps not as muscular. His hair was a shade or two lighter than Wade's and not quite as wavy, but he shared the same stunning eyes, the same chiseled features.

She could only wonder at the genetics that produced three such remarkably good-looking men in one family. The Dalton gene pool certainly didn't look like a bad place to swim.

While she was studying Jake Dalton, his attention was drawn to the table with its festive decorations and the thickly frosted cake. "Wow. A party for me? You shouldn't have!"

Natalie giggled as he set her back on her feet. "It's not for you. It's supposed to be Dad's birthday party since we forgot it yesterday. Only I bet he's not coming."

"All the more cake for me, then," Jake teased his niece, although Caroline thought for a moment there she saw just a hint of irritation flicker in his gaze.

Did he also notice his brother's careless attitude toward his children? she wondered.

He turned to her and offered a smile she somehow found calming and kind.

"Hello. You must be Caroline. I'm Jake Dalton, Wade's brother. Wade told me you offered to stay on for a few days and help him with the boys. I can't decide if you're insanely nice or just insane."

"A little of both, I guess." She smiled. "Since you're here, why don't you stay for dinner? I was just about to call your brother to see when he's going to make it back."

"I just dropped in to take a look at Tanner's hand but I could probably be convinced to stay and eat."

"And I thought the days of the house call were over."

"I give special service for five-year-old rascals in desperate need of a sucker transfusion." He pulled a lollipop from his shirt pocket and waved it like a magic wand.

She played along. "I only hope you're not too late, Doctor."

"Been that kind of a day, has it?" His expression was both sympathetic and understanding. Dr. Dalton must have a heck of a bedside manner with that calm, competent manner, she thought.

"He's a young boy in pain. A little crankiness is to be expected."

"You're an angel to put up with him. If your father's anything like you, no wonder he swept Marjorie off her feet."

She had spent her entire life trying *not* to be like her father, charming and feckless and irresponsible, but of course she couldn't say that to another of Marjorie's concerned sons.

"He hasn't been too bad, as long as I keep him busy," she said.

"Let's have a look at it, shall we? Climb on up here, cowboy."

Tanner made a face but obeyed his uncle, scrambling up to sit on the breakfast bar.

"Caroline, if you're not too busy with dinner, can you play nurse for a moment?" Jake asked her.

"Of course. Let me wash my hands."

She scrubbed hard then helped Jake as he started unwrapping the bandage. To Caroline, the boy's injury looked red and ugly but Jake smiled. "You're doing great. Everything looks good."

"When can I stop wearing the stupid bandage?"

"Another few days. Maybe a week. You can hang on that long, can't you?"

"I guess." Tanner didn't look thrilled at the prospect, but his uncle told him a couple of knock-knock jokes to take his mind off it while he pulled some ointment from his bag and applied it with gentle care, then put a new bandage on.

While he worked, Caroline couldn't help comparing the three Dalton brothers.

Where Seth had been flirtatious and charming to her at breakfast, the kind of man who knew his own tremendous appeal and reveled in it, in just a few moments Caroline had determined that this middle Dalton brother seemed to be the thoughtful, introspective brother.

That must make their oldest brother the grouchy, unreasonable one.

Her sudden smile drew Jake's attention. "So you're the life coach my mother's been working with."

Her smile turned wary. "Yes," she said, not at all eager for another confrontation with one of the Dalton brothers.

"You must be doing something right. The last few months Marjorie has seemed—I don't know, more centered, focused—than I've ever seen her."

"I don't know how much of that is my influence or how much is from her email romance with my father—a courtship, by the way, that I knew nothing about until yesterday."

Wade didn't believe her but for some reason she felt it important to convince at least one of the Dalton brothers of her innocence.

"A sore spot, is it?"

She hadn't realized how much her professional pride had been stung by Marjorie and Quinn's elopement until just that moment. Until the day before, she had been so pleased with Marjorie's progress in the six months she'd been working with her.

She supposed it was arrogant to think she'd been making a difference in the woman's life, but she had seen her client blossom as she'd started to break free of destructive patterns and take control of her own life.

Now she had to wonder how much of Marjorie's transformation had been due to her coaching and how much was from Quinn's attentions.

Jake was waiting for an answer, she realized. She sighed, checking to be sure the children's attention was occupied elsewhere. Tanner was busy with his lollipop in hand and had wandered over to the refrigerator where Natalie and Cody were busy making words out of alphabet magnets. Natalie was spelling out *horse,* Caroline noted with little surprise.

"Your brother thinks my father and I are running a scam to bilk mature women out of their retirement nest eggs," she finally said.

Jake leaned against the counter and folded his arms. "Are you?"

"Of course not! I have a legitimate business. You can check my Web site with my complete résumé, articles I've written and dozens of client testimonials!"

"You have a masters in social work, spent five years working in the field then graduated from an accredited coaching school. You've had articles published in various women's magazines, have an active affirmation email newsgroup and will soon be publishing a book from Serenity Press on how to tap into the healing energy within. Sounds great, by the way. I'm going to want to order autographed copies since I've got plenty of patients who can use all the healing energy they can find."

She stared at him. "How do you know all that?"

He smiled as he shrugged. "I checked you out months ago when Marjorie started working with you.

Wade isn't the only overprotective son in this family. You can find out all kinds of things about a person just by Googling them."

Caroline wasn't sure what to think about this middle son of Marjorie's. Part of her wanted to be offended that he had run a background check on her, but she expected her clients to fully investigate before signing up for her services. She couldn't be annoyed when their family members did the same thing.

How far back did his background check go? she wondered. Her record should have been expunged when she'd been cleared, but he might still find evidence that she'd served jail time while awaiting trial. No, he wouldn't be looking at her with such a friendly smile if he knew about that part of her past.

"You have a solid business," Jake went on, "a healthy reputation and the recommendation of many very satisfied customers. When your book hits the stands, I'm sure you'll have people knocking down your doors wanting your services."

"I've worked hard for what I've earned."

And everything would be ruined if Quinn decided to grift someone he'd found on her client list. But she couldn't let herself worry about that now.

"It shows."

"Apparently not to your brother."

"Wade will come around. He's a hard man but he's not completely unreasonable."

Her doubtful look earned a laugh from Jake but he quickly grew serious again.

"He's a hard man," he repeated. "But he's had to be. He took on the whole responsibility for running the ranch when he was eighteen years old and helped

Mom finish raising Seth and me, not an easy job. These last few years since Andi died have been tough in a lot of ways. If he's abrupt and surly, he has reason to be. Don't take it personally."

"Thanks. I'll try to remember that. A doctor who makes house calls and doles out advice, too. You must do a booming business."

"All part of the service."

He smiled and she couldn't help but return it, but before she could respond, she heard a noise and turned to find Wade standing in the doorway.

Hard, indeed. Right now the oldest Dalton brother looked tough enough to chew nails.

Chapter 7

Wade registered two things when he walked into his kitchen.

The first was the table adorned with balloons and other festive decorations and a birthday cake covered in chocolate icing. His damn birthday party, he remembered. So much for his hopes of grabbing a quick bite to eat and going back to work.

He didn't like the other thing he saw any better. His brother Jake was there, as solemnly handsome as ever. Normally he enjoyed having Jake around but he wasn't thrilled to see Caroline smiling up at his brother in a way she'd never looked at *him*.

His mood darkened further when she caught sight of him and her smile instantly melted away like icicles on a tin roof.

His reaction was irrational, he knew it, but it bugged

the hell out of him that she couldn't spare him so much as a tiny smile, when she seemed to have more than enough for his brothers.

He wasn't jealous, he told himself. Just protective of his brothers. Sure, they were grown men, but he didn't need either of them to get tangled up with her until they knew what she and her old man were up to.

Somehow the rationalization rang hollow but it was the best he could come up with.

Before he could give even so much as a terse greeting, the kids caught sight of him.

"Daddy birthday!" Cody exclaimed gleefully. "Birthday, birthday, birthday!"

"You made it!"

Why did Nat have to sound completely astonished? he wondered. "Sorry I'm a little late. The vet showed up an hour ago and we had a few things to take care of."

They weren't close to being done either. Wade had planned just to slip away for a moment to eat and say good-night to the kids, but now he wondered if he ought to tell Dave to come back in the morning.

"That's all right." Caroline's voice was calm but impersonal. "The important thing is that you're here now. The children have been so excited to celebrate your birthday."

"We made you a cake," Tanner said. "It's chocolate. I got to put on some frosting but only if I used my hand that doesn't hurt."

"I bet it's delicious."

"We're having roast beef since I told Caroline it's your favorite dinner," Natalie announced.

Was it? He liked plenty of different foods—anything put in front of him, usually—and he wasn't quite sure why his daughter thought roast was his favorite.

"Sounds delicious," he murmured.

"We didn't make mashed potatoes, though. I told Caroline that was your favorite but she decided to do a different kind of potato. What's it called again?"

"Twice-baked," Caroline said. For some reason she looked a little embarrassed. "It's a lot like mashed potatoes, just a little fancier."

"Everything smells great. Um, just let me wash some of the dust off and then we can eat."

He would rather have just washed his hands and sat down in all his dirt but he couldn't, not with Jake sitting in there looking so suave and professional and *doctorly* in tan pants and a button-down shirt.

The thought made him wish, conversely, that he had time to shower, but he knew he didn't, not with the vet waiting, so he quickly settled for changing his shirt, combing his hat-flattened hair and washing his face and hands.

On the way back to the kitchen, he called Dave to tell him what was up and invite him for dinner.

"I ate before I came over. Linda's on swing shift this week so we ate before she left for work."

"Well, come on up for cake then," he mumbled, embarrassed all over again about the whole thing.

Dave laughed. "Thanks but I think I'll pass. I've got plenty to keep me busy until you come back down and we can finish up."

"I'll get away as soon as I can," he promised, then disconnected, squared his shoulders, and headed into the kitchen.

Once there, he discovered Seth had come in while

he'd been gone, and his younger brother *had* taken time to shower, apparently.

His hair was damp and he looked his usual charming self. He and Jake were both watching Caroline bustle around the kitchen like a couple of fat toms eyeing a nice juicy canary.

He couldn't blame them for it. With that apron and her hair up in some kind of ponytail thing, she looked sexy and rumpled. Her cheeks were flushed, her eyes bright and she had a tiny smudge of what appeared to be chocolate icing on her chin, like a beauty mark.

His sudden desire to reach forward and lick it off just about had him heading right back out of the kitchen.

"Sit down, Daddy," Natalie ordered, in what Andi used to call her lady-of-the-manor tone.

He obliged, taking his place at the head of the table.

"You have to put on your birthday hat," Nat commanded. "Tanner and me made 'em ourselves."

He studied it by his plate, a spangled creation that looked like something a mad magician would wear. A shower of multicolored glitter fell off when he picked it up and he figured he would have rainbow sparkles in his hair for weeks.

Nat, Caroline and the boys all had similar but less gaudy creations on but both his brothers were looking on with bare-headed amusement.

"Why don't you have hats?" he growled.

Seth shrugged, but there was a gleeful look in his eyes that made Wade want to pound something. "You're the birthday boy."

He felt like an idiot but he couldn't disappoint his kids. With a resigned sigh, he pulled on the creation, snapping his chin with the elastic in the process.

"Let's eat, then," he said.

* * *

Caroline had to give credit to Wade for being a good sport.

Though he looked as if he would rather be sitting in church in his underwear, he wore the birthday hat without further complaint all through dinner; he endured the off-key singing of "Happy Birthday" from his children; he suffered through his brothers' jokes on his behalf about his advancing age.

He even made a birthday wish before blowing out the candles on his sagging cake—though if she had to guess, she suspected his wish most likely involved figuring out some way to escape the unwanted attention.

If not for his frequent looks at the clock or the faint, embarrassed expression or the increasingly hard set of his jaw, she might have thought he was even enjoying himself.

He lasted nearly forty minutes before sliding his chair back and removing the birthday hat.

"This has been great, guys. Really. The best thirty-sixth birthday party I've ever had."

Nat made a "duh" kind of face. "It's the only one you've ever had!"

"Well, I'm afraid I have to go," he said. "I can't keep the vet waiting any longer."

Seth stood up. "It's your birthday celebration. Why don't you stay and I can go out and help Dave?"

Caroline saw surprise register briefly on Wade's tanned features at the offer before he shook his head. "Not this time. We're working out the breeding schedule for next year and it's not something I can miss."

Seth's jaw worked for a moment, but he slouched

back down to his seat and reached for his drink, saying nothing.

Did Wade completely miss the sudden restless light in his brother's eyes? she wondered. How could he completely shoot down his brother's offer of help, especially during his own birthday celebration with his children?

The way he ran his ranch *or* his family was absolutely none of her business, she reminded herself as he kissed his children and bid them good-night.

To her shock, before he left the kitchen, he paused beside her chair, looking big and rangy and slightly uncomfortable.

"Thank you for the nice birthday dinner. I can't remember roast beef ever tasting so good and those potatoes were wonderful. It was a lot of trouble to go to and I, um, appreciate it."

She blinked several times but before she could summon a response, he shoved on his Stetson and headed out the door.

"You're welcome," she murmured to his back.

What a complicated, contradictory male, she thought. Just when she thought she had him figured out, he threw a curveball at her, leaving her completely unsure what to expect.

He obviously still distrusted her but they'd managed an entire meal in peace. She supposed she should be grateful for that.

After Wade closed the kitchen door behind himself, Caroline turned back to the table to find Jake standing up as well. "I should go, too. I've got a patient having surgery tomorrow and I promised I'd stop by tonight to answer any of her last-minute questions."

"Really? You do that for all your patients?" She couldn't believe a doctor would go to so much trouble.

"If they need it."

"That's wonderful! It's so refreshing to find a doctor who genuinely cares for his patients as more than just a few dollar signs."

Jake made a face. "When the patient also happens to be my ninth-grade English teacher, I have to be on my best behavior. Agnes Arbuckle was a holy terror. I barely squeaked past her class as it was and I live in dread that if I don't treat her well, she'll give me a pop quiz about gerunds, and when I freeze and botch it she'll find some way to revoke my diploma."

"What's a gerund?" Natalie asked.

"Beats me." Jake winked. "I was never very good at studying."

Caroline laughed. "That was a gerund right there, Natalie. Studying. It's a verb ending in *ing* that acts as a noun. Like, *I love dancing.*"

"Really?" Seth stepped into the conversation, though there was a militant light in his eyes. "We ought to go sometime. I can do a mean two-step."

She gave him a look. "Or *I dislike teasing.*"

"I wasn't teasing," he said with a smile, though she thought his heart didn't seem to be in his light flirtation. "Just say the word and I'll show you a night out on the town."

Even with his odd mood, Seth was a remarkably good-looking man. So was Jake, she thought, wondering why on earth she couldn't experience even a little sizzle of the awareness for either of them that surged through her when Wade was in the room.

"Well, hate to break up this grammar lesson but I

really do have to run," Jake said. "I'll echo what Wade said. It's been a long time since I've enjoyed a meal like that. Thank you."

Seth slid his chair back. "Yeah, I've got to go, too."

"Where?" Jake asked with a mildly critical look. "The Bandito?"

"What of it?" Seth stalked to the sink, his plate in hand. "Sorry I don't have somewhere more important to go. Like maybe paying house calls to old biddies who only want the attention of a red-blooded young doc like yourself. Or the oh-so-important decision to inseminate the cows by June 1, just like we've been doing at the Cold Creek for fifty years."

The bitterness in his voice shimmered in the air and she saw Jake open his mouth, then apparently think better of whatever he was going to say. He closed it again as Seth headed for the door.

"Thanks for dinner, Caroline," the youngest Dalton brother said, with none of his customary charm, then he slammed the door behind himself.

"Sorry about that." Jake looked annoyed. "Out of all of us, Seth seemed to get most of our father's temper."

She shrugged. "It wasn't aimed at me."

In truth, she felt sorry for him. She wasn't sure why but Wade seemed to discount Seth's ability to help shoulder more of the burden of running the Cold Creek.

None of it was her business, Caroline reminded herself again as she said goodbye to Jake then helped the children through their bath routine—washing hair, finding bath toys, wrapping Tanner's arm and helping him keep it above the water.

As she went through their routine, she thought about

the things she had observed that day, of the three motherless children starving for their father's attention.

They each exhibited behaviors she believed were directly linked to Wade's distracted parenting. Natalie had stepped up to mother and boss everyone around; Tanner was a bundle of energy who seemed to find trouble everywhere he went; Cody was clingy, hungry for affection.

And then there was Wade, who buried himself in work, and Seth, who would like to.

Not that she planned to jump to any rushed judgments, Caroline thought wryly.

She had only been here thirty-six hours. She couldn't expect to know and understand all the dynamics of the Dalton family in such a short time. Besides, even if she was spot-on with her assessment, none of it was her business. She was only the temporary help.

After she settled the boys in bed, she crossed the hall to tell Natalie good-night. She found the girl in her bed, her long dark hair still damp and a book propped on her knees.

Nobody walking in this room could ever doubt the girl was horse crazy, Caroline thought with a smile. The walls were covered in horse posters, a knickknack shelf that ran around the entire perimeter of the room about eighteen inches from the ceiling held dozens of horse figures in all colors and sizes, and the bedspread covering those little knees was, of course, equine in design.

"May I come in?" Caroline asked from the doorway.

"Yeah."

She sat on the edge of the bed, drawn to this little girl despite her bossiness. Something about Natalie reminded Caroline of herself, though she wasn't quite sure why.

She had been quiet, almost shy, something that certainly couldn't be said of Natalie. Heaven knows, even if Caroline had shared a similar obsession for anything like Nat's with horses, she and Quinn had never stayed in one place long enough for her to have a collection like this one.

"What are you reading?" she asked.

"Misty of Chincoteague."

"That's a great one."

Natalie shrugged. "It's okay. I've read it three times before."

"Don't you think the very best books are those you can enjoy more every time you read them?"

"I guess."

They lapsed into a not-uncomfortable silence and Caroline wondered what it would be like to have a daughter of her own. It wasn't an unreasonable idea since she had friends with children this age. Still, her mind boggled at the thought.

"The birthday party for your father was very nice. Your hats showed great creativity. I set them aside while I was cleaning up the dishes. I thought maybe we can put them away and save them for whoever's birthday is next in your family."

"That's Grandma," Natalie said. "Her birthday is in November. Mine's not until March."

"We can put them in a box for your grandmother's birthday party, then. She'll love them."

Natalie closed her book, shifting her legs under the comforter.

"My grandma's not coming back, is she?" she said after a moment.

Caroline drew in a sharp breath at the unexpected question. Where did that come from?

And wasn't this the kind of thing Wade should be discussing with his daughter? she thought, irritated at him all over again. If Natalie needed reassurance, she should be able to turn to her father for it, not to a virtual stranger.

But she was here and Wade wasn't, so it looked like she was nominated. "Oh, honey. Of course she's coming back."

The girl's hair rustled as she shook her head. "I heard Uncle Jake and Uncle Seth talking about it. They said how she eloped with your dad. Is it true?"

Caroline squirmed under Natalie's accusing look. She *had* been the one to tell the girl only that Marjorie had gone on a trip with a friend.

"Yes," she finally admitted.

Natalie nodded, her eyes solemn and sad. "So she's not coming back, then."

"Why do you say that?"

"My friend Holly's big sister eloped. She ran away to get married and she never came back. She lives in California and she's gonna have a baby. What if that happens to Grandma?"

Despite the gravity of the conversation, Caroline had to bite back a smile at the idea. "I think I can safely promise you that's not going to happen, honey."

"But what if it does? What if she doesn't come back? Who's gonna take care of me and Tanner and Cody?"

"You still have your dad," she pointed out.

"My dad's too busy with the ranch. He doesn't have

time to take me to Girl Scouts or make cookies for my class when it's treat day or fix my hair in the morning. Grandma does all that stuff. If she doesn't come back, who's going to do it?"

"Your grandma's coming back. She said so."

"But what if she doesn't?" Natalie persisted.

"Well, your dad will probably hire somebody to help him."

Natalie didn't look at all thrilled by that idea. "Like a babysitter for all the time?"

"Something like that."

The girl peeked at Caroline under her lashes. "Would you do it if he hired you? You fixed my hair today and the braids looked even better than Grandma's. And your roast beef was the best we ever had, even my dad said so."

"Oh, honey," Caroline said helplessly, not sure how to answer.

"That means no, doesn't it?"

"I can't just stay here. I have a job and a house back in California."

"You could if you wanted to. You just don't want to."

"That's not true. Anyway, you don't have to worry about this, Natalie. Your grandma says she's coming back. Has she ever lied to you before?"

"Yes. She promised she would take me to Girl Scouts today to make scrunchies and she didn't."

Okay, Nat had her there. Caroline sighed. "I know your grandma and I know she loves you very much. She said she's coming back and she will. Whatever happens, I also know your dad will make sure you have somebody nice to take care of you and your brothers."

She brushed a kiss on Natalie's forehead. "Now go to sleep and stop worrying."

Though she still looked unconvinced, Nat nodded and rolled over, her cheek pressed against yet another horse on her pillow.

Chapter 8

Wade had been working eighteen-hour days from about the time he'd hit puberty. It was a fact of life on a ranch, something he was used to. When work needed to be done, a man didn't sit around complaining about it, he knuckled down and did it.

If you put off doing what was needed, you only ended up having twice as much to do the next day.

He was used to days when he didn't have five minutes to grab a sandwich, when the minute he finished one task, a dozen more crept up to take its place on his to-do list.

Still, by the time he returned to the ranch house the evening of his birthday dinner, he was more than ready to find his bed. His muscles ached from a hard day of physical labor and his brain was weary from racing around in circles trying to work out the last-minute details before the camera crew arrived on Monday for the pre-interview shots.

He would have loved nothing better than lounging in front of ESPN with a beer and the remote right about now. But since not too many football games were played at eleven on a Thursday night, he figured he would just have to settle for a hot shower and Letterman, while he gave his mind and body time to settle down.

Maybe he could find a piece of birthday cake left, he thought as he parked his pickup at the house and flicked off the headlights. It had been a mighty good cake, even though he'd been too rushed earlier to really savor each bite.

He would have to make sure he remembered to tell Nat she'd done a good job with it, even if Caroline had helped her. As he was pretty sure his daughter would still be in bed before he left in the morning, he'd probably be best to leave her a note about it.

The thought left him feeling vaguely guilty, but he pushed it aside. Another few days and the TV interview would be done. He would still be busy, but at least he wouldn't have that hanging over him, too.

The house was dark except for a small light glowing in the kitchen. It was a silly thing but somehow seeing that glow and knowing Caroline must have left it burning for him warmed him and managed to ease the ache in his muscles just a little.

The night was cool and crisp as he walked into the house, and all was quiet on the Cold Creek.

Wade hung his hat and jacket on the mudroom hook then walked into the kitchen, his mind on cake and, regrettably, on Caroline.

He found both delectable things in the kitchen, the cake on the table and Caroline sitting at the breakfast bar with a laptop open in front of her and papers fanned neatly around her.

She looked up when he walked in, her forehead creased with concentration. Her hair was slipping free from her ponytail and a honey-brown strand lay across the curve of her jawbone, he noticed. She brushed it away, giving him a distracted smile.

In the pale glow from the laptop and the light above the stove, she looked soft and sweet and delicious, and his body instantly jumped with hunger.

"You're still up." It was a stupid thing to say, but for some reason he couldn't seem to hold a coherent thought.

She nodded. "I had some work to catch up on. This seemed a quiet time to do it."

They were alone in the kitchen, the children presumably asleep long ago. "What kind of work?"

"Notes on some of my clients to help me prepare for sessions with them when I return next week."

He almost made a derogatory crack about her work but the words caught in his throat.

He might not see the use in paying somebody else to tell you how to live your life but she was staying in his house, taking care of his kids, and it didn't feel right to give her a hard time about her career.

It was one of those clumsy moments when he couldn't say the first thing that came into his head but couldn't think of anything else to take its place, and they lapsed into an awkward silence.

He was about to excuse himself and head to bed when she finally spoke. "Are you hungry?" she asked.

"There's roast beef left and plenty more cake. I could make you a sandwich if you'd like. With the roast, of course, not the cake."

His mouth watered and dinner seemed a long time ago. On the other hand, he had a funny feeling it wouldn't be exactly the smartest idea he'd ever come up with to fix a snack and sit down to eat it across from Caroline Montgomery, just the two of them in the middle of the night in a warm, cozy kitchen.

Not when he couldn't seem to shake his crazy, unwanted attraction to her.

Since he didn't see any other choice besides grabbing his cake and running away like a coyote-spooked yearling, he opted to pass on the whole thing.

"I'm good. But thanks. You, uh, did a good job with dinner."

"I only made the roast and the potatoes. Natalie did the rest. She worked very hard to give you a memorable birthday dinner."

Did that carefully bland voice hide censure or was it only his guilty conscience?

"Yeah, I was just thinking I should drop her a note about it before I took off in the morning. Tell her what a good job she did and all."

"I suppose you could do that," she said slowly.

"You have a better idea?"

He did his best to keep any trace of defensiveness out of his voice but he wasn't sure he succeeded.

"I just wonder if perhaps it would mean more to her if you could take the time to tell her in person."

A lecture from this woman would be just the thing he needed to cap off a perfect day. He braced himself.

"Maybe, except I'm usually gone before she gets up for school."

"I've noticed." She carefully slid the cap onto her pen and rose from the bar stool. "You're gone before your children awake and not back until long after Natalie and the boys are in bed. I can't help wondering when you do see your children."

Here we go. By force of will, he shoved back the wall of guilt that threatened to crash over him. "I see them."

"When?" she persisted.

"I try to make sure I'm home with them at dinnertime, unless I absolutely can't break away."

"And then you go again."

"Sometimes." Most of the time, he admitted. Not that it was any of Caroline's business. "I also usually have the chance to see the boys for a couple minutes at lunchtime and take them on errands with me when I can."

"Do you think that's all they need from you?" If her voice was at all sarcastic, he would have blown up at her. But she spoke calmly, rationally, and somehow that made it seem worse.

"It's all I have to give them right now. I'm sorry if that doesn't fit your storybook image of what a perfect father ought to be but I'm a little busy here trying to provide for my family."

"You seem to be doing an excellent job of that. Your children don't lack for anything, except maybe your attention."

"Thank you for that two-second analysis, Dr. Montgomery. You'll be the first one I'll turn to if I want an opinion on how to raise my children from a total stranger who has no children of her own and who knows nothing about my situation."

She drew in a sharp breath and her soft, lovely skin seemed to pale a shade.

His guilt kicked up a notch but he shoved it back down. No. This wasn't his fault. She'd asked for it, butting in to things that weren't her concern. If she couldn't take his reaction, she shouldn't have yanked his chain.

He waited for tears or any of those other dirty tricks women used when they were challenged during an argument, but she only nodded. "Fair enough. You're right. I've only been here a day and can't pretend to know all there is to know about you and your family. But let me ask you something. What does Natalie want to be when she grows up?"

Another feminine tactic—throw in a non sequitur. What the heck did one thing have to do with the other?

This he had to think about for a minute. "A nurse?" He heard the question in his voice and quickly repeated it with more confidence. "She wants to be a nurse."

"Maybe. But what she most wants to be at this moment is a barrel racer, like her mother."

Really? He hadn't even realized Nat knew of Andi's high-school rodeo days.

Before he could answer, Caroline went on. "What's her favorite color? What friend asked her to sleep over tomorrow night? What grade did she get on her math test, the one that was the highest in her class?"

He glared at her, angry at himself for not knowing the answers to her interrogation and angry with her for pushing him on this when it was none of her damn business.

Though it strained his self-control to the limit, he managed to contain his temper.

He wasn't about to engage in a shouting match with Caroline Montgomery in his own kitchen. No good could possibly come of it. And besides, there was a very real chance he would lose, since everything she'd said was right on the money.

"I don't know," he finally said quietly. "I'm sure it just makes your day to hear me admit that. I don't know those things about my daughter. I guess that makes me the world's worst father."

To his considerable dismay, she reached out and touched his arm, and he felt the heat of it through every nerve ending. "Of course it doesn't make you a bad father. I never meant to imply such a thing. You're busy. It must be hard work running a ranch of this size. I understand that."

To his relief, she withdrew her hand and frowned. "But I'm not so sure your children do."

"They will. My brothers and I figured it out."

He didn't add that he and his brothers hadn't much minded their father being consumed by the ranch all the time as long as it had kept the son of a bitch away from them.

He couldn't be a completely lousy father—how could he be, since he wasn't anything like Hank Dalton? He was never cruel to his children; he didn't taunt them, or berate them or make them feel lower than the lowliest vermin on the ranch.

"Did you?" Her voice was soft but it still cut through his memories like a buzz saw.

"Did I what?"

"Understand about your father?"

His glare sliced at her. "What's that supposed to mean?"

She shouldn't have said anything. This wasn't at all what she'd wanted to talk to him about tonight. She was concerned only for his children, only Nat and the boys.

Still, in the day and a half she'd been on the ranch, she had begun to wonder if anyone at the Cold Creek was truly happy. Wade certainly didn't seem to be, and this evening at dinner she had witnessed firsthand Seth's unhappiness.

She couldn't put her finger on why she thought this, but there was a kind of sadness to the ranch, a deep and profound melancholy that seemed to permeate the air.

She'd thought it was because he and his children were still grieving for the wife and mother they had lost, but now she wondered if it went deeper than that.

For a moment there after he'd mentioned his father, she had seen something in Wade's eyes, an old pain that suddenly made him seem big and lost and lonely, and that tore at her heart.

"Nothing," she murmured. "I'm sorry. None of my business."

He leaned forward suddenly and was once more the hard man she'd come to know.

"No, you started this. You might as well finish it. What did you mean by that snide little 'did you'?"

She hadn't meant it to sound snide. Obviously his father was a sore subject and she chose her words carefully.

"Marjorie told me something of your father's personality during our coaching sessions. Not much, but enough that I know he wasn't an easy man to live with."

"That's one word for it. My father was a stone-cold

bastard, there's no secret about that. He figured he owned everything and everyone on the Cold Creek. We all had to walk his line or else. I used to think he invented that old phrase about my way or the highway. He sure liked to use it enough."

He shook himself a little. "But I'm not my father. I would never be deliberately cruel to my kids."

"Not deliberately, no. But they notice your absence in their lives far more than you might think. When parents are too distant and distracted, no matter what the reason, children can't help but view it as a rejection. They begin to wonder what makes them so unlovable and find themselves doing all kinds of crazy things to find that attention they need."

Like cutting off all her hair when she was twelve or getting her nose pierced the year she'd turned fourteen, all in the hopes that Quinn might look at *her* once, instead of the next deal.

Somehow Wade must have picked up on her thoughts.

"That sounds like the voice of experience." He moved forward slightly, his eyes an intense blue in the low lighting.

She forced herself not to flinch. "We're not talking about me," she said coolly, wondering how this conversation had suddenly twisted around to her.

"Maybe we should be."

"My childhood isn't very interesting and has no bearing on this discussion," she said, then mentally cringed at the cool, prim note she heard in her voice.

"I think it does. What kind of a father was Quinn Montgomery? The doting kind who adored your every move and let you get away with murder? Or the stern, authoritarian type who laid down the law and insisted you follow it?"

Neither. Quinn had been just like Wade. Distracted, distant. Disinterested. Maybe that's why it was so painful for her to watch. Her father loved her, but on his own schedule, when he could fit her in between scams. Not when she needed him most.

She certainly wasn't going to share that with Wade, though.

"I'm sorry," she said, gathering up her notes and closing up her computer. "I shouldn't have said anything. It's been a long day and we're both tired. I'll see you in the morning."

"Running away?"

Her gaze flashed to his and she wasn't sure how to read the expression there.

"No. I just…"

"You should be. It would be better for both of us."

Before she could figure out that odd statement, he stepped forward, his eyes dark and stormy, and an instant later his mouth descended to hers.

For one shocked second, she froze as his powerful arms captured her and tugged her against his unyielding strength, as his mouth moved slowly over hers.

He tasted dusty and male, a combination she somehow found irresistible, and she softened in his arms, giving in to the attraction that had been buzzing through her like an insistent hummingbird from the moment she'd arrived at the Cold Creek.

She shivered as every cell surged to awareness, to a sweet and heavy arousal, and she was lost to everything but this—the taste and scent and feel of him surrounding her with heat and strength.

What had brought them to this? She wasn't quite sure. One moment they'd been arguing, the next here they were, mouths tangled together, both breathing hard as they tasted and touched and explored.

He didn't like her and thought she was a nosy busybody. So why was he holding her with a kind of desperation, one hand buried in her hair, the other at the small of her back drawing her close enough she could feel the hard jut of his arousal?

She was vaguely aware of the world outside their embrace, of the pig-shaped clock ticking above the stove and a sudden breeze rattling the glass panes and the hard countertop of the breakfast bar digging into her back as he pressed her against it.

But none of it mattered.

Her entire world had condensed to this moment, to this man with his solid strength and the sadness in his eyes.

"You smell so good." The low whisper in her ear was more arousing even than his touch. "Like homemade vanilla ice cream fresh from my grandma's old tin ice-cream maker."

She shivered as his mouth slowly slid down her jawline then found the rapid pulse in her neck.

He kissed her there, then his mouth found hers again and Caroline decided she could cheerfully die right here in the Cold Creek kitchen as long as Wade Dalton could kiss her to heaven.

One of her clients had reached a goal earlier in the year of parachuting out of an airplane for her fiftieth birthday. She'd described a freefall to Caroline as incredible, not so much a sensation of falling as flying, soaring above the earth with arms outstretched and the wind rushing to meet you.

For the first time, here in Wade's arms with his mouth hard on hers, Caroline began to understand what she'd meant by that and she never wanted this twirling, whirling freefall to stop.

One of his hands moved to her waist and slid beneath her shirt just enough to touch the bare skin above the waistband of her jeans. She moaned, her arms tight around his neck, and leaned into his slow, arousing touch, desperate for more.

She wasn't sure what sound intruded first, the scrape of a boot on the steps outside the kitchen door or the low, tuneless whistling—she only knew someone else was coming.

No. Go away, she thought, but the sounds drew nearer. She didn't know how, but at the last moment she managed to organize her scattered brain cells just enough to yank out of Wade's arms half a second before the door opened with a squeak.

Seth stood in the doorway, a basket of laundry in his arms and those heartbreakingly blue eyes wide with surprise. His gaze shifted from her to Wade and then back again, and she knew hot color was soaking her cheeks. Beside her, she could hear Wade's ragged breathing and she was mortified to see the surprise in Seth's eyes give way to speculation.

"I didn't think anybody else would be up. Sorry to interrupt."

"You didn't," Caroline said quickly, compelled for some insane reason to protect Wade from his brother's knowing look. "We were, um, talking about the children."

Not exactly a lie, she told herself. They *had* been talking about the children right before that earthshaking kiss.

"Right. Must have been a pretty heated conversation. You're both looking a little flush. What were you doing, comparing your philosophies about corporal punishment? That's bound to get anybody a little hot. Personally—and I hope this doesn't make me sound like a cretin—I come down on the side that sometimes a little swat on the behind is the only thing you can do to get the little buggers' attention. You can give all the timeouts in the world but they won't be as effective as one well-timed hand to the tush. Don't you agree, Wade?"

"Whatever," Wade snapped, looking so completely stunned by what had just happened that Caroline wanted to die of mortification.

"Well, I was only going to throw in a load of laundry," Seth said. "But I can certainly come back later if you're not done, uh, talking."

"Leave it alone," Wade growled to his brother.

To her immense gratification, Seth held his tongue, though he did nothing to hide his amusement.

Caroline decided she had no option left but to flee. "Do your laundry," she said to Seth. "I was just heading to bed. Good night."

The last was directed to both of them but she hurried from the kitchen without daring to look at Wade.

She might never be able to look at him again, not after the way she had responded instantly in his arms as if he'd set spark to dry tinder.

Chapter 9

Wade watched Caroline rush from the kitchen and wondered if he would ever be able to taste vanilla ice cream again without remembering those incredible few moments she had burned in his arms.

"You're an idiot," he growled, though he wasn't completely sure whether his words were aimed at his brother or himself.

"That's the rumor." Seth grinned, unoffended, and headed for the laundry room just off the kitchen.

"I *am* sorry I interrupted," he called over his shoulder. "I should have knocked first. I just never expected to find my cold and passionless older brother locking lips with our beautiful new stepsister."

"She's *not* our stepsister, damn it!"

This seemed to amuse Seth even more. Grinning like a fool, he started the wash cycle.

Wade thought about going upstairs for that shower he so desperately needed—the one that would now by necessity have to be frigid—then decided he might as well settle at least one of his hungers.

He was cutting a slice of leftover birthday cake when Seth wandered back in.

"Oooh, cake. Mind sharing a piece of that?"

He would have preferred for Seth to take that amused, knowing look and cram it. But it was hard to smirk and eat at the same time, so he gestured to the cake server with his fork. "Help yourself."

"Thanks. I worked up one hell of an appetite down at the Bandito tonight. Bunch of women from New York are staying out at the Swan Valley Dude Ranch, sort of a girls' week out, I guess. They were in the mood for a little cowboy boogie, if you know what I mean. I couldn't let them go home disappointed."

Sometimes he wondered if Seth had been born knowing how to irritate him or if he'd honed the skill through years of study and practice. His brother knew how much he disliked hearing about his exploits so, of course, he delighted in sharing at every opportunity.

He was damn sure not in the mood tonight to hear them, so he decided to change the subject.

"Do you think I'm a poor father?"

Seth froze, the fork halfway to his mouth, then he set it down like it was handblown china. "Is that what Caroline says?"

"Not in so many words."

Seth cocked his head, his eyes baffled but moderately impressed. "Okay so explain to me how a woman goes from questioning your parenting skills to swapping saliva with you?"

To his dismay, Wade could feel his ears turn red. "We were just talking," he mumbled.

"Right. That's why when I came in, her sweet little mouth was all swollen and her cheeks matched the pink of Mom's climbing roses. All that talking, huh?"

Served him right for thinking he could ever have a serious conversation with Seth. "Just drop it. Forget I said anything."

"No, you want to know if I think you're a poor father." To Wade's surprise, his brother didn't offer any more wisecracks and he even appeared to give the matter some thought. "I don't think I've ever heard you say a harsh word to Nat and the boys, unlike our own dear old dad."

"That has to count for something."

"Something," Seth agreed, taking another bite of cake. "You're not half the bastard he was."

"Gee, thanks."

"On the other hand, you do tend to leave a lot of the work to Mom, when it comes to the kids."

First Caroline now Seth. He sighed. "What else am I supposed to do? Can somebody just tell me that? I don't have much choice. The ranch won't run itself."

Seth's too-handsome features seemed to harden a little and for a moment Wade almost thought he saw bitterness flicker in his eyes. "No, it won't. But your kids won't raise themselves, either. What if Mom decides not to come back?"

"Don't think that hasn't been keeping me up at night." And now he would have memories of kissing Caroline to help do the job. "I don't know. I guess I'll have to figure something out. Hire a housekeeper or something."

"Or a ranch manager."

"Can't say I'm crazy about either one of those ideas." He sighed again and took a sip of water. "This wasn't the way things were supposed to turn out. This whole single-father thing sucks."

"Imagine your life without the kids, though," Seth pointed out.

For one brief second, Wade considered how much less stress he would have in his life right now.

Yeah, his life might be less frenzied. But it would also be bleak and miserable.

No Natalie, with her rapid chatter and her freely offered opinions, no Tanner and all that energy, no Cody to cuddle up with him on Sunday afternoons while they napped and watched fishing shows. It didn't even bear thinking about.

He loved his children but it was still tough raising them on his own, wondering if every move he made was the wrong one.

Caroline didn't help things, coming here, stirring him up, making him question himself even more.

"So while you and Caroline were, uh, talking, did she offer any advice for you?"

Not at the time, but he was willing to bet she had a few choice suggestions for him after that kiss. A few of them might even have something to do with the kids.

"I'm sure she's working up to that," he murmured. "I imagine before she goes back to California, I'll have an earful of advice. The woman's not exactly shy about expressing her opinions."

He wanted her gone, he told himself.

So why did his chest feel hollow just at the thought of it?

* * *

How could she ever face him again?

The sun hadn't yet managed its rigorous daily climb above the Tetons but Caroline was already dressed. She wasn't quite ready for the day, though, as she curled up in the window seat of her bedroom, a blanket across her knees, gazing out at the quiet, dark ranch.

Her eyes burned, gritty and tired, and she wondered if she had managed any sleep at all. Her mind couldn't seem to stop racing around and around that stunning kiss.

It was just a kiss, she reminded herself. Nothing to get so worked up about.

But that wild conflagration certainly seemed on a completely different level from your regular, everyday kiss. One moment they had been arguing about the children, the next they'd been tangled together, wild and hungry. If Seth hadn't wandered into the kitchen, she could only imagine how far they might have taken things.

Unless Wade was a better actor than she, both of them had been lost to the world, to propriety, to the sheer *insanity* of the sudden shocking heat between them.

Where had it come from? What strange command did he have over her? She had scarcely recognized herself in that needy, hungry creature in his arms the night before.

She was thirty years old, far from a giddy teenager, and though her love life wasn't exactly the stuff of legend, she'd enjoyed a few relationships she considered serious.

Each of them had been pleasant in its own way.

Yes, that was exactly the word. *Pleasant.* Calm, comfortable, easy.

The heat she and Wade generated had been something else entirely, something completely out of her experience.

It had been raw and fierce and wild, almost frightening in its intensity. She had never had any idea she could burn like that and she wasn't sure she liked it.

Perhaps because of her chaotic childhood, she preferred the comfort of order and calm in her relationships. What she'd experienced in Wade's arms the night before had been anything *but* ordered and calm.

She supposed her reaction disturbed her most because she didn't understand it. Wade was so different from the usual sort of man she dated. He was powerful, forceful, the kind of man who seemed to consume all the oxygen molecules in every room he entered. Despite that, there was also a deep loneliness about him that drew her like a magnet.

She was a sucker for anyone in need, always had been. She wanted to comfort and heal, to hold him close and absorb his pain.

What must he think of her for responding so passionately to him? She cringed just thinking about it.

He already seemed to think she had ulterior motives for coming to the ranch, that she and Quinn were part of some complex scheme to drain the Cold Creek coffers. What if he thought her response to him was another indication that she had somehow set her sights on him as part of their twisted plans?

Nothing could be further from the truth.

Yes, she was attracted to him. But that heated kiss in the kitchen was the only thing they could ever share, even if Wade was interested in more. She had coached enough people struggling through bad relationships to know that one based only on attraction would never survive. And though she'd only known the man a few days, what she had seen didn't lead her to believe he was a good fit for her, relationship-wise.

She could never let herself care for a man who ranked his own children so low on his priority list. She had lived through it herself and knew the pain firsthand.

So how did she make it through the next few days? she wondered as she yawned and stood up. She couldn't avoid the man—it was his house, after all. In a few moments, she would probably see him over breakfast, when she would have to smile and be polite and pretend nonchalance about their scalding embrace.

Though she wanted just the opposite for his children, for her own sake, she had to hope he would be even more busy the next few days as the television interview approached. With any luck, he would be too distracted by that to pay much attention to her.

And while he was busy ignoring her, she would work on shaking free of her unwanted attraction toward the man.

How hard could it be?

Her resolve to keep her distance lasted all of an hour—and then she saw him again.

She had to admit, she had been relieved not to find him in the kitchen when she finally made her way there, though Seth showed up a few moments after she started frying bacon and mixing pancake batter. She assumed Wade had already left for the morning, as someone had made a fresh pot of coffee on the coffeemaker and left a dirty cup in the sink.

The most she had to contend with before the children came down was Seth's flirtation, though it seemed more mechanical than sincere. She didn't know the youngest Dalton brother well but this was the first time she'd seen him so pensive.

The compliments he gave her were almost benign, with none of his flowery prose. He also didn't make any cracks about the scene he had to know he'd interrupted the night before.

She almost asked if he was feeling well but decided that would seem presumptuous.

The children woke soon after Seth had left with a subdued thank you for breakfast. After that, she didn't have time to worry about either Dalton brother, she was too busy taking care of the next generation.

For the next hour she ran nonstop—helping Nat find her library books, rewrapping the bandage on Tanner's burn that had slipped loose in the night, and changing and dressing Cody, who for some reason decided to cling to her like an orangutan baby while she fixed plates of pancakes and bacon for the children.

She was on the floor mopping up the second spilled orange juice of the morning due to Tanner's awkward use of his bandaged hand when she heard the door creak behind her.

Some instinct told her who had come in and she froze, mortified at being caught on her hands and knees, her rear end in the air and Cody leaning against her hip.

Grabbing Cody to keep him upright as she shifted position, she rose quickly to her feet and faced Wade.

Why did the air seem high and thin suddenly? She couldn't seem to breathe, her mind jumping with images of the last time she had faced him here in this kitchen.

"Morning."

Wade's deep-voiced greeting encompassed the room and his progeny. He took off his hat as he walked inside but, instead of hanging it up on the customary hook, he kept it in his hands. She assumed that indicated he didn't plan to stay long.

"Hey Dad, guess what?" Tanner started in with his favorite phrase. "Caroline put a new bandage on my hand and she had to wrap it three times because I was moving too much and she said it was grosser than a whole room full of stinky socks."

"I hope you told her thanks for helping you," he said gruffly. "Not everybody would be willing to face something grosser than a room full of stinky socks first thing in the morning."

"I did."

"Good."

After an awkward pause, he shifted his hat to his other hand and finally met Caroline's gaze.

Her insides twirled and she could swear the temperature of the room had just kicked up at least ten degrees.

"Did I already miss Nat's bus?" Though he directed the question to her, he didn't maintain eye contact and she had to wonder if this encounter was as awkward for him as she was finding it.

"No. She just ran upstairs to change her shirt. Tanner spilled orange juice on the one she was wearing."

"Oh."

She was staring at his mouth, she realized, remembering in vivid detail how it had moved over hers the night before, licking and tasting and exploring....

She quickly jerked her gaze away, horrified at herself as heat soaked her cheeks.

"Um, would you like some breakfast?"

"I grabbed some bread and jam with my coffee this morning before I headed out. I don't have much time, just a few minutes, really."

Big surprise there, she thought, but before she could say anything, Nat burst back into the kitchen.

She stopped when she saw her father. "Hi, Dad! I thought you guys were bringing down the range cows from Hightop today."

"We are. We're leaving in a minute."

He rubbed the back of his neck. "I, uh, just wanted to catch you before you left for school. I didn't have a chance to talk to you much last night but I wanted you to know the birthday cake you made was great. I had another piece last night before I went to bed and so did Uncle Seth. We both said as how the second piece was even better than the first. I just wanted you to know."

He said all this without looking at Caroline and she had to admit, she was grateful. She couldn't have said anything past the lump in her throat, stunned that he took her advice about speaking to Natalie in person.

She'd forgotten that part of their conversation because of what had come after, but obviously Wade hadn't. Here he was first thing in the morning, his hat in his hands, taking time away from his busy schedule to give his daughter some of the attention she craved from him.

Caroline could swear she heard the bump and clatter of her heart tumbling to his feet at the look Wade's simple words had put on Natalie's face. The girl's smile couldn't have stretched any wider and she looked like she was ready to take flight.

"You're welcome."

Backpack forgotten, Nat ran to her father, throwing her arms around his waist. Wade returned her hug, then waited patiently while she grabbed up her jacket and her school things, talking a mile a minute.

"It wasn't hard to make," she gushed. "I just followed the recipe like Grandma showed me and Caroline helped me crack the eggs and put on the frosting. I knew you would like it. I *knew* it. Grandma says your sweet tooth is just as bad now as it was when you were Tanner's age. She said you could finish off a cake all by yourself if you put your mind to it."

"Between Seth and me, we did a pretty good job with yours," he said, though he didn't look thrilled at either his daughter or his mother for sharing that information.

"Do you want me to make you another one today? I can. I can make one anytime you want. I think I can even do the eggs by myself next time."

"Thanks, honey. I think one is enough for now but I'll let you know when I'm ready for more."

"You'd better go or you're going to miss the bus," Caroline murmured, though she was loathe to interrupt the girl's excitement.

Natalie hurried toward the door, where she paused and turned back, still glowing. "Dad, when I come home from school can I help you unload the cows? I won't get in the way, I promise. I just want to watch the hazing."

He opened his mouth and Caroline could see the refusal forming in his expression, but he surprised her by nodding after a moment. "If we're still at it, you can come down to the pens."

Natalie gave a delighted shout, then rushed out the door toward the bus stop.

"Can I help, too, Dad?" Tanner jumped down from his chair. "Hey, can I come up to the mountains with you to bring 'em down, too? I won't get in the way either."

Caroline couldn't contain a smile at that bald-faced lie. She was learning Tanner's best skill was getting in the way.

She stepped in so Wade wouldn't have to be the one to say no. "I need your help around here. We're going to run into town and do some grocery shopping."

"Shopping's stupid. I want to help with the roundup."

"Next time, partner," Wade spoke firmly. "When your arm's all better, okay?"

"Why does Nat get to watch?"

"Because she's older—and because she doesn't have a bum hand she needs to keep clean."

"You said bum, Dad!" Tanner chortled.

"Right. And I'll smack yours if I catch you down at the pens today, you hear me? Those range cows are quick and mean. You stay clear."

Tanner pouted. "I know. I'm not a baby like Cody."

"Then you're old enough and smart enough to obey me, right?"

"I guess." Tanner looked disappointed but didn't push it as he turned back to his breakfast.

Wade stood there another second then shoved his hat back on. "I've got to run. The crew is waiting for me."

This time he met Caroline's gaze directly and she could swear she saw something fierce and hot leap into those blue eyes before he shielded them again. "I meant what I said to Tanner. We'll be bringing two hundred head down today in a couple of batches. Best if you keep the boys clear of them. They can be vicious."

"I will," she promised.

Wade turned to go but she stopped him with a hand to his arm. Heat sparked between them and she quickly dropped her fingers. "Sorry. I just… I wanted to tell you I was touched by what you just did for Nat."

He looked more than a little embarrassed. "It wasn't anything."

"Don't say that. It might have been a little thing but surely you could see it meant the world to her."

He opened his mouth to say something then seemed to change his mind. "I've got to run," he said abruptly, then hurried out of the kitchen without another word.

Chapter 10

The lovebirds finally called to check in just as Wade was following the last semitrailer full of range cows back to the ranch later that day.

He almost didn't pick up his cell phone when it rang, distracted by all he still had to do that day, and it took a moment for his mother's voice to register.

He barely recognized it. She sounded about a dozen years younger.

"Where the he—heck are you?" he asked.

"Reno, honey. Didn't you get my note?"

"Yeah, I got it. I just still can't believe you'd run off like that."

"I'm sorry, honey, but we just couldn't wait another day to be together. You understand, don't you?"

Not in the slightest, but he decided saying so would be mean so he kept his mouth shut.

"Are you coming back?" he asked instead.

"I told you I was, didn't I? Actually that's what I'm calling about. We were planning to be back Monday or Tuesday but now we're talking about driving over to the coast. We thought we'd spend a few days packing up Quinn's place in San Francisco and then drive down to see his daughter in Santa Cruz. Will you and the kids be all right for a few more days if we do that?"

Mentally, he was pounding his head against the steering wheel a couple dozen times. In reality, he just grimaced. "We'll survive. But you won't find Montgomery's daughter in California."

"Sure we will. That's where she lives."

"Not at the present. She's here."

"Who's there?"

"Caroline. She showed up the morning after you left."

"Caroline Montgomery?"

"That's what I said, isn't it?"

"Why, that was two days ago. She's still there?"

Only two days? It felt like forever. He sighed. "Yeah. She offered to stay and help with the kids."

"And you let her?"

The shock in her voice made him defensive. "You picked a hell of a time to run off, Mom. The crew from the network is showing up in three days and things here are a mess. I didn't know what else to do."

He heard silence on the line, then Marjorie's muffled voice telling someone—her huggy bear, he assumed—about Caroline. A moment later, his mother returned to the line.

"It's just like her to see you needed help and settle right in to do what she can. Isn't she wonderful?"

He was still reserving judgment on that one. "She's something, all right," he muttered.

"I just *knew* you'd like her once you met her. I'm sure Nat and the boys adore her already."

Too much. They were going to miss her when she left. "You didn't give me too many choices," he repeated.

"I'm losing the signal here, honey. I didn't quite catch that."

"You left things in a mess here, Mom," he said loudly. "What kind of example do you think that sets to the kids when they see their grandmother run off with some guy she never even met in person?"

"Sorry I can't hear you. These darn cell phones. Works fine one minute, then you feel like you're talking to yourself the next."

Marjorie still sounded giddy and he had to wonder if she really couldn't hear him or if she was faking because she didn't want to listen to any of his lectures.

"Hope you can still hear me because all I'm getting on my end is static," she went on. "Since you've got Caroline there, I know the kids are in good hands. I guess that means we can go to San Francisco without worrying. We'll be back by Wednesday. Thursday at the latest. Tell the kids I love them and I'll see them soon."

Before he realized it, she had severed the connection. He tossed the phone on the passenger seat, though what he really wanted was to chuck the damn thing through the windshield.

Somebody suddenly rapped on his window and he turned to find Seth on the other side. He rolled down the window.

"What's the holdup?" Seth asked.

Wade winced when he realized the crew was all lined up behind him waiting to get through and unload the cattle.

"I love that woman but sometimes, I swear she makes me absolutely crazy."

Seth looked confused. "What woman?"

"Mom. That was her on the phone. Apparently she and her Romeo are having such a wonderful time on their honeymoon they've decided to extend it."

Seth winced. "I don't even want to go there, man. It's an image I don't need in my head."

"They're not ready to come back by Sunday since they want to drive to the coast. Now it's looking like they won't be back until Wednesday or Thursday, which leaves us stuck with Caroline for a few more days, if she's up for it."

"No real hardship there. You don't often find a woman who is sweet as sugar, can cook like that and who looks great while she's doing it. I like her."

"You like anything that doesn't have a Y chromosome."

Seth grinned. "True enough. But I especially like Caroline. You have to admit, she has plenty of grit to pitch right in like she did. Most women would have taken off running the first time they caught sight of your little Dalton gang."

She did seem to be good for the kids. All three of them had taken to her immediately.

He thought of the way he'd seen her that morning when he'd walked into the kitchen, with Cody leaning on her while she worked, like the boy didn't want to let her get two feet away.

"I like having her here," Seth said again, then he grinned. "And judging by that scene in the kitchen I so rudely interrupted last night, I can't help but think you do, too."

Yeah, that was the whole problem and the reason he wanted her gone as soon as possible.

He did like her, entirely too much. He hadn't stopped thinking about her all day. Of her mouth, soft and warm and welcoming, of the soft, sexy sounds she'd made when he'd kissed her, of her small hands buried in his hair, sending shivers of pleasure down his spine.

He shifted in the seat, furious at himself for going down that road again. The night before had been a colossal mistake, one he would make sure never happened again.

"I would like having Mom back where she belongs a hell of a lot more," he muttered, then threw the truck in gear and drove through the gate, leaving his brother watching after him.

Caroline had to admit that even after five years of coaching people to break old patterns and alter old habits—years when she had seen some of her clients make remarkable changes—she found it amazing how quickly she adapted to a new way of life.

Four days after that stunning kiss, she stood at the kitchen window washing lunch dishes and looking out at a clear, beautiful October day. The trees outside the window were ablaze with color and leaves fluttered down on the breeze.

Beyond them, the jagged, snow-capped Tetons provided their magnificent backdrop to the scene and she thought how lucky the Daltons were to enjoy that view every day.

She had been at the ranch for six days and her life in Santa Cruz seemed far away.

She never would have expected to find such contentment here. The children had already wiggled their way into her heart and she found each day with them a delight.

Over the weekend, she'd found Nat to have a funny sense of humor, a sweet girl who mothered her little brothers and who missed her own mother. Tanner was so bright and so inquisitive, he had a million questions about everything. And she adored Cody for his sweet disposition and eagerness to love.

She would miss them all when she returned to California, even Seth with his teasing flirtations and the three quiet, polite ranch hands she had met briefly.

And Wade. Would she miss Wade?

She sighed as she dried the last dish and returned it to the cupboard. Most definitely.

She already did, as she hadn't seen him for more than a few minutes at a time since that night in the kitchen.

With his impeccable timing, Tanner wandered into the kitchen just as she finished. "We're bored. There's nothing to do."

That was the biggest challenge with this one. His attention span was painfully short and keeping him entertained and occupied had been a great challenge, especially with his burned hand and the precautions they had to take because of it.

"Can we go play in the sandbox?" he asked now,

his big blue eyes wearing a pleading expression that was tough to resist.

She stiffened her spine and shook her head. "Honey, you know you can't until your bandage comes off. But you only have to wait one more day, remember? That's not so bad. Your uncle Jake said everything's looking good with your burn and you won't have to have the mummy claw of death much longer."

Tanner made his trademark menacing lunge at her and she played along, shrieking and backing away as he advanced. When she couldn't go backward any more, she caught him in a quick hug, which he returned with a willingness that warmed her heart.

"You can hang on one more day, can't you?"

"I don't want to," he complained. "Why can't you just take it off now so I can go outside and play? You take it off to change it."

"Because then your uncle would be mad at me."

Tanner's expression turned crafty. "He won't spank you, though, 'cause you're a girl and my dad says boys don't hit girls."

She laughed. "Nice try. But even with that threat out of the way, I'm not going to take off your bandage, kiddo. I'm under orders."

His sigh was heavy and put-upon, and she hid a smile as she reached for Cody to keep him from dumping the garbage can.

"Care, Care," the toddler chanted, throwing his arms tightly around her neck.

"Why don't we find jackets and your hats and we'll go outside for a walk?"

"Can we go see Sunshine?" Tanner asked.

"Of course. But we have to stay out of your dad's way, right?"

Tanner nodded. "Yeah, 'cause the TV people are here."

"That's right. And this is important to your father."

The actual interview wasn't until the next day, but the network had sent an advance crew to lay the groundwork for it and to shoot visuals around the ranch of Wade and his crew working.

It was a beautiful day for a walk and for a video shoot, Caroline thought as she followed the two little bobbing cowboy hats outside. The sky was almost painfully blue, with only a few high clouds. It was cool, though, and she was grateful for her sweater.

On their way to the barn and Tanner's pony, they crunched through leaves and tried to catch them in the air as they fluttered down under the spreading branches of the big maples along the fence.

Maybe she ought to ask Wade where to find some rakes and she and the boys could spend the afternoon making piles and jumping in them.

Cody's pony nickered when he saw them and came trotting over for a treat.

"Please can I ride him, Care-line? Please? I'll forget how if I don't."

She debated it. His hand was much improved and, if he wore a glove, she didn't see the harm in allowing it. "Maybe when Nat gets home to help you saddle him, okay?"

"Yes!" Tanner made a triumphant fist in the air just as she heard adult voices.

She turned to find Wade walking around the barn with three others, two men carrying camera equipment and a young woman in jeans and new-looking boots with a clipboard and a cell phone.

She pondered how best to sneak out of their way before Wade and his companions spotted them. Before she could, though, the boys caught sight of their father.

"Daddy, Daddy!" Cody wriggled out of her hold like a budding Houdini and raced to his father, Tanner right on his heels.

Caroline hurried after them, arriving just in time to watch Cody hold his arms out for his father to lift him up.

"Sorry," she said a little breathlessly. "They're faster than me."

Wade's features looked annoyed but he didn't say anything, only gave in to Cody's demands and picked him up.

She had to admit, they made a charming picture— the sexy cowboy and his two very cute little buckaroos in their matching cowboy hats.

Apparently, she wasn't the only one who thought so. The woman with the clipboard seemed to melt into a gushy pile right there next to the horse pasture.

"Oh my gosh, they are *so* precious. We have to include them in the shoot."

Wade blinked. "The boys?"

"Absolutely!" The woman was young and attractive and had a look in her eye that reminded Caroline of some of her clients who became so totally one-dimensional they weren't able to focus on anything but work.

If she were one of her clients, Caroline would probably tell this young woman to quickly find a hobby outside work before she burned herself up like Caroline had done at social work.

"Just thinking out loud here," the woman went on, "but maybe we could do something along the lines of building a legacy for your children's future or something, as those who make their living from the land have been doing for generations. I'll have to run it past the reporter."

She turned to Caroline suddenly, her features friendly. "I'm sorry. I'm Darci Perez, Mrs. Dalton. I'm producing the story about your husband and the Cold Creek."

Caroline froze, unexpected heat flashing through her at the idea. Her gaze collided with Wade's and she found the aghast expression on his face the height of humiliation.

"He's not my husband," Caroline said quickly—too quickly, she realized, when the producer looked surprised at her vehemence.

The woman winced. "Sorry. I should know better than to jump to conclusions like that."

"Tanner, don't touch anything," Wade broke in sharply and Caroline saw that one of the cameramen had set his equipment on a bale of hay and Tanner, of course, had homed in on it like a bee on a honeysuckle bush.

Tanner froze and Wade turned back to the conversation. "I'm a widower," he told the producer. A muscle flexed in his jaw, as if just saying the word was difficult.

Darci Perez looked even more uncomfortable. "That's probably in the background information I have about you. I should have read it more closely. I'm so sorry."

"Don't worry about it," Wade said, then glared again at Tanner, who, despite his father's warning, had sidled closer to the equipment. "What did I tell you about not touching anything?"

If Caroline hadn't survived six days with the boy, she might have been taken in by his angelic expression. "I'm just looking, Daddy. With my eyes, not my hand or my mummy claw of death."

"Keep it that way, bud."

The producer was studying her expectantly so Caroline stepped forward, her hand outstretched. "I'm Caroline Montgomery, a friend of the family. I'm staying here for a few days to help Wade with the children while his mother is out of town."

The woman shook her hand. "That name is familiar. Have we met?"

"I don't believe so."

Darci frowned and then her expression brightened. "I know! Didn't you write an article for *Glamour* a few months ago about the top ten best ways to guarantee yourself a happy, fulfilling life?"

Caroline was flattered, she had to admit. "I did. I'm shocked you remembered the byline. Most people skip right over them."

"Only because I practically have the thing memorized." The woman grinned. "I've done the exact opposite of at least half of the things on your list but I'm working on it."

Caroline smiled. "Progress is good."

"Don't you think you should be going back to the house now?" Wade asked and she saw that it was all he could do to hold onto Cody, who'd decided he wanted down now and was wriggling for all he was worth.

Darci observed the boy's struggles with interest. "He looks like a handful. That must be an interesting challenge, a single father trying to raise his young children and run a ranch of this size as well."

"*Interesting* is one word for it," Wade said.

"I'll mention that to the reporter, too. He might want to follow up on that angle."

Wade would absolutely detest discussing his personal life on camera, Caroline knew. She wondered how to help him avoid it, then remembered it was none of her business.

"Come on, boys. Let's go," she said. She took Cody from Wade and turned around for Tanner, then drew in a quick breath when she found him trying to heft the large camera off the hay bale.

"Tanner! Put that down!" Wade barked. The boy jumped at his tone and hurried to obey but the camera slid out of his bandaged hand and landed in the dirt with a heavy, sickening thud.

"Tanner! I told you not to touch anything." Wade's features looked harsh and angry. "Now look what you've done!"

Tanner's lip trembled. "I'm sorry, Daddy. I didn't mean to. It slipped out of my hand."

"You shouldn't have been messing with it in the first place. When are you ever going to learn to listen to me?"

Tanner gazed around at the circle of adults looking down at him, then at his father's glower. He let out a little distressed cry then took off running around the side of the barn.

Wade stared after him like he wasn't quite sure what to do. Exasperated, Caroline handed Cody back to him and started out after the boy.

Chapter 11

Caroline followed the upset boy around the corner of the barn, wondering how on earth his little legs could move so fast.

She assumed he was heading for the house but then he seemed to catch sight of something distracting. Suddenly, in mid-stride he switched directions and headed toward the pens to the east of the barn.

Caroline stopped dead, her blood suddenly coated in a thin, crackly layer of ice, when she saw what was inside the corral. At least a dozen range cows and their calves munched hay, their wickedly sharp horns gleaming in the afternoon sun.

She remembered Wade's warning about the range cows and what she'd learned in the few days she'd been on the Cold Creek. The cows were bred to be tough and aggressive to survive predators and weather conditions in the mountains, and she remembered Wade's warning that they could be nasty and bad tempered.

Tanner knew that. What on earth was the rascal thinking to go anywhere near them?

"Tanner, get back here," she yelled, but he either chose to ignore her or didn't hear over the cattle's lowing.

He moved closer to the corral, his attention fixed on something inside and Caroline had a sudden terrible foreboding that left her sick. He wouldn't go inside. He *couldn't*.

She held her breath as she raced after him but Tanner had at least a ten-yard head start. Even if he hadn't, she had learned during her time at the ranch that the boy could be quick and wily.

"Tanner Dalton, you get back here," she called again.

To her relief, this time he slowed a little and looked back at her.

"Stop," she called out.

Her relief was short-lived when he shook his head. "One of the kitties is in there," he called. "I have to get him."

She tried to see where he was looking but all she could see were milling, deadly looking hooves.

"No you don't! Let your dad go after him."

"He'll die in there and then the mommy kitty will be sad."

She was within ten feet of him now. "And if you go in there and get hurt, your dad is going to be sad *and* mad. You don't want that."

Bringing up Wade was apparently the wrong tack

completely. Even from here she could see the sudden stubborn light in the boy's eyes.

"He's already mad at me," Tanner said as he reached the corral fence.

She was close, so close, but just as she reached out to grab his shirt, he slipped under the wooden slat and was inside the pen heading toward the tiny gray kitten she could now see trembling in the middle of the milling cattle.

"Tanner, get back here," she snapped, keeping a careful eye on the cows, who were paying them no attention for now.

"I will. Soon as I get the kitty."

Caroline stood on the other side, torn about what to do. Should she go after him or go get help? She didn't know the first thing about range cattle other than they were huge and horned and scared the stuffing out of her. But she didn't dare leave even to call for Wade's help.

She had no choice. She was going to have to go after him. Oh, she was going to have a head full of gray hair by the time she made it back to Santa Cruz, she thought, then drew in one last terrified breath and slipped through the slats of the fence.

They seemed even more huge on this side of the fence, as big as small cars, and those horns looked sharp and deadly. She moved through them carefully, as slowly as she dared, her eyes on Tanner as he finally reached the tiny kitten safely after what felt like a dozen lifetimes.

"I got you," she heard him murmur, holding the little creature in his bandaged hand and stroking him with the other. "You're okay now. Nobody's going to treat you like a big baby anymore."

Caroline wanted to scream and yell and shout Hosanna when he started toward the other side of the enclosure. She followed, doing her best to keep her body between his and the animals, who so far were paying them little heed, to her vast relief.

Twenty yards had never felt so endlessly long. Finally they were within five yards of the fence, safety almost in reach. She could taste it, feel it, even as she wondered whether she would ever be able to breathe again.

After this, she was swearing off beef forever, she decided.

They were almost there when the stupid, self-destructive kitten suddenly jumped or slipped out of Tanner's arms. He gave a cry that drew the attention of a few of the nearby animals, then went down on his hands and knees to grab it.

"Come on. We've got to get out of here," Caroline ordered.

"I know. I've almost got him. There!" he pounced on the wriggling kitten then stood up again.

Caroline grabbed for his hand—at this point she would damn well carry him *and* the blasted kitten out of here—but just as she caught his fingers, she heard a snort behind them. She turned slowly and found herself facing the beady eyes of a cow, not placid and gentle as she'd always imagined, but red-rimmed and wild and not at all happy to have them in her space.

The cow started loping toward them and Caroline's stomach dropped. "Tanner, move!" she ordered, but before the last word was out of her mouth, the cow came toward them so fast she never would have believed it if she hadn't seen it herself.

"Run!" Caroline yelled harshly and the startled boy obeyed. She half dragged him, half carried him as they headed at full speed for the corral fence and safety.

They weren't going to make it, she realized grimly. The blasted cow would get to them a split second before they reached the fence.

She didn't think about it, she just reacted totally on instinct, picking up Tanner and the kitten and shoving him in front of her, then she pushed him through the wooden slats of the fence.

She had time only to breathe a quick, frightened prayer before the cow reached her.

When Wade caught up with that kid, he was giving him a serious lecture on following orders. A ranch could be a dangerous place for children who didn't learn early to mind their parents the first time.

If they hadn't gotten that message yet, maybe he'd been too soft on Natalie and the boys in his efforts to be as unlike his own father as possible. Tanner obviously didn't understand, so he was just going to have to drill it into the kid's head that when Wade spoke, the kid had to jump. The consequences of doing otherwise could be deadly.

He didn't have time for this today, not with the TV crew there. He almost just let Caroline deal with Tanner and his tantrum. But as he had been the one to yell at his son, he also knew he needed to be the one to explain why. They had a head start on him, though. It had taken a few minutes for him to take Cody to the outbuilding they used as a machine shop, where Seth was fixing a tractor part.

He'd given the baby to a greasy-fingered Seth, had asked him to watch him for a minute, then had taken off after Caroline and Tanner.

As he rounded the corner of the barn, he heard a shout. He jerked his head around and his heart stuttered in his chest when he saw Caroline and Tanner in the middle of a small herd of range cows he'd culled to take to market first.

Inside the pen, Caroline's butter-yellow sweater was a small splash of color in the middle of a sea of huge russet bodies, and he could barely see Tanner.

What the hell were they doing? Did the woman not have a single brain cell in her head? He'd *told* her range cows were dangerous and here she was wandering through them like she and Tanner were tromping through a field of daisies.

At least they were heading out, he saw. They were moving toward the opposite side of the pen from where he was; he had just started around the perimeter when he saw Tanner bend down for something. A few seconds later, Caroline picked him up and headed fast toward the fence.

Just before they made it through, one of the cows got excited by the ruckus and headed toward them, head down.

His blood iced over and he yelled at them to move.

He vaulted the fence where he was, though he was still half the length of the corral away, and raced toward them, waving his hat and yelling to try to distract the angry cow.

She didn't even turn her big head, focused only on

Caroline and Tanner, and Wade could do nothing but watch, horrified, as she charged.

As he ran through the milling cattle, he saw Caroline bend down and shove something through the slats—Tanner, he realized—but an instant later the cow reached her and tossed her into the air like she was a sack full of straw.

She landed with a hideous thud against the fence and the cow lowered her head, her nostrils flared. She snorted and bawled, looking for any excuse to charge the unwanted intruder again, and Wade didn't stop to think.

He raced in front of the cow, scooped Caroline up in one arm as gently as he could under the circumstances, and used the other to haul them both up and over the fence.

He made it over to the other side just as the huge cow slammed into the fence, shaking it hard.

He felt like *he* had been the one to take that crushing hit—every ounce of oxygen in his lungs seemed to have been sucked out and, for one horrifying minute, he felt shaky and light-headed as he lowered a limp Caroline to the ground.

With effort, he forced himself to stay calm, especially as Tanner seemed hysterical enough for the both of them, his eyes huge and scared in his pale face.

"What's wrong with Caroline, Daddy? Why are her eyes closed? Is she sleeping?"

"Something like that."

"Should I go find Uncle Seth?"

"No!" With visions of all the trouble the chaos-magnet could get into on his own, Wade spoke to him sternly. "You should sit down right there and stay put."

"But I…"

He didn't have time to deal with two crises right now, not when Caroline's eyes were still closed, but he knew his son well enough to see by the obstinate jut of his jaw that a little child psychology was in order.

"Look," he tempered his tone. "I might need your help, so it would be better for Caroline's sake if you stick close to me for now, okay?"

That seemed to do the trick. Tanner nodded and settled onto the dirt outside the pens, a kitten Wade assumed to be at the heart of this whole damn fiasco still clutched tightly in his arms.

No, *he* was at the heart of this fiasco. If he hadn't yelled at Tanner, the boy wouldn't have run off and none of this would have happened.

He pushed the guilt away for now and focused on Caroline, sick all over again to see her pale, chalky features and the blue tracery of veins in her closed eyelids.

"Come on, honey. Wake up," he ordered as he did a rapid medical assessment.

Growing up on a cattle ranch had, unfortunately, given him plenty of experience in first-triage and he quickly put those skills to work. Her pulse seemed fast but strong and he hoped she had just had the wind knocked out of her.

No bones seemed to be broken but her head had taken a pretty hard crack and it wouldn't surprise him if she had a concussion. A couple of bruised or cracked ribs weren't out of the question either.

If that was the worst of it, she'd be lucky, he thought, but when he was checking her legs for fractures, he felt something sticky at the back of her thigh. He pulled his hand away and his stomach dropped when he saw it was covered in blood.

What was it from? he wondered, not sure whether he dared turn her over to see.

His mind replayed the scene in his head, relived that sickening moment when the cow had charged, and he realized exactly what must have happened, where the blood was coming from.

The cow's horn must have caught the back of Caroline's thigh as she'd tried to get away.

He swallowed a raw oath, not wanting to scare Tanner any more than he already was, and turned her over slightly so he could see what he was dealing with.

His worst fears were confirmed at the jagged puncture wound in her thigh. Blood was already pooled underneath her and the sight made his own blood run cold.

Knowing it was vital he stop—or at least slow—the copious bleeding, he yanked off his work shirt for the relatively clean T-shirt underneath to use as a pressure bandage.

He was punching in 911 when Seth and the news crew came around the corner of the barn, probably to see what was taking him so long.

When Seth caught sight of them, of Wade without his shirt and Caroline stretched out on the ground, he hurried over, Cody in his arms.

"What happened?"

Tanner suddenly started bawling and turned to his uncle for the comfort Wade didn't have time to give.

"I went to get this k-kitty in the corral and Caroline came after me," the boy sniffled. "One of the c-cows got mad and ran to get us and Caroline pushed me out of way but the cow hurt her and now she won't wake up and it's my fault."

Seth pulled him close. "Okay. It will be okay, bud."

Wade hoped so. With all his heart, he hoped so. The 911 operator finally answered and he recognized a woman he'd gone to high school with, one of Andrea's cousins on her mother's side.

"Hey Sharon, this is Wade Dalton. I need an ambulance up here at the Cold Creek for a thirty-year-old female who's been gored by a range cow. She's unconscious, with a possible concussion and likely a couple bruised ribs as well as a puncture wound in the back of her left thigh."

"Is she breathing?"

Wade watched the steady rise and fall of her chest and took some small comfort from that. "Yeah."

"Is she out of harm's way?"

"You think I'm going to leave her in a corral with an angry cow? Yeah, she's safe. Dammit, Sharon. Just send an ambulance fast!"

"Sorry, Wade but I have to ask the questions. Stay on the line while I call the guys."

It would be at least ten minutes before the volunteer paramedics could make it here from town, he figured. A moment later, Sharon returned to the line. "Okay, they're on their way."

"Thanks, Sharon. Call Jake at the clinic, okay? Tell him it's Caroline and have him stand by."

"Will do. Want me to stay on the line until the crew gets there?"

"No. I've got it from here."

She was waking up, he saw. She moaned a little and started to move restlessly, trying to roll from her side where he'd moved her, to her back. He held her still and he watched her eyes blink open as she tried to get her bearings.

He saw the pain and confusion in her eyes as she looked blankly at the camera crew and Seth, then she turned her head slightly, probably so she could see what was keeping her from rolling back.

The minute her gaze found him, the distress in her features eased and her body seemed to relax.

"I guess I wasn't fast enough," she murmured.

"Told you those range cows can be ornery buggers."

He was astonished at the tenderness soaking through him, though it couldn't quite crowd out all the fear.

She closed her eyes for a moment but opened them a second later and he saw they were wide and panicky. "Tanner! Where's Tanner?"

"Over there with Seth, see? All safe and sound."

She followed the direction he pointed and the relief in her eyes touched some deep chord inside him. She was battered and bloody, but her first thought was still for his son.

At the sound of his name, Tanner approached them, his cheeks tearstained. He knelt down and grabbed hold of Caroline's hand. "Are you mad at me?"

"Oh, honey. Of course not." She squeezed his fingers and Wade felt like some icy band around his heart he hadn't realized was there had started to loosen.

"I'm sorry I went inside the pens where I'm not supposed to go. I'm sorry you got hurt."

"How's the kitten?"

"Good."

He held it up for her and she sighed. "A lot of trouble for a little ball of fur. Good thing he's cute."

The T-shirt Wade was using as a bandage was soaked with blood and he could see her features were getting paler. The kids didn't need to see all this, he thought, and he had a feeling Caroline would feel more comfortable without the crowd of onlookers.

"Seth, maybe you should take the boys and our guests up to the house until the ambulance gets here."

"You sure there's nothing we can do?"

"Send somebody back with something clean I can use as a fresh bandage."

Seth nodded and herded everyone toward the house.

When they were gone, Wade folded his work shirt and tucked it under her cheek so she didn't have to lie in the dirt.

"Thank you," she murmured, her voice weak and thready.

"Hang on. The ambulance is on its way."

Her eyes fluttered open and connected with his. "Oh, is that really necessary? I don't want to be a bother."

"Honey, you've been gored by an eight-hundred-pound range cow. Trust me, it's necessary."

She blinked and the pain in her eyes tore at his heart. He would do anything to take it away, but he was completely helpless. "Gored," she murmured. "That must be why my leg feels like it's on fire."

"Afraid so."

"I thought I just went the rounds with a freight train."

"Yeah, a close encounter with a cow will do that to you."

"You sound like you speak from experience."

"A few times. You can't grow up on a ranch without your share of bumps and bruises."

"Have you been gored?"

She was talking to distract herself from the pain, he realized, and he felt another band around his heart loosen.

"Once. I was fourteen and Jake dared me to do a little bull riding. Dad had this ornery bull he was selling to one of the neighbors, so he had it penned waiting for them to come for it. Somehow we managed to chase him into a chute and I climbed on. We didn't have a rope or anything, just me being an idiot. I probably lasted half a second before I went flying into the air. I was like you, I almost made it out before he caught me."

The worst part of the whole ordeal had been Hank's fury when he'd found they had used an expensive animal for sport. He hadn't worried so much about his son as he had about the bull. Hank had even made him walk up to the house through agonizing pain, he remembered.

Marjorie had almost left the bastard over that one, he remembered, then he realized Caroline's eyes were closed again and pushed the memory away.

"Come on, honey. Hang on."

"Hurts."

He brushed her hair out of her eyes. "I know, sweetheart. But listen, there's the ambulance. Can you hear it? They'll be here in a minute to take you to Jake and he'll fix you right up. He's a hell of a doctor."

"Will you come with me?"

Her quiet words ripped out what was left of his heart. "I doubt they'll let me ride on the ambulance but I'll bring the boys and follow it to the clinic, okay?"

She nodded just as the ambulance arrived.

A moment later, the place bustled with paramedics. Wade stood up, shirtless and suddenly freezing in the cool wind.

His hands were bloody, his chest ached, and he felt like he'd aged at least ten years in the last ten minutes.

Chapter 12

Two hours later, Wade decided he'd aged more like twenty years since seeing that cow heading straight for Caroline and Tanner.

Now he sat across the desk from his brother in Jake's pathologically clean office at the clinic, where Wade had sat for the last two hours thumbing through journal articles on topics about which he had no interest or comprehension.

"So what can you tell me? Are you done with her yet? Will she have to transfer to the hospital in Idaho Falls or can I take her back to the Cold Creek?"

Jake leaned back in his chair twirling a pen in both hands with something perilously close to a smirk on his features. "I'm afraid that as you're not a blood relative of Ms. Montgomery, I'm not at liberty to give you any information about her condition unless she signs a release."

He glared. "I'm *your* relative and I can still pound your smart ass into the ground without breaking a sweat."

"Sorry, but self-preservation is not adequate justification for me to break the law. Bring it on, brother."

Wade suddenly remembered just why Jake used to drive him crazy when they were kids. "You're enjoying this, aren't you?"

"You've been pacing in here like a nervous father for the last two hours. I have to say, I haven't seen you this upset since…" His voice trailed off, along with his grin, and his mouth tightened.

"Since Andrea's illness," Wade finished for him grimly.

Compassion and regret flashed across Jake's features. "I'm sorry for giving you a hard time. I wasn't thinking about how all this must bring back memories of Andi."

"It's not the same. Andi was my wife. My life. Caroline is just…just…"

He couldn't seem to come up with the right word for the place she had filled in his life. Sometimes he wasn't even sure he liked her very much, then others he couldn't stop thinking about her, remembering that kiss they had shared, her crooked little smile that seemed to brighten the whole house, her endless patience with his kids.

Despite his protestations to Jake, he had to admit that his emotions of the last two hours had been eerily similar to those terrible, helpless days he had prowled that hospital room in Idaho Falls while his wife had tried and failed to fight off the infection that had finally claimed her life.

How could he even compare the two experiences? It made no sense and yet his worry and fear felt the same.

"Caroline's a trooper," Jake said. "No tears, no hysterics. She even made a few jokes while she was under the local and I was sewing up the puncture wound. Forty-five stitches, all told, but she's doing fine."

"I thought you couldn't talk about her condition with me."

Jake pulled a paper out of a file and tossed it on the desk, his expression a little shamefaced. "Oh, look. A release form. I must have forgotten Connie had her sign it when they were filling out her insurance papers."

Wade glared at him in disgust. "You always were a son of a bitch."

Jake smirked. "How could I be otherwise when I had such a fine example in my older brother?"

"So what can you tell me? What's the extent of her injuries?"

Jake suddenly became all doctor, no longer a teasing younger brother trying to yank his chain. "Your triage assessment was right on. The X-rays showed two cracked ribs, just as you suspected, I'm guessing from hitting the fence. From what I can piece together, the cow came at her from behind, head down, and caught her in the leg."

"Yeah, I know that part. I was there."

Just remembering it sent cold chills down his spine. He knew he would never forget that horrible moment when she'd gone flying through the air. No doubt he would relive it in his nightmares for a long time.

"Well, she was relatively lucky. It could have been

much worse. As it is, she has a deep laceration in the back of her thigh. It went through the biceps femoris but missed the popliteal artery by a fraction of an inch. If it hadn't, she probably would have bled to death at the Cold Creek before you were able to summon help."

Wade felt cold, light-headed, just thinking about the idea of a world without Caroline in it.

How had she come to be so important to him in just a few days? He let out a ragged breath then covered it by coughing a little as if he were only clearing his throat.

"What kind of a recovery time is she looking at?"

Jake studied him closely and Wade hoped like hell none of his emotions were showing on his face.

"Well, I can't lie to you, she's going to hurt for several days. The ribs are going to be the worst of it but deep tissue trauma like a gore wound isn't easy to bounce back from."

"Yeah, I remember."

"That's right, I forgot you've been there, El Matador."

He narrowed his gaze. "You should be damn grateful you're a good doctor, otherwise you'd be too obnoxious to tolerate."

Jake laughed, unoffended. "We gave her a local anesthetic while I was sewing things up and she's still a little numb from that but I don't think there's any need to transfer her to Idaho Falls to the hospital. I can keep a closer eye on her here. She'll have to stay off it completely for a couple days and I've urged her not to travel for at least a week. I figured she can stay at my place until she's ready to go back to California.

I can take turns checking on her throughout the day with my clinic nurses."

"Forget it. She's staying at the Cold Creek."

His vehemence seemed to surprise Jake as much as it did him.

He wasn't sure why he hated the idea of her staying with his brother so much. It probably made more sense all around. She would certainly be able to get more rest without his kids in the way and she would be closer to expert care with Jake in the same house, but he hated the whole idea.

Jake folded his arms. "And why is that? Because, as usual, you think you're responsible for the whole world?"

"Not the whole world. Just people who are injured on *my* ranch, by one of *my* cows, while they happen to be in the process of saving *my* son's life. I'd say that gives me some responsibility to see she's cared for properly."

"You don't think she would be at my house? See that diploma on the wall? I do happen to be the doctor here, remember?"

"As if you would ever let me forget. But just because you're the one with the fancy degree doesn't automatically make you the best one to take care of Caroline," he said. "You work eighteen-hour days and she would be alone all day except for the few times you sent people to check on her. She'd be miserable."

"You're a great one to talk about working long hours! Your kids see you for five minutes a day if they're lucky."

What was it with everybody telling him what a lousy father he was, all of a sudden?

"Look," Jake went on, "I'm sure Caroline understands you're grateful to her for going after Tanner like that. But she also has to know you have your hands more than full at the Cold Creek. I haven't forgotten how crazy autumns on the ranch can be. And with Caroline on the injured list, you're back to where you were when Mom left, without anybody to help you with the kids."

Wade clenched his teeth. "I'm well aware of that, but thanks for the reminder."

"I'm only pointing out that you can't handle the load you've already got. What makes you think you can take on the care of an injured woman, too?"

"We'll manage. I'll just have to take a few days off."

Jake stared at him like a fat, wriggling trout had just popped out the top of his head. "A few days off what?"

He shrugged. "Seth can handle things around the ranch and I'll stick close to the house and take care of Caroline and the boys until she's back on her feet."

He braced himself for more arguments but whatever his brother threw at him, Wade refused to let himself be deterred. He had absolutely no intention of letting Caroline recover anywhere but at the Cold Creek.

He owed her this for what she had done for Tanner—hell, what she'd done for all of them the last six days. She had stepped up when he needed help and he couldn't do any less for her.

Something else had been bothering him these last two hours and Jake bringing up Andi's illness finally helped him crystallize it in his mind.

When his wife had been so sick, he could do nothing for her but haunt the hospital, hound the doctors and spend every spare minute on his knees praying for God not to take her.

He was a man used to doing, not sitting back and watching others, and it had been hell to stand by while his wife had grown sicker and sicker.

Here was something concrete he could handle, something he hadn't been given the chance to do for Andi. And maybe by helping to nurse Caroline, in some way, another of the scars crisscrossing his heart might heal.

"I'm taking her home," he said firmly.

To his surprise, Jake—the same one Marjorie used to say would argue with her if she said his eyes were blue—completely folded.

After another long look at Wade, he nodded. "Fine. I'll give you a list of discharge instructions before you take her back to the ranch. She's being fitted for a pair of crutches and I'll have to call in a prescription for painkillers and heavy-duty antibiotics, then after that she should be good to go."

Despite his relief at not having to engage in hand-to-hand combat with his brother over the rights to care for her, he suddenly felt a spurt of panic at the task in front of him.

"Just like that? Are you sure you don't need to keep her longer for observation or something?"

Jake seemed to be fighting a smile. "Oh, I think I've seen all I need to see."

"What's that supposed to mean?" he snapped.

"Oh, nothing." Jake stood up, stretching a little as he did. His surgical scrubs were sweat-stained and he suddenly looked as tired as if he'd spent all day in the saddle roping steers.

"Never mind," Jake said. "I'll go let the nurses know you're ready."

Ready? He wasn't sure he'd go that far. Still, he'd made his choice and he backed his words up with action.

Hours later, Caroline dragged herself out of an uneasy, pill-induced sleep to a muted bass voice, a higher-pitched whisper and pain in every single molecule of her body.

Mercy, she hurt. For several moments after she awoke, she concentrated only on breathing past the pain until she could think straight. Even breathing hurt and she couldn't figure out why until she remembered the cracked ribs. Wade's brother had warned her they would probably hurt worse than anything else at first and she discovered he'd been telling the truth.

Her leg burned and throbbed but she could endure that. What she hated was not being able to take a deep breath into her lungs for the pain.

She did the best she could, keeping her eyes closed while she focused. Through the layers of pain, she listened to the voices—Wade and Tanner, she realized.

"If you can't remember to whisper, you'll have to leave," Wade admonished his son.

"I'll be quiet, I promise," Tanner said and Caroline almost smiled at that impossible claim. She wasn't sure Tanner could be quiet even if his mouth were taped shut.

Her eyelids were just about the only part of her that wasn't sore right about now, so she propped one up just enough to see she was alone with Wade and Tanner in a room she recognized as one of the empty bedrooms on the main floor.

Nat and Cody were nowhere in sight but Wade sat at the old-fashioned writing desk in the room with Tanner on his lap. The boy had a blueberry-colored crayon in his hand—his *unbandaged* hand, she saw with some delight, and his cute little face wore a frown of concentration, his tongue clamped between his teeth, as he peered down at what he was coloring.

"You sure you want that horse's tail to be blue?" Wade asked, his voice low.

"Do you think I should change it?"

"I guess it's your horse so you can do whatever you want. If you want it to be pink with purple polka dots, have at it."

"It's for Caroline, not for me, and she likes blue. She told me. It reminds her of the ocean in the summer. She lives by the ocean, did you know that?"

"I did."

"I asked her if she could go swimming anytime she wants and she said the water is kind of cold where she lives but she still likes to walk on the beach and look for seashells and sand dollars and take her shoes off so she can jump over the little waves."

"That sounds fun."

"And she said we could come visit her sometime in California and she would take us to find starfish and stuff. Can we, Dad?"

"We'll see," Wade whispered, an odd look in his eyes. "Looks like you're about done there."

"Yeah. It's a get-better card. Grandma and me made one for Molly Johnson when she had the chicken pox. You think Caroline will like it?"

Before she could answer that of course she would, she saw Wade give a slow smile then kiss the top of

Tanner's head. "She'll love it because you made it for her," he said in that same low voice.

As she studied those two male heads so close together, one so masculine and dark and strong, the other small and darling, Caroline's pain faded for just a moment, overwhelmed by a stunning realization.

She was in love with him.

It poured over her, through her, an inexorable, undeniable wash of emotion.

In love with Wade Dalton. Of all the idiotic things for her to do!

Her chest hurt, but she was certain the pain had nothing to do with her cracked ribs and everything to do with her cracked head. She had to be crazy to let things come to this.

What was she thinking? Why hadn't she protected herself better? Made some effort to toughen her spine, her mind, her heart?

She tried to tell herself that was just the painkiller talking, giving her all kinds of weird delusions, but she couldn't quite make herself buy that explanation.

The worst of it was realizing she'd been sliding down this precarious path a little more each moment since she'd arrived at the Cold Creek. Surely she could have switched direction at some point along the journey if only she'd been awake enough to see in front of herself.

She had ignored the signs along the way, unwilling to face the truth until she'd been literally knocked off her feet.

Oh, this was bad. Seriously bad. She was going to end up more battered and broken by loving Wade Dalton than just a few paltry cracked ribs and a gouged thigh.

She thought of the article Darci Perez had mentioned earlier in the afternoon, another lifetime ago, it seemed. "Top Ten Best Ways to Guarantee a Happy, Fulfilling Life."

She had written it several months ago and couldn't remember everything in it but she was fairly sure that nowhere in there did she mention that one of those ways to guarantee happiness was to fall head over heels for a workaholic rancher who didn't trust her, didn't like her, and who was still grieving for his late wife.

She must have made some sound of distress—she wasn't entirely sure but she must have done something to draw attention because both of the males at the writing table swiveled their heads in her direction at the same time.

"Caroline! You're awake!" Tanner beamed with delight.

Wade studied her intently and she flushed, praying her emotions weren't exposed somehow for all to see. He approached the bed and she dug her fingers into the quilt.

"Did we wake you?" he asked. "We tried to be quiet but I'm afraid that was a losing battle."

Her mouth suddenly felt as if she'd been chewing sandpaper in her sleep and she could do nothing but shake her head.

He instinctively seemed to sense her need. From the bedside table next to her, he picked up a pitcher and ice rattled as he poured a glass of water and handed it to her. She took it gratefully and sipped until she thought she might be able to squeeze out a word or two.

"Thank you," she murmured and her voice sounded rough, scratchy.

How long had she been sleeping? she wondered. It was dark and Tanner was in pajamas, so it must have been more than a few hours.

"How do you feel?" Wade asked when she lowered the glass.

"Like I should have tire tread marks somewhere on my person."

He gave a sympathetic smile. "No tread marks that I can see. Maybe a hoofprint or two."

She winced and tried to move to a more comfortable position. She realized as she moved that she was wearing her nightgown. She frowned trying to remember how she had changed out of the clothes she'd been wearing when she'd been gored, but she couldn't grab hold of it.

She had worn what was left of her clothes home from the clinic, hadn't she? Much of the afternoon felt like a big blur. Someone here at the ranch had to have helped her change into her nightgown. Wade? she wondered and flushed at the thought.

"Where are the others?" she asked to distract herself.

"Cody didn't have much of a nap so he crashed right after dinner. And Nat's in doing homework."

"What time is it?"

"Almost eight. I gave this one a few more minutes but it's just about bedtime for him, too."

Tanner walked to the side of the bed, his picture in his outstretched hand. "I made you a get-better card."

He set it carefully on the quilt and she picked it up,

touched by his effort. "It's beautiful. I especially like the blue tail on the horse."

He grinned at his dad. "See? Told you she'd like it!"

Wade rubbed his hair. "So you did. Maybe Caroline would like us to tape it up somewhere that she could see it all the time. How about there by the bed?"

"Perfect," she said as Tanner rummaged in the desk and emerged triumphant with some tape. The next few minutes were spent watching him hang it crookedly on the wall.

"Thank you so much," she exclaimed when it was done. "You know what? It's working! I feel better already."

He beamed and fluttered his hands. "Hey, guess what? Uncle Jake took off my bandage when he came to check on you a while ago and he said I could leave it off since it's looking good."

"Great news!"

"Yeah, and I can get it wet and everything! I had a bath and I could play with my boats with both hands."

Wade stepped in and placed a hand on the boy's shoulder. "Okay, bud. Time to hit the sack. We've got a big day tomorrow."

Something important was happening the next day. She knew it but she couldn't seem to grab hold of what that might be.

"We're gonna play basketball and clean out the toy box and maybe make brownies if Dad can figure out how."

No, that wasn't it. She closed her eyes but still couldn't figure it out.

When she opened them, Wade was watching her, his blue eyes dark with concern.

"Go on up and find a book and I'll be up to read to you in a minute," he told his son.

The boy nodded, then smiled. "Night, Caroline."

She reached out and squeezed his fingers. "Good night."

Tanner hesitated for a moment by her bedside then, before she knew what he intended, he bent over and kissed her cheek, leaving behind the sweet smell of just-washed little boy.

"Thanks for helping me save the kitten. I would have been sad if a cow stepped on her but I'm real sorry you got hurt."

"Me, too. But I'm glad you were safe."

After Tanner left, Wade pulled his chair to her side, watching her with a strange, inscrutable expression on his face.

"You need another pain pill. I'm on strict orders to make you eat something before you take one. I can't claim to be a great cook but Mom left some soup in the freezer and I can heat you some. Beef barley."

She didn't want to eat and she certainly didn't want another pill. But already the pain was building and she knew it would only get worse if she didn't take something for it.

"I'm sorry to be a bother," she said. "I know you have so much to do...."

Suddenly it hit her and she remembered the scene with the TV crew that had led up to her accident. "The interview. You've got the news interview tomorrow. You don't have time to babysit me."

"It's all under control," he assured her.

"How?"

"Don't worry about it. I'm going to go in and warm up some soup for you then you can take a pill and rest."

She laid back on the pillow, too weak and sore and heartsick to argue.

Chapter 13

Twenty-four hours after leaving the clinic, Caroline felt as if that blow to the head she'd taken had permanently jostled her brain.

Either that or she had somehow slipped through the rabbit hole into some alternate universe.

She studied Wade standing in the doorway with a tray of more of the ubiquitous soup and scarcely recognized him. Who was this man and what had he done with the distant, taciturn rancher she'd come to know since arriving at the Cold Creek?

Wade had been nothing but solicitous and concerned since her accident. All day he had played nursemaid, fetching and carrying and even just sitting with her.

She had awakened in the night from a terrible dream where a vast herd of cows with glowing red eyes chased her down the beach, their heads down and their horns swinging until she had no choice but to dive into the surf to evade those vicious horns.

When she jerked her eyes open, gasping for breath, she found Wade dozing in the chair, his stocking feet propped on the bed beside her and a ranching magazine open across his chest.

She found him surprisingly vulnerable in sleep, without the hard edges and harsh lines on his features during the day.

Without the burdens and cares he carried when awake, he looked young, relaxed, and she grieved for this man who had lost so much and who could only release the load of his responsibilities while he slept.

She watched him for a long time, wondering how many opportunities she would have to share this kind of quiet moment with him. Her feelings for him were a heavy ache in her chest and she wondered what she would possibly do with them after she left the Cold Creek.

Sometime during her scrutiny, his eyes opened and she was completely disarmed when his cheeks colored and he dropped his stocking feet to the carpet.

"Sorry." He rubbed a hand through his hair. "Guess I fell asleep."

"What are you doing here?" she asked.

He shrugged. "You've had a concussion. I'm supposed to check on you through the night."

"I don't think that requires an all-night vigil, do you?"

"I promised Jake I would follow orders. He said to keep an eye on you through the night, so that's what I'm doing. Or that's what I'm supposed to be doing anyway. I won't fall asleep again."

Completely astonished, she stared at him, not knowing how to respond. "You can't stay up all night! I'm sure that's not what Jake meant. Tomorrow's a big day for you, with the TV interview and all. You need your sleep."

He closed the magazine and set it on the desk, not meeting her gaze. "Seth and I decided he would take care of the interview. He knows as much as I do about ranch operations. They shot plenty of footage of me spouting off today before your accident. I told Darci the reporter will just have to use that if he wants me included in the story."

Maybe if her brain weren't so fuzzy from the pain and the pills, she could figure this out. As it was, nothing he was saying made sense. "So you're not going to do the interview?"

"No. Seth is."

"But why? This is an important opportunity for you to showcase the Cold Creek and the improvements you've made."

"Yeah, and Seth can do that as well as I can. Better, probably. He's young, good-looking and has a hell of a lot more charm. All that will play well on camera."

She wondered if Wade had any idea that while Seth was extremely good-looking and probably flirted in his sleep, he reminded her of a young, playful pup compared to his older brother.

Wade was rugged, masculine, *compelling*. No woman who saw him on or off camera would ever be able to forget him.

Why had Wade suddenly decided to delegate the important interview to his brother?

While she tried to puzzle it out, she shifted to find

a better position and wanted to smack her forehead when the answer came to her.

Her. He was doing this because of her. "You think you need to stay here and babysit me. *That's* why you're having Seth do the interview."

"Don't worry about it. We've got everything worked out."

"I will worry about it. I can't let you make that kind of sacrifice for me. I can take care of myself, Wade."

"You can't even get out of bed by yourself right now."

"You don't have to feel responsible for me!"

"I *am* responsible for you."

"Since when?"

He met her glare with a level look. "Since you nearly died saving my son's life."

She let out a breath, embarrassed by the depth of gratitude in his eyes. "Don't be silly. You don't owe me a thing."

"I owe you *everything.*" His voice, low and intense, sent shivers down her spine. "If you hadn't been there, Tanner would have been trampled or worse in that corral."

"Wade—"

"No sense arguing about it. Seth is going to take over for me for a few days while the kids and I get you back on your feet. That includes doing the interview."

A few days? Wade Dalton was taking time off work during what she had quickly come to learn was his busiest time of the year for *her?*

"I… You can't do that."

"It's done." Suddenly he gave her a disarming smile. If she weren't already in bed, he would have knocked the pins right out from under her with it. "Besides, my mother—your new stepmother—would never forgive me if I didn't take proper care of you, especially with the circumstances of how you were injured. I can hear her now lecturing me all about bad karma and all that. Now let's get you something for the pain I can tell is coming back nastier than a one-legged dog with fleas."

She hadn't known how to answer him the night before and she still didn't know what to say as she studied him in the doorway, the boys on either side of him. Tanner held a pitcher in his hand and Cody had what she assumed was an empty plastic cup.

"Lunch time." Wade smiled.

"Hi, Caroline," Tanner chirped. "We made soup and a cheese san'wich. My dad made it and everything."

Wade shrugged, his cheeks suspiciously ruddy. "I opened a can and threw a piece of cheese and bread under the broiler. Sorry, but that's about the best I can do unless I'm standing in front of a barbecue grill."

"I'm sure it will be delicious," she said.

"Sit by Care." The youngest Dalton beamed, holding his arms up for her.

"You'll have to have your dad help you up," she told Cody.

Wade set the tray on the table by the bed. "Better not. He might bump your ribs or your leg."

"Then I'll scream bloody murder and hand him back to you."

He shook his head. "It's your funeral."

He lifted the toddler up and Cody gave her a big, toothy smile like he hadn't seen her in months. He held out his arms and hugged her, tucking his head beneath her chin. It did hurt but she decided a little pain was a small price to pay to hold a sweet, loving little boy who smelled of sunshine and baby lotion.

"Hey Dad, can I sit up there with Caroline, too?" Tanner asked.

"You'd better not. You're a little bigger and tougher than your brother."

Tanner's heart didn't seem to be broken by that news. "Well, can I go back and watch *Blue's Clues* then?"

Wade considered. "Stay by the TV, though. No wandering around outside and no going in the kitchen."

"Okay," Tanner promised and hurried out of the room with a quick wave to Caroline.

"Can you eat like that?" Wade asked.

Caroline settled the boy next to her, on the other side from her injured leg. "We'll be just fine, won't we, Cody?"

The toddler nodded and cuddled closer. To her surprise, Wade pulled up a chair while she tackled her lunch.

"You don't have to stay," she murmured, a little uncomfortable at him watching her eat.

"I'd better, just so I can keep the kid there from giving you a judo chop to the leg."

"He's fine. I think he's going to be asleep in a minute."

Sure enough, before she even tasted her soup, his eyes were half-closed and a moment later he was out for the count. He moved a little closer, bumping her leg, but she wasn't about to complain.

"He's a beautiful boy," she said with a smile. "All three of your children are. You know, I can see bits of you in Nat and Tanner but Cody is his own little man."

She paused, debating the merits of pressing forward, then took the plunge anyway. "From what I can tell, he resembles the pictures I've seen of your late wife."

Wade said nothing for a long moment, then he nodded slowly. "He does. If you looked at baby pictures of Andrea, you would swear you're looking at Cody. She had the same brown eyes and blond hair, the same dimples, the same full bottom lip."

He paused. "And you know, their personalities are similar in a lot of ways. He's got the same sunny disposition and same easygoing attitude toward life. I'm sure you've noticed Cody is a cuddler and Andrea was happiest when we were all sprawled together on the couch watching a movie."

She smiled, touched that he would share this piece of his past with her. "What a wonderful blessing that you've been given these three beautiful children so you can remember your wife whenever you look at them. Especially this one."

"They are a blessing. Every one of them." He paused, a faraway look in his eyes. Not pain, precisely. Just memories.

When he spoke, his voice was low and she sensed instinctively he was telling her something he didn't share easily.

"I couldn't even look at Cody for a week or so after Andi's death," he said slowly. "It was such a crazy time and I was...lost inside. Totally messed up. My wife was gone and here was this bawling newborn baby who needed so much, along with Tanner who wasn't much more than a baby himself and Natalie who was old enough to know what was going on."

"She must have been devastated."

"We all were. This sounds awful," he went on, "but I kept thinking, I hadn't wanted another one in the first place. I'd been perfectly content with Natalie and Tanner. Andi was the one who wanted another child. I guess part of me blamed Cody. It wasn't fair, I know, but I thought, if not for him, she wouldn't have caught that staph infection during the delivery. She would have been healthy and strong, ready to take on the world, like always. My other two kids would have still had their mother, I still would have had a wife. If only she hadn't pushed so hard to have another one, everything would be just fine. I don't know if I blamed God, Andi or the baby more for her death."

"Oh, Wade."

He looked at the boy and the softness in his eyes brought tears to her own.

"Thank the Lord my Mom stepped in to help because I wanted nothing to do with him. I don't think I would have let him starve but I sure didn't want to see him or touch him or anything. But about a week after the funeral, Mom was in taking a shower when Cody woke up howling. I almost left the house right then, I couldn't stand it, but I finally made myself go in to see what he needed."

She almost reached for his hand but she didn't want to move, to breathe, afraid any interruption might compel him to stop talking. He was giving her a rare window into his world and she was touched beyond words that he would share this with her.

"It was like something out of the movies. You know, one of those unbelievable moments." He smiled a little. "One minute he's shrieking loud enough to knock the house over, but as soon as he caught sight of me, he shut right up, stuck a little fist in his mouth and just stared at me out of Andi's eyes for the longest time."

He didn't add that when Marjorie had finally come in to check on the quiet baby after her shower, she'd found Wade in the rocking chair clutching Cody tightly and bawling his eyes out like he hadn't been able to do since Andi's death.

He also didn't add that in those first horrible months after she'd died, the only peaceful moments he remembered—the moments he'd somehow felt closest to Andi—were when he'd been holding their baby. On nights when he couldn't sleep for the pain, he even used to sometimes go into Cody's room in the middle of the night, just so he could pick the sleeping baby up out of his crib and rock him until he could remember how to breathe again around the vast, endless grief.

He looked up from his thoughts to find Caroline watching him, a tear trickling down her cheek. Guilt swamped him. "You're in pain and I'm in here yakking your leg off. I'm sorry."

She reached out and squeezed his arm, and the simple touch almost made him feel like bawling, too, for some crazy reason.

"No. I'm fine," she insisted. "I just can't imagine what it must have been like for you."

She was crying for *him?* He wasn't exactly sure how he felt about that but he did know that when she pulled her hand away, part of him wanted to reach for it again.

"The hardest thing was the kids. It still is, really," he said. "Trying to do right by them is tough on my own, even with Marjorie's help. Whatever you might think— whatever my mom thinks—I love my kids. They're first in my heart, even if I don't always act like it. Everything I do is for them. I might not be able to give them as much time as I should, but I love them."

He heard that blasted defensiveness creep into his voice, but he couldn't seem to help it. He wanted so much for her to understand. It seemed suddenly vitally important that she not see him as a father trying to shirk his duty by his children.

She wiped at her eyes. "I know you do. I know. It was presumptuous of me to ever imply otherwise and I'm sorry for what I said the other night. I have this bad habit of thinking I know what everyone in the entire world should be doing to improve their lives. I forget that my help isn't always wanted or needed."

"I guess that's why you're a life coach, then. So people will pay you to boss them around."

She laughed softly at that and, for some reason, it moved him that she could still laugh even when she was in pain—and at herself, no less.

"My dad always told me that if you're lucky enough to find something you're good at, you have to hang on to it with both hands and not let go no matter what the world throws at you."

He decided in the spirit of goodwill between them, he would put aside his animosity toward her father and try to understand what his mother might have seen in the guy.

"What does your father do for a living? I never thought to ask Marjorie. I guess that's something I should know if I'm to perform my son-in-law duties effectively."

What had he said to put that strange, edgy light in her eyes? he wondered.

"Oh, he's retired," she said quickly.

"From what?"

Her fingers tightened on the quilt. "A little of everything. Sales, support, research and development. I guess mostly sales, you could say."

Now that sounded like a whole lot of nothing. He wanted to push for more specifics but he could plainly tell she was uncomfortable with the subject and he didn't want to press her when she was hurting.

He didn't want their conversation to end, though, he realized, so he fished around for another subject.

"Where are you from originally? I assumed California but I just realized I never bothered to ask."

Again, he got the strange impression she was picking her words carefully. "I'm one of those unfortunate people who doesn't really have a hometown, except the one I've chosen for myself as an adult."

She smiled a little but it didn't reach as far as her eyes.

"I'm not like you, born and bred in one place like the Cold Creek. We lived in Texas for a while when I was a kid—Houston and San Antonio, mostly—and then my mother died when I was eight and after that we moved around a lot."

"Just your dad and you?"

She gave a sharp, tight-looking nod and he wondered if she was hurting. "I was an only child."

"I'm sorry."

She looked surprised at his word. "When I was a kid, other kids at school always told me how lucky I was to have my dad all to myself. But I always wanted a couple of older brothers and an older sister or two."

"My brothers drive me crazy most of the time but I can't imagine not having either of them."

"You're very lucky," she murmured. "And your children are as well. No matter what else happens, you all have each other."

"You have your dad," he pointed out.

She seemed to find that amusing in a strange sort of way. "Right. My dad."

"And according to Seth, you're now our stepsister."

He meant it as a joke to lighten her odd mood but she gave him a long, charged look that had his palms sweating.

"I don't think either one of us wants to think very seriously about that, do you?" she said quietly.

He suddenly couldn't think of anything but the kiss they had shared, of her arms wrapped around him, of the wild heat flashing between them like a summer lightning storm.

He shifted, wishing he could get those blasted images out of his head. But every time he looked at her mouth, every time she smiled, every time her soft vanilla scent drifted to him, they came flooding back.

The room instantly seemed to seethe with tension and he regretted the loss of their brief camaraderie.

He had never told anyone about Cody, probably because he was ashamed of that initial anger he'd felt toward a helpless, completely innocent little baby. Marjorie was the only one with any inkling and even she didn't know the whole of it.

He wasn't sure why he'd told Caroline, he only knew that once the words had started, he couldn't seem to hold them back.

He had learned a few things about her but he wanted more. He wanted to know everything. The name of her second-grade teacher, her favorite kind of candy bar, her happiest memory.

The realization scared the hell out of him. He had no need to know those things about Caroline Montgomery—or to share his deepest, innermost secrets with her.

That was the kind of thing a man did with a woman he was dating, a woman he thought he might have feelings for.

A woman whose kiss he couldn't get out of his head.

Wade rose abruptly. "I'd better go check on Tanner. Who knows what kind of trouble he might get into if I don't."

"Right. Good idea," she said, her voice quiet.

"Do you want me to take Cody out of your way?"

"No. Let him sleep."

Her smile looked a little strained, he thought with concern. "Are you sure he's not hurting you?"

"He's fine," she insisted, running a gentle hand over Cody's blond curls. The boy made a sound and moved closer. "I'll call if I need you to come get him."

He nodded, picked up the lunch tray and headed for the door, wondering as he went how on earth he could be so jealous of a two-year-old.

Chapter 14

By the afternoon of the second day after her injury, Caroline decided she'd had enough of pain pills that left her loopy and disconnected, and she stopped taking them, at least during the day.

Though the result was a low, throbbing ache in her ribs and stabbing pain in her leg, she decided it was worth the price to feel moderately like herself again.

She also reached the firm conclusion that if she had to spend one more moment in her room—lovely though it was—she just might have to throw one of her crutches through the window.

She nearly planted a big, juicy kiss on Jake when he came to check on her and said there was no reason she couldn't sit on one of the recliners in the great room with Wade and the children.

"Those sore ribs are going to make it tough to work

the crutches," Jake said. "I'll go get Wade so he can help you move to the other room."

Before she could ask Jake why *he* couldn't help her, he left with a peculiar smirk on his handsome features.

She hadn't seen much of Wade since their encounter the day before. She couldn't decide if he was avoiding her or simply wrapped up in the children and the ranch paperwork she knew he tried to catch up on anytime he had a spare minute.

He had brought her meals and checked every hour or so to see if she needed anything—or sent one of the kids in to check—but there had been no more opportunities for revealing conversations.

She was glad, she told herself. She was afraid she had already revealed too much about herself. Better if he left her alone so she had no more opportunity to make a fool of herself or to slide deeper and deeper in love with him.

For an instant, she regretted asking Jake if she could start getting up and around. Maybe she should stay in her room, despite the boredom, for the sake of her heart.

The decision was taken out of her hands a moment later, though, when Wade walked through the open doorway. He wore jeans and a soft gray chamois shirt, and he looked big and hard and gorgeous.

She sighed, wishing she were wearing something a little more attractive than her old nightgown and robe.

"I'm under orders to help you into the other room," he said, gazing at some point above her head.

"Jake is afraid I'm not quite ready to handle the crutches on my own because of the bruised ribs."

For some reason, she was compelled to make it clear

to him this had been entirely his brother's idea that Wade come in to help her.

Wade finally met her gaze and her stomach twirled a little at the strange expression in his eyes. She would have given just about anything right at that moment to know what was going on inside his head.

He moved toward the bed and, before she realized what he was doing, he scooped her up gingerly. Not expecting the move, or the sudden shock of finding herself held so gently in his powerful arms, she couldn't contain a quick gasp.

"Did I hurt you?" He looked aghast at the idea.

"No. I just don't think this was what Jake meant!"

A muscle flexed in his jaw. "Oh, I'm pretty sure it was, since his exact words were *go carry Caroline from her bedroom to the recliner in the great room.*"

"He should have at least warned me what the master plan was here," she said.

"Yeah, me, too," she thought she heard him mutter but it was so low she couldn't be sure.

"I can probably make it on the crutches if you'll just spot me," she said, though she wanted nothing more than to stay right here, nestled into his heat and strength.

He smelled divine, of some kind of outdoorsy aftershave, and his shirt had to be the softest material she'd ever felt as her arms slid around his neck to hang on. He was close enough that she could have drawn his head down to hers without much effort at all....

"You could have said something if you were bored in there."

She blinked, hoping he didn't notice the sudden color

she could feel creeping over her features. "I didn't want to bother you. You're already doing so much for me."

"What? A few meals, that's about it. Doesn't seem like much in return for saving my son's life."

Before she could respond to that, they made their way far too quickly to the great room.

The moment they walked through the doorway, the children reacted in different ways to the sight of her in their father's arms. The boys both shrieked her name as if they hadn't seen her in months and raced to her side.

While she was greeting them with laughter, she caught sight of Natalie sitting at the table with Jake, her math book spread out in front of her. She looked stunned at the two of them together, as if she'd never considered the possibility of ever seeing another woman in her father's arms.

Caroline wanted to assure her Wade was just helping her, that there was nothing between them, that she would never take her mother's place, even if she could.

She could say nothing, though, with everyone else looking on.

Still, she was aware of Natalie's hard stare the whole time Wade carried her to the recliner then set her down as carefully as if she were fragile antique glass.

"Is that good?" he asked gruffly and Caroline shifted her gaze from the daughter to the father. His jaw looked tight and she saw his pulse jump there and she wondered if he'd been affected by their nearness as much as she had been.

"Yes. Wonderful—thank you so much. It's amazing how a simple change of scenery can lift my spirits."

"Don't overdo it," Jake warned. "You'll pay the price if you try to take on too much."

"I know, Dr. Dalton. I'll take it easy, I promise."

He rose from the table. "Sorry I can't stick around but I've got to run to the hospital in Idaho Falls to check on one of my patients who had surgery this morning."

"What about my homework?" Natalie asked, a plaintive note in her voice. "I still have, like, ten problems to go."

Wade frowned at her. "I'm still here," he reminded her. "Uncle Jake's not the only one who knows long division, you know."

"Yeah, but he always explains it better," she muttered.

"I'll do my best to muddle through," Wade said dryly.

"Care read?"

Caroline glanced away from the homework drama to find little Cody hovering near the arm of her chair, a favorite picture book in his chubby fingers.

She smiled. "Of course."

"No, not that one," Tanner objected, not far behind. "That one's a baby book. I'll find a better one."

He raced out of the room, most likely to scour his bedroom bookshelves for something more to his liking, leaving Cody standing by her side, his picture book held out like an offering to the gods.

She smiled at him and patted her uninjured leg. "Come on up here, kiddo. Maybe we can get through this one before your brother comes back," she said.

Cody giggled as if they shared a particularly amusing secret and climbed from the footrest onto her lap.

"Is he okay?" Wade asked. The worry in his eyes warmed her even more than Cody's sturdy little body.

"Wonderful." She wedged a throw pillow between her aching ribs and the little boy, then opened the book.

They turned the last page just as Tanner skipped in, his arms loaded with at least a dozen books.

"These are better," he announced, dropping them all to the floor. "Start with this one."

He handed her a rhyming book about trucks she had already read to him at least a dozen times during her time at the Cold Creek, then he pulled an ottoman next to her recliner and perched on it with all the anticipation of a baby bird awaiting nourishment.

The next hour would live in her memory forever as one of those rare, sweet moments when all seems perfect with the world.

A soft rain clicked against the window but a fire in the huge river-rock fireplace took away any chill from the October night and lent a cozy, snug feeling to the gathering room.

While Wade and Natalie slogged their way through the intricacies of arithmetic, Caroline read story after story to the boys, repeating a few of them several times. Tanner wasn't often able to sit still through long bouts of reading but for now he seemed content to settle in next to her, trying to pick out letters he recognized.

A few times she felt the heat of someone watching her and looked up to find Wade studying her intently. As soon as she would meet his gaze, he would quickly turn his attention back to Natalie, but not before she thought she saw an odd, baffled kind of look in his eyes.

Though she knew it wasn't productive and would only lead to more heartbreak when she returned to Santa Cruz, she couldn't prevent her imagination from playing make-believe, if only for a moment. Was this how things would be if they were a family? If she belonged here at the Cold Creek with Wade, with his children?

Autumn evenings spent in front of the fire, winter nights with a soaring Christmas tree there in the corner, springtime with the windows open and the sweet smell of lilac bushes wafting in.

They would sit here, the five of them, sharing stories and memories and laughter.

And then after the children were asleep, Wade would turn to her, those blue eyes bright with need, his strong hands tender on her skin....

She blinked, stunned at herself.

The last little part of her fantasy wasn't so surprising—since that kiss and probably even before then, sexual awareness simmered between them. She couldn't manage to look at him without remembering his mouth, firm and warm on hers, and those large, powerful hands buried in her hair, at the small of her back.

But the rest of it totally took her by surprise. She had no idea such desires lived inside her.

She had made a rewarding career out of helping people discover the true dreams of their heart.

Contrary to what many of her clients thought when they first contacted her, coaching was not about telling people how to live, gleefully doling out advice to anyone who would listen.

She tried to help her clients dig deep into their psyches to discover their potential and break down all the barriers people erected to keep themselves from risking everything to touch those dreams.

How had she so completely missed this deep-seated need inside herself, then? This intense craving for home and hearth?

She thought she was fulfilled by her life in California but as she listened to the rain and the pop and hiss of the fire and studied the sweet faces of the Dalton children, she realized how much she envied Wade.

He had this all the time, this constant, unwavering love from his children and this unbreakable connection.

She wanted it all—not just the idea of children but the idea of *these* children. Tears burned in her eyes at the warm weight of Cody on her lap and Tanner leaning against her arm. She loved them, all three of them, as much as she loved Wade.

Her heart would rip apart into a thousand jagged pieces when she had to leave the ranch and the Daltons.

She couldn't think about that now. For now, she would sit here and listen to the rain and enjoy the night and these sweet children.

She must have closed her eyes for a moment. The next thing she knew was Wade's voice in her ear, low and disconcertingly close.

"How in the world did you pull that off?" he asked and she blinked her eyes open and found him standing by the recliner.

"Sorry?"

"Must have been a pretty boring story," he murmured.

It took her a moment to realize both boys were asleep—Cody nestled under her chin and Tanner with his cheek resting on her forearm. She probably had dozed off, too. "No wonder nobody complained when I stopped reading."

He smiled, drawing her gaze to his mouth. A deep, intense yearning to taste him again washed through her and she had to clench her fists to keep from reaching for him.

"Where's Natalie?" Her voice sounded hoarse and a little ragged but she had to hope he didn't notice or would attribute it to lingering sleepiness.

"We finished homework so I sent her off to bed."

"No matter what she said, I thought you explained her homework very well."

His smile was a little lopsided and made her want to trace a finger at the corner of his mouth. "So I guess I could always be a math tutor if the whole ranch thing doesn't work out."

She could just imagine the women of Pine Gulch lining up to have him teach their children.

"What do you think my odds are of getting these guys up to bed without waking them?" he asked.

"I didn't realize you were a betting man."

"Every rancher and farmer I know is a gambler. It's part of the package. You gamble every time you plant a crop or buy an animal or take your stock to market."

"Well, I'll give you a fifty-fifty chance on the boys. I'd have to put my money on Tanner to be the one who wakes up."

"That's what you call a sucker bet." He grinned. "I'd have to be stupid to take it and I try not to be stupid more than once or twice a week. I'll get them settled and then I'll come back and help you back to bed."

"No hurry," she assured him. "I'm still enjoying the change of scenery. Would you mind if I stayed a while?"

"No. Seth is coming in a few minutes to fill me in

on what went on today. We'll probably bore you to tears with all our shop talk."

"I don't mind. I enjoy learning about what goes into running a big ranch like the Cold Creek. Anyway, if I get bored, I have a magazine I can read. As long as you don't mind if I stay."

"No. That's fine."

She smiled and he looked as if he wanted to say something, then decided against it and reached down for Cody. His arm couldn't help but touch her breasts as he scooped the boy off her lap and she was suddenly hot everywhere he touched.

She had almost managed to cool down by the time he returned from carrying Cody upstairs. Her arm was asleep, with the weight of Tanner's head pressing it against the armrest of the recliner, but she hadn't wanted to risk waking him by moving.

Still, she was grateful when Wade returned for him. "One down, one to go," he said softly.

"Good luck."

"I think I'll need it with this one."

Just as he had done with Cody, he lifted Tanner into his arms, and though the boy murmured something and flung an arm across his father's chest, he didn't appear to wake up.

She watched them go, the tall, handsome rancher and his busy little son, quiet only in sleep, and pressed a hand to her heart as if she could already feel it begin to crack apart.

He would miss her when she went back to California.

It was a hard admission but Wade had never let himself shrink from things that were tough to face.

He stood in Tanner's bedroom, which his mother had decorated with everything cowboy, and watched as the boy nestled into his bucking-bronco sheets, rump up in the air like a potato bug.

Focusing on Tanner didn't help him avoid looking the cold, hard truth right in the eye.

Somehow in the few days she'd been on the Cold Creek, Caroline had managed to worm her way into their lives with her softness and her sweet smile and her gentleness with the boys.

The kids adored her, even Nat—though his daughter had seemed a little on the cool side tonight. Cody and Tanner thought she was the best thing to come along since juice boxes. He had watched their eyes light up when he'd carried her into the great room, the eager way both boys had come running just to be near her.

She seemed to adore them, too. Watching her spend the evening reading to his sons had given him a weird tug in his chest. He couldn't explain it and he wasn't sure he liked it, but he couldn't deny that his children had come to love her.

Having her there seemed *right*.

He stared at the rope border Marjorie had nailed around the room. How could that be? Caroline had only been at the Cold Creek a few days but already she seemed to belong, as if she'd been there forever, and he was having a tough time imagining how things would be when she left again.

Alone.

That's how he would be. Not just alone but lonely, and that seemed far, far worse.

He had been empty these last two years since Andi had died. Hollow, joyless, cold. There was a spring on their grazing allotment in the mountains that had suddenly dried up a few years ago when a severe drought had hit the West. But when he had taken the cattle up earlier in the summer, he'd discovered that by some miracle of nature, the wet winter had suddenly revived it and now it was pumping water again just like it had done for generations, clear and pure and sweet.

Since Caroline had come to the ranch, he felt like that spring. He had thought his life was all dried up after Andi had died, that anything good and pure was gone forever.

Now all those empty, dry places inside him seemed to be filling again.

He wasn't sure he was ready to come back to life—nor was he really thrilled about the fact that Caroline was the one who seemed to have brought about the change.

She wasn't at all the sort of woman he needed in his life. She didn't know anything about cattle, she had the same wacky New Age ideas Marjorie did about some things, and she had a busy life and career a thousand miles away.

But she seemed to love his kids, so much that she'd risked her own life to save Tanner's. She was kind and funny and she made his pulse jump every time she smiled at him.

He blew out a breath and tucked the covers closer around Tanner.

He would miss her like crazy.

Chapter 15

When Wade returned to the great room, he found his youngest brother sprawled on the same ottoman Tanner had pulled up next to Caroline's recliner earlier for story time.

Seth appeared so close, Wade was surprised he didn't have his chin perched on Caroline's arm just like Tanner had done.

He couldn't seem to control a quick spurt of jealousy. With his charm and good looks, Seth could have any woman he wanted—and he usually did. If he set his sights for Caroline, she wouldn't stand a chance.

Right now she looked like every other woman who ventured into Seth's orbit—completely charmed. She was laughing at something his brother said and she looked bright and animated and as pretty as a mountain meadow ablaze with wildflowers.

He had to admit, he was slightly gratified when she turned as soon as he entered the room and her crooked little smile actually seemed to kick up a notch or two.

"You can't be done already," she exclaimed. "Did Tanner really stay asleep?"

He shrugged, wondering what Seth would do if he shoved him off the ottoman to the floor and took his place next to her. "So far. I admit, I cheated a little."

"I knew there had to be something underhanded!"

"I didn't put him all the way in his pajamas, just traded his jeans for pajama bottoms and left him in his T-shirt."

"Sneaky," she said in an admiring tone.

"It's one of those survival skills every parent figures out early."

"You were sneaky long before the kids came along," Seth interjected. "You were the one who figured out how to rig that rope in the old maple tree so you could climb out your bedroom window, swing over to the tree and climb down the trunk. It was genius, something I used many a time after I took over your bedroom when you moved out."

"Only I used to sneak out and get in a little late-night fishing while you used it to go make out with SueAnn Crowley. Anyway, I'm sure Caroline isn't interested in this old family history."

"Oh, I am! Did either of you ever get caught?"

Seth grinned. "Nope. That rope is still probably there."

"Guess I'd better take it down before Tanner discovers it and figures out how to use it," Wade said.

He didn't want to go sit on one of the couches and

leave Seth here in close proximity to Caroline, so he opted to remain standing by the side of her recliner.

"So are you ready for me to take you to bed?"

At his abrupt question, her lips parted just a little and Seth made a sound that could have been a laugh or a cough.

It took a moment for Wade to realize what he'd said. When he did, he felt the tips of his ears go hot and red.

"I meant, can I help you back to your bedroom now?" he said quickly, making a mental note to teach Seth some manners next time the opportunity arose.

"Not yet. Do you mind terribly if I just sit here a while longer? The fire is so comforting and I'm enjoying the change of scenery. I promise, you two can take care of your business and you won't even know I'm here."

Right. And maybe tomorrow his horse would suddenly recite the Pledge of Allegiance. He had no doubt whatsoever that he would be aware of every sigh, every breath, every movement.

"You'll probably be bored to tears listening to dry ranch talk."

"I told you, I find it all interesting. Seth was telling me about the TV interview before you came down. It sounds like it went well."

"He did a good job representing the ranch," Wade said. "And the producer was fine about the change in plan."

How could she be otherwise, with Seth pouring on all his charm? He wouldn't be surprised if his brother had Darci Perez's phone number tucked away right now with all his others.

"I'm still sorry you missed it, especially when you didn't have to on my account," she said.

"She said they got enough footage of me explaining things around the ranch and they'll use that."

"When does it air?" she asked.

"Two weeks from yesterday," Seth provided. "At least that's what Darci said."

"I guess I'll be back in Santa Cruz by then," she said. "I'll have to be sure to watch it."

Her casual reminder that she would be out of their lives soon put a definite damper on Wade's mood.

"It's late," he said curtly to Seth. "Let's go through the log so we can all get to bed."

They moved to the table Nat used for homework and Seth pulled out his report of the day's activities.

For the next half hour they discussed feed schedules, which animals to cull for the winter and Seth's encounter with a neighboring rancher disputing water rights.

"Sounds like you handled Simister just right. He needs to know where we stand on this. I wouldn't have done a thing differently."

"Thanks." Seth looked surprised at the comment and Wade wondered if he'd been too stingy with the praise over the years. If so, it was something he'd picked up from old Hank Dalton.

He had worked alongside his father every day until Hank had dropped dead of a heart attack. He could count on one hand the number of times Hank had offered anything to him but criticism.

Had he become like his father in other ways without realizing it? He thought of the extra work Seth had done these last few days with an eagerness that had surprised him, then made him feel guilty, especially when he realized Seth was more than capable of the job.

His brother made sound decisions, treated the ranch hands with fairness and decency, and had clear ideas about what they were trying to accomplish at the ranch.

Wade should have been delegating to him more, especially these last few years after Andi had died, he suddenly realized. Lord knew, he could have used the help and Seth seemed willing to step in.

Wade wasn't sure why he hadn't seen it, but somehow he had fallen into the habit of thinking of Seth as the same irresponsible kid he'd been when Wade had taken over running the ranch. Maybe because his brother was still a very swinging bachelor, still running around with his friends from high school, still hanging out at the tavern in town.

He acted like he was still in college, though he'd graduated and come back to the ranch five years ago. Seth never seemed to take anything seriously and when Wade compared his brother's life to his own, full of responsibility after responsibility, Seth came out looking reckless and carefree.

Now he wondered how much of his brother's wildness stemmed from Wade's own lack of trust in him.

It was a stunning revelation for him.

Since the day his father had died, Wade had taken his responsibilities to the ranch and his family very seriously. It was tough for him to surrender that burden to someone else because he loathed the idea of anyone thinking he was shirking his duties.

But maybe by failing to delegate more to Seth, he had caused both of them harm.

"You've done a good job these last few days," he said slowly. "I'm sorry for the extra work."

Seth started gathering up the papers he'd brought. "I'm not. It's been a major learning experience. I've gotten a whole new perspective being the big hombre for a few days."

"You're a good cattleman, Seth. Maybe you ought to give some thought to running your own herd."

Where before Seth had looked astonished at Wade's appreciation, now he looked flabbergasted. His mouth sagged open and he stared for a full moment before he composed himself.

"I've thought about it some," he admitted, then paused. "What would you say if I told you I'm more interested in training horses?"

Wade couldn't say he would be surprised. Seth had been horse-mad since before he could walk. Wade and Jake both enjoyed horses, but Seth had always been passionate about them.

His brother had been a team roper on the college rodeo circuit and had even spent a couple summers on the pro circuit. It seemed like he always had a horse he was working with.

"What kind of operation?"

"Cutters." Seth said the word so fast, Wade realized his brother had indeed given this some thought. "Breeding and training them."

"I thought that was just a hobby with you."

"A hobby I'm damn good at. You know Calliope never met a cow she couldn't work and I trained her from a colt. And remember, I worked that gelding for the Stapeley kid and he got a buckle at the PRCA finals out of the deal."

"What sort of business plan have you considered?"

"Find a good stud, to start with. I've got my eye on one from over at the Diamond Harte in Star Valley. If I could come up with the capital, I think Matt Harte would give me a good deal on it."

"The man has quality horses, that's true."

Seth went on for another ten minutes about what he would do if he ran a breeding-and-training operation, and with every word, Wade felt more and more ashamed.

He had completely undervalued his brother, had been so wrapped up building his own legacy at the Cold Creek that he hadn't seen Seth had dreams of his own.

He wouldn't make that mistake again.

A few weeks ago, he might not have seen the value in a man holding onto his dreams. But things seemed different now. He risked a glance at the recliner where Caroline sat, a magazine propped open on her lap as she gazed into the fire.

You don't think following your dreams is important? she had asked that first day she'd shown up at the ranch.

At the time, he'd thought a man would do better to focus on fulfilling his responsibilities. Now he realized that the work he did at the Cold Creek was both his responsibility *and* his dream. He loved the ranch and had poured his heart into making it a success.

How could he deny Seth the same opportunity?

"You know, you do own a quarter share of the Cold Creek," he said slowly. "Seems to me if you've got your heart set on working with horses, you ought to stop sitting around thinking about it and get serious."

Seth narrowed his gaze. "What are you saying?"

"Off the top of my head, I can think of at least two or three spots on the ranch that would make a good location for stables and an indoor training arena."

His brother had the look of a man afraid to hope. "The Cold Creek has always been about cattle."

"Well, maybe it's time we shake things up a little."

Wade and Seth talked for another half hour about the risks and the challenges of stretching the ranch in a second direction. Seth had thought things through in great detail, and Wade wondered if his brother ever would have acted on those ideas or if he would have been like Wade, so consumed with the daily minutia of running the ranch that he'd lost sight of the bigger picture along the way.

Caroline had helped him refocus, he realized. On his kids, on himself, on more than just the ranch.

The thought distracted him from the business at hand enough that he looked over at the recliner and found her asleep, her cheek resting on one hand.

Seth followed his gaze. "I guess we bored her right to sleep."

"I better take her back to bed."

"And I'll take that as my cue to get out of here. I've got plenty to think about tonight."

If his thoughts involved more than women and whiskey, Wade had to be grateful.

Seth tugged on his denim jacket but paused before putting on his Stetson, his features serious. "At the risk of having you bash my face in, can I offer some advice?"

"You might as well, since I'm pretty sure I'm not going to be able to stop you."

Seth cocked his head toward Caroline. "I don't pretend to know all there is to know about women—"

"And yet you seem to be doing your best to screw up the learning curve for the rest of us."

Seth grinned. "I do what I can."

A second later, his grin slid away as he looked at Caroline again. "Take it from a man who knows women. Caroline is different. She's funny and sweet and smart. She listens when you talk, she's not one of those people who just waits until you wind down before they launch into their own life story. She cares about people, you can tell."

Wade glared, not liking that look in his brother's eyes. "And you're telling me this because...?"

"There's something going on between the two of you. I don't pretend to understand that either, but nobody could miss the vibes the two of you are sending out. She watches you all the time and when she's not watching you, you're watching her. It's a good thing we're into the rainy season because the two of you put out enough sparks to start a forest fire."

Wade flushed, hoping like hell she was really sleeping and not just pretending, and embarrassed that Seth had noticed the attraction he apparently hadn't been able to conceal. "You're crazy."

"Maybe. But I've got to tell you, brother, if a man is lucky enough to find a woman like that, he'd be a damn fool if he didn't hang on to her and never let go."

Before Wade could respond, Seth shoved on his hat and headed out the back door toward his place.

Wade watched him go, a weird ache in his chest as his brother's words rolled around in his head.

Hang on to her and never let go.

Suddenly he wanted desperately to do just that.

How could this have happened?

He slid down to the much-used ottoman next to Caroline and watched her sleep in the flickering glow of the firelight. How could she have come to be so important?

Looking at her always seemed to take his breath away a little.

She was like something out of a painting hanging in one of the fancy galleries over the mountains in Jackson Hole, all soft, muted colors and elegant lines.

He hated to admit it but Seth was right. Caroline was different.

She had brought laughter and light back to the ranch, had given him hope again in a future that consisted of more than just next year's yield and what interest rates the bank would charge him.

He thought of his talk with Seth and realized suddenly that it was no coincidence they had never had that kind of conversation before. It was more than just Caroline opening his eyes to the importance of having something good to hold onto.

He hadn't talked with Seth about his dreams before because Wade had been so consumed with surviving the present—with the ranch and the kids and all of his many obligations as head of the family—that he hadn't allowed himself to give much thought to the future.

He hadn't wanted to think about the future, not when the present was so bleak.

Now it was as if a door in his mind and heart had opened somehow, showing him a world of possibilities. The only question was whether he was willing to take the chance of walking through that door.

The log in the fireplace finally burned through and broke apart with a loud crackle and a shower of sparks, and the sound seemed to jerk Caroline from sleep.

She blinked her eyes open slowly, like a tiny kitten exposed to light for the first time.

At first she looked confused and he saw the dull wash of pain there before awareness crept in and she sat up a little with just a tiny wince.

"Oh, dear. I've been asleep, haven't I?"

"Yes. I should have taken you back to bed earlier. You need a pain pill, don't you?"

She made a face and looked around the room, ignoring his question. "Did Seth leave?"

"Just barely."

"Before I drifted off, I heard you talking with him about training and breeding horses."

"It's a good idea. Seth has always been a hell of a horseman and if anyone can make it work, he can."

"He was certainly excited about it. More focused than I've seen him since I've been here. It was wonderful to see."

"Well, we've got a lot of planning to do before we bring in the first horse but we'll work up a business plan and see if it's feasible."

"You'll do it even if it's not a huge moneymaker for the ranch, won't you?"

She sounded so confident of it, he flushed that she could read him so accurately. "Probably. It's always good to diversify as long as it's not a big drain on our resources. And I've suddenly realized Seth needs something to call his own. I should have seen it before. Even though he works alongside me on the ranch, his heart has never really been in it. Not like mine is, not like Jake's is with his clinic."

She reached out and touched his arm. "You're a good brother, Wade."

More than he wanted his next breath, he wanted to tug her into his arms and kiss that soft smile. But she was hurting, he reminded himself. He could see it in her eyes. "Come on. Let's get you back to bed so you can take a pill and stretch out."

She must have been hurting more than she let on because she let him scoop his arms under her to lift her carefully from the recliner.

Her arms slid around his neck for balance and she tucked her head under his chin, and it was all he could do not to bury his face in the vanilla-ice-cream scent of her hair.

"I'm sorry you have to do this," she murmured.

I'm not, he almost said, but caught himself just in time. He didn't know how many more chances he would have to be close to her like this.

Hold her close and never let go. Seth's words echoed in his mind. If only things were that easy. Yes, he had feelings for her. But that didn't mean she returned them or that she could ever be happy at the Cold Creek.

He would do well to remember that.

He carried her into her room and set her carefully on the bed. "I'll get you some water so you can take a pill."

"I don't want any more pills."

"I can understand that but you'll sleep better if you do."

"Just tonight, though, then I'm throwing the bottle away."

He poured her water from the pitcher by her bed and

handed it to her. "Do you need me to, uh, help you into the bathroom or anything?" he asked after she swallowed the pill.

She shook her head, color rising on her cheeks. "I think I can make it that far on my own. Thank you, though."

He had a million things he wanted to say to her but couldn't think of the right words for any of them.

"Well, good night, then. Call if you need anything."

"I will."

He turned to leave but froze when she reached out and touched her fingers to his arm again. She often touched him to emphasize a point, he was discovering. He didn't care why she did it, he just found he liked it, that he was hungry for any kind of contact with her.

"Wade, I...thank you so much for all you've done for me since I was injured. I know it's been hard for you to turn so much over to Seth but I'm grateful."

"I've learned some things through the experience. My kid brother can handle a whole lot more responsibility than I've been willing to give him over the years. I guess you could say your little run-in with that cow has been good for me and for my brother."

"I'm so pleased I could help you both out," she said dryly.

He laughed out loud and she gazed at him, a strange light in her eyes.

"What?" he asked, intensely aware of her hand still touching his arm.

"I've never seen you laugh before."

He stared at her, thinking back over the week she'd been at the ranch. He hadn't laughed once? It seemed impossible. "Am I really that much of a humorless curmudgeon?"

"You smile at the children sometimes but you don't laugh. And there's always a sadness in your eyes." She was quiet for a long moment, then she spoke softly. "It breaks my heart."

His heart seemed to tumble in his own chest at her low words. "Ah, Caroline."

For a moment, he was terribly afraid she was going to cry. Her mouth tightened and her eyes glistened but a moment later she smiled, though her eyes were still a little watery.

"Now that I know you have the ability to laugh, I'm going to do everything I can think of to make you do it again."

Her confident statement surprised another laugh out of him and she grinned triumphantly and squeezed his arm. "See? Whatever I'm doing is working already."

"Something is working," he murmured, then he couldn't help himself. He had to kiss her again.

As soon as their mouths tangled, reality rushed in and he froze, stunned at his impulsiveness. He would have jerked back but she slid her arms around his neck with a soft sigh he found incredibly sexy and returned his kiss with fierce intensity, as if she'd been waiting just for this.

Chapter 16

Caroline forgot about the pain digging into her ribs, the throbbing from her leg wound. She forgot about the differences between them and her inevitable heartbreak when she left the ranch.

All she could focus on was Wade touching her, tasting her, like he couldn't seem to get enough.

He murmured her name in that slow, sexy drawl she had come to adore, the one she discovered he only slipped into once in a while when he forgot himself.

She wanted him to forget. She wanted him to think only of her, not the past or the future. Just this moment.

He was bent at an awkward angle, still standing while she was stretched out on the bed, so she slid over to make room for him and tugged him down to the bed beside her.

He pulled her across his lap, supporting her weight

with his arm, and his hands were breathtaking in their gentleness as he traced her chin and tilted her face for his kiss.

His mouth explored her, tasting each hollow, each curve, until she wanted to weep from the emotions pouring through her—love and longing and terrible fear that she would never know this sweet wonder again.

She couldn't speak any of those feelings so she tried to show him with her mouth and her hands what was in her heart.

She couldn't have said how long he held her. A few moments? An hour? Time seemed to have lost all meaning; the only thing that mattered to her was Wade.

Finally, when she was beginning to seriously wish they could share more than these kisses, wonderful though they were, he wrenched his mouth away. "Stop. We have to stop."

"Why?"

His laugh—that sound she adored so much—sounded hoarse, strangled. "You want that list of reasons in alphabetical order or prioritized in order of importance?"

"Neither. I don't want you to stop kissing me." With her arms around his neck, she tried to pull his face down but he was far stronger than she was. He pulled her hands free and held them in his.

"Carrie, we can't. You're just loopy from the pain pill. It's wrong for me to take advantage of you like this."

Okay, maybe she was starting to feel a little buzz. The world suddenly seemed like a beautiful, shiny place, but she didn't know how much of that was from the pain pills and how much came simply from being in Wade's arms again.

"That's ridiculous. I've been dying for you to kiss me again since the last time."

When a muscle flexed in his jaw, she smiled and traced it with her forefinger, loving the rough texture of late-night shadow against her fingertips.

"Since the first night I stayed at the ranch, I've thought about it. Dreamed about it," she whispered.

His breathing caught and she watched his Adam's apple work as he swallowed hard. "You don't know what you're saying right now. You're not yourself."

She certainly couldn't seem to make her brain work the way she wanted it to, but still she smiled softly and reached for his hand. "Here's a confession for you, Wade. I'm more myself when I'm with you than I've ever been in my entire life."

He looked stunned, so shocked she wondered if she should regret being so open with him. No. She meant her words and she wouldn't take them back. Instead, she leaned forward and kissed him. He didn't move for several seconds, then he returned the kiss with tenderness and almost unbearable sweetness.

Finally he pulled away again, resting his forehead on hers. "You make it hard to leave."

"You don't have to."

"We both know I do. You're hurting and you need to sleep and I …" He paused. "I need to think about all this."

"About what?"

He pulled away, sitting on the edge of the bed, and said nothing for a long time.

When he finally spoke, his blue eyes were solemn.

"About the two of us. About where this might be heading and whether that's a journey I'm prepared to take right now."

She nodded, sensing the admission was not a comfortable one for him. She leaned back against her pillows, suddenly exhausted.

"I don't know if this will make any of that thinking easier or harder," she murmured, "but I should tell you that it would be very easy for me to have feelings for you."

"Caroline—"

"I just thought you should know, that's all."

He watched her for a long moment. "And I should tell you that while it would be very easy for me to return those feelings, I'm just not sure whether I'm ready to let myself do that."

She could be content with that, she thought as she closed her eyes and gave in to the exhaustion. It was far more than she'd ever expected.

Caroline woke the next morning with a sweet and giddy anticipation singing through her veins.

For the first few hazy moments after waking, she couldn't quite understand how it was possible to feel so happy when every inch of her body ached, and then recollection flooded back.

She settled back on the pillow and a smile blossomed as she remembered the tenderness of the night before, the intense, smoldering kisses.

Wade cared about her. He couldn't have kissed her, touched her so sweetly if he didn't.

Oh, she knew they still had much to work through and he could very well decide he wasn't ready for a new love yet. But she would wait. She had waited thirty years to discover what she really wanted out of life. She could wait a while longer for those dreams she hadn't known lived inside her to come true.

How could she ever have imagined when she'd set off on this impulsive journey to try dissuading Quinn from a hasty marriage that she would end up falling in love with a gruff rancher and his three adorable children? With the wild, harsh beauty of the Cold Creek?

She and Wade had a future together. She was sure of it. Now she just had to convince him.

But not without a shower first, she decided. She had contented herself with quick sponge baths since her accident but she needed the full deal today before she could face the day.

Wade had brought in a sturdy plastic lawn chair to give her added support in the bathroom and she maneuvered it into the shower then positioned her injured leg outside the shower curtain so the bandage wouldn't get wet.

It was tricky work and by the time she finished, her ribs ached and her head was pounding, but she was blessedly clean.

When she turned off the spray, she heard a loud banging on the door, so insistent she had to wonder how long it had been going on.

"Caroline?" The voice was low, male and furious. "Caroline, what the hell are you doing?"

She reached for a towel off the rack. "Drying off."

"You've got no business doing that on your own!"

Was he offering to help? she wondered, her stomach trembling at the thought. Still she was compelled to refuse. "I think I can handle wielding a towel by myself, thanks."

"Not that part," he growled. "I meant the shower. You're going to fall and break your neck."

"I'm done now and I handled things just fine. I'm feeling much better this morning."

It was only a little lie, she told herself. She *did* feel better, but the qualifier was perhaps a bit on the excessive side.

"Why didn't you wait for someone to help you?"

She patted her hair with a towel. "I didn't need help. Everything's under control. I'll be out in a moment."

Suddenly she remembered with chagrin that she'd left her clean clothes on the bed in the adjoining room, thinking it would be much easier to maneuver out there where she had a little more room.

Under normal circumstances, she would wrap in a towel and grab them, but she wasn't entirely sure she could manage to stay covered and work the crutches at the same time.

She finally decided she had no choice but to throw on the robe she'd been wearing. She put it on again and ran a quick comb through her hair, then picked up her crutches.

When she hobbled out, doing her best to stay covered, she found Wade standing outside the door, his arms crossed over his chest. He looked so forbidding she had to wonder if she imagined the heat of the night before, some painkiller-induced fantasy.

No. Her imagination simply wasn't productive enough to conjure up something so magical.

"Where are the kids?"

"Nat's already on the bus and Seth took the boys

into town with him to get some fencing. They always love a trip to the hardware store."

They were alone in the house, she realized, and her insides seemed to shiver as she wondered if he would take this rare opportunity for privacy to kiss her again.

Not with that distant expression back on his features, she feared.

"You do look like you're getting around okay on those," he said, instead of pledging his undying love, as some silly corner of her mind had hoped he had come to do.

"I've been practicing. I'm still not proficient but I'm trying."

"Does it hurt your ribs to use them?"

"A little. But it's worth it to feel mobile again."

Okay, maybe not as mobile as she thought. The shower had sapped her energy more than she'd realized and her knees were trembling a little with the effort to stay upright, so she hobbled to the bed and lowered herself down.

"You don't have to do everything by yourself. Call me next time. That's why I'm here."

"You're sweet to worry about me but I'm fine," she insisted. "A little weak but fine."

"I'm not sweet." He said the words so harshly she blinked. "I don't want you getting the wrong idea because things have maybe been a little different these last few days. The truth is, I'm bad tempered and pigheaded and impatient. I get caught up in a project and I lose track of time. I can be thoughtless and stubborn and I've never been one for much social chitchat."

"That sounds like a disclaimer."

He focused on a spot above her left shoulder. "I just

wanted to make sure you knew these last few days have been outside the norm, that's all. And anything you might have said last night about…about feelings or anything else, I didn't take it seriously."

Ah. Now his words made more sense. "I was never more serious in my life. I haven't taken any pain medicine this morning. My brain is clear and unclouded. And my feelings for you haven't changed."

If anything, she thought, they had deepened with this show of awkwardness. How could a man so big and strong and confident in matters of his ranch be tentative and uncomfortable about this? she wondered.

"Caroline—" he began, his eyes a dark, intense blue. But before he could finish the thought, they heard what sounded like the front door open, then a familiar woman's voice.

"Wade? Caroline? Kids? Anybody home?"

Her gaze locked with Wade's as she recognized the voice from her coaching sessions. What horrible timing for Marjorie and Quinn to return.

The honeymoon was over.

A week ago, Wade would have been doing handstands and jumping in circles to hear his mother's voice. But now he wished she would just go away for another week.

In their crazier moments, he and his friends used to cliff dive at a reservoir a few miles away and, talking with Caroline just now, he'd had that same shaky, pulse-pounding feeling he used to experience just before soaring toward the water.

"Caroline—" he said again, not sure what he intended to say.

"Later," she murmured. "Maybe you should go out and say hello while I finish dressing. I'll be out in a moment."

"I'll just go let them know I'm here then come back and help you out, all right?"

She nodded and he walked out in search of his run-away mother.

He found the newlyweds in the great room, looking at the display of family pictures on one wall.

Quinn Montgomery was tall, handsome and athletic looking, with a California tan and a full head of salt-and-pepper hair. He stood with a casual arm around Marjorie and, even from here, Wade could see she looked a decade younger.

She had her hair styled a different way, lighter somehow, and there was a glow about her he was sure he hadn't ever seen before.

Both of them turned when he walked into the room. Marjorie stared. "Wade! I didn't expect to find you home at this hour."

"I do live here," he reminded her dryly.

"I know, but I assumed you would be out working." She looked around. "Where are the boys?"

"Seth went to the ranch supply store in town for some fencing and they decided to ride along."

"Are you sick? Is that why you're home at this hour?"

He didn't want to launch into a complicated explanation about Caroline's injury until she was there so he changed the subject by looking pointedly at her new husband.

Quinn Montgomery had his daughter's eyes, he discovered. They were the same warm brown and right now they were scrutinizing Wade just as intensely, with curiosity and a healthy mix of amusement.

"I believe your son is waiting for an introduction, Marjie."

His mother tittered—she actually *tittered* like some kind of teenager!—and threaded her arm through Montgomery's. "I'm sorry, dear. I don't know where my manners have gone."

She then performed a polite introduction as if they were strangers meeting at a garden party.

Wade had never felt so awkward in his life. Just how was he supposed to respond to the bastard who had eloped with his mother—especially when the bastard in question happened to be the father of the woman Wade…had feelings for?

"Montgomery," he said tersely.

Quinn Montgomery's smile also looked remarkably like his daughter's. "Dalton," he responded in kind. "You have a beautiful ranch here. I'd love to have a tour."

I'll just bet you would, he thought.

"We're very proud of it," he said instead. "The Daltons have been ranching here at the Cold Creek for four generations. We're one of the biggest cattle operations in eastern Idaho."

And we're not about to let some aging, slick-eyed Lothario swindle his way into a share of it, he thought.

"I'm afraid I know next to nothing about cattle ranching, although Marjorie has done her best to give me a primer while we were driving out here. She says you've built the ranch into a real force in the beef industry."

"We're working on it."

"And succeeding, from what your mother says."

Wade scowled. Was Montgomery's interest mere curiosity or something more sinister?

Whatever it was, he didn't want to talk about the Cold Creek's success—or lack thereof—with some total stranger, even if the man was married to one of the ranch's partners.

"So what are your plans, now that the honeymoon is over?" Wade asked pointedly.

His mother giggled. "Oh, it's far from over, believe me," she said with so much gleeful enthusiasm that Wade wanted to cover his ears. He absolutely didn't want to know that much information.

"Marjie, this whole thing is no doubt tough enough on your boys," Montgomery chided gently. "You're not making things any easier."

To his surprise, for a moment, Marjorie looked taken aback, then apologetic. "You're right. I'm sorry, dear," she said to Wade. "As far as our plans, we're going to have to work out the details but I told Quinn I still intend to help you with the children as long as you need me. We were thinking about selling my house in town and building a place of our own out here. That way we're close enough to help you but would still have a little privacy."

If it meant he wouldn't have to have her new husband underfoot all the time, Wade would build the place with his own bare hands.

Montgomery smiled. "There will be time to work out all these details. No need to rush into any decisions today." He paused. "Tell me, is my daughter still here?"

"I'm right here, Dad."

Wade turned to see Caroline standing in the doorway on her crutches.

"Good Lord!" Marjorie exclaimed, her eyes wide and horrified. "What happened?"

"I had a little accident a few days ago, but I'm feeling much better now and Jake says everything is healing nicely."

"Sit down before you fall over on those things," Wade growled. "You were supposed to get dressed and wait for me to come back and get you, not come trekking in here like Sir Edmund Hillary."

"I walked twenty feet, I didn't climb Mount Everest. That may have to wait a while."

She looked wobbly to him, her features pale and her weight leaning a little too heavily on the crutches. He shook his head but hurried forward and scooped her up, then set her carefully in the recliner.

He was rewarded with a blush. "You can stop babying me anytime now, Wade. I'll never learn how to use the crutches if I don't practice. You can't carry me everywhere."

"You think I'm going to let you kill yourself when I'm standing right here to help?"

"You're not always going to be standing right there," she pointed out. "I have to figure it out on my own sometime."

She changed the subject by looking past Wade to Montgomery. "Hello, Dad." There was a reserve in her eyes Wade wasn't expecting, though he thought he saw love there, too.

Quinn stepped forward and kissed her cheek. "Hello, baby. I was surprised to learn you were here at the ranch."

"Were you?" The coolness in her voice again surprised Wade. Since she'd come to the ranch, she'd been nothing but warm and friendly to everyone, from the ranch hands to Natalie's bus driver.

"There was no reason for you to come chasing after me. I thought I explained everything sufficiently in my email. You shouldn't have been so concerned."

"When you decided to run off with one of my clients without a word to me beforehand, you really didn't have the slightest inkling that I might consider that a cause for anxiety?"

"Carrie—"

"No, tell me Dad. Why didn't you mention to me that the two of you were corresponding?"

"We knew you would be upset," Marjorie broke in. "Quinn knew he had done the wrong thing answering your work phone that day you weren't home but we had such a lovely conversation, neither of us wanted to see it end. There was nothing underhanded about it, it was just too precious to share with anyone at first, especially when we knew you wouldn't be happy about how we met."

Caroline said nothing to that, only gave her father a long look. There were undercurrents zinging between her and her father that Wade couldn't pretend to understand. He did know she looked upset, though, and for that alone he decided to step in.

Before he could, Marjorie did the job for him. "I'm starving," she said suddenly. "We've been driving all night and didn't take time for breakfast. Would anybody else like an omelet?"

Caroline shook her head but her father smiled. "An omelet sounds great. Can I help you make it?"

"No, no. Why don't you stay here and talk to your daughter? I'm sure the two of you have a great deal to say to each other. Wade, why don't you help me in the kitchen and fill me in on everything that's happened around here since I've been gone?"

That particular conversation would take far longer than the time needed to whip up a couple of omelets, but he followed Marjorie anyway, impatient to talk to his mother.

"Isn't he wonderful?" Marjorie asked as soon as they were out of earshot. "He's kind and thoughtful and by some miracle, he's as crazy about me as I am about him."

Wade shook his head. "What the hell were you thinking, to run off with a man you only knew from the Internet, a man none of us had ever met? For all you knew, he could have been an ax murderer. Or worse!"

Marjorie grabbed a carton of eggs from the refrigerator. "I'm not some desperate old lady who just fell off the turnip truck, Wade. You don't think I considered that possibility?"

"But you married the bastard anyway!"

She narrowed her gaze at him. "Be careful, son. That bastard is my husband." The steel in her voice might have been coated in velvet but it was still most definitely steel.

He sighed. "Let me rephrase, then. You considered the possibility that the man you were sharing a clandestine long-distance relationship with might have a criminal past but you went ahead and married him anyway. Explain how an intelligent, progressive woman like you claim to be can make that choice."

"Because I love him," she said simply. "Quinn is a good man, honey. I knew that right away. Yes, he's had some run-ins with the law but he's paid his debt to society and moved on."

He stared at her, his blood suddenly running cold. "What do you mean, run-ins with the law?" he asked carefully.

She made a careless, dismissive gesture, an egg in her hand. "Just that. He was a little wild in his past but that's all behind him now. And before you think I was some naive old bat who let myself be charmed by a handsome face and a smooth talker, Quinn himself told me of his past the very first time we talked on the phone. He didn't have to—we were only casual acquaintances at the time—but he did."

Wade couldn't seem to think straight with the rushing in his ears and he was suddenly filled with a bone-deep foreboding. "Mother. Exactly what did he do?"

"Oh, this and that." She whipped the egg beater. "Ran a few schemes that went bad, a little grifting here and there. He was a bit of a rascal in the past and the law finally caught up with him. But I'll have you know, he's turned over a new leaf and has been a clean, productive member of society since he was released from prison four years ago."

Prison? *Prison?* Just when he thought this situation couldn't get worse. Now he had the delightful added complication of learning his mother was married to an ex-con.

He let out a long, slow breath, so angry he didn't trust himself to speak. A criminal. His new stepfather was a criminal.

Why was he just learning about this now? Caroline had been in his home for more than a week and not once had she whispered a single word about her father's dubious past.

He had a right to know, damn it. She should have told him. He had trusted her, had told her things no one else in the world knew. With all they shared, how could she have kept this part of her life a secret?

The deep ache of betrayal settled in his gut and he wasn't sure which was more powerful, that or the fury seething through him.

His instincts had been dead-on. A grifter. A scam artist. In Marjorie, the bastard had found a nice, juicy widow, then he'd wooed and wed her before her family could do a thing about it.

Caroline must have been in on the whole scheme. Otherwise, wouldn't she have told him about her father's past?

His stomach hurt suddenly like he'd been sucker punched, and he had to fight to press a hand there to help him catch his breath.

"Quinn deeply regrets the wrongs he did and has worked hard to make restitution," Marjorie went on, heedless of his turmoil. "Personally, I believe it shows a great strength of character to admit to his wrongs and try to repair the harm he caused. If you give him a chance, I know you'll love him."

She smiled as she added the eggs to the frying pan. "I'm sure you and the kids already love Caroline, don't you? She's such a sweetheart and she's so much like her father."

Yeah. He was finally beginning to figure that out.

Chapter 17

By the time he returned to the great room, Wade was fairly confident he had the worst of his rage and hurt contained behind a vast wall of ice.

Even though he wanted to pick up his new stepfather and throw him through the big picture window, he forced himself to be polite.

He was also polite to his mother, even though his second impulse was to lock her in her room until she rediscovered her brain.

Caroline, he mostly ignored, even though what he most wanted was to grab her and shake her and ask her why the hell she had to go and make him feel again, just so he could bleed.

Finally, just when he thought he might explode if he had to pretend another second, Marjorie finished her omelet and smiled at her new husband. "Why don't we go bring in our luggage and then have a look around the ranch?"

Quinn agreed with alacrity, just as Wade would have expected. Eager to get an eyeful of his score, Wade thought bitterly, grateful he'd had the foresight to contact the ranch attorneys right after Marjorie's fly-by-night wedding to make sure the Cold Creek assets were protected.

Caroline and her scheming father wouldn't see a penny.

"They seem genuinely happy, don't you think?" Caroline said as soon as they left. Her tone conveyed a relief and surprise he didn't quite understand and couldn't take time to analyze.

When he didn't answer, she gave him a searching look and then her smile froze.

"You don't agree that they seem happy?"

"Oh, they seem delirious," he snapped. "It's a regular lovefest here at the Cold Creek."

Her smile slid away completely. "What's wrong?"

His fury finally managed to burn a hole in the ice covering his emotions and he couldn't stop it from seeping through, even if he wanted to.

"Were you ever going to tell me?"

At his low, bitter tone, her face paled. "Tell you... what?"

"About my new stepfather and his interesting little hobbies. Oh, and, I don't know, perhaps you might have thought to mention the time he spent behind bars."

She drew in a sharp breath and her features lost even more of their color. "Wade—"

"What? Did it slip your mind? After all, he's such a fine, upstanding citizen now."

She folded her hands in front of her and, through his howling pain, he saw they were trembling slightly.

"What do you want me to say?" she asked in a small voice.

"What's your game, Caroline? Your father is easy to read. He finds a wealthy but vulnerable widow and charms his way into her life. It's an old and familiar story but I'm afraid this time it's not going to work. My mother can't cash in her share of the ranch unless the other three shareholders agree and I can guaran-damn-tee that neither I nor my brothers will ever do that. No matter how clever he might be, your swindler of a father won't see a penny of Cold Creek money."

Her dark eyes seemed huge, bruised, in her pale face and he had a twinge of anxiety but quickly discarded it.

"Your father's role is easy to figure out. But what is your part in this little drama? What were you hoping to gain by all this? By coming here and insinuating your-self into my life, into my children's lives?"

"Nothing," she whispered.

"Oh, come on." He bit out the words and had the hollow satisfaction of seeing her flinch. "If you were purely innocent, why didn't you ever mention your fa-ther's past crimes? You hoped I would never find out, didn't you? Because you knew that once I learned the truth, your little game would be over."

He wanted her to defend herself, to tell him he was crazy, to explain, but she said nothing, her mouth com-pressed in a tight line.

He let out a harsh breath. "If your father's half as good at the grift as you, no wonder my mother fell for him. You'll be happy to know, whatever game you were running, it worked. I fell for all of it, the whole sweet, nurturing act."

He couldn't remember ever being so angry—most of all at himself. He should have listened to his own instincts at first, his suspicions of her. If he had held on to them and protected himself a little better, he wouldn't be feeling this terrible, crushing sense that he had lost something rare and precious.

"I trusted you, Caroline. I let my children come to care for you, let *myself* care about you. For the first time in two years, the world seemed bright and shining and new. I thought you were someone good and decent, a woman I could love."

His last word came out savage and ugly and she made a small, wounded sound.

She was crying, he saw, and the sight of it arrowed right through his fury to his heart. Damn her. He couldn't let her get to him. He wouldn't fall for it, even though part of him wanted to hold her tight, to tell her he was sorry, to kiss her tears away.

She was only crying out of frustration because her plans had been ruined, he told himself.

"The tears are a nice touch," he snarled. "Too bad I've got your number now. You can shut them off anytime."

"Oh, can I?" she whispered, blinking hard.

Tears shimmered on her lashes and one more slid down the straight plane of her nose. She swiped at with a jerky, abrupt motion, but another one quickly took its place.

Suddenly his anger washed away, leaving only a deep, yawning sense of loss and he couldn't look at her anymore, with her soft eyes and her pretty features and her lying mouth.

"The minute Jake says you can travel again, I want you off my ranch," he said quietly.

"Of course," she murmured.

He turned away, thinking of how baffled and lost his children would be when she disappeared from their lives. Though he hated to ask her for anything, he knew he had no choice, for their sakes.

"I would appreciate it if you'd stay away from Nat and the boys during the rest of your time here. They're going to be hurt enough when you leave. I don't want them to suffer more for my stupidity."

He didn't trust himself to say anything more, just turned and walked out without looking back.

She certainly wasn't going to wait for permission from any of the Dalton brothers.

As soon as the door slammed behind Wade, Caroline allowed herself only a few ragged breaths for strength, then grabbed her crutches and pulled herself to her feet, welcoming the physical pain if it would take some of this terrible ache from her chest.

By sheer force of will, she made it to her bedroom and by the time Quinn wandered in a half hour later in search of her, she was sweating and pale but her suitcases were packed and waiting on the bed.

Quinn stopped in the doorway, his gaze taking in her luggage. "What's this about?" her father asked.

Though it cost just about everything she had left, she managed to speak in a calm, even tone. "I need a ride to the airport in Idaho Falls. I'm not physically able to drive yet."

Quinn looked surprised. "Do you really think that's wise? Hate to break it to you, baby, but you're not looking so hot right now. Maybe you ought to sit down and rest. Think this through a little."

"No. I need to leave."

Something in her tone or her expression must have given away her distress. Quinn's too-handsome features dissolved into concern and he stepped closer.

"What's the matter? Come here. You look like you just lost your best shill."

He wrapped her in his arms and for an instant she leaned her weight against him, surrounded by the familiar scent of his aftershave and the cinnamon mints he was never without.

The combination of smells made her feel ten years old again, and she wondered how she could love her father so much and still carry this heavy burden of anger.

She stepped away, balancing on her crutches. "Quinn, I haven't asked you for anything. Not anything, not even that time I spent four months in jail for something we both knew I had nothing to do with. I'm asking you now, calling in every marker. I need a ride to the airport. I can't stay here another minute."

To her chagrin, her voice broke on the last word and tears burned in her eyes again.

Quinn studied her for a long moment. "Oh, baby. I've never been much of a father to you, have I? There are plenty of sins Saint Peter can pile at my feet when I reach those pearly gates, but the worst will be the harm I've done to my little girl."

He slid his thumb over her cheek. "I was given a rare and precious gift, better than any score I could dream up, and I treated it like pigeon bait."

She couldn't deal with this. Not now.

"I need to go home. Please, Daddy."

Her tears were falling freely now and Quinn pulled her into his arms again. When he released her, he looked sad and tired and years older.

"Let me go find my keys."

Caroline wasn't sure how she survived the two weeks after she left the Cold Creek. She had little memory of the torturous plane ride home or of that first terrible night when she had wept until she'd thought for sure she must have no tears left. The intervening days all seemed to run together, a hazy blur of sorrow and loss.

Physically, she felt much better. Though her doctor in Santa Cruz still advised her not to put weight on her leg, she was moving around on her crutches with ease and the pain had abated significantly.

Her chest still ached but she wasn't sure if that was from her broken ribs or her broken heart.

She sighed now, gazing out the window at the little slice of ocean that was all she could see from her cottage.

A cold rain blew against the glass, as it had been doing nearly every day since she'd returned from the Cold Creek. She was so tired of it. If the sky would only clear, maybe she could feel warm again. She might even remember that the sun always came out again, even after the darkest night.

There was no sunshine in sight today. From here, the sea looked a churning, angry green, and the sky was heavy and dark.

In hopes of cheering herself up, she had opened a

jar of the tomato soup she'd canned with produce from her own garden. It was warming on the stove, sending out a hearty, comforting smell, and a fire burned merrily in her little fireplace, but she still felt cold, empty.

Somehow, she had to learn to go on, but the thought of a future without Wade and the children seemed unendurable.

She missed the children so much she could hardly bear it. Nat, with her rapid-fire conversation and her bossiness, Tanner and all that mischievous energy, Cody the cuddler, who was never as happy as when he was sitting on a warm lap with a book and his blanket.

And Wade.

Her finger traced a raindrop's twisting journey on the other side of the glass. She missed Wade most of all. She missed his strength and his slow smile and the sweet tenderness of his touch.

She had to snap out of this misery. Her work was suffering—it was very difficult to help others face their problems and weaknesses when her own life was such a shambles.

She'd had two sessions that morning and had to reschedule both, with great apologies to her clients, because she just hadn't been able to focus.

Tonight would be better, she told herself. She would have her soup, turn on some cheerful music, then try to finish some of the paperwork she had been neglecting since her return to California.

She had just dished up a bowl and set it on the table to cool when her office telephone rang. She waited for the answering machine to pick up but the ringing continued.

Rats. In the distracted state she seemed to permanently inhabit since leaving the Cold Creek, she must have forgotten to switch it back on after sending a fax earlier.

With an exasperated sigh, she grabbed her crutches to hobble in and turn it off. The ringing stopped just as she made her slow way to her office door, but it started up again before she could reach the phone. Whoever it was had persistence going for him.

She could turn on her machine and let technology catch the call or she could pick it up.

Maybe human contact would shake her out of her melancholy, make her feel a little less alone. She lowered herself to her office chair and picked up the phone.

"Light the Stars."

A long pause met her words and she heard a burst of static, then a male voice spoke, sounding like it was coming from some distant planet.

"Yes. Hello. I'm interested in your coaching services."

She almost told him to call back in the morning during business hours. But even through the dicey connection, she thought she heard a hint of desperation in the voice.

"Have you ever used a life coach before?" she asked, trying to gauge a little background on the potential client.

"No. But I need some serious help and you come highly recommended. I understand you're the best."

Not anymore, even if that were ever true. Right now she was a mess and she wasn't sure she could coach a mosquito to bite.

"There are many good life coaches out there. Finding the right one is always a little tricky. I always recommend that my clients talk to several before finding the one they want to work with."

"I don't want to do that. It's you or nobody else. I'm desperate here, ma'am."

She didn't need that kind of pressure—not now, when she was filled with self-doubt. But something about that staticky voice struck a chord within her.

"All right. We can set up a time for a trial session if you'd like—"

"Can't we do that now?"

She laughed a little, though it sounded hollow and tinny to her ears, and she wondered how long it had been since she'd found anything genuinely amusing.

"I'm afraid it doesn't work that way. After we schedule an initial session, I usually have my clients fill out a somewhat lengthy questionnaire on my Web site and email it to me so I have a little background information going into our session."

"What kind of questions?"

"Basic things, really. Name, occupation, your family dynamics. The areas of your life you're unhappy with...."

"I can tell you that one right off. My life is a mess, mostly because I've been an idiot."

Oh, I bet I've got you beat on that one, she thought.

"I've been stupid and mean to someone who didn't deserve it and in the process I threw away something that could have been wonderful. I'm miserable. The woman I love left me and I need your help trying to figure out if there's any chance I could win her back."

Caroline closed her eyes. Why couldn't his problem be something simple like a midlife crisis or dissatisfaction with his career choices? Why did it have to be a romance turned sour?

She couldn't deal with this right now, not with the shambles her own life was in.

"I don't think I can help you," she said quietly.

"You have to. Look, I'm desperate. This woman brought joy and laughter back to a cold and lonely world. She made me feel again, when I wasn't sure I ever would again. I can't face a future without her in it. I can't."

Even through the bad connection, the raw emotion in his voice came through clearly and Caroline was shocked to feel tears burn behind her eyelids. She definitely couldn't take on this client—or any client dealing with a relationship disappointment right now.

"I'm sorry," she said after a moment, "but I'm afraid you're going to have to find someone else to work with you. I can give you some referrals to some excellent coaches—"

"No. I don't want anybody else. I want you."

"I don't think I'm the right person to help you at this time."

The man gave a ragged-sounding laugh. "I'm afraid you're the only one who can help me."

"I don't—" she began but the doorbell rang before she could complete the sentence, then rang again more insistently just an instant later.

"You should probably get that," the voice on the phone said.

"Yes. I'm sorry. Could you hold on a moment?"

"As long as it takes," he responded.

Cordless phone in the crook of her shoulder, she

hobbled the few steps to the door and looked out the peephole, then nearly lost her balance on her crutches.

"Wade," she breathed.

He stood on her stoop, his Stetson dripping rain, looking big and gorgeous and wonderful.

And holding a cell phone to his ear.

"Caroline," the voice on the phone murmured and she wondered how she had possibly mistaken that slow drawl for a stranger's voice.

Her heart stuttered in her chest and she could do nothing but stare at his distorted image through the peephole. He was here, not a thousand miles away on his Idaho ranch, but right here on her doorstep.

After two weeks of misery, of missing him so badly she couldn't breathe around it, he stood in front of her. She almost couldn't believe it.

"Are you still there?" he asked after a long moment.

"I...yes. I'm here."

"I'm sorry, Caroline," he said softly in her ear and she saw the truth in his eyes. "I'm so sorry. I should have trusted you. I should have trusted myself, my own instincts. In my heart, I knew you were just what you seemed but I jumped at the chance to push you away. It's a poor excuse, but I can only tell you I was scared."

"Scared?"

"When I lost Andrea, I didn't think I would survive the pain of it and I sure never dreamed I might be able to love again. And then you showed up at the Cold Creek. Somehow you started to thaw all those frozen corners of my heart and it scared the hell out of me."

"Wade—"

"It still scares me," he admitted. "But the thought of living without you scares me more."

She pressed a hand to her stomach, to the swirly, jittering emotions jumping there.

"I love you, Caroline," he said quietly. "With all my heart. Are you going to open the door? Or will you leave me standing out in the rain for the rest of my life?"

With pounding heart and trembling hands, she worked the locks as fast as she could, dropping the phone in the process. Finally, after what felt like forever, the last bolt shot free and she jerked open the door.

It wasn't a mirage, some heartache-induced dream. He was real. And he was hers.

Using her crutches as a fulcrum, she launched herself at him, laughing and crying at the same time. He caught her, as she knew he would, and pulled her tight against him.

"Carrie," he murmured, his blue eyes bright and intense in the gloom, then his mouth found hers.

It was a kiss of redemption, of healing. Of peace and hope and joy, and she never wanted to stop.

"I love you," she said against his mouth. "I've missed you so much."

He made a low sound in his throat and kissed her fiercely, until she was dizzy from it.

"We're getting soaked," he murmured some time later.

"I don't care."

His laugh was raw. "You'll catch pneumonia, then your father will never forgive me. He's already spent two weeks telling me what an idiot I am."

She blinked. "Quinn?"

"My new stepfather is not too thrilled with me right

now. Nobody on the ranch is, if you want the truth. For the last two weeks, I've been getting the cold shoulder from just about everybody. Even Cody."

She couldn't believe that. The little boy adored his father.

"The kids aren't speaking to me, my brothers only talk to me to tell me what a damn fool I am, and your father finally threatened bodily violence if I didn't get a brain in my head and come after you."

"He…he did?"

Without waiting for an invitation, Wade carried her through the door to her couch, then sat down with her in his lap. They would drip all over it, but she didn't care.

"That man might have made some mistakes where you're concerned but he loves you. He told me everything, all his years of running cons, how you used to beg him to stop but he was always after the thrill of the next deal. He told me you were the most honest person he'd ever met and would rather cut out your tongue than join him in a con."

"You believe him?"

He cupped her chin. "He told me about Washington."

She closed her eyes, mortified that he knew about her time in jail, but they opened again when he kissed her lightly.

"He told me none of it was your fault, that he dragged you into the whole mess against your will."

"I couldn't testify against him. I would have been out in a day but I couldn't do it. I'm weak when it comes to him."

"Not weak. You love him. And so does Marjorie,

by the way. He seems to be crazy about her, too. After two endless weeks of living with their constant billing and cooing, I have to believe it's the real deal. Nobody could be that good an actor, even your father."

"Do you mind? About his past?"

He was quiet for a moment, his hand doing delicious things to the small of her back. "He makes her happy. She didn't have much of that, married to my father, so I can't begrudge her this."

He made a face. "And to tell you the truth, though I hate to admit it, your dad is growing on me."

"Yes, he seems to have that effect on people," she said dryly.

"I know I hurt you and I'm sorry, sweetheart," he said after a moment. "If you can find it in your heart to forgive me, I swear I'll spend the rest of my life trying to make it up to you."

"Oh, Wade. There's nothing to forgive. Nothing! I should have told you about Quinn the moment I arrived at the ranch. That's the whole reason I came after him. I was in a panic that he might be running another con game, with Marjorie as his mark."

"He signed a prenuptial agreement. Apparently he insisted on it. Marjorie showed it to me and Quinn willingly gave up any current or future claim to any ranch assets or income."

Caroline sagged against him, as the last of the worry over Quinn's motives—the worry she hadn't even realized had been lurking inside her—seemed to seep away, leaving a vast relief.

"I guess it takes a man in love to recognize another one, and I think what Quinn and Marjorie have is the real deal."

"Oh, that's wonderful."

He smiled, then kissed her softly. "I love you. On behalf of everybody on the Cold Creek—but especially for the sake of this lonely, miserable shell of a man—I'm asking you to come back. The kids miss you. I miss you and I need you more than life, Caroline. You showed me how to dream again and I don't want to give that up. Will you come back to the Cold Creek and to me?"

She touched his face, this gorgeous strong man who was looking at her with such tenderness, then she smiled and pressed her mouth to his. "There's nowhere on earth I'd rather be."

* * * * *

THE FARMER NEXT DOOR

Patricia Davids

This book is dedicated with deep love
and affection to my mother, Joan,
a true wise-hearted woman.

And all the women that were wise hearted did
spin with their hands, and brought that which
they had spun, both of blue, and of purple,
and of scarlet, and of fine linen.
—*Exodus* 35:25

Chapter 1

If the Amish farmer standing outside her screen door would smile, he'd be a nice-looking fellow—but he certainly wasn't smiling at the moment. His fierce scowl was a sharp reminder of all her life had been before—tense, fearful, pain-filled.

Faith Martin thrust aside her somber memories. She would not allow the past to follow her here. She had nothing to fear in this new community.

Still, the man at her door made an imposing figure blocking out much of the late afternoon sunlight streaming in behind him. His flat-topped straw hat sat squarely above his furrowed brow. That frown put a deep crease between his intelligent hazel eyes.

Above his reddish-brown beard, his full lips barely moved when he spoke. "*Goot* day, *Frau*. I am Adrian Lapp. I own the farm to the south."

His beard told her he was married. Amish men were clean-shaven until after they took a wife. He had his pale blue shirtsleeves rolled up exposing brawny, darkly tanned forearms folded tightly across his gray vest. A familiar, nauseous odor emanated from his clothes.

Faith's heart sank. It was clear he'd had a run-in with one of her herd. What had he been doing with her animals?

She managed a polite nod. Common courtesy dictated she welcome him to her home. "I'm pleased to meet you, neighbor. I am Faith Martin. Do come in."

He made no move to enter. "Is your husband about?"

It seemed the farmer next door wasn't exactly the friendly sort. That was too bad. She had prayed it would be different here. "My husband passed away two years ago. It's just me. How may I help you?"

Her widowed status seemed to surprise him. "You're living here alone?"

"Ja." She brushed at the dust and cobwebs on her apron and tried to look like a woman who managed well by herself instead of one who'd bitten off far more than she could chew.

His scowl deepened. "Your creatures are loose in my fields. They are eating my beans."

Faith cringed inwardly. This was not the first impression she wanted to make in her new community. "I'm so sorry. I don't know how they could have gotten out."

"I tried to catch one of them by its halter, but it spat on me and ran off with the others into the cornfield."

She saw the green, speckled stain across the front shoulder of his shirt and vest. Alpaca spit, a combination of grass and digestive juices, was unpleasant but not harmful. What a shame this had to be her new neighbor's first introduction to her alpacas. They were normally docile, friendly animals.

Faith never tired of seeing their bright, inquisitive faces waiting for her each morning. Their sweet, gentle natures had helped her heal in both body and spirit over the past two years.

"The one wearing a halter is Myrtle. She's the expectant mother in the herd. You must have frightened her. They are leery of strangers."

"So I noticed," he answered drily.

"Spitting is their least endearing habit, but it will brush off when it dries." Faith's encouraging tone didn't lighten his scowl. Perhaps now wasn't the time to mention the smell would linger for a few days.

"What did you call them?"

"Alpacas. They're like llamas but they have very soft fleece, softer than any sheep. Originally, they come from South America. How many did you say were in your field?"

"I counted ten."

"Oh, no!" Fear blotted out any concern for her neighbor's shirt. If all of her animals were loose in unfamiliar country, it would be difficult, even impossible, to round them up before dark.

Her defenseless alpacas couldn't spend the night out in the open. Stray dogs or coyotes could easily bring down one of her half-grown crias, or they might wander onto the highway and be hit by a passing car. She couldn't afford the loss of even one animal. She had everything invested in this venture and much more than money riding on her success.

Please, Lord, let me recover them all safe and sound.

As much as she hated to be seen using her crutch, Faith grabbed it from behind the door. It was wrong to be vain about her handicap, but she couldn't help it. It was a personal battle she had yet to win.

The pickup truck that had crashed into their buggy two years ago had killed her husband and left her with a badly mangled leg. Doctors told her it would be a miracle if she ever walked again, but God had shown her mercy. After a long, difficult recovery she was able to get around with only her leg brace most of the time. But chasing down a herd of frisky alpacas required exertion and speed. Things she couldn't manage without added support.

She pushed open the screen door, forcing Adrian Lapp to take a step back. She didn't miss the way his eyes widened at the sight of her infirmity.

Let him stare. It wasn't something she could keep secret. She knew her crippled leg made her ugly and awkward, a person to be pitied, but she wouldn't let it be her weakness. Right now, the safety of her animals was the important thing, not her new neighbor's opinion of her. "Where did you see them last?"

"Disappearing into the cornfield beyond the orchard at the back of your property."

"I will need to get their halters and lead ropes from the barn." She left him standing on the porch as she made her way down the steps.

Adrian quickly caught up with her. "I'm sorry, I didn't know… I will take care of the animals for you. There is no need for you to go traipsing after them."

His offer was grudgingly given, but she sensed he meant well.

"I'm perfectly capable of catching them." She didn't want pity, and she wasn't about to leave her valuable livestock in the hands of a man who didn't even know what kind of animal they were.

Hobbling ahead of him across the weedy yard, she spoke over her shoulder. "Once I catch them, can you help me lead them home?"

"Of course."

Faith headed toward the small, dilapidated barn nestled between overgrown cedars some fifty yards from the house. In the harsh August sunlight it was easy to see the peeling paint, missing shingles and broken windowpanes on the building. The Amish were known for their neat and well-tended farmsteads. She had a lot of work ahead of her to get this place in shape.

She didn't know why her husband had never mentioned owning this property in Ohio or why he had chosen to leave it sitting vacant all these years, but finding out a month ago that she owned it couldn't have come at a better time.

She pulled open the barn door. Copper, her mare, whinnied a greeting. Faith spoke a few soft words to her as she gathered together the halters and lead ropes that were hanging on pegs inside the doorway.

Adrian took them from her without a word and slipped them over his shoulder. She was grateful for his help but wished he wasn't so dour about it. Why couldn't her alpacas have chosen to eat the beans of a cheerful neighbor? Maybe she didn't have any.

She led the way around the side of the barn to the pens at the rear. The gate panel that should have been wired closed had been pushed over, offering the curious alpacas an easy way out. Why hadn't she paid more attention when her hired help set up the portable pen and unloaded the animals? Now look what her carelessness had wrought.

Adrian removed the thin wire that had proven to be an ineffective deterrent. "Do you have a heavier gauge wire than this or some strong rope?"

"I'm sure there's something in the barn that will work."

"Then I should find it." He turned back toward the barn door.

Faith called after him. "Shouldn't we find my animals first and then worry about how to keep them in? It's getting late."

He didn't even glance in her direction. "It won't do any good to bring them back if they can just get out again."

She pressed her lips closed on a retort. She had learned the hard way not to argue with a man. Her husband had made sure she understood her opinions were not valued.

Leaving her new neighbor to rummage in the barn, Faith headed toward the rows of trees that stretched for a quarter of a mile to the back edge of her property, knowing he could easily overtake her. It was slow going through the thick grass, but at least she knew her alpacas would be well-fed through the summer and fall once she had her fences in place.

It didn't take long for Adrian to catch up with her. As she expected, his long legs made short work of the distance she had struggled to cover. A twinge of resentment rippled through her before she firmly reminded herself it didn't matter if someone could walk faster than she could. All that mattered was that she walk upon the path the Lord had chosen for her without complaint.

Adrian wasn't sure what to make of the woman charging ahead of him through the tangled grass of the old orchard. Her handicap clearly didn't slow her down much. He'd been curious about his new neighbors as soon as he'd spotted the moving van and large horse trailer inching up the rutted lane yesterday.

The farmstead had been deserted since he'd been a lad. It hurt his soul to see the good farm ground lying fallow and the peach orchard's fruit going to waste year after year. He could do so much with it if only he had the chance.

Even though he'd seen he had new neighbors, he hadn't gone to introduce himself. He didn't like meeting people or answering questions about his life. He liked being alone. He preferred to stay on his farm and work until he was bone-tired and weary enough to fall asleep as soon as his head hit the pillow at night.

Too tired even for dreams…or for nightmares.

He wouldn't be here today if Faith Martin had kept her animals penned up properly. This was costing him an afternoon of work that couldn't wait.

He glanced sideways at her. She was a tiny slip of a woman. She didn't look as if she could wrest this land and buildings back into shape by herself. A stiff wind could blow her away. Why, the top of her head barely reached his chin whiskers.

A white prayer *kapp* covering her chestnut-brown hair proclaimed her to be a member of the Plain faith, but he didn't recognize the pattern. Where had she come from?

She wore a long blue dress with a black apron and

the same type of dark stockings and sturdy shoes that all the women in his family wore. As she walked beside him, the breeze fluttered the long ribbons of her *kapp* about her heart-shaped face, drawing his attention to the slope of her jaw and the slender curve of her neck. She was a pretty little thing with eyes bright blue as a robin's egg. She had long eyelashes and full pink lips.

Lips made for a man to kiss.

He tore his gaze away as heat rushed to his face. He had no business thinking such thoughts about a woman he barely knew. What was wrong with him? He'd not taken this much notice of a woman since his teenage years.

He used to look at Lovina that way, used to imagine what it would be like to kiss her. When they wed he discovered her kisses were even sweeter than he'd dreamed. After her death, he'd buried his heart with her and raised their son alone until…

So what was it about Faith Martin that stirred this sudden interest? He studied her covertly. She pressed her lips into a tight line as she concentrated on her footing. Did walking cause her pain?

Her eyes darted to his face, but she quickly looked away as if she were uncomfortable in his presence. Her glance held a wary edge that surprised him. Was she frightened of him?

He hadn't meant to scare her. He quickly grew ashamed for having done so. He wasn't used to interacting with new people. Everyone in his family and the community knew of his desire to live alone. He truly had no reason to be surly with this woman. Her alpacas hadn't actually damaged his crop.

He glanced at her again. How could he set this right? How could he bring back her smile?

Adrian abruptly refocused his attention to the task at hand. He had a corncrib to finish and more work waiting for him at home. He didn't have time to worry about making a stranger smile. He would help her gather her animals and then get back to his labors. A few moments later they reached the end of the orchard.

The fence that separated her land from his had fallen down long ago. Only a few rotting uprights remained to mark the boundary. Beyond it, his cornfield stood in tall, straight rows. There was no sign of her odd creatures. They could be anywhere by now.

Faith cupped her hands around her mouth and called out, "Myrtle, Candy, Baby Face. Supper time."

He listened for any sound in return but heard only the rustle of the wind moving through the cornstalks. What did an alpaca sound like? Did they moo or bleat?

She took a step farther into the field. "Come, Socks. Come, Bandit."

Suddenly, a wooly white face appeared at the end of the row a few yards away. He heard Faith's sigh of relief.

"There's my good girl. Come, Socks." The animal emerged from the corn and began walking toward her with its head held high, alert but wary. It was butternut-brown in color with a white face and four white legs. Its head was covered with a thick pelt of fleece, but the long neck and body had been recently shorn, leaving the animal with an oddly naked appearance. It approached to within ten feet, but wouldn't come closer.

Faith glanced at Adrian. "Give me one of the halters and a lead rope and wait here."

He had no intention of venturing closer. Although the animal looked harmless, he still reeked of Myrtle's earlier disapproval.

Faith walked toward Socks with her hand out. The animal made a low humming sound, then ambled up to her and wrapped its long neck around her in a hug.

"Were you lost and scared? It's okay now. I know the way home." She crooned to it like a child as she slipped the halter on, then scratched behind the alpaca's ear.

A second animal stepped out of the corn. It already wore a halter. Adrian recognized it as the one that had spit on him. As soon as she caught sight of him, she turned back into the cornfield.

Faith led Socks to Adrian and handed him the lead rope. "Try not to scare her. If one gives an alarm cry, they may all scatter."

Faith took several halters and ropes from him and disappeared into his cornfield without another word. Adrian found himself alone with the strangest animal he'd ever beheld.

He studied the creature's face. It was calmly studying him in return with large, liquid black eyes fringed with long black lashes. Besides doe-like eyes, Socks had a delicate muzzle with two protruding lower teeth. Her narrow, perked ears reminded him of a rabbit. Her round body was similar to a sheep, but she had long legs like a deer. Looking down, he saw two large, hooked toenails on each front foot that could have belonged to a giant bird.

When Socks tried to nibble his beard, he drew back abruptly, uncertain of her intentions. "I have orders not to scare you."

Socks hummed softly and didn't spit.

So far, so good.

Reaching out, Adrian scratched behind her ear as he'd seen Faith do. Socks closed her eyes and nuzzled into his hand. Her thick wool was as soft as anything he'd ever touched. He smiled at the sound of her hum. They might be odd-looking creatures, but they had a certain appeal. When they weren't spitting.

He ran a hand down her camel-like neck. She stood, patient and unconcerned. With his confidence in her temperament restored, he gave free rein to his curiosity. He wanted a closer look at her strange feet.

As soon as he grasped her leg, Socks lifted her foot as any well-trained horse would do. To his surprise, the bottoms of her feet were soft pads much like a dog's foot, not a hoof at all.

Straightening, he stroked her nose and chuckled. "It appears the Lord assembled you from leftover animal parts."

Socks looked past him and called softly. He turned and saw another alpaca, this one black as night, emerge and look in his direction. Should he call out to Faith or would that scare the animal?

It looked more curious than frightened. He gave a gentle tug on the lead rope and walked with Socks toward her friend. He made a soft humming sound, hoping to soothe the animal and not frighten it into running away. Was he going to help Faith, or was he about to make things worse?

Tired, hot and discouraged, Faith emerged from the forest of corn thirty minutes later with only two of her alpacas in tow. The sun was touching the horizon. It would be dark within the hour. How would she find the others then? She would need dozens of people to comb this acreage properly in the dark.

It seemed she was destined to meet more of her neighbors tonight and not under the best of circumstances.

She had no doubt they would come to help. That was the Amish way. She would not be prideful. She would ask Adrian Lapp to gather a group to help in her search.

To her surprise, Adrian wasn't where she had left him. She glanced around, wondering if she had come out of the corn in the wrong place. No, this was the spot. Had he gone back to his own work? What kind of neighbor was he, anyway?

"I shouldn't be judgmental. Perhaps his work is as pressing as mine." As usual, Myrtle proved to be a good listener and followed obediently behind Faith.

"All I have to do is round up my missing animals, start a business and ready a dilapidated house to pass inspection in a week's time so I may become the guardian of my brother's child. I'm sure Mr. Lapp is equally as busy."

Tears pricked the backs of Faith's eyes as she struggled through the long grass. The past two years had been incredibly hard. First, there had been the terrible crash and her husband's death. She'd spent weeks in the hospital afterward. Her small savings had covered only a fraction of her medical bills. Thankfully, the congregation at her church had taken up a collection to pay the rest, but it left her little to live on. It had taken her more than a year to get back on solid financial ground.

Then, three months ago came word that her brother and his wife had been killed in a flash flood, leaving their five-year-old son an orphan. As the boy's only relative, she was willing and eager to take Kyle in. She'd been halfway through the maze of paperwork and home studies needed to approve his adoption when her landlord had informed her he had to sell the farm she'd been renting.

Her adoption plans fell apart. She couldn't take in a child when she was about to lose the roof over her head.

But in the midst of her despair, the Lord had delivered what seemed like a miracle. A delinquent property tax statement had arrived in the mail addressed to her husband. It was then that she'd learned she owned a house and farm in Ohio. She'd spent every penny she could scrape together to pay the bill and move.

She hadn't expected to find the place in such deplorable condition.

Was this God's way of telling her Kyle didn't belong with her? Did He want Isaac's child raised in the English world her brother had chosen instead of in her Amish faith?

Why would God see fit to give Isaac's child into her care when He had denied her children of her own?

She had no answers to the questions and doubts that plagued her. It would be all too easy to sit down and bawl like a baby, but what would that fix? She sniffed back her tears and blinked hard, refusing to let them fall.

Tears hadn't made her husband a kind man. They wouldn't bring back her brother or undo any of the pain she had endured. They certainly wouldn't build fences for her alpacas, clean her house or make it a home for a lonely little boy.

She stopped to rest her aching leg and looked heavenward. "I know You never give us more than we can bear, but I could use Your strength right now. Help me, Lord. I beseech You."

As always, she felt the comfort of God's presence in her life whenever she turned to Him. She must not let her despair or her fears gain the upper hand. God was watching over her.

Had not the letter come in her hour of need telling her she owned this land? So what if it was going to take hard work to make it livable? She knew how to work. God would provide. She had faith in His mercy. Here in Ohio she had started Kyle's adoption process again. Now she had to prove to a new agency worker that she had a safe home and a stable income.

Which was exactly what she didn't have yet.

Drawing a deep breath, she started forward again. The time for tears was past. This was the new path the Lord had chosen for her. She had to believe it would be better than the life she'd left behind.

Chapter 2

When Faith emerged from the trees, she stopped short in surprise. Adrian Lapp stood beside her barn with all eight of her missing alpacas clustered around him in their pen. It seemed her prayers had been answered, and apparently her grumpy neighbor had a way with animals.

Not two minutes ago she had been piling unkind thoughts on his head.

Forgive me, Lord. I judged this man unfairly. I won't do it again.

Walking up to Adrian, she said, "I can't believe it. You found them."

"It was more like they found me."

Bandit stood close beside him, sniffing at his beard. He gently pushed the inquisitive black alpaca away and opened the gate so Faith could add her two to the herd. Adrian said, "I fixed the pen. They shouldn't get out again."

"Thank you. I was so worried I wouldn't be able to find them before dark. This move has been hard on all of them."

"And on you?"

Her gaze locked with his. Did she look like such a mess? She must. Embarrassment sent heat flooding to her face. Socks chose that moment to nibble at the rim of Adrian's straw hat. He pushed the alpaca gently aside. Faith concentrated on removing the halters from her pair.

"Where have you come from, Faith Martin? Surely not South America like your animals."

His interest seemed genuine. Some of her discomfort faded. "Originally, I'm from Indiana, but on this move I came from Missouri."

"That's a lot of miles."

It was, and many more than he knew. Her husband had been affected with a wanderlust that had taken them to twelve different communities in the ten years they'd been married. Faith was determined that this farm would be her final home. She wanted to put down roots, to become a true member of a community, things she'd never been able to do during her marriage.

Besides, she had to make a home for Kyle. A place where her brother's child could recover from the tragedy of losing his parents and grow into manhood. This was her last move. If it was God's will, she didn't plan to leave Hope Springs, Ohio, until He called her home.

"I'm grateful for your help, neighbor. I have fresh lemonade in the house. Can I offer you a glass?"

He opened the gate and slipped out, securing the

panels with a quick twist of heavy wire, then double checking it to make sure it would hold. "*Nee.* I must get back to my work."

With her overture of friendship soundly rejected, she nodded and started toward the house.

He hesitated, then fell into step beside her. "What are your plans for this place?"

Oddly pleased by his interest, she said, "I want to enclose the orchard area with new fence. In the future I will divide it into separate pens so I can rotate where the alpacas graze. In spite of their behavior today, the fencing is really to keep predators out. My babies won't try to wander once they become accustomed to their new home. After that, I need to fix up the barn well enough to store winter hay for them." She walked slowly, more tired than she cared to admit.

"So my beans will be safe in the future?"

He hadn't really been interested in her plans, only in making sure his crops wouldn't be destroyed.

"*Ja,* as soon as I have the fences up. Of course, I will pay for any damages my animals caused."

"That won't be necessary. Do you plan to do all this work yourself?"

Faith paused and drew herself to her full height of five-foot-one. "I'm stronger than I look. I'm not afraid of hard work. With God's help I shall manage."

His eyes grew troubled. "I was going to offer the names of some young men who could use the work. That is why I asked. I did not mean to offend."

He had a gruff manner, but he was clearly sorry to have upset her.

Her defiance drained away, leaving her embarrassed. "I don't have the money to pay a hired man.

Once I sell the yarns I am spinning, I will consider hiring someone."

"A light purse is nothing to be ashamed of."

"You're right, but I don't want people here to think I will be a burden on them."

"We would not think such a thing, Faith Martin. It would be un-Christian." There was a hint of rebuke in his words.

Amish families and communities supported all Amish widows and orphans. It was everyone's responsibility to care for them, but Faith needed to be able to take care of herself.

At her age and with her disability, she had no hope of marrying again. Even if such an offer came her way, she would never place her fate in the hands of another man. No, never again. The thought of doing so sent cold chills down her spine.

She looked up to see Adrian studying her intently. His frown had returned, but she wasn't frightened by it now. It was more bluff than substance.

He said, "If you find this farm is more than you can handle, I'll be happy to take it off your hands. For a fair price."

"I'm not interested in selling. I plan on staying here a long, long time."

"Then I pray you fare well among us, but do not forget my offer."

Faith watched as he strode away with long, easy strides. She saw a man at ease in his surroundings and at home on his own well-tended land. Not overly friendly, but not unfriendly. She found him...interesting. If his spouse was pleasant, they might prove to be good neighbors. She liked the idea of having someone close by to count on in an emergency.

She had turned down his offer to buy the place, but she sensed he didn't believe she could make a go of it on her own.

Why shouldn't he doubt her? She doubted herself. For years Mose had hammered into her head what a failure she was as a wife. She couldn't give him children. It was her fault all his business enterprises failed because she didn't work hard enough.

In her heart she knew he was wrong, but after a while it ceased to matter. She had simply accepted the unkind things he'd said and kept quiet.

But Mose was gone now, and she had to believe in herself again. This was the time and place to start.

Watching Adrian cross the field toward his farm, she wondered what it would be like to have a strong, handsome man like Adrian Lapp for a husband? She shook her head at her foolish musing.

A woman could not tell if a man would be a good husband by his looks. Mose had been a handsome fellow, but his good-looking face had hidden a mean nature at odds with the teachings of their Amish faith.

She forgave Mose for the good of her own soul. He was standing now before a just God, answering for his sins while she was free to live a quiet and humble life. It would be enough.

She wondered if other Amish wives suffered silently as she had done. She prayed it wasn't true. In her heart she wanted to believe in the gentle nature of men who professed submission to God in every aspect of their lives—but there was no way to be certain. Only God could see into the hearts of men.

Pushing aside the host of unhappy memories gathered during her marriage, Faith entered her new home determined to finish sweeping away years of debris and clutter, from the house and from her heart. She was ready for her new beginning.

"I heard someone has moved into the old Delker place. Do you know anything about it?" Ben Lapp handed the next set of boards up to Adrian who was perched on the top of the new corncrib.

Adrian knew there would be no end to his brother's curiosity. He might as well tell him everything he knew. "*Ja,* I met her yesterday. Her name is Faith Martin. She is Amish and a widow."

"I don't suppose she has a pretty daughter or two?" Ben asked hopefully. At seventeen, Adrian's youngest brother was in the first year of his *rumspringa,* his running around time, and always on the lookout for new girls to impress.

Adrian hated to dash his hopes. "Sorry, but she said she was alone."

"Too bad. A pretty new face would be welcome in this area."

Adrian recalled Faith's soft blue eyes and the sweet curve of her lips. "She is pretty enough."

"Really?"

Adrian caught the sudden interest in Ben's tone and grinned. "Pretty enough for a woman in her thirties."

Ben's face fell. "She's an old woman, then."

"Do you consider me old? I'm but thirty-two."

Adrian tried not to smile as he watched the struggle taking place behind his baby brother's eyes. Finally, Ben said, "You're not so old."

"Not *so* old. That's good to know for I was thinking of getting a cane when I went to market."

The thought of a cane brought a sudden vision of Faith struggling through the long grass with her crutch. How was she doing today? And why was he thinking about her again?

Ben grinned. "Tell me more about the widow. What's she like?"

Determined, pretty, kind to her animals, wary, worried. A number of ways to describe his new neighbor darted through Adrian's mind, but they all sounded personal, as if he'd taken an interest in her. "She raises alpacas."

"Alpacas? Why?"

"She spins their fleece into yarn for sale."

"I remember grandmother Lapp sitting at her spinning wheel. It was fascinating to watch her nimble fingers at work even when she was very old."

"I remember that, too."

"I never understood how chunks of wool became strands of yarn. Whatever became of her spinning wheel?"

"I suppose it's in *Mamm*'s attic if one of our sisters doesn't have it."

"It's sad to think someone is living at the Delker farm now."

"Why do you say that?" Adrian hammered the last board in place.

"Because we could eat all the peaches we wanted from those trees. No one cared. Now, we'll have to get permission. Is the house still in decent shape?"

"From the outside it doesn't look too bad. I'm not sure about the inside." Maybe he should stop in again and see if there was something Faith needed done around the place. That would be neighborly.

Not that he was looking for an excuse to see her again. He wasn't. He grew annoyed that she kept intruding into his carefully ordered world.

Ben backed down the ladder. "Do you even remember the people who lived there before?"

Adrian followed him. "I remember an old *Englisch* woman yelling at our cousin Sarah and I when we were helping ourselves to some low-hanging fruit. I must have been ten. She scared the daylights out of us. I think she went to a nursing home not long after that. When she passed away, the place stayed vacant."

"Is the new owner a relative?"

"That I don't know."

"Didn't you try to buy the place a few years ago?"

"More than once. I got a name and address from the County Recorder's office and sent several letters over the years, but no one ever answered me. I even tried to buy it from her yesterday, but she wasn't interested in selling." He could still hear the determination in her voice when she turned him down.

Determination was one thing. A strong back was another. She'd need both to get that place in working order.

"It's odd that she'd show up after all this time. I wonder why?" Ben mused.

Gathering together his tools, Adrian started toward the house. He'd spent more than enough time thinking about Faith Martin. "It's none of our business."

"Not our business? Ha! Tell that to *Mamm*. She'll be wanting every little detail, and she'll have it by Sunday next or I'll eat my hat." Ben fell into step beside Adrian.

It irked Adrian that he couldn't get Faith off his mind. What was she doing? Were her alpacas safe? Was she having trouble putting up fences for them? It would be a big job for one woman alone.

Ben wrinkled his nose in disgust. "What's that smell?"

Adrian swiped at the shoulder of his vest. The dried juice had brushed off, but not the aroma. "Alpaca spit."

"That's nasty. I didn't know they spit."

"Only if you scare them."

"I'll avoid doing that."

"Me, too, from now on."

"Before I forget, *Mamm* wanted me to remind you to come to supper tomorrow night."

Alerted by the sudden uncomfortable tone in Ben's voice, Adrian stopped. "Why would I need reminding? I come to supper every Wednesday evening with the family."

"That's what I told her."

Adrian closed his eyes and sighed deeply. "Who is it this time?"

"Who is what?" Ben looked the picture of innocence. Adrian wasn't fooled.

Leveling a no-nonsense, tell-me-the-truth look at his brother, Adrian repeated himself. "Who is it this time?"

"Edna Hershberger," Ben admitted and flinched.

"Edna? She's at least fifteen years older than I am."

"Her cousin is visiting from Apple Creek. Her younger female cousin. I hear she's nice-looking."

"Why does Mother keep doing this?" Adrian started walking again. He wasn't interested in meeting marriageable women. He would never marry again. He had sworn that over his young wife's grave when he'd laid their son to rest beside her.

"Mother wants to see you happy."

"I am happy." The moment he said the words he knew they were a lie.

"No, you're not. You haven't been happy since Lovina and Gideon died."

The mention of his wife and son sent a sharp stab of pain through Adrian's chest. He bore wounds that would not heal. No one understood that. "I'd rather not talk about them."

"It's been three years since Gideon died, Adrian. It's been eight years since Lovina passed away."

"For me, it was yesterday."

God had taken away the people he loved, leaving Adrian an empty shell of a man. An empty shell could not love anyone, certainly not God, for He had stripped away the most important parts of Adrian's life.

Adrian went through the motions of his faith, but each day it became harder to repeat the platitudes that no longer held meaning for him. Disowning his Amish faith would only lead to being separated from his remaining family. For their sakes he kept his opinions about God to himself.

Ben laid a hand on Adrian's shoulder. "You can't blame *Mamm* for worrying about you."

Adrian met his brother's gaze. "Mother needs to accept that I won't marry again. You can tell her I've made other plans for tomorrow evening."

"What plans?" Ben called after him.

Adrian didn't answer him. Instead, he walked to the end of his lane and up the road for a quarter of a mile to where a small field of tombstones lay enclosed by a white wooden fence. A fence he painted each year to keep it looking nice.

He opened the gate and crossed the field to where an old cedar tree had been cut down. The stump made a perfect seat for him to sit and visit with his wife and son.

The breeze blew softly across the open field. Beyond the fence he saw fat black-and-white cattle grazing in a neighbor's pasture. Overhead the blue sky held a few white clouds that changed shape as they traveled on the wind. He took off his hat and looked down at the small tombstones that bore the names of his wife and child.

"It's another pretty day, isn't it, Lovina? I remember how much you enjoyed the summer evenings when the days stretch out so long. I miss sitting with you on the porch and watching the sun go down. I miss everything about both of you."

Tears filled his eyes as emotions clogged his throat. It took a minute before he could go on.

Clearing his throat, he said, "We've got a new neighbor. Her name is Faith Martin. I think you'd like her. You should see the strange animals she has. They spit. I think I like sheep better and you know how much I dislike them."

Clasping his hands together, he leaned forward with his elbows propped on his knees. "*Mamm* is at it again. She's trying to fix me up with a cousin of Edna Hershberger. I wish she would learn to leave well enough alone. I don't want anyone else. You will be my only wife in this life and in the next. If Gideon had lived, it might have been different."

The tears came back, forcing him to lift his head. "A

boy needs a mother, but he's with you now. I know that makes you happy because it gives me comfort, too."

He sniffed once and wiped his eyes with the heels of his hands. "I'm not going over to *Mamm*'s for supper tomorrow. I'm sorry if that disappoints you. I've decided to go over to Faith Martin's. That place needs too much work for a woman alone to do it all. I can spare an hour or two in the morning and again at night. The days are long now," he added with a wry smile.

The memory of Faith declaring she wasn't afraid of work slipped into his mind. "She reminds me of you a little bit in the way her chin comes up when she's riled. She said an odd thing yesterday. She said she didn't want people here to think she would be a burden. It makes me wonder who made her feel that way in her last community."

Having said what he needed to say, he rose to his feet. "Enough about our neighbor. Give Gideon a kiss for me. I miss you, Lovey."

So much so it was hard to put into words. "Sometimes, I wake at night and I still reach for you. But you aren't there and it hurts all over again."

As he walked away, he wondered if Faith Martin woke in the night and reached for the husband who was gone.

Chapter 3

Faith woke to the sound of a persistent clanking coming from outside her house. Squinting, she could just make out the hands of the clock on her dresser. Six thirty-five.

Her eyes popped open wide. Six thirty-five! Panic sent her heart racing. Mose would be so angry when he discovered she'd slept late.

Throwing back the sheet, she sat up and stopped as every muscle in her body protested the quick movement. Had he beaten her again? What had she done wrong this time? She couldn't remember.

Swinging her feet off the mattress, she reached for her clothes. They weren't on a chair beside the bed. Looking around the strange room, she saw them hanging from a peg on the wall. Her panic dropped away like a stone from her chest. She drew a deep breath.

Mose might be gone, but his imprint remained in her life. In moments of mindless panic like this one. In nightmares that left her weak and shaking in the night.

Faith began to recite her morning prayers, letting the grace of God's presence wash away her fears and restore her peace.

Dear Lord, I give You thanks for this new day, for my new home and for the strength to face whatever may come my way. I know You are with me, always. Watch over Kyle and keep him safe. If it is Your will, Lord, let him join me here, soon. Amen.

A few years ago her morning prayers had been much simpler. *Please don't let me make Mose angry today.* Sometimes, she wondered if she would ever be truly free of him.

She stood and crossed to the open window. The sound of hammering started up again. It was coming from her orchard, but she couldn't see anyone. What was going on?

She dressed and set to work quickly brushing out her hip-length hair. When it was smooth, she parted it straight down the middle and began to make a tight roll of it along her hairline pulling all of it together and finally twisting the remainder into a tight bun, which she pinned at the back of her head. With her hair secure, she donned her *kapp* and pinned it in place. Outside, the clanking continued.

Sitting on the edge of the bed, she buckled on her leg brace, wincing as the padded bands came into contact with her chafed skin. She was paying for all the time she'd spent working and sweating the past few days. She needed to apply more salve to the reddened areas, but that would have to wait. Her priority was finding out what was going on outside.

After leaving the house, she limped to the barn to check on her animals. Copper dozed in her stall. The alpacas, all ten of them, as Faith quickly counted, stood or lay in their pen outside. Relieved, but with mounting curiosity, Faith made her way into the orchard.

A few yards from where she had stopped building the fence the evening before, Adrian Lapp was pounding a steel fence post into the ground. He'd already added several stakes along the string she had laid out to mark the boundary of her pen.

What was he doing here? She hadn't asked for his help. As quickly as her objections surfaced, she swallowed them. Humility was the cornerstone of her Amish faith. Being humble also meant accepting help when help was offered.

Adrian hadn't seen her yet. She watched as he effortlessly drove in the stakes with a metal sleeve that fit over the top of each post. Compared to the heavy maul she had used to painstakingly pound each post into the ground, his tool made the job much easier. And he didn't even have to stand on the wooden box she had used just to reach the top of the six-foot-tall t-posts.

All right, he was strong and tall. It was a great combination when building fences, but that didn't mean she needed to stand here staring. She had half a mind to go back to the house and let him finish the row, but her conscience wouldn't let her. This was her property now. She was the one who needed to take care of it.

"Guder mariye," she called out in her native Pennsylvania Dutch, the German dialect spoken by the

Amish. "You've done a lot of work while I was lazing abed. *Danki.*"

He stopped pounding, wiped the sweat from his brow with his shirtsleeve, and nodded in her direction. "Good morning to you, too. You have accomplished quite a bit here yourself."

His gaze swept across the posts that she'd put in yesterday, the yard she had mown into order with an old scythe and the fresh laundry waving on the clothesline she'd strung between two trees beside the house.

"I could have done more if I'd had a fence post driver such as you have there." She walked toward him to look at the tool.

"They aren't expensive. You can pick them up pretty cheap at farm auctions."

"I will keep that in mind."

It seemed to Faith that he wanted to say more, but instead, he returned to pounding the post he was working on until he'd sunk it another two feet into the ground.

"I appreciate your help, Mr. Lapp, but I can manage on my own. I'm sure you have plenty of work to attend to."

"Call me Adrian. I've got a few free hours today. Do you have a wire stretcher? I can put up the fencing after I get these posts in if you do."

"It's in the barn along with the rolls of woven fence wire I want to use. Are you sure you have time to do this? I hate to impose."

"I'll do the posts this morning and come back this evening to finish putting up the wire. Unless you object?" He grabbed another stake, measured off the distance with a few quick steps and began hammering the post into the ground.

"That will be fine." Other than taking care of her animals, she would have the whole day free to work on the house. Adrian's help was a blessing she hadn't anticipated.

Still, she had plenty to do to get the house ready for the social worker's arrival next Wednesday. Would God understand if she did a little extra work on Sunday? Sundays were days of rest and prayer and a time for visiting with friends and family even if there wasn't a service.

Since Amish church services were held every other Sunday, she would have another week before she had to face the entire congregation. Would they all be as kind and helpful as her new neighbor? He had a gruff way about him, but his actions spoke loudly of a kind heart.

After watching Adrian work for a few more minutes, Faith realized there was nothing she could do to help him and she was wasting time. She left him to his work and returned to the house giving thanks to God for her neighbor's timely intervention.

Inside the house she applied salve to her chafed leg, then set about making breakfast and a pot of strong coffee. An hour later, just as she was pulling a pair of cinnamon coffee cakes from the oven, Adrian came to the screen door.

She fought back a smile. With the windows wide-open to the morning breeze, she had been sure the smell of her baking would reach him.

He said, "I finished the row of posts you had laid out."

She set the second hot pan on the stovetop. "Already? You've saved me a lot of work. *Danki.* Would you like some coffee?"

He hesitated, then said, "I would."

When he came inside, her kitchen instantly felt small and crowded. Unease skittered over her skin. She moved away to make more room between them.

He looked for a peg to hang his hat on, but there wasn't one. He settled for tossing it on the sideboard and took a seat at her table. When he wasn't looming over her, Faith could breathe better.

He motioned toward the wallpaper with its faded yellow flowers. "You will have a lot to do to make this a plain house."

"*Ja*. It will be a big task. Every room is wallpapered." She tapped the floor with her foot. "This black-and-white linoleum will be fine but there is pink-and-white linoleum in the bathroom."

The colorful flooring and wallpaper would all have to be taken out. The Amish lived in simplicity, as they believed was God's will. They avoided loud colors and worldly things such as electricity in order to live separate from the world. Hopefully, the bishop in her new community would give her plenty of time to make over the house from English to Amish.

She would have the option of painting her walls blue, green or gray. The brightly patterned linoleum on the bathroom floor would have to go. She could leave the planks underneath bare or replace the linoleum with a simpler, more modest color. It was all on her list of things to be done. A list she was whittling down much too slowly.

She cut two pieces of coffee cake and carried one of them along with a cup of coffee to the table. Adrian accepted her offering with a nod of thanks. "The county will take down the electric lines leading to the house, but you will have to take down the ones leading to the barn."

"I know. At least the gas stove still works and I was able to have the propane tank filled before I arrived."

Fetching a cup of coffee and a piece of cake for herself, she said, "I've cooked on a wood-burning stove, but I'm not a good hand at it."

Adrian's look of sympathy said it all. She sat down at the table with a heavy sigh. "I take it the *Ordnung* of this church district doesn't allow propane cook stoves?"

"*Nee,* we do not. The stove must be wood-burning or coal-burning. But you may have a propane-powered refrigerator and washing machine."

The thought of chopping wood or hauling coal on top of her other chores was enough to dampen her spirits. She glanced sadly at the stove. It was old, but it worked well. She would hate to see it go.

It was always this way when she moved to a new community. Each Amish church district had their own rules about what they allowed and what they didn't. Each bishop in charge of a district often interpreted those rules differently.

She had lived in several communities that used tractors in the fields instead of horses. When they'd lived in Mifflin County, Pennsylvania, their church district permitted members to drive only yellow buggies, another place only gray ones. Here in Hope Springs the buggies were black.

She would have to make all new *kapps* for herself, too. The women of each district wore distinctive patterns. She would get around to that if, and only if, she met with the approval of this community and they voted to accept her as a new church member.

If they didn't accept her, she would have to look for another nearby district who would or live as an outsider. "I must meet with your bishop soon."

"Bishop Zook is a good man. He will help you learn your way among us."

"Is he a good preacher?" she asked, half in jest. Church services often lasted three or more hours.

"I've only fallen asleep twice during his sermons." Adrian didn't crack a smile, but she saw the twinkle of humor in his eyes. It surprised and delighted her.

"Then he must be *wunderbarr.* I'm looking forward to my first church Sunday already."

Adrian changed the subject. "Are you a relative of Mrs. Delker, the woman who used to own this place?"

"No, but Mose, my husband, was a grandchild of hers. I inherited this farm after he passed away. It's odd really, because he never once mentioned owning a farm in Ohio."

"I tried to buy it from him about five years ago."

"Did you? That must have been when we were raising chickens in Nebraska. Why did he say he wouldn't sell?"

They had certainly needed the money. The chicken houses had been another of her husband's failed business ventures. They'd left Nebraska owing money to everyone from the feed store to their landlord. Only Mose's last venture, buying her first four alpacas, had actually turned out well.

She never understood how her husband talked people into loaning him money for his wild ideas or how he could just pick up and walk away without looking back or even feeling badly for those who'd lost money because of him. Every time they moved, they left hard feelings behind.

Would this new community receive her into the church if they knew her husband had left debts unpaid all across the Midwest? She was sorry now that she had mentioned Nebraska to Adrian.

"Your husband didn't give a reason why he wouldn't sell. He never answered my letters."

She wanted to tell Adrian how lucky he was *not* to have done business with her husband, but she wouldn't speak ill of the dead. She rose and took her cup to the sink. "We moved around a lot. Perhaps your letters missed him."

"Perhaps. Do you find it hard to talk about him?" he asked quietly.

"Yes." She kept her back to Adrian. It was hard to talk about Mose because there was so little she could say about him that was good.

"I understand."

The odd quality in his tone made her look at him closely. The pain in his eyes touched her heart. Why was he so sad?

He rose abruptly and crossed the room to pick up his hat. "I must be going."

"Wait a moment." She quickly wrapped the remaining coffee cake in a length of cheesecloth and added a small package wrapped in brown paper and string to the top. She held it out to him. He stared at her as if he didn't understand.

"It's a small token of my appreciation for all your hard work. A pair of socks made from my alpaca yarn. Please tell your wife that she is welcome to visit anytime. I'm sure she and your children will enjoy meeting my animals."

Adrian blinked back the sudden sting of tears. Gideon would have loved to have seen Faith's animals and Lovina would have liked this new neighbor with her determined ways. It was so unfair that their lives had been cut short. So unfair that he had to go on living without them.

"Is something wrong?" Faith inquired softly.

He took the packages from her. "My wife and son passed away."

"I'm so sorry. You must miss them very much."

Adrian met Faith's sympathetic gaze. Oddly, he found he wanted to talk about Lovina and Gideon. Somehow, he knew Faith would understand.

"I miss them every day. My son would have liked your alpacas. He had a way with animals, that boy did. He was always finding lost and hurt creatures and bringing them home for me to make well."

"Little boys believe their fathers can do anything."

"Too bad it isn't true."

He hadn't been able to save his wife or his son. That bitter truth haunted him day and night.

He blinked hard to clear his vision. Faith's face swam into view. She understood. He saw it in her eyes. It was more than sympathy and compassion. She had been in the same dark place that surrounded him.

"How old was your son when he died?" she asked.

"Four."

"You mustn't think me cruel, but four years is a gift. I wish I might have had four years, even four days, with my daughters."

"You've lost children, too?"

"Twin daughters who were stillborn. I always wondered if that was why Mose was never able to settle in one place. If we'd had a family, maybe things would have been different. Only God knows."

"I wanted at least six children. Lovina wanted a dozen or more. Gideon was the first and he was perfect."

Adrian couldn't believe he was talking to this woman about his family. He hadn't been able to talk to anyone about them since Gideon's death. Maybe it was because she'd known the same kind of tragedy that he felt she understood what he was going through. Maybe it was because Ben had brought the subject up yesterday.

Whatever the reason, Adrian suddenly decided not to bare more of his soul. Remembering was too painful.

He said, "The coffee cake is appreciated. I'll be back tonight to help finish your fence. I need my bean crop kept safe from your overgrown rabbits."

"Your help has been most welcome, neighbor."

He settled his hat on his head and walked outside into the summer sunshine. At the foot of her steps, he stopped and looked back. She stood framed in the doorway, her arms crossed, a faraway expression in her eyes. He wondered what she was thinking about.

Was she thinking about the children and husband she had lost or the work that needed to be done? Did she find it hard to go forward with her life? Somehow, he didn't think so.

Faith Martin was a remarkable woman.

The moment the thought occurred to him, he began walking, putting as much distance as he could between himself and his disturbing neighbor.

He'd come to Faith's home today to do his Christian duty by helping a neighbor, but he'd also been interested in seeing exactly what shape the place was in. The more he saw, the less he expected she would be able to manage it alone.

He might yet be able to buy the land. If he made some improvements for her, well, that would mean less work for him later.

Having a fence around the orchard was a good idea. Letting the alpacas graze down the overgrown grass would make it easier to mow later, or he could put sheep in to do the same job.

At the edge of his hay meadow, he stopped and glanced toward Faith's house once more. Helping her might turn out to be a good idea—from a business point of view. Not because he wanted to spend time in her company.

His wife might be gone, but he wouldn't be untrue to her. Lovina had been the one love of his life. He had no business thinking about spending time with another woman.

He had come to Faith's place to lend a hand. He hadn't been looking for sympathy or a shoulder to cry on. He hadn't planned on finding someone who could understand the pain he lived with. Yet, that was exactly what he'd found with Faith Martin.

Was that why he found her so attractive? His feelings toward her troubled and confused him.

He had already promised to help her. He wouldn't go back on his word. As promised, he would help her get her home in order as a good neighbor should, but he wouldn't spend any more time alone with her.

Chapter 4

It was shortly before noon on Saturday when Faith heard the sound of a horse and buggy approaching the house. She dropped the sponge she'd been using to wash grimy windows into her pail, dried her hands on her apron and waited to see who had come calling.

The buggy stopped in front of her gate, and three Amish women stepped out. They all carried large baskets over their arms.

"Guder mariye," called the oldest woman. She wore a bright, beaming smile of welcome. Behind her came a young woman with black hair and dark eyes followed by another woman with blond hair.

"Guder mariye," Faith replied. A faint flicker of happiness sparked inside of her. She was free to make new friends here—if they would have her. She wouldn't have to hide her bruised face or bear pitying looks from those who suspected her husband's cruelty.

The leader of the group stopped at the bottom of Faith's steps, adjusted her round wire spectacles on the bridge of her nose and switched her heavy basket to her other arm. "Welcome to Hope Springs. I am Nettie Sutter."

She indicated the dark-haired girl standing behind her. "This is my daughter-in-law, Katie."

"And I am Sarah Wyse," the blonde added. "My cousin is your neighbor to the south."

"Adrian?"

Sarah nodded. "When I heard he'd met you, I thought it best to rush over and assure you the rest of Hope Springs is more hospitable than Adrian is."

"He has been most kind and welcoming."

"He has?" Sarah exchanged astonished glances with her companions.

Faith swept a hand toward the front door. "Do come in, but please excuse the condition of the house."

"None of us can keep our houses free of dust in the summertime. With all the windows open to catch any breeze, the dust piles up before you know it."

Faith had more than a sprinkling of dust to contend with. She had twenty years worth of accumulation to haul out. She was thankful that she had made a coffee cake for herself while making one for Adrian that morning. At least she had something to offer her guests.

The women gathered around the kitchen table, each one setting her basket on it. Sarah opened the lid of the one she carried and began to pull out its contents. "We brought a few things to help you settle in and get this old house in order."

Out of her basket, Sarah brought cleaning supplies,

plastic pails, pine cleaner, rags, sponges and brushes. "Where shall we start?"

Faith was speechless. She hadn't expected help from the community so soon.

Nettie picked up the pail and carried it to the sink. "I will finish these windows for you. Sarah, why don't you take a broom to the front porch and steps? Elam, Eli and his boys will be here to paint this evening."

"I'll get this food put away." Katie opened her basket and brought out two loaves of bread and a rhubarb pie with a gorgeous lattice crust just begging to be eaten. A second later she began unpacking mason jars filled with canned fruits and vegetables.

Faith was overwhelmed by their kindness. "*Danki.* This is far too much."

"No thanks are needed," Nettie assured her.

Perhaps not needed but gratefully given. Faith asked, "Who are Elam and Eli?"

Nettie smiled broadly. "Elam is my son and Katie's husband. Eli and his sons live down the road a piece. Our farm is a little ways beyond that toward Hope Springs."

"Where do you need me to start?" Katie asked, looking over the kitchen.

Faith took a second to gather her thoughts. "I've cleaned out one bedroom upstairs, but the others haven't been touched in years. If you want to start in one of them, that would be great. Sarah, perhaps you could help me drag the mattresses outside so I can beat the dust out of them."

Sarah held out her hand. "Lead the way."

The house quickly became a beehive of activity. Old bedding was taken out, walls and floors were scrubbed free of grime and rubbish was hauled out to the burn barrel. Everywhere inside the house, the crisp scent of pine cleaner filled the air. In one afternoon the women managed to do more inside the house than Faith had accomplished in four days on her own.

Her heirloom clock was striking five when the women gathered in the kitchen once more. Faith wiped her forehead with the back of her sleeve. "I don't know about you, but I've worked up an appetite. I believe I will sample this pie. Would anyone else care for a piece?"

Nettie smiled brightly. "I thought you'd never ask."

"Where are your plates?" Sarah was already moving toward the cabinets.

"To the left of the sink." Chuckling, Faith turned to Katie. "Would you like some?"

"Yes! I could eat the whole thing."

Nettie grinned. "That's because you are eating for two."

Faith endured a sharp stab of wistfulness but quickly recovered. "Congratulations. When is your baby due?"

"The last week of November."

"Is this your first?" Faith gathered forks for everyone and brought them to the table.

Katie shook her head. "It will be my second. We already have a little girl, so we're hoping for a boy."

Nettie sliced into the pie and slipped a piece onto the plate Sarah supplied. "Either will be fine with me as long as it is a healthy grandbaby."

Faith decided it was the perfect opening to share something about herself. "I am expecting a little boy soon."

Everyone's glances fell to her trim waist. She chuckled as she appeased their unspoken curiosity. "I'm hoping my nephew can come to live with me soon. That's why I have to get this house in some kind of order."

"Is he visiting for the summer?" Sarah asked. The women all took a seat at the table.

Sadness put a catch in Faith's voice. "*Nee,* he is not coming for a visit. I hope he will live with me until he is old enough to marry and have a family of his own. My English brother and his wife were killed recently in a flash flood in Texas when their car was swept off the road. Fortunately, Kyle, their son, wasn't with them at the time. I'm all the family he has now."

Sarah reached across the table and laid a hand over Faith's. "I'm sorry for your loss. I lost my sister not long ago, so I understand your grief."

"*Danki.* I had not seen my brother for many years. He fell in love with an English girl and left our faith. I've never met his son. I'm trying to adopt him, but the process is painfully slow."

Nettie finished dishing out the pie and handed the plate to Faith. "It will be a hard change for him coming from an *Englisch* life to live in an Amish home."

"I am worried about that. What if he says he doesn't want to live here?"

Sarah gave Faith an incredulous look. "What little boy wouldn't love to live on a farm?"

"One who is used to television and video games." Faith was giving voice to one of her biggest fears. That Kyle would hate living with her.

"To worry about such things is to borrow trouble," Nettie chided. "God is bringing this child into your life. He knows what is best for all of us."

"You're right. I will put my trust in Him." Faith took

a bite of her pie and savored the sweet tart flavor and tender, flaky crust. Nettie Sutter really knew how to make good pie.

"Tell us about yourself," Katie prompted. "I hear you have some unusual animals."

"I have ten alpacas. I raise them for their fleece. I spin it into yarns. Once I get this house in order, I will start looking for a place to sell my work."

Sarah brightened. "I work at a fabric store and we sell many types of yarn. The store owner's name is Janet Mallory. You should speak to her."

"In Hope Springs?" Could it possibly be this easy to find a market for her work? Faith dared not get her hopes up.

"Yes, we are on Main Street, downtown. You can't miss it. It's called Needles and Pins. Janet is always looking for things made by the local Amish people to sell in her store. We get a fair amount of tourists in Hope Springs. Amish handmade items sell very well, although most of our yarn is bought by local Amish women for use at home."

Faith said, "I'm grateful for your suggestion. I will come in once I have my house in order."

Sarah leaned forward. "Is it true that your animal spit on Adrian? His brother Ben said he smelled as bad as a skunk."

Faith felt the heat rush to her cheeks. "Myrtle did spit on Adrian. I don't blame him for being upset."

Sarah laughed, a sweet light sound that made Faith smile, too. "I would have given anything to see Adrian lose his composure. What did he say?"

Faith crossed her arms over her chest and mimicked his deep stern voice. "Your creatures are eating my beans."

"*Ja,* that is just the way he talks." Sarah giggled again, then took another bite of her pie.

Faith couldn't let them think Adrian had been unkind. "He was upset, but he helped me catch them. Except for Myrtle, the others seem to like him. He's also been helping me build fences to keep them in."

Sarah sobered. "Adrian is coming over to help you build fences? That's interesting. He has stayed mainly to himself these past few years."

Faith's curiosity was piqued. Wanting to learn more about her stoic neighbor, she asked, "Why is that?"

Sarah glanced at the other women, then back to Faith. "Adrian's wife died shortly after their son was born. He raised the boy by himself. His son was his whole world. One afternoon, Adrian was walking home from his field that lies across the highway from his house. His son saw him coming and raced out to greet him. He ran right into the path of a car and was killed in front of Adrian."

Faith's heart twisted with pity knowing the pain he must have felt. "No parent should have to bury a child."

Nettie sighed heavily. "There is no greater sorrow. That is how we know God loves us. For He allowed His only son to die for our sins so that we may rejoice with Him in heaven for eternity."

From the tone of her voice and the sadness in her eyes, Faith knew that Nettie was speaking from first-hand experience. She said, "It is our solace to know they are waiting to greet us in heaven."

"Indeed it is," Nettie agreed.

Katie was the one to break the ensuing silence. "I

have never seen an alpaca up close. May I take a look at yours?"

"Of course." Faith took pity on the expectant mother having to listen to such a somber conversation. Rising to her feet, she motioned for Katie to follow her. Nettie and Sarah deposited the dirty plates in the sink and quickly joined them.

Outside, they crossed the yard in a tight group. Nettie eyed the sad state of the barn. "You will need to find a strong husband to get this farm in shape. We have several bachelors in our church district who would make a good husband to you and a father to your nephew."

Quickly, Faith said, "I have no plans to marry again."

"Not even if the right fellow happens along?" Katie teased.

"I'm too old to remarry," Faith added firmly.

Nettie started laughing. "No, you aren't. I'm getting married in a few weeks. If I found someone at my age, you can, too. It is all up to God."

Katie asked Nettie a question about preparations for the upcoming nuptials, and the two women began an animated discussion.

Faith slowed her pace and hoped that would be the end of her part in the conversation, but Sarah shortened her stride and dropped back beside her. "Nettie is right. It's up to God."

"It is up to me, too. I see no need to marry again."

She felt Sarah's keen eyes studying her intently. Finally, Sarah said, "Your marriage wasn't a happy one? I understand. We won't speak of it again."

Faith could only wonder if Sarah's experience in marriage was the same.

As they rounded the barn, Faith saw her alpacas were all grazing except for Myrtle. She stood alone near the barn door. Faith called out to them. "Come here, babies. I have people who want to meet you."

They all raised their heads to look at her, but only Socks ventured close.

"Will they spit at us?" Katie asked.

"They only spit if they are startled. Sometimes they will spit at each other if they are annoyed, but for the most part they all get along."

"They are so cute," Katie gushed.

Faith had had the same reaction the first time she'd seen one. "They are wonderful animals. They are docile and they are quite smart."

"Which one spit on my cousin?" Sarah leaned her arms on the top of the gate.

Faith pointed. "That was Myrtle. She's the gray one standing by the barn door. She is expecting in a few weeks."

Katie started laughing. "I know just how she feels. Being pregnant makes me moody, too. Some days I feel like spitting at my husband. Poor Elam knows to stay out of my way when I get in a temper."

Nettie and Sarah joined in Katie's laughter. Myrtle moved as far away from the noise as she could get. She huddled by the corner of the barn and watched them all with a wary expression.

Faith felt a glimmer of hope begin to grow in her heart. She would enjoy having these women for friends. It seemed things were beginning to look up for her in this new place.

"Here you all are!"

Faith looked past Myrtle as a woman walked into view from around the corner of the barn. Myrtle took quick exception to the stranger coming so close. She spat and galloped to the far side of the pen, giving an alarm call that sent the entire herd milling in panic.

The middle-aged woman stood frozen with a shocked expression on her face as alpaca spit dripped from her chin.

Katie clasped her hands over her mouth. "Oh, no, not her."

"Who is it?" Faith asked, knowing full well she didn't want to hear the answer.

"The bishop's wife," Katie whispered.

"You should have seen the look on Esther Zook's face." Sarah started giggling again. "I'm sorry, I can't help it. It was the funniest thing. Poor Faith, I've never seen anyone so contrite."

Adrian, sitting in the corner of his living room, continued his pretense of reading the newspaper while he listened to his cousin regale his mother with her story. Sarah was a frequent visitor in his home. They had been close since they were children.

"What did you think of her?" his mother asked.

"Adrian's new neighbor or the bishop's wife?" Sarah began giggling again.

Glancing over top of the paper, Adrian saw his mother frown at Sarah's levity. "I meant Faith Martin."

Sarah shrugged. "She seems nice enough. She is certainly a hard worker."

His mother transferred her gaze to him. "It's a pity she is handicapped for there are several bachelors around who are on the lookout for a new wife."

Compelled to defend Faith, he said, "She walks with a barely noticeable limp. It isn't a handicap."

"I'm sure there is someone who is willing to overlook such a minor imperfection." She gave him a pointed stare.

He turned the page and ignored her broad hint. He wasn't on the lookout for a wife. His mother would eventually learn to accept that.

Sarah, a widow herself, rolled her eyes. "*Aenti* Linda, if you mean Toby Yoder and Ivan Stultz, I don't think they would mind a wife who walks with a limp. Not as long as she can cook and clean, mend clothes, run a farm and milk twenty cows twice a day while they spend their time gossiping at the feed store. Why, they would both be thrilled to have such a woman."

"You might be right," his mother admitted.

Adrian couldn't stay silent any longer. "Maybe she doesn't want to marry again. Did you think of that?"

"What woman doesn't want a husband and children of her own?" his mother countered.

"The love between a husband or wife doesn't die because one of them is with God. It lives on." He didn't care if she knew he was talking about himself.

Her gaze softened. "Of course not, but we can love more than one person."

I know. I loved a wife and a child and God took them both.

"Sarah hasn't remarried," he pointed out, keeping his painful thoughts to himself. His cousin ducked her head. Her smile vanished. He was sorry he'd brought the subject up. Sarah's husband had passed away from cancer over three years ago.

Glancing from Sarah back to Adrian, his mother

gave him a fierce scowl. "Sarah has not closed her heart to love. It will find her again when God wills it. Hopefully, before she is too old to bear children."

He went back to his paper, knowing his mother would always have the last word.

Sarah said, "Faith doesn't have to worry about that. She already has a child on the way."

"What?" Adrian and his mother demanded together in shocked surprise.

Sarah couldn't keep a straight face. "She is adopting her brother's child."

"Well, that changes things a little," his mother mused. "Not all men want a wife and a child at the same time."

Sarah propped her elbows on the table. "Faith insists she won't marry again, and I believe she means it."

Linda waved aside her comment. "Nonsense. Once she has had the chance to meet a few of our fellows she'll change her mind. Let me think. Micah Beachy might be just the one. He's got a nice little farm over by Sugarcreek and he's never been married. I'll have to invite him over for a visit next month."

Intrigued by Sarah's comments, Adrian asked, "She specifically said she won't remarry? Does she intend to raise a child alone?"

Sarah turned in her seat to face Adrian. "*Ja.* What did you think of Faith when you met her?"

"I think she is going to have a hard time making a go of that farm. She doesn't have the money to hire help."

He understood Faith's reluctance to marry again. Suffering the pain of losing a spouse and child was more than anyone should have to bear. Loving someone meant risking that pain again. He wasn't willing to take that chance.

"The peaches in her orchard should be nearly ripe. If she sells her fruit, she'll be able to make some money, won't she?" Sarah asked.

Adrian shook his head. "The place is so overgrown, she'll have a hard time even getting to the fruit. Those trees haven't been pruned in twenty years. Most of them are so old they may not even bear fruit anymore. The peaches she does have will be small because no one thinned out the fruit when it was setting on."

"I told her to bring some of her yarns into Needles and Pins. I'm sure Janet will allow her to sell them there."

He turned the page of his paper. "It will take a lot of yarn to fix up that farm."

His mother left off cleaning the kitchen counter and began wiping down the table. "What kind of shape is the house in?"

Sarah brightened. "It's not too bad. I didn't see any water damage inside, so the roof must still be sound. But it was so grimy. It took us hours to get the walls and floors clean. Elam Sutter, Eli Imhoff and his two sons managed to get the outside of the house painted but not the barn. I'm afraid it's in need of a few repairs first."

"More than a few," Adrian added, unable to stay out of the conversation.

His mother folded her arms over her ample bosom. "Then everyone will have their work cut out for them. It is clear our sister is in need. We cannot turn our backs on her."

Folding his paper and laying it aside for good,

Adrian said, "Do you really think everyone will feel the same way? She isn't even a member of our church. Clearly, she didn't make a good impression on the bishop's wife."

His mother waved aside his objection. "Esther Zook will get over being made a laughingstock. She won't hold our new neighbor to blame for the actions of her animals. Esther knows her Christian duty, and when she forgets it, her husband will remind her."

Adrian exchanged glances with Sarah. She obviously wasn't in total agreement with his mother. She knew Esther Zook's opinion could sway many of the women in the community if she chose to rebuff Faith.

He rose to his feet. Grabbing his straw hat from the peg beside the front door, he slapped it on his head.

"Where are you going?" his mother asked.

"To see a woman about some peaches."

He left the house and headed for the hay meadow that separated his property from Faith's farm as fast as his feet could carry him. With him out of the way, his mother could finish fussing in his kitchen and talk about him freely. Not that his presence ever stopped her.

She meant well, he knew that. He appreciated that she came by to cook and clean for him each week even though he didn't need her help. What he didn't like was her interference.

Twice he'd found Lovina's and Gideon's clothes had been packed away in a trunk in the attic. He never said a word to his mother. He simply put the clothes back into the bureau beside his own. He wasn't ready to let go.

Adrian's rapid steps slowed as he approached Faith's

house. He wasn't sure exactly what he wanted to say to her. He wasn't even sure why he'd come. As he neared the front of her house, he saw she had moved her spinning wheel onto the front porch, probably to take advantage of the cooler evening breezes.

Her head was bent over the wheel as she concentrated on her task. With deft fingers, she pulled fleece from a bundle into long slender strands. Her feet pumped the pedals and made the wheel fly, spinning the fleece rapidly into yarn that wound around a pair of spindles.

It wasn't so much the art of her work that caught his attention. It was the look on her face. The worry and pain he'd seen before were gone, replaced by an expression of serenity. A sweet, soft smile curved her lips. He caught snatches of a song she was humming. So this was how Faith Martin looked when she was happy.

He couldn't bring himself to interrupt. Instead, he leaned on her rickety gate and simply enjoyed watching her work.

He had once wished to see her smile. He had no idea the sight could steal his breath away.

As much as he wished to let her work in peace, he had come here for a reason.

Chapter 5

"You make that look easy."

Faith jerked upright, searching for the source of the voice that startled her. She relaxed when she caught sight of Adrian leaning against her front gate. What was he doing here this late in the day? Her fence was finished.

How long had he been watching her?

Did he disapprove of the song she'd been humming? Mose had always hated it when she'd sung or hummed.

Faith slowed her spinning wheel to a stop. It wasn't fair of her to compare Adrian to Mose. They were two very different men. Even from the small amount of time she'd spent with Adrian, she could see that. She had to learn to let go of the past.

She said, "It is easy when you find the right rhythm. What can I do for you this evening?"

"I have come with another proposition for you."

Disappointment stabbed her. He'd come to make another offer on her land. Was she foolhardy to hang on to her dream of a place of her own?

She gathered up her loose fleece and placed it back in a blue plastic laundry basket. "I am still not interested in selling my land."

"What about your peaches?" He opened the gate and walked to the foot of her steps.

She shifted her basket to her good hip. "You want to buy peaches from me?"

"Not exactly. I'm willing to harvest your fruit and sell it for shares."

Faith pondered his surprising offer. She already had more work to do than she could possibly get done before Kyle arrived. That was, if the adoption when through. Selling peaches hadn't entered her mind. She had thought only of canning some for herself.

The extra income would be most welcome if Adrian was willing to do the work. "What share would you be asking?"

"I was thinking of a seventy/thirty split."

That was generous. "Seventy for me, thirty for you?"

He cracked a smile as he shook his head. "*Nee.* I would be doing the majority of the work."

Maybe so, but she wasn't going to *give* her produce away. "The fruit is all mine. If you will do fifty/fifty, I'll consider it."

"The crop will go to waste if I don't pick it for you. In that case, you'll get nothing."

He spoke the truth and she knew it. "Very well, sixty/forty and we have a deal."

Nodding once, he said, "*Goot.* We have a deal."

She expected him to leave, but he didn't. The heat of the day had waned. A cool breeze slipped past her cheeks and rustled through the leaves of the trees beside the house. For her, evenings were the best time of the day. She said, "I have some sweet tea made. Would you care for a glass?"

He hesitated. She thought he would refuse, but to her surprise, he said, "*Ja.* That would be nice."

"Let me put my fleece away and I'll be right back with some."

She hurried inside the house, feeling strangely lighthearted. When she came out again, he was sitting on the bottom step. After handing him the glass of tea, she awkwardly sank down on the step beside him. His hand shot toward her. She flinched away before she could stop herself.

He withdrew his hand slowly. The frown she was beginning to know so well settled on his face. He regarded her with a quizzical look in his eyes.

Faith stretched her bad leg out in front of her and tried to pretend nothing had happened. "I hope the tea is sweet enough."

"Does it hurt much?" he asked softly.

She rubbed her thigh and swallowed hard, uncomfortable with his sympathy. "Not as much as it used to."

"How did it happen? If you don't mind my asking?"

She didn't mind talking about the accident. It was talking about her marriage that she shied away from. "A pickup struck our buggy when we were on our way home from church."

Adrian took a sip of his tea, then stared out across the yard. "Is that how your husband died?"

"Mose was killed instantly." Faith stared into her glass as she relived those painful days.

"My son was struck and killed by a car. The English, they go so fast in their big machines. What in their lives makes them rush so?"

"It seems to me they are afraid they will miss something important."

"What was more important than my son's life?"

"Nothing." She wanted so much to reach out and comfort him. What would he think if she did? She tightened her grip on her glass.

After a moment of silence, Adrian shook off his somber mood. "I understand Myrtle met the bishop's wife today."

Faith pressed a hand to her cheek. "Please don't remind me. It was horrible."

"Sarah thought it was quite funny."

Faith cast him a sideways glance. "That was the worst part. Everyone was trying so hard not to laugh while I was stuttering my apologies."

"I'm sure you told her alpaca spit will brush off when it dries."

"Of course I did."

"Did you also mention how long the smell lingers?"

"I suggested she wash her clothes with baking soda to cut the odor as soon as she got home."

"I don't recall you giving me that information."

She tried to look innocent. "Didn't I?"

"*Nee.* I will assume you were too worried about your animals to pass along that important piece of advice."

"*Ja,* don't think for a minute it was because you were scowling so fiercely that the words flew out of my head."

"Did I frighten you that day?"

She shrugged. "A little."

"Are you frightened of me now?"

She knew he was referring to the way she had flinched from him a few moments ago. She stared down at the glass in her hand, avoiding his gaze. "You have been most helpful to me. I could not ask for a better neighbor."

It wasn't an answer to his question, but it was the best she could do. He said nothing more. The sounds of cicadas rose and fell as they started their noisy evening songs. As abruptly as it started, their song stopped, and the silence stretched on for another awkward minute.

Faith racked her mind for something to say, but Adrian beat her to it. "I will go through your orchard on Wednesday and see if the fruit is ripe enough for picking."

"It's a mess. There are downed branches and dead trees all through it."

"We had a bad ice storm a few years back. I imagine most of the damage is from that. However, many of the trees are getting old. Peach trees only live about twenty years and these were planted at least that long ago."

"Do you know if they are freestone or clingstone peaches?"

A hint of a grin tugged at the corner of his lips. "The ones I snitched as a *kinder* were all freestone and extra sweet."

She smiled at his confession. It was easy to imagine him as a mischievous child. "*Goot.* Those are the best kind for selling at market."

Faith smoothed her skirt with one hand. It should have felt strange to be sitting beside Adrian and discussing the work that needed to be done on the farm, but it didn't. It felt comfortable. It was only when the conversation turned personal that she grew uncomfortable.

The shadows had grown long, and the cicadas resumed their evening serenade. Adrian finished his drink and rose to his feet. "It's getting late. I should go home."

Faith tried to stand but didn't quite make it. Embarrassed, she gathered herself to try again. Adrian stepped close and held out his hand to aid her.

Faith's heart began hammering so hard she was sure he could hear it. Fear made her mouth dry. Adrian wasn't Mose. She didn't have to be afraid anymore. They were brave words but hard to live by. She ignored his hand and pulled herself upright using the railing.

Adrian saw the change that came over Faith when he offered his hand. Was it pride that made her struggle to her feet alone? He didn't think so.

He saw the flash of fear in her eyes, although she hid it quickly. What reason would Faith Martin have to fear him?

He let his hand fall back against his side. If his presence was unwelcome, he would not force it upon her. "I will see you Wednesday, then."

She twisted her hands together as she avoided looking at him. "I may not be here. I'm taking my yarns into town. Your cousin Sarah was kind enough to invite me to bring my work into her shop. After that, I will be here, but I'm expecting the social worker from the adoption agency. I'm trying to adopt my brother's child."

Was that why she seemed so worried? Was she

afraid her adoption wouldn't go through? He tried to picture her with a babe in her arms. She would make a good mother.

He said, "You don't need to be here while I survey your orchard. We can discuss what I find another time. I promise I won't eat up your profits."

She smiled halfheartedly at his humor. He wanted more. He wanted a real smile from her. "How are your beasts adjusting to their new home?"

"They seem quite happy in the pen you built for them. Thank you for your help with that. They are growing fat on the thick grass in the orchard."

"Will I disturb them working in there?"

"I do not think so. They may disturb you for they are quite curious. You're likely to find them underfoot and investigating everything you do."

He nodded toward the barn. "Has your expectant mother had her calf?"

"A baby alpaca is called a cria, not a calf." She relaxed as she talked about her animals. The haunted look faded from her eyes.

"Cria." He rolled the unfamiliar word on his tongue. "Has Myrtle had her cria?"

"Not yet. I think it will be few more weeks before she becomes a mother again."

"This is not her first babe?"

"Bandit and Baby Face are both her offspring."

"You have chosen unusual names for your unusual creatures."

"My husband and I rented a farm from an English family when we lived in Missouri. I let their daughter name all the new babies."

"You will be able to name this one yourself."

She glanced shyly in his direction. "Perhaps I will give you the honor."

He stroked his beard as he considered her offer. "I could name it for its mother. *Shmakkich.*"

"Smelly? I will not call my new baby Smelly."

"Then you must find a better name yourself for that is my only suggestion." He handed her his empty glass.

She took it without hesitation. Her eyes crinkled with humor. "I did not think you would shirk from a difficult task."

"A challenge, is it? Very well, I shall name it Stinky."

"Nee." She shook her head.

"Foul Breath."

Faith giggled. *"Nee.* I will not call any creature Foul Breath. If that's the best you can do, it will remain nameless."

Her smile was back and Adrian was content. "I shall give it some more consideration. Good night, Faith Martin."

"Guten nacht, Adrian."

He started toward home but stopped a few yards away. Turning around, he called out, "What about Skunk?"

"Nee! That's the worst name ever."

"But what if it's black with a white stripe down its back?"

"Not even then. Be off with you, foolish fellow." She shooed him away with one hand, but she was smiling.

It wasn't until he was nearly home that he realized he was still smiling, too.

Faith guided Copper onto the highway and headed toward Hope Springs. The horse kept to a brisk trot, but it wasn't long before several cars were backed up behind Faith's buggy waiting to pass her on the next open stretch of road. The driver of the first car that went around her gave her a friendly wave. The second car drew alongside but didn't pass. When Faith glanced their way, she saw the passenger had the window rolled down and was aiming the camera in her direction.

Faith quickly turned her face away. No matter which Amish community she lived in, it was always the same. There were always a few tourists who just had to snap a photograph of an Amish person. They never seemed to realize it was rude.

The second car sped away, and Faith was free to enjoy the green rolling countryside. It was easy to see how fertile the land was as she passed farm after farm with tall cornfields and fat cattle grazing near the roadside.

The outskirts of Hope Springs came into view after several miles. Faith had no trouble finding her way to the fabric store. She pulled Copper to a stop in the parking lot beside three other buggies.

As soon as she pushed open the front door of Needles and Pins, she was greeted with the scent of a floral and vanilla potpourri and the sound of chimes. The store was small, but it was crammed from floor to ceiling with bolts of fabric in every color. At the rear of the store a white-haired woman stood behind the counter. She looked up from her work and smiled in greeting.

"Welcome to Needles and Pins. Is there something I can help you with?"

Faith worked to quell the nervousness making her stomach queasy. She needed to find a market for her work as soon as possible. One of the things Kyle's social worker would be looking at was her financial situation. Faith needed proof that she earned enough to care for a child. Sending up a quick prayer, she said, "I'm looking for Janet."

"Then look no further. I'm she."

Faith approached the counter. After introducing herself, she opened her bag and pulled out a sample of her yarn. "Would you be interested in purchasing some hand-spun baby alpaca yarn?"

"I might be." Janet took the skein to examine closely.

"The black color is natural. It's from one of my crias."

Janet looked up in surprise. "You raise your own alpacas?"

"*Ja,* I have ten animals. Some are white, I have one black, several grays and two that are butternut-brown. I can die the wool for you if you have customers that want a particular color. It's very soft yarn and very strong." Faith forced herself to stop babbling.

Running her hand over the skein, Janet said, "I can see this is quality work, Mrs. Martin. I would be interested in buying all you have in black and dark gray. I'm not sure about the other colors. Perhaps I will take a few of them and see how they sell."

Faith struggled to hide her excitement. She had prayed to make a big sale today, and her prayers were being answered.

Janet continued, "If you are interested, I could post your yarn for sale on my website. I get a fair number of internet orders."

"That would be *goot, danki.*" This was better yet.

Faith sorted her yarns for Janet and pocketed the money with a happy heart. She was preparing to leave when Sarah came out from the back room. Smiling,

Sarah came forward carrying several large bolts of powder-blue material. "Faith, how are you? Have you brought in your yarn?"

"*Ja.* Janet was kind enough to purchase several dozen skeins. If they sell well, she will buy more."

Sarah leaned close. "I will do my best to steer our customers toward them."

"I appreciate that."

"I have been instructed by Nettie Sutter to invite you to our widow's meeting on Friday night."

Such meetings were common in Amish communities where widows sought to remain active and productive members of the community even into old age. Faith had been a member of such a group in her last church district.

As much as she wanted to say yes, Faith didn't have time to devote to social visits. "Perhaps I can join you when I've settled in."

"Fair enough. We are finishing two quilts that will be auctioned off next month. We help support an orphanage in Haiti with the money we raise and we give to the church to help our members who have medical bills and such. Several times a year we hold a large auction. Some of the women in our church have started a co-op to help members market and sell their work."

"I'm not much of a hand at quilting," Faith admitted.

"Don't worry, we will find something for you to do. We meet at the home of Naomi Wadler. Her daughter and son-in-law run the Wadler Inn and Shoofly Pie Café. You passed by it on your way in town. Naomi's home is behind the inn."

Faith remembered the Swiss-chalet-style inn at the edge of town. "What time are the meetings held?"

"Five o'clock."

"I look forward to the day I can meet with you."

"Wonderful. Have you decided to join our church?"

"I plan to ask the bishop about it soon."

"I must warn you that once you are accepted, you will be fair game as far as Adrian's mother is concerned."

Perplexed, Faith asked, "Why do I need a warning about his mother?"

"*Aenti* Linda fancies herself a matchmaker. Adrian and I are her only current failures. I admit she does have a knack for putting the right people together. You will provide her a new challenge. Hopefully, I can get a break from chance meetings and uncomfortable suppers at her house where I feel like a prize hen on display."

Faith shook her head. "She may matchmake all she wants. I have no intention of marrying again."

"That is exactly what Adrian says."

Faith began to rearrange the yarns left in her basket. "It is a shame he feels that way. He would make a good husband."

"He's a handsome fellow, I'll give him that."

"He's much more than that. He's kind and generous, strong and hardworking. He's everything a woman could desire in a mate."

As soon as she realized she was rambling, Faith looked up in embarrassment. Sarah stared back with a look of compassion on her face.

Faith wanted to sink through the floor. She hadn't realized how much she had come to admire Adrian or how much she wanted to be admired by him.

Sarah reached out and laid a hand on Faith's arm.

"Adrian still grieves deeply for his wife and son. He says the love he holds in his heart for his first wife doesn't leave room for another. He speaks with conviction when he says he will never love again. A woman who sets her heart on my cousin is likely to find heartache instead."

Adrian started his assessment of Faith's orchard under the close supervision of her alpacas. The herd followed him everywhere, observing his activity with wide curious eyes. Their heads bobbed back and forth on their long necks as they tried to figure out what he was up to.

Before long, the group grew tired of simply watching him. They began a new game, bounding away, then racing back at him, dodging aside at the last second to avoid a collision. Soon, several mock battles broke out between the youngsters. They chased each other around the trees, kicking and knocking their long necks into one another. Socks and Baby Face reared up and began a boxing match as they hopped about on their rear legs.

Adrian chuckled at their antics. It was like being surrounded by five-foot-tall puppies. He began to understand Faith's attraction to them. They were adorable. Like their owner.

Only Myrtle refused to join the fun. She spit at those brave or foolish enough to encroach on her space. Adrian had no trouble staying away from her.

He finished his task and was letting himself out the gate to the orchard when he saw Faith returning. His spirits lifted instantly. She was sure to smile when he recounted her animals' antics.

She drew her horse to a stop beside the barn door. He held the mare's headstall as Faith descended from the buggy. "Did you sell all your yarn?" he asked.

She pulled a large hamper from the backseat. "Not all of it but a large portion. I hope you have some good news about my orchard."

"You have very curious animals prowling out there."

Her face filled with concern. "Did they give you trouble?"

"I was able to dodge their charges and most of the spit."

"I will wash your shirt if need be."

"*Nee,* I'm only teasing. You have about ten trees that should be cut down. They are too old and diseased to bear fruit. They can be cut up and stacked for firewood. They should dry out enough through the fall to burn well this winter."

Faith set her basket on the ground. "Should I replant more peach trees in their place?"

"If I were you, I'd diversify with some plum and apple trees. Since they flower at different times, you will be less likely to lose the entire crop if we get a late freeze in the spring.

Her eyebrows shot up. "So you think I will be here in the spring? Have you decided I can make a go of this place?"

"You have made a good start," he admitted.

"Only because you've done the majority of the outside work. Your help has been a godsend."

Adrian grew uncomfortable with her gratitude. He hadn't started out to help her earn a living. He'd had his own selfish reasons for doing the work needed. He had hoped she would sell her farm to him.

Did he still want her to leave?

No…and yes.

He hadn't once thought of Lovina all through this day. He'd thought only of what Faith would say, what would make her smile. Faith made him forget his pain.

He didn't want to feel this sense of wonder when she was near, but he did. Seeing her smile shouldn't make him happy, but it did.

Adrian turned away and started to unhitch the horse. Faith made him feel things he didn't want to feel. Things that had died in him when Lovina died.

Faith said, "I can manage. I'm sure you have your own work to see to."

"I've wasted the best part of the day here. I might as well stable your horse. It won't take that much longer." His voice sounded unnaturally harsh even to his own ears.

Faith took a step back and ducked her head. "I should get these things up to the house. The social worker will be here soon."

As she hurried away, Adrian could've kicked himself for stripping the happiness from her eyes. Had he been wrapped up in his own grief so long that he'd forgotten how to be kind?

Chapter 6

Faith put her yarns and baskets away and worked up the courage to return to the barn. She had upset Adrian, but she didn't know how. Was it something she said? He'd done too much for her to let him go away angry.

She paused at the kitchen door, remembering Adrian as he had first appeared to her, dark and scowling. In spite of his fierce appearance, he'd been nothing but kind to her. She had come to care for him, to see him as a friend, yet she had scurried away from his displeasure like a sheep running from the wolf. Why was it still so hard to stand up for herself?

Because I'm afraid.

Was Adrian's kindness only an act or did her old fear make her suspect evil where it didn't exist? If she couldn't be sure, how could she do business with him, accept his help, allow him into her life?

Learning to trust again was harder than relearning to walk had been. Perhaps that was the reason God had brought her to this place. Because she had to begin somewhere. If this was her first test, she had failed miserably.

No, that wasn't true because she wanted to trust Adrian. The real problem was that she no longer trusted her own judgment.

Dear Father in heaven, give me strength and wisdom. Let me not judge others lest I be judged in return. Help me to see the good in men and not suspect evil.

Bolstered by her prayer, Faith left the house, crossed the yard and pulled open the barn door. Adrian was busy forking hay into Copper's stall. He hadn't seen her return.

Unobserved, Faith took a moment to admire the way he made the work look easy. His strong arms and shoulders drove the fork deep into the hay and lifted a bundle with ease. Beneath the sweat-dampened shirt he wore, she could see the muscles tightening and rippling across his back. Her breath quickened as she realized she wasn't seeing him as a friend should. Embarrassed, she looked away.

He was a strong, handsome man, and he was proving himself to be a good friend and neighbor. That was all. She wouldn't let it be anything else.

He caught sight of her. "I'll be done in a minute."

He didn't seem angry now. She took a step closer. "I'm sorry I upset you earlier."

His eyes widened in surprise. "You did nothing to upset me. I'm the one who should be sorry. I let my ill humor ruin your day. That was wrong. The help I gave you was for selfish reasons. Please forgive me."

"You are forgiven. For what selfish reason have you worked here day in and day out?"

He hesitated, then sighed. "I thought if you couldn't make a go of this farm, I could buy it from you. The work that I've done here would have had to be done anyway when I took over."

"I see. Thank you for telling me this."

"I no longer think you will fail, Faith Martin. You have the will to succeed, and as you once told me, you aren't afraid of hard work."

A sound outside drew her attention. Faith's heart leaped into her throat when she saw the automobile pulling to a stop in front of her house. In the front seat she could see a woman surveying the property. "That must be Mrs. Taylor, Kyle's social worker. What do I do?"

Adrian came to stand beside her. Gently, he said, "Go and welcome her."

His simple reply made her realize how silly she was being. "Kyle was raised in an *Englisch* home. I'm worried that this *Englisch* woman won't think he belongs in an Amish home."

"You cannot discover the answers you seek by hiding here in the barn."

"Are you sure?"

"*Ja,* I'm pretty sure." He smiled and motioned her toward the door. "Go."

Gathering her courage, Faith walked out of the barn and toward the car, knowing this was the moment she had been dreading and praying for. She had had several letters from Mrs. Taylor, but she had no idea what to expect from the *Englisch* social worker.

The car door opened, and a tall, slender young

woman got out. She wore a plum-colored suit and matching high-heeled shoes. Her hair was short and dark. It curled tightly against her skull. She held a briefcase in one hand.

Faith managed a smile. "*Velkumm.* Are you a Mrs. Taylor?"

"I'm afraid Mrs. Taylor no longer works for our agency. I'm Miss Watkins. Caroline Watkins. Are you Faith Miller?"

"Martin," Faith corrected her.

"My apologies." Caroline's gaze was fastened on Adrian standing by the barn. "Is that Mr. Martin?"

"No. That is my neighbor, Adrian Lapp. I am a widow. I thought you knew that."

"I'm sure it was in the file. I apologize if I sound unprepared. I've been swamped with work. Yours is my third home visit this week. Mrs. Taylor left on very short notice and I'm playing catch-up."

"Do come in the house." Faith gestured toward the front door.

Would her home pass inspection? Was it clean enough? Was it big enough? Would Faith pass as a prospective parent, or would this woman decide she didn't deserve her nephew? Worry gnawed at her insides. Exactly what would this home study entail?

Inside the house, Faith led the way to the living room. It was sparely furnished with a small sofa placed in front of a pair of tall windows. Two reading chairs flanked the couch. A small bookcase sat against the wall opposite the windows. Miss Watkins settled herself on the sofa while Faith perched on the edge of a chair facing her.

Miss Watkins must have seen the concern Faith was

trying to conceal. "Please don't be nervous, Mrs. Martin. I'm here to make sure your home is a suitable, safe place for your nephew, not to pass judgment on your housekeeping or personal tastes."

"I am Kyle's only family. What could be more suitable than that?"

"I agree it is almost always best to place a child with a relative, but placing a child in a safe and loving home is our top priority, even if that means placing them with someone other than a blood relative."

The social worker searched through her papers. "First, I need to see two forms of identification. I have to make sure I'm talking to the right person. Confidentiality laws and all that, you know. Your driver's license and a Social Security card will be fine."

"I do not have such documents."

Miss Watkins frowned. "You don't have a Social Security card?"

"I do not. The Amish do not believe in Social Security. It is the responsibility of everyone to care for the sick and elderly. We do not depend upon the government to do that for us. I do have my birth certificate and my marriage license, if that will do?"

Faith rose from the chair and crossed to the small bookcase in the corner. She opened her Bible and took out several pieces of paper and handed them to the social worker.

"Under the circumstances, I think these will be fine. Today, I'd like to gather some information about your background, family life, child care expectations and about your parenting philosophy. I know you must be frustrated at having to repeat some of this process since you began your adoption in Missouri, but now that you are in Ohio, you will have to abide by Ohio law."

"I understand my move came at a bad time, but it couldn't be helped."

"I will do what I can to expedite your home study. A few things won't have to be repeated. Your background check and criminal search records have been forwarded to us by the Missouri authorities."

"I only wish to have Kyle with me as soon as possible. He has been with strangers for two months."

Miss Watkins opened a folder. "Kyle King is in foster care in Texas, is that right?"

Faith nodded.

"And you've not been to visit him, is that correct?"

"I've spoken to him on the phone several times and written letters to him twice a week, every week, but I've been unable to travel to Texas." It wasn't much, but it was all she could do for now.

"I will admit I know very little about the Amish, so please forgive my ignorance. You are the first Amish client I've worked with. I understand you do not use electricity."

"We do not."

"And you have no phone and no car."

"There is a phone shack at the end of the lane that I and my Amish neighbors may use. It is permitted for work and for emergencies. I have a horse and buggy for ordinary travel, but I may hire a driver if I must travel a long distance."

"I'll make a note of that. After our interview, I'll make a brief safety inspection of your home. Typically, this first visit lasts from three to four hours."

"Four hours?" Faith thought of all the work that she had waiting for her.

"Yes. Is that a problem?"

"*Nee,* of course not."

"If I can't gather all I need today I will schedule a follow-up visit. I don't see a statement from your doctor. Did you receive the paperwork we sent you?"

"I haven't had a chance to schedule an appointment."

Miss Watkins frowned. "Ohio law is very clear on this. In order to adopt a child, you must be in good health."

"I am. My limp is the result of an accident, not an illness. I'll take care of it this week." A doctor's visit was another expense Faith didn't need. The money from her yarn sales wouldn't go far.

"All right. Let's get started. Are there any other adults or children living in this home?"

"*Nee.*"

"Do you have adequate room to house a child?"

"*Ja,* this house has four bedrooms upstairs, although I don't yet have a bed for Kyle."

Miss Watkins jotted down some notes. "I will have to see all the accommodations prior to his arrival. Do you suffer from any physical or mental illnesses?"

"Only the limp you see."

"What is the reason for your disability?"

"I was injured when a pickup struck our buggy. My husband was killed."

"I'm sorry for your loss."

"It was God's will." Faith couldn't pretend there was sorrow in her heart, for there was none. Only relief and guilt for not loving Mose as a wife should.

"Do you have a history of alcohol, drug or substance abuse, even if it did not result in an arrest?"

"Nee."

"Do you have a history of child abuse, even if it was not reported?"

"Nee."

"Do you have a history of domestic violence, even if it did not result in an arrest or conviction?"

Faith's heart jumped to her throat. Would Mose reach out from the grave and snatch away her only chance to raise a child? She couldn't let that happen.

Never again would she place herself, or Kyle, in such a situation. She answered carefully for she didn't want to lie. "I have never abused anyone nor have I been accused of such behavior."

"Have you ever been rejected for adoption or foster care?"

Faith relaxed. "I have not."

For the next several hours, Faith answered all the questions put to her. Finally, Miss Watkins said, "Why don't we take a break and you can show me the house."

"Of course. I have only recently moved in. There is still much work to be done."

"I understand. Let's start with the kitchen."

Faith led the way. Miss Watkins made notes as she walked. To Faith, it seemed that she took note of every flaw, every uneven floorboard and even the stains on the wall behind the stove. The house might not be perfect, but it was a roof over her head.

In the kitchen, Miss Watkins went straight to the refrigerator and opened the door. The shelves were bare except for a few staples—butter, eggs and some bacon. She turned to Faith. "You don't have much in the way of food here."

"I have only myself to cook for. I don't need much."

"Will feeding a growing boy be difficult for you?"

"Not at all. Come. I will show you the cellar." Faith took a lamp from inside the cupboard and lit the wick. Opening a door at the back of kitchen, Faith descended the steps, cautioning Miss Watkins to use the handrail.

Down in the cool, damp cellar, Faith raised her lamp to show shelves full of canned fruits, vegetables and meats. It had taken her two solid days to clean out the cellar, repair the shelves and stock them. "I brought most of this with me from my previous home in Missouri. Some of my new neighbors have brought more as gifts."

"Impressive. Can we go back upstairs now?"

Clearly, Miss Watkins didn't care to remain in a small dark space. She frowned as she eyed the lamp Faith held. "I have some concern about the use of kerosene lamps around a small child."

"Amish children are all taught how to use lamps safely."

"Open flames are very dangerous. You will have to provide an alternate source of light."

"Would battery-powered lights be acceptable?"

"Absolutely."

"Then I shall purchase some." Faith smiled. More expenses.

After leaving the cellar, Faith gave the social worker a tour of the yard and outbuildings. Once again, Miss Watkins was scribbling furiously in her notebook. The alpaca herd came to the fence to observe the newcomer. Faith assured the social worker that they were not dangerous animals, but she gave Myrtle a wide berth. The rest of the herd remained well behaved, much to her relief.

Back in the house, Miss Watkins gathered together her papers. She closed her briefcase and handed Faith two additional pieces of paper. "I think that will do it for today. As far as paperwork goes, you will need to complete the health summary and you will need to have a fire safety inspection."

Was that a free service or was it something else she would have to pay for?

Miss Watkins held out her hand. "I will be back the same time next week. Hopefully, you will have everything completed by then."

Twisting her hands together, Faith asked, "What if I don't?"

"If there are deficiencies, it does not automatically mean you can't adopt your nephew. It simply means that these are things we will have to work on."

As Faith watched the social worker drive away, she had no idea if she had passed inspection or not.

Why should they feel she deserved a child if God had not seen fit to answer her prayers for one? Simply because she was Kyle's aunt didn't mean she was the best person to raise him.

Glancing toward the orchard, she wondered if Adrian was still working out there or if he had gone home. An intense need to see him took hold of her.

Faith let herself through the gate behind the barn. Only Socks was grazing near the building. The rest of the herd had disappeared. Lifting her head, Socks ambled slowly in Faith's direction. When she reached Faith, she stopped and rubbed her head against Faith's side.

"What are you doing here all by yourself? Where is the rest of the herd?" Faith peered into the trees but couldn't see the animals. Giving Socks a quick pat, Faith headed deeper into the orchard.

She hadn't gone far when she spotted the rest of the group. They were clustered around a single tree and all gazing upward. A ladder stood propped against the trunk. She could just make out Adrian's legs halfway up the rungs.

She was startled when he called out, "How did it go?"

"I wish I knew."

A large, dead branch came crashing to the ground, sending the alpacas dashing in circles before they clustered again beside the ladder. Adrian descended from the tree. "How soon will you know if your nephew can live with you?"

"For all the hurry, hurry, hurry in *Englisch* lives, their child placement process moves slowly. If all goes well, it may be two or three weeks."

"Where is he until then?"

"In a foster home."

"I'm sure they are taking good care of him."

"I pray so."

If the *Englisch* woman didn't find Faith acceptable, what would happen to Kyle? Was there someone else waiting and longing to adopt a child the way she was? Perhaps they deserved him more than she did.

She looked at Adrian. "Am I doing the right thing trying to bring an *Englisch* child here?"

"Why would you ask that?"

She crossed her arms and hugged herself as if she

were cold. "Because in all the years I was married, God never saw fit to give me a child of my own."

Adrian heard the pain in Faith's voice. He saw the disappointment and loss in her eyes. He wanted to take her pain away, but he didn't know how. "Will you love this child?"

"I will."

"Then you are doing the right thing."

"If only I could be so sure. I must put my trust in God."

He said, "*And they that know thy name will put their trust in thee: for thou, LORD, hast not forsaken them that seek thee. Psalm 9:10.*"

"You are so very right. He has not forsaken me."

Adrian wasn't sure why that particular Bible verse popped into his head. God had turned away from him. He had been forsaken. Faith, too, had suffered a great loss, and yet she still drew comfort and hope from God's word.

Why was her faith so strong when his was so weak?

Chapter 7

On Sunday morning, Faith turned Copper off the highway and onto a farm lane two miles north of her home. At the edge of the road a homemade white sign with a black anvil painted on it said, "Horse Shoeing. Closed Wednesdays."

The church service was being held at the farm of Eli Imhoff, the local blacksmith, and the generous neighbor who, along with his sons, had painted the outside of her house.

Overhead, low gray clouds scuttled northward. The overcast sky was a welcome relief from the oppressive heat of the past few days, but the clouds were hanging on to any rain they held. Hopefully, any showers would remain at bay until after she was back home again.

At the other end of the long lane, Faith saw a two-story white house with a smaller *dawdy haus* built at a right angle from the main home. Both the grandfather house and the main house had pretty porches with white railings and wide steps. Three large birdhouses sat atop poles around the yard ringed with flower beds. Someday, her home would look like this.

Across an expanse of grass now crowded with buggies and groups of churchgoers stood a big red barn. In the corral, a pair of caramel-colored draft horses shared round hay bales with several dozen smaller horses. Copper whinnied a greeting. Several horses in the corral replied in kind.

A man came forward to take the reins from Faith. He tipped his black hat. "Good morning, *Frau.* I am Jonathan Dressler. I will take care of your horse." Although he looked Amish, he spoke in flawless English without a hint of the Pennsylvania Dutch accent she was accustomed to hearing.

"*Danki,* Jonathan." Faith stepped down from her vehicle and smoothed her skirt. Her stomach churned with nervous butterflies. More anxious than she cared to admit, she pulled a picnic hamper from beneath the front seat and stood rooted to the spot.

He pointed toward the farmhouse. "You may take your basket to the house. Karen Imhoff is in charge of the food today. It's nice to meet another newcomer to the community. Thanks to you, I'm no longer the new kid on the block."

"You are new here, too?"

"Yes. I guess I should say, *ja.*"

"You are *Englisch,* yet you dress plain."

"God has called me to live this simple life. Every day I give thanks that He led me to this place."

The smile on his handsome face was contagious.

She asked, "Have you any advice to share with this newcomer?"

"The people of Hope Springs are wonderful, welcoming souls."

As they were speaking, another horse and buggy came trotting into the yard. She recognized Adrian at the reins. With him were an older man and woman, two younger women in their early twenties, and a teenage boy.

Jonathan said, "I best get back to work, but I have to ask you one question. Did your alpaca really spit on the bishop's wife?"

Her shoulders slumped. "Has everyone heard of this?"

Jonathan chuckled. "It is not kind of me to say, but your alpaca sounds like a wonderful judge of character."

He laughed again as he unhitched Copper and led her to the corral.

Faith's heart sank to a new low. She would have to attend services several times in this church district before the congregation would be asked to accept her. Neither the bishop nor his wife was likely to want a new member who'd made Mrs. Zook a laughingstock.

Faith looked toward the house and saw the women from Adrian's buggy join a large group of women gathered on the porch. She recognized the bishop's wife standing among them. All eyes were turned in her direction.

She wanted to run home and hide.

"If I were you, I'd go in with my head up and smile as if nothing were wrong."

Faith glanced over her shoulder and saw Adrian unhooking his horse from the buggy. He wasn't looking at her, but she knew he was talking to her. There was no one else around.

He patted his horse's flank and spoke again, just as softly. "She will appear mean and petty if she snubs you when you are offering friendship, but if she senses fear, she won't have any trouble ignoring you. The other women will follow her lead."

"I should walk up to her and pretend my animal didn't spit in her face, is that what you suggest?"

"You have already apologized for that, haven't you?"

"More than once."

"Then it's over. Go, before they start to think you're *naerfich*."

She was nervous. But he was right, bless the man. His encouragement was exactly what she needed. Raising her chin, Faith limped forward and pasted a smile on her face.

As she approached the house, she nodded to Mrs. Zook. "Good morning. The Lord has blessed us with a fine morning, has He not? I look forward to hearing your husband's preaching for I hear God has graced him with a wonderful understanding of the Bible."

Mrs. Zook's smile wasn't overly warm, but at least she didn't cut Faith dead. She inclined her head slightly. "My husband speaks as God moves him. Joseph takes no credit for himself."

"That is as it should be. Where shall I put this?" Faith patted her basket, glad her voice wasn't shaking for her fingers were ice-cold.

A second woman spoke up. "Inside. Karen Imhoff will show you where she wants things."

Faith nodded her thanks, pulled open the front door

and went inside with a huge sigh of relief. Behind her she heard the women's lowered voices begin to buzz. She knew they were discussing her. Unfortunately, she couldn't make out what they were saying.

Inside the kitchen, Faith was thrilled to see Nettie, Sarah and Katie at work arranging the food on the counters and long tables set up against the walls. Everything appeared ready for the meal the congregation would share after the service was finished.

A tall, slender woman came in from a back room with a box of glasses. She added them to the table where the plates were stacked. Her eyes lit with mischief when she spied Faith. She said, "Hello. I'm Karen Imhoff. You must be Faith Martin. I have been hearing so much about you."

Faith gave a quick glance around the room and saw Sarah and Katie trying to hide their grins. She looked back at Karen. "*Ja,* I am the one with the spitting alpaca."

Sarah and Katie dissolved into giggles. Nettie gave them both a stern look. The young women quickly pulled themselves together.

Karen said, "I hope you enjoy the service today. We are always glad to see new faces."

The front door opened and Jonathan stuck his head in. He said, "Everyone is here now."

Faith noticed the way his gaze rested on Karen. There was a softness in his eyes that bespoke great affection.

"*Danki,* Jonathan," Karen replied. "We will be there shortly." There was no mistaking the love that flowed between them.

What would it be like, Faith wondered, to love wholeheartedly and be loved in return?

Jonathan started to close the door but stopped as a little girl of about nine slipped beneath his arm and into the kitchen.

After he closed the door, Faith said, "Jonathan is a most unusual young man. I have never known an *Englisch* person to join our faith."

Smiling fondly, Katie folded her hands atop her bulging tummy. "You should have Karen tell you the whole story of how Jonathan came to be with us. It is the most romantic tale."

"I should tell it. I saw him first," the little girl declared. She was the spitting image of Karen and clearly not shy.

Karen laid a hand on the child's head. "You are forgetting your manners, Anna. This is Faith Martin. She is new to Hope Springs, and we must make her welcome. Faith, this is my sister, Anna."

Faith smiled at her. "I'm pleased to meet you, and I'm dying to hear the story."

Anna eagerly launched into her tale. "Just before Christmas, Karen was taking us to school. I looked out the buggy window and I saw a dead man in the ditch. Only, he wasn't dead. He was only hurt, but bad. God made him forget who he was, so we called him John. He stayed with us until God let him remember his name. And now he knows who he is and he wants to marry my sister."

Anna grinned broadly, Karen blushed rosy red and the rest of the women grinned.

Karen cleared her throat. "That about sums it up."

Nettie said, "It's almost time for the service to start. Girls, take Faith down to the barn. I'll be there shortly."

"I'll show you the way," Anna said as she bounced toward the door.

Outside, the solidly overcast sky gave way to intermittent sunshine. The women followed Anna to the far side of the barn where a sloping earthen ramp led to the barn's loft. The huge doors had been propped open to catch the cool morning breeze.

Inside, rows of wooden benches in the large hayloft were filled with worshipers, men on one side of a center aisle, women on the other, all waiting for the church service to begin. Faith took a place beside Sarah, Karen and Katie. Anna wiggled her way in between Faith and Karen.

Glancing across the aisle to where the men sat, Faith caught Adrian's eye. He didn't smile, but he gave a slight nod to acknowledge her. He'd overheard her conversation with Mrs. Zook, and Faith had the feeling he approved. A moment later, Anna asked Faith a question, forcing her to look away from Adrian.

As everyone waited for the *Vorsinger* to begin leading the first hymn, Faith closed her eyes. This was a solemn time, a time to prepare her heart and soul to rejoice and give thanks to the living God. She listened intently, willing her soul to open to God's presence, preparing to hear His word.

She heard the rustle of fabric on wooden benches as people shifted on the hard seats. In the trees outside, birds sang cheerfully, as if praising the Lord with their own special voices. In the barn below, Faith heard the movement of horses and cattle in their stalls. The smell of alfalfa hay and barn dust filled the air. She drew a deep breath. Contentment filled her bones. This was where she wanted to be. This was where she had always belonged.

She remembered how nervous she'd been the morning she took her vows. At nineteen, she had been the youngest of the group preparing for baptism. In that final hour before the service, she had searched her heart, wondering if she was making the right decision. It was no easy thing to live Amish.

She knew she had made the right choice.

The song leader, a young man with a red beard, started the first hymn. More than a hundred voices took up the solemn, slow-paced cadence. There was no music, only the stirring sounds of many voices praising God. Two ministers, a deacon and the bishop took their places on benches facing the congregation.

When the first song ended, the congregation sat in silence waiting for the preaching to begin. For Faith, it was a joyful moment. This was her first service in her new district and it felt as if she had come home at last.

Adrian did his best to listen to the sermon being preached, but his eyes were drawn constantly to where Faith sat. At the moment, her eyes were closed. There was such a look of peace on her face that he envied her.

He had not known peace or comfort during services since his son was killed. As hard as he tried to find consolation in the words being spoken, all he felt was anger.

Anger at God for robbing him of those most precious to him.

If he had his way, he would have stopped coming to church, but to do so would only bring more heartache to his family. If he avoided services, he would soon find himself under the ban, shunned by those who loved him in the hopes that he would mend his ways.

His brothers and sisters, his mother and father, none of them understood the anger that filled his heart, so he kept it hidden. He went through the motions of his faith without any substance. His life, which had once been filled with daily prayers, was now filled with hollow silence. God knew Adrian Lapp had not forgiven Him.

Adrian glanced at Faith. Was she even better at pretending faith than he was, or had she discovered the secret of letting go of her anger and hurt?

Beside him Benjamin fidgeted. His brother was eager to see the preaching end so he could visit with the Stultz sisters. The pretty twins were nearly the same age as Adrian's little brother. They were always willing to share their sweet smiles and laughter with him. Benjamin would soon be of courting age.

Adrian no longer believed in asking God for favors, but he hoped Benjamin would be spared the kind of pain he had endured, if and when Ben chose a wife.

Three hours later, when the service came to an end, Benjamin practically leaped from his seat and rushed to join his friends outside. Adrian stayed behind to help convert the benches into tables for eating by stacking them together. As he worked, he visited with his friends and neighbors. He listened to his father catching up on who had a sick horse, how everyone's corn was doing and what they planned to sell or buy on market day.

As the groups moved out of the barn toward the house, Adrian kept an eye out for Faith. He wanted to see if she was fitting in with the women of the district. He'd seen how scared she was when she first arrived. He'd offered his advice without thinking twice. It was strange how easily he read her face and demeanor. Stranger still was how often he found himself thinking about her. She was an unusual woman.

Since there wasn't enough room to feed everyone inside the house, the ordained and the eldest church members ate first at the tables set up for them inside. The rest of the congregation took turns getting their food and carrying it out to the barn.

When it was Adrian's turn, he saw Faith had joined Nettie, her daughters and several other women and was working alongside them in the kitchen.

He relaxed when he saw her at ease, visiting with Sarah and Katie Sutter, holding Katie's baby on one hip as easily as any seasoned mother. It was good to see her happy and smiling.

He caught Nettie Sutter's eye. She smiled and nodded once. She was a good woman. She would do everything in her power to see that the women of the community welcomed Faith.

Adrian glanced away and caught Sarah studying him. She looked from him to Faith and then back again. Her grin widened. She beckoned him over. He immediately took his plate and went outside.

He finished his meal and was taking his plate back to the house when he saw Faith deep in conversation with Bishop Zook over on the front porch of the *dawdy haus*. Joseph motioned to Adrian. This time he had no choice but to obey.

The bishop smiled a broad welcome. "Adrian, I have been filling Faith in on our *Ordnung*. I suggested she refer to you if she has any doubts about changes to her home or business as you are closer than I."

Faith remained silent, but a rosy blush stained her cheeks.

"I will do what I can to help." He didn't need a new excuse to see Faith, but he accepted the responsibility. It was important that she be accepted in the community. To do that, she had to live within the rules of their church.

The bishop thumped Adrian on the back. "Bless you. I knew I could count on you. A few of the men are getting up a game of quoits. Will you join us?"

Similar to horseshoes but played with round metal rings, quoits was a game Adrian used to enjoy, but he rarely took part in such activities now. "I will go find Ben. He has the best aim in the family."

After passing the message to his brother, Adrian put Ben in charge of getting the family home. With his duty discharged, Adrian left early and walked the few miles back to his farm.

At the house, he took a sharp knife and cut two bunches of flowers from the garden. With a bouquet in each hand, he walked out to the small cemetery where Gideon and Lovina waited for him.

Kneeling between their graves, he placed his gift beneath each headstone. "I brought some daisies for you, Lovey. I remember how much you loved them. You always said they were the bright eyes of your flower beds. They've bloomed all summer for you."

He sat back on his heels. "We held church services at Eli Imhoff's place. That *Englisch* fellow is still attending. I didn't think Jonathan would stay but he has a plain way about him now. Our new neighbor was there, too."

Pausing, he considered what to say about Faith. "She

smoothed things over with Esther Zook right nicely. Course, I gave her a hint on how to handle Esther. I hope that's okay. She's a smart one, that Faith is."

Suddenly, it didn't feel right to be talking to his wife about another woman. He rose and took his usual place on the cedar stump.

The silence pressed in on him. The wind tugged at his hat, and he settled it more firmly on his head.

"Gideon, you should see the crazy animals that live next door to us now. Alpacas. They're cute, but they spit on people and each other if they get annoyed. Faith has ten of them. The yarn she spins from their fleece is mighty soft. She gave me a pair of socks. The ones I'm wearing now, in fact."

He pulled up his pant leg and fingered the material. The warm softness reminded him of Faith's smile when he'd caught her humming as she worked her spinning wheel on her front porch.

Pushing thoughts of her out of his head, he said, "I'm glad I'm not the fella who has to shear those beasties come spring. I'll bet he gets spit on a lot."

Adrian chuckled as he imagined anyone trying to clip the wool from Myrtle's neck.

The wind carried his mirth away. There was no answering laughter here. No one to share the joke with. Only two gray headstones among many in a field of green grass. Sadness settled in his chest, making it hard to breathe.

Adrian rose to his feet, shoved his hands in his pockets and started for home. It wasn't until he reached his lane that he realized he hadn't said goodbye.

On Monday afternoon Faith walked to the end of her lane and crossed the highway to the community phone. A small gray building not much bigger than a closet sat back from the road near a cluster of trees. A solar panel extended out from the south side of the roof. She could see through the window that it was unoccupied. She opened the door and stepped inside.

The shack held a phone, a small stool and a ledge for writing materials along with an answering machine blinking with two messages. She listened to them in case the agency had left a message for her, but they hadn't. Adrian had a message that his mower part was in, and Samuel Stultz had a new grandbaby over in Sugarcreek. It was a girl.

A local phone directory hung from a small chain at the side of the ledge. Picking it up, she searched for and found the number for the medical clinic in Hope Springs. She pulled a pencil and a piece of paper from her pocket to make note of the number for later. As she laid her pencil down, it rolled off the ledge and fell under her stool.

In the cramped space she couldn't reach it. She blew out her breath in a huff of disgust, then awkwardly squatted down, bracing herself against the door. A second later the door opened and she tumbled out backward, landing in a heap at Adrian Lapp's feet.

"Faith, are you all right?" He immediately dropped to one knee beside her.

She looked up into his face filled with concern and could have died of embarrassment. "I'm fine, but my dignity is a little bruised."

He helped her to her feet. "I'm sorry. I didn't see you. What were you doing on the floor?"

His hands lingered on her arms. She could feel the warmth and strength of them through the thin fabric of her dress. He was so close. His masculine scent enveloped her, sending a wave of heat rushing to her face that had nothing to do with embarrassment or fear. She wasn't frightened of him. His touch was strong but gentle. She was frightened by how much she wanted to move closer, to step into the circle of his arms and rest there.

She took a step back. He slowly let her go, his hands slipping from her elbows to her wrists in a soft caress. She said, "I dropped my pencil."

"What?" He seemed as confused as she was by the tension that shimmered between them.

"I was trying to reach my pencil. I dropped it and it rolled under the chair." She brushed at the back of her dress. Her blood hummed from his nearness and the way his gaze lingered on her face. Suddenly, she saw an attractive man in the prime of his life. A single man.

She crossed her arms and looked down, hoping he wouldn't read this new and disturbing awareness in her eyes.

"No wonder I didn't see you." He stepped inside the building and retrieved her pencil.

He held it out and she took it gingerly, careful not to touch him. *"Danki."*

"I will let you finish your call."

"I'm only making a doctor's appointment. If you need the phone, you may use it now. I can wait."

His brow furrowed into sharp lines. "Are you sick?"

She was flattered by the concern etched on his face. *"Nee,* it is nothing like that. The adoption agency I'm using requires me to have a physical. I need to have a fire safety inspection of my home, too. Do you have any idea who I would call to see about that?"

"Michael Klein is our local fire chief. I'm one of the volunteer firemen. His number is in the book."

"Michael Klein. I will remember that. What would I do without you, Adrian? You have helped me at every turn."

"I have no doubt you would manage. Make your calls. I can wait."

He walked away to stand in the shade, giving her some privacy. She went back inside the phone booth, quickly placed her first call and was happy to find out the doctor's office could see her that afternoon.

The second call went smoothly, as well. The fire chief agreed to come by the following day and inspect her home. With her appointments made, she stepped outside. "I'm finished, Adrian."

He walked over, but instead of taking a seat inside the phone booth, he leaned against the doorjamb. "How is your adoption going?"

Faith struggled against the urge to linger here with Adrian and lost. She liked his company; she liked spending time with him.

"Things are going well, I think. The doctor can see me today and the fire chief can come tomorrow. The social worker did not run screaming from my house, although when we were in the cellar, I thought she might."

"You have not introduced her to Myrtle, have you?" There was a glint of humor in his eyes and in his voice.

Faith grinned. "*Nee,* I made sure Miss Watkins stayed away from her."

"That's *goot.* The bishop's wife and I are forgiving of such an insult, but an *Englisch* woman in her fancy suit might not be."

The clip-clop of a horse and buggy approaching made them look toward the highway. Samuel Stultz pulled to a stop. "Are you using the phone?"

Faith grinned for she already knew his good news. "You have a message, Samuel."

As he hurried to get down, Faith turned to Adrian. "I must be going. I will have to hurry if I am to find the clinic in time for my appointment. Poor old Copper isn't as fast as she once was."

"I need to take a harness into Rueben Beachy's shop for repairs. I go right by the clinic if you want to ride with me."

"That is very kind of you, but I have no idea how long I will be."

They moved aside to let Samuel use the booth.

Adrian said, "I have several other errands to run. I need to pick up some bushel baskets and the new blades for my sickle mower should be in."

"They are. I heard it on the message machine." She leaned closer. "And Samuel has a new grandbaby."

Adrian chuckled, "I'm glad my blades have come in. It will be time to put up hay in another few days and I must be ready."

"Is the work in my orchard taking up too much of your time?"

"*Nee,* I'm glad of the extra work. I don't mind waiting for you at the doctor's office as long as you don't mind waiting there if you are done ahead of me."

A ride into town seated beside Adrian was more appealing than it should have been. Should she accept? What was the harm in it? There was no need for both their horses to make the trip. "I accept your offer, gladly, and I won't mind waiting."

"*Goot.* I will be back with my wagon in half an hour."

"I will be ready."

Samuel stuck his head out the door, a wide grin on his face. "I have a granddaughter."

Faith laughed. "I know. Congratulations."

When she looked back, Adrian had already started toward his farm. Faith bid Samuel good day and hurried as fast as she could to her house.

Once there, she quickly freshened up. She changed her worn and stained everyday dress and apron for her best outfit. After patting down a few stray hairs, she decided she looked well enough to go into town. The blue of her good dress brought out the color of her eyes. Would Adrian notice? The thought brought her up short. Now, she was being foolish.

Her practical nature quickly reasserted itself. It wasn't that she wanted to impress Adrian. She merely wanted to look presentable when she met the doctor. Having rationalized choosing her best dress, she gave one last look in the mirror, pinched some color into her cheeks, put on her bonnet and went out to wait for Adrian with excitement simmering in her blood.

Chapter 8

Adrian called himself every kind of fool as he drove his green farm wagon up to Faith's gate. He was about to give his nosy neighbors and his family food for speculation by driving the widow Martin into town. Knowing smiles and pointed questions would be coming his way for days. What had he been thinking?

Cousin Sarah would be sure to hear about this. She would make certain his mother knew before the day was out. He began lining up explanations in his head so he would have them ready. His mother was certain to drop by his house before nightfall.

He tugged at his beard as the source of his coming discomfort limped down the walk and crossed behind the wagon to the passenger's side. He glanced down at her as she prepared to step up into the wagon. Something of what he'd been thinking must have shown on his face.

A look of concern furrowed her brow. "Is something wrong?"

There was no point in ruining her afternoon with his glum thoughts. He extended his hand to help her in. "*Nee*. I've much on my mind. That's all."

She laid her hand in his without hesitation. He realized it was the first time she hadn't flinched away from him. A sense of satisfaction settled in the center of his chest.

Her hand was small and delicate in his grasp. His fist completely engulfed it. She was light as a feather when he pulled her up. She might be a tiny thing, but what she lacked in size she more than made up for in determination. He admired her tenacity. She had done a lot with her run-down inheritance. She was making the place into a home.

He turned the wagon around in the yard and set his gelding to a steady trot when they reached the highway. The drone of the tires on the payment, the clatter of the horse's hooves and the jangle of the harness were the only sounds for the first few minutes of the ride.

Adrian suddenly found himself tongue-tied. He hadn't spent time alone with a woman since his single days. What should he talk about? Or should he keep his mouth shut?

He glanced at Faith sitting straight as a board on the seat beside him. The wide brim of her black bonnet hid her face from his view. What was she thinking? Did she regret accepting his offer? Was she worried that gossips might link their names?

She spoke at last. "What is your horse called?"

"Wilbur."

"He has a fine gait."

Wilbur was a safe enough topic. "He was a race-horse in his younger days, but he was injured. His *Englisch* owner didn't want to waste money caring for him. You met Jonathan Dressler, didn't you?"

"The *Englisch* fellow who has become Amish?"

"*Ja.* He works for a group that takes in abandoned and injured horses. He nurses them back to health and retrains them for riding or buggy work."

"I'll remember that. My Copper is getting old and slowing down. I will need a new horse in a few years."

"Perhaps you can teach your alpacas to pull your buggy."

She giggled and shot a grin his way. "Can you see how many tourists would want my picture if I did such a thing?"

"Not many once they met Myrtle."

Faith laughed outright. His discomfort evaporated as warmth spread though his body. She had a way of making him forget his troubles. He said, "You should laugh more often."

Their eyes met, and she quickly looked away. "How soon will our peaches be ripe?"

"Another two or three weeks."

"Will you sell them from a roadside stand or take them into the market in town?"

"To market unless you want to run the stand?"

"I've been thinking about it. Do we get enough traffic on this road to make it worthwhile?"

Adrian relaxed and started to enjoy the ride as Faith asked about his plans for the orchard. A few pointed questions from him set her to talking about her alpacas and her plans for expanding her spinning business. It wasn't long before the town of Hope Springs came into view. As far as Adrian was concerned, the ride was over all too soon.

He left her at the door to the medical clinic and quickly set about completing his own errands so she wouldn't have to wait when she was done seeing the doctor. With a jolt, he realized he was eager for the trip home.

Faith entered the Hope Springs Clinic, a modern one-story blond brick building, with a sense of dread. She had spent more than enough time in hospitals and doctors' offices over the past two years. What if they found something new wrong with her? What if they thought she wasn't strong enough to take care of a child?

Inside the building, she checked in with the elderly receptionist and took a seat in the crowded waiting room. When her name was called, she followed a young woman in a white lab coat down a short hallway and took a seat on the exam room table.

The young woman introduced herself. "I'm Amber Bradley. I'm Dr. White's office nurse and a nurse-midwife. Can you tell me what kind of problems you've been having?"

"None." Faith withdrew her papers from her bag. "I am adopting a child, but first, I must have a physical."

Amber's smile widened as she took the paperwork. "Congratulations. The doctor will be with you in a few minutes. We will need to get any previous medical records you have. I'll bring you the forms to sign so we can get them faxed to this office."

"I'm very healthy. I did not see a doctor until I was in an accident two years ago." Faith opened her mouth for the thermometer Amber extended.

"That doesn't surprise me. Many Amish go their entire lives without seeing a doctor. We see a fair number here because of Dr. White's reasonable rates. I tell him he's just plain cheap." Amber chuckled as she recorded the temperature reading, then wrapped a blood pressure cuff around Faith's arm.

The outside door opened, and a tall, silver-haired man walked in. "Good afternoon, Mrs. Martin. I'm Dr. Harold White. What can we do for you today?"

Faith again explained her situation. The doctor listened carefully, then took the forms from Amber. "This looks pretty straightforward. We'll get a chest X-ray, draw some blood and give you a complete physical while you are here today. My office will send you the results in a few days. Do we have your address?"

Faith recited it, and the doctor wrote it down. He said, "Isn't this the old Delker Orchard?"

"Ja."

Dr. White said, "That place has been empty for twenty years. I didn't know it was for sale."

"I inherited it when my husband passed away. He was the grandchild of the previous owner."

The doctor's eyebrows shot up. "He was that boy?"

Confused, Faith asked, "Did you know my husband?"

"I only met him once. I often wondered what happened to him. The whole thing was very hushed up at the time. Back then child abuse simply wasn't talked about."

Faith shook her head in denial. "You must be mistaken. He never spoke of such a thing."

"Was your husband's name Mose?"

"It was."

The doctor began counting to himself using his fingers, then said, "He would be forty-five years old if he were alive today."

She nodded. "He would."

"Did he have scars on both his wrists?"

"From where he was dragged by a runaway team of horses when he was small."

"I wish that were true. I'm not surprised he never spoke of it. Children who suffer such abuse often block it from their memory. His wrists were scarred from where he was tied up in his grandmother's basement. Apparently, he came to live with her when his parents both died of influenza. Old Mrs. Delker hated the Amish. Her only daughter ran away from home and wound up marrying an Amish fellow who left the faith for her."

"My husband said he was raised by his Amish grandparents after his parents passed away."

"Eventually, he was. I was called out to the farm when a utility worker reported he'd seen a boy chained in the cellar. The poor child was wearing only rags and he was thin as a rail. It was clear he'd been beaten and neglected. He hit and bit at anyone who came close to him."

Faith wrapped her arms around herself. "How terrible."

If only she had known. If only Mose had shared his pain instead of keeping it hidden all those years. Would their lives have been different? Surely they would have been.

Dr. White stared at the floor, as if watching that long-ago scene. "It was terrible. Eventually, the sheriff located his father's Amish parents and the boy was sent to live with them. Mrs. Delker spent some time in a mental hospital, but she came back within about six months. She was even more of a recluse afterward. She had a stroke and passed away ten years later."

Dr. White looked up, suddenly contrite. "I'm so sorry. I shouldn't go on like that. Sometimes we old people don't know when to stop reminiscing. The past can seem clearer than the present for us. This must be quite a shock for you."

"It explains a lot about my husband. He wasn't a happy man."

"I'm sorry to hear that. Let us talk of more cheerful things. You are adopting a child. That's wonderful. The sooner we get done here, the sooner that can happen. The first thing we need from you is a medical history." He became all business.

Faith answered what seemed like a hundred questions, had her X-ray taken and suffered through getting her blood drawn, but the whole time she kept seeing Mose's face. He had been a harsh man without peace in his life. She prayed he was at peace now.

When she left the doctor's office, she saw Adrian waiting for her. The sight of him lifted her spirits.

"Are you finished?" he asked.

"*Ja.* And you?" She climbed up onto the wagon seat.

"All done. Shall we head home?"

"Would you mind if we stopped at the fabric store? I need to see if I should bring in more yarn." She was in no hurry to return to the house that had seen such pain.

A fleeting look of reluctance flashed across Adrian's face. "*Ja,* we can stop at the fabric store."

"If it's too much trouble, I can wait," she offered, not wanting to upset him.

"It's no trouble at all," he drawled. Slapping the reins against Wilbur's rump, he set the black horse in motion.

When they reached Needles and Pins, Faith scrambled down from the bench seat. "I'll just be a minute."

A wry smile twisted his lips. "Take your time and say hello to Sarah for me. Tell her I'll be expecting *Mamm* this evening."

Faith wasn't quite sure what to make of his odd mood. He glanced toward the shop door as it opened and said, "Never mind. Here she comes now."

Faith turned around, expecting to see Sarah, but saw instead a short, gray-haired woman coming out of the shop. She stopped abruptly when she caught sight of Adrian, then smiled broadly.

"Hello, my son. What are you doing here?"

"I had some errands to run. *Mamm,* have you met Faith Martin?"

"I have not." His mother subjected Faith to intense scrutiny.

Faith was glad she'd taken the time to change her dress and put on her best bonnet. "I'm pleased to meet you, Mrs. Lapp. Your son has been wonderfully helpful to me. He has been the best neighbor anyone could ask for."

"Please call me Linda. It does a mother's heart good to hear such things about her son. I saw you briefly at the last church service, but I failed to introduce myself. I've been remiss in not welcoming you. Please forgive me."

"There is nothing to forgive. Excuse me, I must check to see if Janet needs more yarn from me. I won't be long, Adrian."

"No hurry," he replied.

Linda's grin widened. There was a distinctive twinkle in her eyes. "Your papa and I must stop by for a visit one of these evenings, Adrian. We have some catching up to do."

He knew where she was going and sought to cut her off. "Don't read more into this than there is. I'm helping out a neighbor. That's all."

Her smile faded. "It's time you put your grief away and took a close look at your life, my son. Many wonders of God are missed by a man who will not open his eyes."

As his mother walked away, Adrian mulled her words. How did he put away his grief even if he wanted to? Did he want to?

His grief had become a high fence he used to hold others at bay. In spite of his efforts, and without meaning to, Faith Martin had made a hole in that fence. To close it back up meant pushing her out of his life. Was he willing to do that?

Even if he wanted to, he wasn't sure he could. There was something special about her, something more than her pretty face and expressive eyes. When he was with her…he felt alive for the first time in years.

True to her word, Faith was back in a few minutes. He glanced at her seated beside him as they rode homeward. She was unusually quiet. Her eyes held a faraway look, as if she were viewing something sad from her past.

Was she remembering trips she'd taken with her husband seated beside her? Had the doctor given her bad news? Did her leg hurt? Was she tired?

There were so many things he wanted to know about her, so many questions he wanted to ask, but he shied away from them because they might reveal the real question nagging at the back of his mind.

Did Faith enjoy being in his company as much as he enjoyed being with her?

The afternoon sun beat down on them as they traveled along. Faith untied her dark bonnet and laid it on the seat between them. He asked, "Are you warm?"

"A little."

Stupid question. Of course she was or she wouldn't have taken off her bonnet. Why did he revert to acting like a tongue-tied teenager around this woman?

They made the rest of the journey to her home in silence. When he pulled to a stop in front of her gate, she didn't get down but sat staring at the house like she'd never seen it before. She asked, "Did you know the woman who lived here before I came?"

"Vaguely."

"Was she evil?"

What a strange question. "I don't think so. She was old, and *ab im kopp.*"

"Off in the head? Crazy?"

"*Ja.*"

"She must have been," Faith whispered.

He covered her hand with his. "Is something wrong?"

She didn't look at him. Her eyes remained fixed on the house. He checked out the building but didn't see anything amiss. What was going on?

Gazing back at Faith, he studied her face intently. It was as if she couldn't see or hear him. He squeezed her fingers. "Faith, what's the matter?"

Her gaze slid to their hands and then to his face.

She pulled away sharply and climbed down from the wagon, mumbling, "Goodbye."

Stunned by her abrupt departure, Adrian stared after her. Had he done something wrong? Had he upset her with something he said? Should he follow her and ask or leave her be?

The safe thing to do was to leave her be. He was becoming far too caught up in Faith Martin's life. He'd been neglecting his own work to help her, something he never did. This had to stop.

He turned the wagon and started for home. He'd only gone a hundred yards when he noticed her bonnet on the seat beside him.

Stopping the horse, he picked up the bonnet and held it in his hands. The dark fabric was warm from the sun. He lifted it to his face and breathed in. It held her scent.

He looked over his shoulder toward her house. Perhaps he was too caught up in her life, but he was ready to admit he was deeply drawn to Faith. He saw no way to free himself unless she turned him away.

Looping the reins over the brake handle, he jumped down from the wagon and strode toward her gate not knowing if he was simply returning her belonging or starting down a whole new path in his life.

When he reached the porch, he saw the front door stood open. He climbed the steps and called her name. She didn't answer. Pausing in the doorway, he started to call out again when a sound stopped him. Someone was crying.

"Faith?" He took a step inside. The muffled sounds of sobbing were coming from a doorway at the back of the kitchen. Hesitantly, he walked that way.

The second he realized the door led to the cellar,

he rushed forward. Had she fallen? Was she injured? "Faith, is that you? Are you all right?"

It took a second for his eyes to adjust to the darkness below him. When they did, he could just make out her form at the bottom of the stairs. She sat huddled in a ball on the bottom riser with her arms around her knees. Her shoulders shook with sobs.

He descended quickly, stepping past her to crouch in front of her. He laid his hand gently on her shoulder. "Faith, did you fall? Are you hurt?"

She lifted her head and shook it in denial as she wiped the tears from her cheeks.

His heart began beating again with rapid erratic thuds. "You scared the life out of me. What's wrong?"

Words began pouring out of her. "If only I had known, I would have been a better wife. How could he keep such a thing locked away from me?"

"Faith, I don't understand."

"I married Mose because my parents were gone, my brother had left the faith and I had no one. I didn't love him as a wife should. I tried, but I couldn't, and I'm so ashamed." She buried her face in her hands.

This was way out of his depths. Faith needed another woman to talk to. Someone like his mother or Nettie, but he couldn't leave her weeping in the cellar.

No, that wasn't true. He could leave, but he didn't want to.

Adrian settled himself on the narrow step beside her. His hip brushed against hers. Her shoulder, where it touched his, spread warmth all down his arm. He wanted nothing more than to slip his arm around her and comfort her, but he knew it wouldn't be right. Such closeness between a man and a woman was for husbands and wives.

He had no idea what to say. He simply started talking. "I loved my wife dearly, but I can't remember her face. I try so hard to see her, but she isn't clear anymore. I'm ashamed of that. How can I forget the one I loved more than my own life?"

Faith sniffed and slanted a look his way. "You should not feel ashamed for that."

"Nor should you feel shame. We are only human."

Nodding, she looked away from him, staring into the dark corner of the room. "My husband was a cruel man. I think he tried not to be, but he couldn't help himself. I used to think it was my fault. I thought I couldn't make him happy because I didn't love him enough."

Adrian's breath froze in his chest. "He was cruel to you?"

She looked down at her hands and gave a tiny nod.

Was she saying what he thought she was saying? "Faith, did your husband beat you?"

She nodded again, as if words were beyond her.

His stomach contracted with disgust. No wonder she flinched from his touch. What kind of man could abuse someone as sweet and kind as Faith?

"No man has the right to be cruel to another in such a fashion. It was not your fault."

Scrubbing her face with her hands, she said, "I know."

She drew a deep breath and looked at Adrian. "My husband's grandmother lived here. Her daughter ran away with an Amish lad. When they died, Mose came back to stay with her."

"Are you sure? I don't remember a boy living here."

"Mose was twelve years older than I. You wouldn't have been old enough to know him, but, in truth, no one knew he was here. His grandmother kept him locked away in this cellar until the sheriff learned of it and took him away. Dr. White told me the whole sad story today."

"That's why you were so quiet on the way home."

"I kept thinking that I was the one person who should have loved him and I didn't. If I had, he might have shared this pain with me and been healed."

"You take too much onto yourself. Only God can know the hearts and minds of men. You would have helped your husband if you could. You have a kind heart, Faith Martin."

She shook her head in denial. "You are the one with the kind heart."

He gently cupped her face and turned it toward him. With the pad of his thumb, he brushed the tears from her cheeks. Her luminous, tear-filled eyes widened, and her lips parted.

She was so close, so warm, so vibrant, and yet so vulnerable. He could kiss her—wanted to kiss her. He wanted to taste the sweetness of her soft lips, but something held him back.

Faith needed a friend now, not another complication. If he gave in to his desire it would change everything between them. She had given him a rare gift. Her trust. He didn't want to do anything to jeopardize that.

Faith closed her eyes and leaned into Adrian's hand, drawing strength from his gentle touch. If only she could hold on to this moment forever. She'd never felt so safe.

Why did this man make her wish for things that

could never be? Long ago she'd given up the notion of having a happy marriage and children of her own. That wasn't God's plan for her. She accepted that.

And now this man had come into her life. A kind, sweet man who made her wish she still believed in a marriage with love between a husband and a wife. She cared for Adrian. Deeply.

As much as she wanted to hold on to this moment, she couldn't. She couldn't allow her growing feelings for Adrian to distract her. She had to think about Kyle. She had to focus on his adoption and on providing him with a safe, secure home.

She pulled away from Adrian. He withdrew his hand. The coolness of the cellar air made her shiver.

Pity filled his voice as he said, "Come upstairs, Faith. You cannot change what happened here. It is all in God's hands now."

Pity for her or for her husband?

She'd shared her darkest secret with Adrian. Did he think less of her for suffering in silence all those many years? Maybe she didn't want to know.

She struggled to her feet. "I didn't mean to burden you with my woes."

"They are no burden, Faith. Sharing your troubles makes them lighter."

She realized he was right. Her unhappy past didn't loom over her the way it once had. Her sense of relief left her light-headed. She started up the stairs. "You have work to do. You should go home."

"There's nothing that can't wait. Are you sure you're okay?"

"*Ja,* a stout cup of tea will fix me right up." She entered the kitchen and crossed to the sink. Her hands trembled as she reached for the teakettle. The room began spinning around her.

Adrian was beside her in an instant. His hand closed over hers as he gently took the kettle from her. "Let me do this. You sit down."

He took her by the elbow and led her to the table. Pulling out a chair, he held it while she sat, then he returned to the sink and began to fill the kettle.

She drew several deep breaths. "Adrian, you don't have to take care of me."

"If I don't, who will?" He carried the kettle to the stove. He turned on the burners and set the kettle over the flames, then started opening cabinets. "Where do you keep your tea?"

"In the green tin on the counter beside the refrigerator."

He found it and soon had a mug ready for the hot water. As he waited for the kettle to boil, he took a seat across the table from her.

She managed a small smile. "God is *goot* to give me a friend such as you. Are you so thoughtful of all your neighbors?"

"Only the ones with animals that spit on me."

She chuckled. "Poor man. What an impression we must have made on you. It's a wonder you ever came back."

"I reckon I came back because I didn't think you could make a go of this place. You proved me wrong."

Lacing her fingers together in front of her on the table, she said, "I've managed to hang on for a few weeks. That doesn't mean I can hang on forever. It doesn't mean the *Englisch* will think this is a good home for my nephew."

"What will happen if they don't let you adopt him?"

Faith closed her eyes. "I can't think such a thing. They *must* let him stay with me. I don't think I could bear it if they don't."

Adrian laid his hand over her clenched fingers. She opened her eyes to find him gazing at her with compassion and something else in his eyes. Longing.

Her heart began beating faster. He started to speak, but the shrill whistle of the kettle cut him off.

He pulled his hand away and rose to fix her tea. Whatever he had been about to say remained unsaid. After bringing her mug to the table, he muttered a goodbye and left abruptly. As the screen door banged shut behind him, Faith was left to wonder if she had imagined the closeness they had shared so briefly.

Chapter 9

Two days after taking Faith into town, Adrian was cutting hay in the meadow when a car turned in his lane. It stopped on the road not far from him, and an *Englisch* lady got out. He drew his team to a halt. She approached but kept a wary eye on his horses. "Are you Mr. Adrian Lapp?"

"I am." He waited for her to state her business.

"I'm Caroline Watkins. I'm the social worker in charge of your neighbor's adoption application. I've just come from my second visit here, and Mrs. Martin has given me permission to speak with some of her neighbors. May I have a few minutes of your time?"

He wiped the sweat from his brow with his shirtsleeve and adjusted his hat. "A few. I must get my hay cut."

"I won't take long, I promise." She opened a leather folder and began to write in it.

Meg, the horse closest to her, stomped at a fly and shook her head. Miss Watkins stumbled back a step and looked ready to run to the safety of her car. Time was a wasting. Adrian said, "What questions have you?"

She gave an embarrassed smile but didn't come closer. "How long have you known Faith Martin?"

"Three weeks, I reckon."

"Is that all?"

"I met her the day after she arrived here."

Miss Watkins kept writing. "Are you aware of any reason why Mrs. Martin should not adopt a child?"

"Nee."

"Do you believe she can provide for a child?"

"I do, but it makes no difference if she can or not."

Miss Watkins's brows drew together in a frown. "Of course it makes a difference."

"An Amish parent does not need to worry about what will happen to his or her family if something tragic befalls them. All our widows and children are well cared for."

"By whom?"

It was clear this outsider didn't understand Amish ways. "Our church members will see that Faith and her child have food, clothing and a roof over their heads if ever they need such help."

"That's very admirable."

"It is the way God commands us to live."

"Have you seen Mrs. Martin interacting with children?"

He thought back to last Sunday. *"Ja."*

"Tell me about it."

"I saw her holding Katie Sutter's daughter, Rachel. She had the babe settled on her hip. It looked as if she had done it many times. I also saw her with Annie Im-hoff. She is nine, I think. Faith gave her attention and directed her to help with the work as was right."

"What are your feelings about Faith's adoption plan?"

"It is a *goot* thing for her to take in her brother's child, or any child."

"How often do you see Mrs. Martin?"

"I've seen her almost daily since she arrived."

"And why is that?"

The question shocked him. Why had he found ex-cuse after excuse to trek across the field to see her so often?

Wasn't it because he was happier when he was near her? Wasn't it because her smile drove away his lone-liness?

Miss Watkins waited for his reply. He said, "Be-cause she needs help and it is the neighborly thing to do."

"Describe her personal qualities and limitations."

At last an easy question. "She is hardworking. She is devout. Modest. She is kind to her animals."

Miss Watkins stopped writing and looked up. "And what about her limitations?"

A not-so-easy question. What could he say that wouldn't undermine her chances of adopting her nephew and yet was the truth? "She sometimes takes on more than she can handle."

"Do you see her physical handicap as a limitation?"

"You and I might see it as such, but she does not," he stated firmly.

"Can you describe her potential ability to parent?"

"She will make a fine mother." Of that he had no doubt.

Miss Watkins folded her notebook tight against her chest. "Will a child of a different faith be accepted in your community?"

He shouldn't be annoyed by her ignorance, but he was. "God loves all His children. How could we do any less? Faith's nephew will be raised to know and serve God, as all our children are. To become Amish is a choice, not a requirement. When he is old enough, he will make that decision for himself. I must get back to work now."

"Thank you for your time."

He clicked his tongue. "Get up, Meg. Go along, Mick."

The team began moving and set the sickle in motion. The clatter of the razor sharp blades drowned out the sound of Miss Watkins's car as she drove away.

It wasn't right that an outsider was the one to decide if Faith could adopt her nephew.

For the first time in many years, Adrian opened his heart and prayed. He prayed for God to smile on Faith and the child who needed her.

In the middle of the week, Faith purchased a used woodstove at a farm sale and had it installed in her home. She bid a sad goodbye to the propane stove but happily pocketed the money from its sale. Her first attempt to use her new stove resulted in a charred meal, but by the third day she had the hang of it again.

The fire chief's favorable inspection report arrived in the mail a week later, the same day her medical report came. Dr. White had found her in sound health.

She mailed the reports along with mounds of paperwork to the adoption agency and waited for a reply.

The following week she opened her mail to find the news she had been waiting for.

Kyle was coming to stay with her…on a trial basis. Finally!

Faith hugged the letter to her chest and twirled in a circle, nearly falling in the process.

When she was calm enough, she read the details again. There would be more follow-up visits by the agency after Kyle arrived, but if all went well, the adoption hearing was scheduled for the last Monday in September.

There could still be stumbling blocks, but Faith didn't care. Kyle was on his way. She was finally going to meet her brother's child.

As she waited impatiently on the porch the day he was to arrive, she worked at carding her fleece. The process of combing sections of hair over and over again between two brushes was a mindless task she could do as she watched the driveway. Each passing minute felt like an hour.

When Miss Watkins's car finally appeared, Faith dropped her work into a basket and walked toward her gate, her hands shaking with excitement. She had waited so long for this moment.

Caroline stopped her car and got out. Without a word, she opened the back door of the automobile. Faith smiled happily at the boy who emerged. With his flaming red hair and freckles, young Kyle was the spitting image of his father at the same age.

The anxiety Faith had been living with for weeks lifted away and vanished into the air like smoke. It took but a moment for love to form in her heart. This was her brother's son, and she would love him as she had his father. As she would love her own child.

"Welcome, Kyle. I am your *Aenti* Faith, and I am very pleased to meet you."

He looked ready to bolt back into the car. His green eyes held sadness and fear. The tragedy had left its mark on him. Faith could have wept for all he had endured. It would be up to her and God to see that Kyle's life was safe and happy from now on out.

Miss Watkins said, "Today is a very special day. It's Kyle's birthday. I didn't know if you knew that or not."

Faith grinned at Kyle. "I didn't know. Happy birthday, dearest. My goodness, you are six. We will have to get you enrolled in school right away if you are to start this fall."

She took a step closer and bent to his level. "I have a surprise for you. Someone else has arrived just this morning and I think he would like to meet you."

Kyle's gaze moved from her face to the house behind her. "Who is it?"

Faith straightened and crossed her arms. "Well, I don't know what to call him. He's down in the barn. Would you like to meet him?"

Kyle eyed the barn with uncertainty. "I guess."

"*Goot.* Come along. Miss Watkins, you are welcome to come, too." Faith nodded in that direction.

The social worker looked from the barn down to her high-heeled shoes. "I believe I'll wait in the house."

Faith extended her hand to Kyle but he didn't take it. She tried not to feel rejected. She knew she needed to give him time to warm up to her. She started toward the barn and glanced over her shoulder. Kyle followed.

Happiness warmed her heart. It had been a long time since she'd dared believe she could be this happy.

At the barn door, she waited for him to catch up. "Have you ever been to a farm before?"

He hooked his thumbs in the waistband of his jeans. "We stayed on a ranch once. The rancher was a friend of my mom's. They had a whole lotta cows and cowboys, too."

Faith smiled at his Southern drawl. He had lived his whole life in Texas and it showed.

She opened the door. "I don't have a cow yet, but we will have to get one soon so you can have fresh milk to drink. There are lots of things you will learn about living on a farm, but one of the most important things is to respect the animals."

A loud whinny came from inside. Kyle's eyes grew round. "You've got a horse?"

She grinned at the excitement in his voice. "It is your horse now, too."

"Can I see him?" His wariness gave way to tempered eagerness.

"It's a she. Our mare's name is Copper. You can see her in a minute. A horse is a very strong animal and can hurt you if you aren't careful. I want you to listen carefully to these two rules. Are you listening?"

He nodded.

"Never run behind a horse. Never. Always speak to them softly so that they know where you are. Can your repeat these rules for me?"

"I never run behind one and I speak softly so they know I'm there."

"That's right. Okay, come and meet Copper." Faith led the way down the narrow center aisle to the first stall on the right. Copper hung her head over the boards to investigate the newcomer.

Kyle took a step closer to Faith. "She's really big."

"Wait until you see my neighbor's draft horses. They are really, really big. They make poor Copper look like a pony beside them."

Kyle started to hold out his hand but snatched it back when Copper nibbled at it. "Does she bite?"

"She is looking for a treat. I just happen to have something she loves in my pocket. I will show you how to feed her."

Faith withdrew a kerchief from her pocket and opened it to reveal several apple slices. Taking one, she laid it in the center of Kyle's palm. "Keep your hand flat. You don't want her to think your fingers are the treats."

He bravely held up the slice. Copper daintily nibbled it up. Kyle wiped his hand on his jeans. "Her lips are soft but her chin whiskers tickle. Can I give her another one?"

"Of course."

He fed her two more apple bits and then grew brave enough to pet her nose. "Can you teach me how to ride her?"

"I can, but Copper is a buggy horse."

"Like the ones I saw on the highway coming here?"

"*Ja,* just like those. Come, I have some more animals for you to meet." She smiled at Kyle and wondered what Adrian would think of her *Englisch* nephew.

Leading the way to the back of the barn, Faith stopped beside the last stall. "This is who I want you to meet."

She pointed through the board to the farthest corner.

Myrtle lay in the thick bed of hay Adrian had spread out for her. At her side, a coal-black cria lay beside her. He raised his long neck that still wobbled slightly and batted his thick eyelashes in their direction.

"Is that a camel?" Kyle climbed up the boards to get a better view. Faith was pleased to see his curiosity pushing aside his unease.

"It's an alpaca. Her name is Myrtle and that is her new son. He doesn't have a name yet. He was just born this morning."

"Sweet. Can I pet him?"

"As long as his mother doesn't object. Come, I will introduce you so that she knows you are a friend."

Faith opened the gate and stepped inside the pen. Her feet sank into the soft hay, making her stumble. Myrtle shot to her feet in alarm. The cria struggled to its feet and ducked under his mother's body to hide on the other side of her legs.

"What's the matter with your leg?" Kyle had noticed her brace.

"I hurt it a long time ago and it didn't heal well so now I have to wear this brace."

"Does it hurt?"

"Sometimes, but not today."

Grasping the gate to steady herself, Faith spoke soothingly to Myrtle in Pennsylvania Dutch. When the new mother was calm, Faith crossed the pen carefully with Kyle at her side. Myrtle allowed them both to admire her baby, but the baby remained hidden behind his mother.

Kyle squatted down in the bedding and held out his hand. "Come here, little fella. I won't hurt you."

"Perhaps he wants a name first. What do you think

we should call him? He's black as night. Shall we call him Midnight?"

"No, that's a girly name."

Feeling put in her girly place, Faith held back a chuckle. "All right, what would you like to call him?"

"I want to call him Shadow."

She considered it. "Shadow. I think that's a very good name for him."

By this time the cria had grown accustomed to their presence and ventured out from behind his mother. Kyle extended his hand. "Come here, Shadow."

Shadow approached slowly, wobbling as he walked. Barely bigger than a tomcat with impossibly long legs, he was still trying to learn to use them.

It was clear he was as curious about the boy as the boy was about him. Kyle inched forward and touched the baby alpaca's head. Shadow frisked away behind his mother but didn't stay there. He returned after a moment to investigate further.

Faith said, "Kyle, I think he likes you."

"I think so, too."

"Since you have chosen his name, would you like to be his owner?"

"Can I?" Kyle looked up with uncertainty in his eyes.

"There are many things you will have to learn in order to take good care of him. It will be hard work. Are you willing to do that?"

"Sure."

"I don't mean for one day. I mean every day."

"If you show me what to do."

Myrtle began stamping one foot and making huff-ing sounds. Faith said, "His mother says he has had enough playtime. We should let him rest."

"He's really neat. Thanks, Aunt Faith."

She held open the gate to let him out of the stall. "You're welcome, Kyle. Let's go back to the house. I'm sure Miss Watkins is wondering where we are."

When they reached the house, Kyle went in ahead of her. Miss Watkins sat at the kitchen table fanning herself with a sheet of paper. Faith said, "Kyle, why don't you go explore the house."

"Okay." He left the room.

Miss Watkins slid several sheets of paper toward Faith. "We have only two more documents to sign, Mrs. Martin. It won't take long. Now, you understand this is a temporary guardianship until the court hearing next month."

"*Ja,* I understand."

"Good. I'll be back to visit Kyle several times before the hearing and see how things are going for the two of you. Expect me at noon the day after tomorrow. These transitions don't always go smoothly, so be prepared for that."

"I will."

After Faith signed the papers waiting for her, she walked with Miss Watkins to the door. "Thank you for all your help."

"I'm just doing my job. The judge will consider my recommendations when making a decision about the adoption."

"Of course." Faith wanted to hug the woman. It was finally sinking in. Kyle was here. At long last, God had given her a child.

"Aunt Faith?"

She and Miss Watkins turned around. Faith asked, "What is it, Kyle?"

"Where's your TV?"

At the end of their first day together, Faith helped Kyle get ready for bed. The scared, lost look she'd seen on his face when he'd first arrived had returned.

Setting his suitcase on a chair beside the bed, she began putting his clothes into the lowest drawers of the dresser against the wall where small hands could reach them easily.

Her hand encountered something hard tucked in between his pajamas and T-shirts. When she pulled it out, she saw it was a photograph of her brother and his wife.

Faith let her hand drift over the glass as she studied her brother's face. He had changed a great deal in the twelve years that he'd been gone. A man looked back at her, not the boy she remembered. The woman with him had dark brown hair and green eyes, a stunning combination.

"That's my mom and dad." Kyle reached for the picture.

"You look just like him." She handed the forbidden image to the boy.

He kissed the picture and looked around the room. "I think I'll want this by the bed so I can see it when I open my eyes."

She didn't have the heart to tell him the photograph would have to be put away. He had lost too much already. She wouldn't take away this reminder of his parents. Not yet.

She patted his head. "On your bedside table will be fine for now."

Turning away, she opened his windows to dispel the room's stuffiness and to hide the tears that stung her eyes. When she had a grip on her raw emotions, she turned around. He was already under the covers.

"You will be too hot under all of this." She drew back the quilt and folded it to the foot of the bed, leaving him with just a sheet.

He looked around, then sat up in bed. "I need a fan to sleep with."

"I don't have one. The breeze from the windows will keep you cool."

He pointed at the lantern she had placed on the dresser. "Can I keep the light on?"

"If you leave it on all night the battery will go dead."

"Please? I don't like the dark."

"I reckon it'll be okay. I have more batteries."

Relief flickered in his eyes. He scooted down in bed and pulled the sheet up to his chin. His red hair and freckles stood out in stark relief against the white bedclothes. Once again she was reminded of his father.

She asked, "Do you want to say your prayers before you go to sleep?"

He pressed his lips together and shook his head. "I don't know any."

Surprised, she asked, "You don't? Did not your mother and father teach you your prayers?"

"I know one but I don't like it anymore."

"I'll tell you what. I will say my prayers and you can listen and add anything you want to say. How's that?"

He didn't consent, but he didn't object so Faith dropped awkwardly to her knees. Pain shot through her leg, but she ignored it. She folded her hands and bowed her head.

"Dear Father in heaven, Kyle and I give you thanks for the blessings You have shown us today. I'm so happy that he is here with me. Thank You for bringing him safely to my home."

"You could say thanks for giving me Shadow," Kyle whispered.

She nodded and closed her eyes. "Kyle and I both want to thank You for the gift of little Shadow. He brings us great joy with his playful ways."

She peeked at her nephew. "Anything else?"

He shook his head. Closing her eyes again, she said, "Bless us and help us to do Your will, Lord. Help us to live as You would have us live, humbly and simply, ever mindful of Your grace as we go about our daily tasks. Forgive us our sins as we forgive those who have sinned against us. Amen."

"Are you done?" he asked.

She smiled softly at him. "I'm done."

"Where are you going to sleep?" Worry crept back into his voice as she struggled to her feet.

Tucking the sheet around him, she said, "I will be right across the hall. If you need anything, just call out. Okay?"

"I guess. Can you leave the door open?"

"Certainly. Try to get some sleep."

"Am I going to stay here a long time?"

"I hope so, darling."

"Who decides if I stay or go to a another house? Do you?"

"It will be up to Miss Watkins and a judge to decide. If God wishes it, you will stay with me a long, long time." She bent down, kissed his brow and went to her own room.

Hours later she came awake with a jolt. Someone was screaming.

"Mommy! Mommy!"

Kyle! She shot out of bed, stumbling without her brace toward his room.

Chapter 10

The door to Kyle's room stood open, but he wasn't in the bed. Frantic, Faith rushed in and searched the room. The lantern's battery was nearly depleted. It gave only a feeble, flickering light, but it was enough to let her see him huddled in the corner by the closet.

Some instinct made her approach him slowly. "Kyle, dearest, what's wrong?"

His eyes were open, but she knew he wasn't seeing her. He turned his head from side to side, sobbing. "Mommy? Mommy?"

Faith lowered herself to the floor. "Kyle, it's *Aenti* Faith. Can you hear me? Everything is all right. You've had a nightmare, that's all."

He sat with his arms around his knees. His little body trembled violently.

Faith moved closer. "It's all right, baby. It's all right. I'm here."

Suddenly, his eyes focused on her. He launched himself into her arms. Faith held him close, rocking him and stroking his hair as she murmured words of comfort.

He said, "I don't like it here. I want to go home."

"You are home, sweetheart. This is your new home, now."

He didn't answer, but slowly, his sobs died away. After a time, he fell asleep.

Faith sat holding him for a long time. Her heart bled for the pain he had endured in his young life. She could only pray that time and her love would heal his wounded soul.

When she was sure he was fast asleep, she struggled to her feet and carried him to his bed. After tucking him in, she lay down beside him in case he woke again and waited for the morning to come.

Miss Watkins would be back to check on him at noon tomorrow. If she learned how unhappy he was, would she take him away?

Late-morning sunshine glinted through the orchard canopy dappling the ground with dancing patterns of light and shadow as Adrian set to work harvesting the first of Faith's fruit. He hadn't been at it long when the hair at the back of his neck started to prickle.

Someone was watching him.

He lowered his fruit-picking pole to the ground. One of the alpacas, perhaps?

A quick check around showed he had Faith's orchard to himself. Shrugging off the feeling, he raised a long pole with a wire basket and a branch snipper on the end up into the branches of Faith's trees. As he worked, he transferred the peaches he'd plucked into a bushel basket at his feet. When he was finished gathering the fruit from one tree, he moved on to another. The feeling that he was being watched didn't leave.

As he emptied the pole basket into a larger one, a shower of leaves made him look up into the tree above him. The sight that greeted his eyes sent a slash of pain through his heart.

A red-haired, freckled-faced *kind* peered down through the leaves of a peach tree. The boy looked so much like his son that for a second he thought he was dreaming.

"Gideon?" He barely breathed the name.

The face disappeared back into the foliage. A small, disembodied voice asked, "Are you going to make me go away?"

The voice didn't belong to Gideon. This wasn't his son come back from the grave. Who was it? Adrian said, "Come down from there."

A few seconds later a pair of sneakers appeared. A boy lowered himself until he hung suspended from a branch with his shoes about three feet off the ground.

The kid shot Adrian a scowl. "Can I get a little help here?"

Adrian's racing heart slowed. Now that he had a better view of the boy, he could see the red hair and freckles were the only things that were similar to his son. This was an *Englisch* boy. He was several years older than Gideon had been. Stepping forward, Adrian grasped the boy's waist and lowered him to the ground.

"Thanks." The kid dusted his hands together, then cocked his head to the side as he studied Adrian. "Well?"

"Well what?"

"Are you going to take me away?"

"Nee."

"Are you going to be my new dad if the judge makes Aunt Faith my new mom?"

Realization dawned on Adrian. The boy was Faith's nephew. He breathed a silent prayer of thanks that God had seen fit to bring her the child she longed for.

"I will not be your father. I'm a neighbor from down the road. I'm helping your *aenti* harvest her peaches."

"Oh. That's okay then. I didn't want a new dad. Aunt Faith is nice and all, but I want my real dad and mom to come back."

"They cannot come back from heaven."

Looking down, the boy kicked a fallen peach and sent it rolling through the grass. "Yeah, I know."

Adrian knew exactly what the boy was feeling. He said, "My name is Adrian Lapp. What is yours?"

"Howdy, Mr. Lapp. I'm Kyle King," the boy drawled.

"If you have nothing better to do, Kyle King, you can help me finish picking this fruit."

He didn't look enthused. "I don't know how. Do you have TV at your house?"

"Nee, it is *veldlich* and is *verboten."*

"Huh?"

"It is a worldly thing and forbidden to us."

"How come you talk so funny?"

"Because I am Amish. How come you talk so funny?"

Kyle's solemn face cracked a tiny smile. "Because I'm a Texan."

"Ah. Do they have peaches in Texas?"

"I guess."

"But you have never picked peaches in Texas."

"Nope. We lived in Houston. Mom got our peaches from the grocery store."

"Houston, is that a big town?"

Kyle raised one eyebrow. "Are you kidding me?"

"*Nee,* I am not."

"What does *nee* mean?"

"It is Pennsylvania Dutch and it means no."

"Then why don't you just say no?"

"Because I am Amish and that is the language we speak."

"Oh. My aunt Faith is Amish, too. That's why she wears those funny dresses and that thing on her head."

"It is called a prayer *kapp.* It signifies her devotion to God."

"I'm not going to wear one 'cause I don't like God. He's mean."

"You must not say such a thing."

"It's true. My foster mom said God wanted my mom and dad with Him in heaven more than He wanted them to be here. That proves He isn't nice."

"I think she meant God *needed* them in heaven more than He needed them here."

Those were the same words Adrian's family and friends had used to try and comfort him, to help explain the inexplicable reasons why first his wife and then his son had been taken away. Like Kyle, Adrian found no comfort in the words.

The boy picked up a peach and threw it against a nearby tree, splattering the soft fruit against the rough bark. "I needed them more."

Faced with the impotent fury of this child, Adrian put aside his own feelings of bitterness and sought a way to help the boy. "You have a good arm, Kyle. Do you like baseball?"

"Sure. My dad was the coach of my team. He taught me everything about baseball. He was going to get me a new mitt when he picked me up after school, but he never came back. Why did God have to take him away?"

Adrian plucked a wormy peach from an overhead branch and threw it. It smashed into bits against the same tree. "We cannot know God's reasons. We can only pray that one day we will see our loved ones again."

"Did your parents die, too?"

"No. God took my wife and my son to heaven."

Kyle chucked two peaches toward the hapless tree. Only one hit the target. He squinted up at Adrian. "So, do you hate God, too?"

Faith faced Miss Watkins across the kitchen table. This was the social worker's first visit to see how Kyle was adjusting to life on the farm. Faith had never been more nervous in her life. She wished Adrian were here. She could use his solid presence beside her to bolster her courage.

Caroline checked the contents of the refrigerator, made a few notes in her folder and asked, "How's it going?"

"As well as can be expected." Faith kept her hands still, trying not to fidget.

"Can you elaborate a little more?"

Faith wasn't sure what the woman wanted to know. "Kyle didn't have much of an appetite yesterday, but he ate a good breakfast this morning. He adores the alpacas, especially the baby. He misses his friends and his foster parents. We went to the phone booth yesterday evening and called his buddies, Tyrell and Dylan."

Should she mention Kyle woke in the night and was crying, or would that count against her?

"Did talking to the boys upset Kyle?"

"Maybe a little. It has to be hard being pulled from all he knew."

"Where is he now?"

"Upstairs in his room. Shall I get him?"

"We can go up together. I'd like to see his room now that he's settled."

Faith led the way up the narrow fight of stairs to the bedroom opposite hers. She opened the door to Kyle's room expecting to see him reading or coloring at his desk. He wasn't in the room. His bedroom window stood wide-open with the screen pushed out.

She rushed to the window. The porch roof beyond was empty. The limbs of the old oak beside the house overhung the porch offering an adventurous boy a way down to the ground.

"He's gone." Faith heard the panic in her voice as she turned to the social worker.

Miss Watkins said, "Maybe he came downstairs and we didn't notice."

It took only a few minutes to search the house and see he wasn't in it. Where could he be? Faith opened the front door and stepped onto the porch with Miss Watkins right behind her. Faith scanned the yard. At least Kyle wasn't lying unconscious on the ground beneath the tree.

"He's likely out in the barn with Shadow." She tried calling his name but got no answer.

Crossing to the barn, Faith pulled open the door and called him again. Still no answer.

Inside, she found Myrtle and Shadow lying together undisturbed. Copper dozed in her stall. Kyle wasn't in here. Faith's worry took flight like the pigeons fluttering in the rafters. Where could he be?

Caroline asked, "Did he talk about running away?"

"He hasn't run away. I'm sure he's playing nearby."

Why would he run away? Was she such a terrible parent that he couldn't bear to live with her?

Faith opened the back door of the barn and went out into the alpaca's pen. They were milling about near the gate to the orchard and looking in that direction. The gate was closed. Faith knew she had left it open that morning so they could go out to graze.

She cupped her hand around her mouth and shouted for Kyle.

"He's with me!"

The booming voice from the orchard belonged to Adrian. Faith relaxed. Kyle was safe if he was with Adrian.

When the pair emerged from the trees, Faith crossed her arms and scowled at her nephew. "Did you climb out your bedroom window?"

"Yes."

"Why would you do such a thing? You could have fallen and been badly hurt."

He glanced from her to Miss Watkins. "I'm sorry. I won't do it again."

Miss Watkins dropped to his level. "Kyle, why did you sneak out of the house?"

He shrugged. "I don't know."

She laid a hand on his shoulder. "I understand that

this is very difficult for you. If you aren't happy here, it's all right to tell me."

Faith held her breath. Would this woman take Kyle away from her so soon? They had barely gotten to know each other.

"It's okay. Sometimes it's boring, but it's okay." His voice wobbled.

Adrian said, "Idle hands are the devil's workshop. The boy needs work to occupy his mind. He can help me pick peaches if he is bored."

A quick frown crossed Caroline's face, but she didn't say anything to Adrian as she rose. Instead, she patted Kyle's head. "I'll be back in a week to check on you. All right? You have your aunt call me if you need anything. Will you be okay until then?"

"I guess." He shoved his hands in the waistband of his jeans.

As Miss Watkins headed for her car, Faith turned to Kyle. "You may help Adrian gather fruit until lunch-time. I'll call you when it's ready."

Kyle ventured a small request. "Can we have burgers and French fries?"

As a reward for climbing out your window and scaring me half to death?

Faith put aside her fright and forgave the boy for his behavior. "I think I can manage that, but it won't be like the fast food you get from town. Adrian, would you care to join us?"

Would he accept? She didn't want to appear too eager for his company, but she had missed him the past several days.

"I reckon I can. My hay is cut and drying in the fields. I have no need to rush home."

"*Goot.* Kyle, you must do as Adrian says."

"I will." The boy's smile returned.

Adrian said, "There are some wooden boxes inside the barn door. Bring them out to the tree where we were working."

"You got it." Kyle took off at a jog.

Faith said, "It's kind of you to let him help."

"You look tired. Is everything all right?"

"Kyle has nightmares. I haven't been sleeping well, either."

"He's had it tough, poor tyke."

"When we unpacked his things, I saw he had a picture of his mother and father. He wanted it on his bedside table. I let him keep it." She chewed the corner of her lip. Would he think she had done the wrong thing by going against their Amish teachings? Photographs were considered graven images and thus banned from Amish homes.

"The boy is not Amish. He does not know our ways. Give him time to learn about the things we believe."

She nodded, pleased that Adrian's advice mirrored her own feelings.

He leaned close. "But don't tell the bishop's wife. You already have one strike in her book."

Faith held back a giggle as Kyle came through the barn, his arms filled with a tall stack of boxes. "Are these the ones you need?"

Adrian said, "*Ja,* those are the ones. Your *aenti* and I will earn a pretty penny if we can fill and sell this many boxes of peaches."

Kyle looked between them. "You should charge more than a penny."

Adrian laughed. "Your nephew has a head for business, Faith. Should we follow his advice?"

Pretending to consider it, she finally said, "I agree. I say we ask for a nickel."

Adrian ran his fingers down his chin whiskers. "Let's think big. We should ask for a dime."

Kyle scrunched up his face. "Are you making fun of me?"

Faith ruffled his hair. "Perhaps a little."

Kyle rolled his eyes. "Whatever."

Adrian said, "Come along. Our work is waiting."

Faith watched them walk away together with mixed emotions. Kyle would need the influence of a man in his life, someone to teach him how to earn a living and work the land. Was she wrong to hope that Adrian could fulfill that role? It was a lot to ask of a neighbor. Those were things a father should teach a son.

Adrian would make a great father. He was kind and patient. She'd never heard him utter an angry word. While she never intended to marry again, if she did, someone like Adrian would be the kind of husband she'd look for. Someone exactly like Adrian.

The idea of being his wife made her blush. She quickly dismissed it as a fantasy that could never come true. Adrian wouldn't marry again any more than she would. The love he held in his heart for his first wife didn't leave room for another.

Wishing things could be different was foolish. Daydreams about Adrian were a sure path to heartache. She knew that.

So why couldn't she put her foolish yearning away?

Chapter 11

Several days later, Faith rose at five o'clock. She dressed, brushed and rolled her hair, fastened on her *kapp* and went down to start a fire in the kitchen stove. Stacking kindling and newspaper inside the firebox, she put a match to it. When she was sure the fire was going, she closed the firebox door.

While the stove heated, she straightened up in the living room. Adrian would be over soon to start work in the orchard. She didn't want him to see her home in a state of disarray.

Grabbing her broom, she began sweeping the floors. Soon she would have to have the offending pink-and-white linoleum replaced. The bishop had generously given her eight months to convert the old *Englisch* house into an Amish home. A home for her and Kyle, where the ghosts of the past could be put to rest and their new lives could flourish. It wouldn't be easy, but it would be worth all her hard work.

She finished her floors, washed up and began making breakfast. At half-past five o'clock, Faith called to Kyle from the bottom of the stairs. "Kyle, time to get up. Breakfast is ready."

She had to call one more time before he appeared in the kitchen, his hair tousled and his eyes puffy with sleep. "What time is it?"

"Almost six o'clock, sleepyhead. We have a lot of work waiting for us."

"We do?" He sat at the table and yawned.

She loaded both their plates with pancakes and scrambled eggs and carried them to the table. "Adrian will be here soon to start picking peaches. You don't want to keep him waiting, do you?"

"No. Is Miss Watkins coming today?" Kyle folded his arms on the table and laid his head down.

"Not that I know of."

"Good."

Outside, a loud whinny came from the barn. Faith said, "Sounds like Copper is wanting her breakfast, too."

Kyle raised his head to squint at Faith. "Can I feed her?"

"*Ja,* but first eat before your eggs get cold." Faith sat beside him, bowed her head to say a quick silent prayer and then began eating.

"Can I feed Shadow, too?" Kyle forked in a mouthful of eggs.

"His mother will give Shadow all he needs for a few months yet, but we need to feed her."

"Okay. Then can I play on the swing Adrian made me yesterday?"

Adrian had turned a length of rope and a broad plank into a swing that now hung from the oak tree beside the porch. Faith said, "After all your chores are done."

"What chores?"

"We must feed the horse and turn her out to graze. We must feed and water the chickens and gather their eggs."

"Then can I play?"

"Not until we feed the alpacas, clean up their pen, pick the debris out of their coats and let them out to graze."

"How long will that take?"

"It takes as long as it takes, Kyle."

It might sound like a lot of work to him now, but wait until next spring when there would be a garden to hoe and weeds to be pulled every day and all before he went to school. Faith smiled. Amish children did not have time to be bored.

Kyle finished his breakfast and waited impatiently for Faith to wash the dishes. When they were done, he dashed ahead of her to the barn. "Remember the rules," she called out.

He immediately slowed down. "Don't run behind a horse and always speak softly to let them know where you are."

"Very *goot*."

She passed Adrian's farm wagon sitting in the shade. The bed of the wagon was half full of boxes of peaches. The scent of the ripe fruit filled the still morning air. Today they would load the rest of the wagon and head into the farmer's market in Hope Springs where Faith hoped her fruit would fetch a good price.

She opened the barn door, and Kyle ducked under her arm to get inside ahead of her. He made a beeline for Shadow's stall. His little buddy rushed away to hide beneath his mother.

Faith showed Kyle how to measure and pour the feed into the troughs for the alpaca. While Myrtle was busy with her breakfast, Shadow ventured close to Kyle and allowed the boy to pet him.

Kyle's bright grin gladdened Faith's heart. She took a small rake and a shovel from their place on the wall and handed them to the boy.

He said, "What's this for?"

"To *redd-up* the stall. To clean it." She indicated the manure piles.

He wrinkled his nose. "Yuck!"

She folded her arms and scowled at him. "Shadow is your responsibility. You said you would take care of him. Do you want him to sleep on a messy floor?"

"No."

She held out the tools. He approached with lagging steps and took them from her. Faith had trouble holding back her laughter as he carefully raked the manure onto the flat shovel. He looked at her. "Now what?"

"I will fetch the wheelbarrow. When we have done everyone's stall we will empty it onto the pile behind the barn."

"We're keeping it? Why?"

"Because it will make very *goot* fertilizer for the orchards and gardens next spring."

It took most of an hour to feed all the animals and clean the stalls. To Faith's delight, Kyle didn't complain or shirk from the work. They let Myrtle and Shadow out into the pen. Shadow raced about in delight at finding himself outside.

Faith and Kyle were crossing back to the house when she saw Adrian striding toward them across the field. He was pulling a small wagon behind him.

He raised a hand and waved. Her heart flipped over with unexpected joy at the sight of him.

Kyle took off toward him. "Hi, Adrian. I cleaned out the barn and fed all the animals and Shadow let me pet him."

Adrian grinned at Kyle. "Then you have done a man's work already this morning. You must be tired."

"No. Well, maybe a little."

"You deserve a rest." Adrian picked the boy up and balanced him on his shoulder. Kyle's squeal of fear quickly turned into giggles of delight.

Faith waited until the two of them caught up with her before falling into step beside them. Adrian immediately shortened his stride to match hers. Something Mose had never done.

She needed to stop comparing the two men in her mind. There was no comparison.

"Aunt Faith says we are going to town later. Are we?"

"We are. It is Market Day. Almost everyone goes to town on Market Day."

"Cool beans. Can you teach me to drive the horse?"

By this time they had reached the porch. Adrian swung Kyle down and deposited him on the steps. "Someday, but not today. We must take my team and they are too big for you to handle."

"I'm strong." Kyle flexed one arm and pushed up his sleeve to show his muscles.

Adrian whistled his appreciation. "We must put those muscles to work in the peach orchard. Are you ready?"

Kyle fisted his hands on his hips. "*Ja.* I'm ready."

Faith pressed her hand to her lips to hide her smile. "Spoken like a true Amishman."

Adrian folded his arms over his chest. "Grab a couple of boxes from the big wagon and put them in this one. We won't have to carry our peaches so far this way. Can you pull this out to the tree where we stopped working yesterday?"

"Sure." The boy took off at a run, the little wagon bouncing behind him.

Faith spoke softly to Adrian. "He has taken quite a liking to you. God was wise to bring you into his life."

"He is a fine boy. He reminds me of my son."

Faith laid a hand on Adrian's arm. "This must be very difficult for you."

Adrian waited for the pain of his son's loss to strike his heart, but it didn't. Instead, he recalled the way Gideon had always wanted to help, sometimes to the point of being in the way. Kyle had the same burning desire to prove his worth.

Adrian glanced at Faith's small hand on his arm. Her touch was warm and comforting. Was she right? Did God have a purpose for bringing him into Kyle's life?

For the past several years Adrian had thought only of what he had lost. He'd never once considered that God might use him as a gift to others.

He gazed into Faith's sympathetic eyes. "Kyle reminds me of Gideon, but he is not Gideon. I see in Kyle a boy with joys and pain, hopes and fears that are all his own. I'd like to think that they would have been friends. I know Lovina would have liked having you for a neighbor."

"I wish I could have known her."

"Me, too."

Adrian moved away from the comfort Faith offered. "We'd better get busy or we'll miss the start of the market."

"You're right. I need the best possible price for my fruit. My yarn is selling fairly well, but not well enough." They began walking toward the orchard.

"I've been thinking about that. Have you any items you'd like to sell at the market?"

"You mean things made from my yarn? I have several baby blankets and two dozen socks ready. Should I take them?"

"Many tourists come for the quilt auction that will be held this afternoon. They might buy your work."

She shook her head. "My plain socks hardly compare to the beautiful quilts they come to buy."

They reached the gate leading into the orchard. Kyle joined them carrying more boxes than he could safely manage. Shadow was prancing and bouncing beside him.

Adrian opened the gate for him. As usual, the curious alpacas came galloping up to investigate this new activity.

Kyle petted his little buddy. "I wish Shadow could come to town with us. I bet he'd like it."

Faith chuckled. "The tourists would stare at an alpaca riding in an Amish buggy, that's for sure."

Adrian stopped in his tracks. "They would, wouldn't they?"

Faith and Kyle walked on until they noticed he wasn't following. Faith stopped and looked back. "What's the matter?"

"Kyle and Shadow have given me an idea."

"We have?" Kyle looked perplexed.

"A very good idea. Faith, can you bring your spinning wheel to market and spin yarn while others are watching you?"

"*Ja*. What are you getting at?"

"Could we take Shadow to town with us?"

She shook her head. "He's only a few days old. It wouldn't be good for him to be separated from his mother for any length of time."

Adrian pondered the problems involved in his scheme. "And Myrtle is known for her spitting skills. That wouldn't work."

Faith's eyes lit up. "You want to take one of the alpacas to market with us as an advertisement for my yarns."

"You said it yourself. People would stop and stare. They might also stop and buy. Which of your animals has the best temperament?"

"Socks," she said without hesitation. "She loves attention and she loves people."

He nodded. Socks was the least likely to spit on an unsuspecting customer. "Would she follow behind the wagon into town?"

Faith's face showed her growing excitement. "I don't see why not. She's halter trained."

He held up his hand. "What's wrong with this plan?"

Faith shrugged. "Nothing that I can see."

Adrian nodded slowly. "Kyle and I will get started on the peaches. You get together the things you'd like to sell."

He turned and scratched Socks between the ears. "Looks like you're going to town, girl. What do you think about that?"

Kyle ran ahead with the wagon into the orchard with Shadow hot on his heels.

Faith once again wore her best bonnet and Sunday dress as she sat on the high seat of Adrian's wagon. Kyle sat between them as excited as any six-year-old child on his way to a special treat. The boy had been awed into silence by the size of Adrian's draft horses but soon recovered his chatty nature.

As they approached Hope Springs, they met dozens of other Amish families all heading in the same direction. The influx of lumbering produce-laden wagons and buggies forced the traffic in town to drop to a crawl. The slow pace allowed many drivers and their passengers to gawk at Socks as she ambled along behind Adrian's wagon.

The alpaca didn't seem at all upset by the commotion going on around her. With her head held high, she surveyed the activity with wide, curious eyes.

Adrian turned off Main onto Lake Street. "The regular weekly markets are held every Friday afternoon in a large grassy area next to the lumberyard up ahead."

"Is it all produce?"

"You will find a wide range of fruits and vegetables sold here including certified organic produce. There will also be homemade baked goods, homemade jams, local honey, meat, eggs and cheeses. You can even find fresh-cut flowers as well as fresh and dried herbs and spices."

Faith could already see the striped canopies of numerous tents being set up. "I'm surprised at the size, given the fact that Hope Springs isn't that big of a town."

"This isn't a regular market day. This is our Summer Festival. It's held every year on the last day of August. The big draw this year is the Quilts of Hope charity quilt auction. My mother mentioned that they have over fifty quilts to sell."

Adrian maneuvered his wagon to a tent marked for fresh produce and fruit. With Faith's and Kyle's help, he began unloading the wagon and stacking their boxes of peaches in neat rows inside the tent. The work would have gone faster if not for the crowd of children and adults who quickly gathered around Socks. Faith answered numerous questions about her animal while helping Adrian and keeping an eye on Kyle.

When they had the wagon unloaded, Adrian parked the wagon near a row of buggies and unhitched his team. He slipped off their bridles and put halters on the pair but left them in their harnesses. He turned to Faith. "Where would you like to set up your spinning wheel?"

"I wish I had a tent." The afternoon sun beating down on her head promised to make her demonstration hot work unless she could find some shade.

"*Ja,* we need to get one for you."

Faith liked the way he said "we," as if they would be doing this together again.

Kyle pulled at her sleeve. "Can I go look around?"

On one hand, she was as eager to explore all the tents and displays as Kyle was, but on the other hand, she didn't want Adrian to be stuck looking after Socks. The alpaca was her responsibility.

She put aside her childish desires and said, "Perhaps Adrian can show you around."

Kyle turned his pleading eyes toward Adrian. "Can you? Please?"

"I must stay with the wagon," he replied.

Faith wasn't about to let him miss out on a fun afternoon. "Socks belongs to me. I will stay with her. Please take Kyle and show him the sights."

A young man made his way though the crowd and straight to Socks. "So this is an alpaca! They are cute. Is this the one that spit on you and the bishop's wife?"

The resemblance between the two men was unmistakable. Faith wasn't surprised when Adrian said, "Faith, this is my *bruder* Ben."

Ben's grin lit up his face. He touched the brim of his straw hat. "I'm pleased to meet you, Faith Martin."

She bowed slightly. "I'm pleased to meet you, as well. Myrtle was the ill-mannered one. This is Socks. She likes people."

"May I pet her?" Ben asked.

Faith nodded. Ben reached out hesitantly and stroked his hand along Socks's jaw. She showed her appreciation by stepping close and wrapping her long neck around him in a hug.

From behind her, Faith heard a pair of girls' voices cooing in unison. "Isn't that sweet?"

The girls, identical twins, joined Ben in petting Socks. Adrian spoke to his brother. "Ben, would you mind watching Socks while Faith and I show Kyle around?"

Ben winked at Adrian. "Not a bit."

"Danki." Adrian looked to Faith and tipped his head toward the nearest tent. "Shall we?"

She nodded and reached for Kyle's hand. As she grasped it, he let out a hiss of pain. Startled, she let go. "Did I hurt you?"

He put his hands behind his back and shook his head. Adrian squatted to his level and said sternly, "Let me see."

Reluctantly, Kyle extended his hands. There were large blisters on both palms.

Faith sucked in a sharp breath knowing how painful they had to be. "Kyle, why didn't you tell me you'd hurt yourself?"

"I was afraid you would make me stay home."

She thought of all the raking and wheelbarrow pushing he'd done as well as the heavy boxes full of peaches he'd pulled through the orchard in the little wagon. Never once had he complained.

"Darling, you mustn't be afraid to tell me when something hurts. We need to find somewhere to wash these and put some bandages on them."

Ben said, "There's a first-aid tent near the front of the lumberyard."

Faith flashed him a grateful smile. *"Danki.* Come along, Kyle. We'll get you fixed up in no time."

She and Adrian guided him through the crowds to the tent run by the local firefighters. A kindly fireman rinsed Kyle's hands, applied an antiseptic cream and a large Band-Aid to each palm. When he was done, he gave Kyle a lollipop. "For being so brave."

Faith thanked him. He said, "No problem. If you go out behind this tent you'll see we are providing free pony rides to all the children attending the market today. Our police and fire departments are giving out snow cones and popcorn, too."

Kyle looked hopefully at Faith. "Can I ride a pony?"

He certainly deserved some fun after all the work he'd done. "You may."

They found the ride without difficulty. Kyle waited patiently until it was his turn. Adrian lifted him aboard a small white horse and stepped back beside Faith as he and several other Amish children went round and round on the plodding ponies.

Standing beside Adrian and watching Kyle enjoying himself, Faith had a glimpse of what her life might have been like if she had married the right man and been blessed with children of her own.

While she might never be a wife again, she now had a chance to raise a son. The thought was bittersweet.

After the ride came to an end, they walked on together exploring the various tents and booths until they came to the largest tent. Two sides of the tent had been rolled up to take advantage of the gusty breeze. Inside, dozens of beautifully crafted quilts hung from wooden frames meant to display them to full advantage. The room was already crowded with *Englisch* men and women examining the quilts closely.

Faith was admiring a wedding ring quilt pattern done in cream, pinks and blues when she spotted Nettie Sutter, Adrian's mother and several other women conferring at a table near the back of the tent.

"Adrian, there's your mother."

"Where?"

She pointed. He quickly turned the other way and took her arm. "Let's go. I don't need any quilts."

Chapter 12

Adrian hoped to avoid his mother's too-sharp eyes but he should have known better. She had already seen them and was headed in their direction with Rebecca Beachy holding on to her arm. His mother's cheeks were rosy red from exertion. Wisps of her gray hair had escaped from beneath her *kapp*.

"Adrian, you are just what we need—a strong son to help me set up these tables. Hello, Faith." His mother's eyes darted between the two of them with intense speculation. No doubt she had already jumped to the wrong conclusion about his business association with Faith.

He said, "We've brought peaches to sell."

She winked at him. "What a clever excuse to bring Faith to our market. Faith, I'd like you to meet Rebecca Beachy. She and her aunt are neighbors of mine. Although Rebecca is blind, she stitches beautiful quilts."

Rebecca held out her hand. "My talent comes from God, it is not of my own making."

Faith stepped forward and took Rebecca's hand. "I'm pleased to meet you."

Rebecca tipped her head to the side. "And who else do you have with you?"

Adrian saw Kyle peeking from behind Faith's skirt.

Faith urged the boy forward. "This is my *Englisch* nephew, Kyle."

Kyle frowned up at her. "I'm not English, I'm from Texas."

Adrian's mother chuckled. "It's nice to meet you, Kyle from Texas."

"Have you had a pony ride yet?" Rebecca asked.

He nodded. "Aunt Faith says I can have a snow cone, too."

Rebecca grinned. "*Ach,* I love them. You must try the pineapple ones. They're the best."

"Adrian, can you spare a few minutes to help us?" his mother asked.

He looked over the number of visitors filing through the tent. This would be the best place for Faith to set up her wheel. "If I may ask a favor in return?"

Mamm nodded. "Of course."

"May Faith use one of your tables to sell her yarn?"

His mother grinned at Faith. "I don't see why not. The more, the merrier. Show Adrian where you want to set up."

Within a few minutes he'd set up the tables his mother needed and placed one for Faith near the open side so that Socks could be tethered out on the grass. His mother promised to keep an eye on Kyle while he and Faith returned to the wagon to collect Faith's spinning wheel and the yarns she had boxed up to sell.

They found the wagon surrounded by a dozen young Amish girls admiring Socks. Ben, seated casually on the tailgate of the wagon, was clearly enjoying the attention.

Faith and Adrian shared an amused glance before Adrian stepped inside the circle of young women. "*Danki,* Ben, I'll take over now."

Standing up, Ben said, "I don't mind watching Faith's pet a little longer."

"If you want to be useful, little *bruder,* you can carry Faith's spinning wheel to the tent where the quilts are being auctioned."

"I can handle that if one of you girls can show me the way." Ben's charming smile gathered him several volunteers.

After Ben left, Adrian stacked together Faith's wares and carried the boxes while she led Socks through the maze of vendor stalls back to the quilt tent.

Adrian staked Socks's lead rope just outside the tent. The alpaca promptly lay down in the thick green grass.

Kyle was waiting for them with a snow cone in his hand. Adrian's mother sat beside him enjoying one, too.

Kyle held his out. "These are really good. You should get one, Aunt Faith."

Faith said, "I hope you thanked Mrs. Lapp."

"I did." He slurped at juice dripping over the paper holder.

Adrian's mother rose and came to stand beside Faith. "He's been well behaved. Is this one of your alpacas? They are cute."

She leaned closer, and Adrian heard her ask, "Is this the one that spit on the bishop's wife?"

Faith blushed a becoming shade of pink. "No."

He took pity on her and tried to distract his mother. "*Mamm,* do you need anything else?"

"Not that I can think of," she replied.

"Faith, can I do anything else for you?" he asked. He needed to get back to the produce and see that it sold for a decent price, but he didn't want to leave her side. He was happy when he was near her.

She smiled sweetly at him. "I will be fine, *danki.*"

He turned to Kyle. "You must keep an eye on Socks while your *aenti* is busy and don't wander off without telling her."

"Okay." Kyle took his snow cone and went out to sit in the grass beside Socks. A number of people had already gathered to stare at the unusual creature. When they saw Kyle sit beside her, they pressed in for a closer look.

Faith, having arranged her yarns by color in small baskets on the table, sat down at the spinning wheel and began pumping the pedals that made it turn. Adrian stood back and watched to see how she would handle being on display along with her work. He didn't have long to wait.

A middle-aged *Englisch* woman with her husband stopped to watch Faith spin. She asked, "Is this all handmade yarn?"

"*Ja,* from my own alpacas." She seemed so nervous. Adrian wondered if he'd made a mistake in suggesting the venture.

The man asked, "What type of dye do you use?"

Faith glanced to Adrian. He gave her a thumbs-up sign.

She turned back to the prospective buyers. "Alpacas come naturally in twenty color variations. I have white, fawn, brown, gray and black, with many shades in between. The fleece dyes beautifully if you'd like colors other than these natural shades."

Nettie Sutter stepped up to the table. "I've heard it's better than wool."

"Alpaca has a softness unlike any other natural fiber. Most people find it doesn't itch like sheep's wool. It is also very lightweight and yet is warmer than wool. I have a receiving blanket made from white alpaca that you might be interested in for Katie's baby when it arrives." She indicated a box at the end of her table.

Adrian could see that the more Faith talked about her alpacas and her spinning, the more relaxed she became.

Nettie withdrew the blanket and gushed, "This is wonderfully soft. Feel it." She held the blanket out to the *Englisch* woman. She exclaimed over the quality, too. In a matter of minutes Faith made her first sale. Adrian turned to leave and found his mother at his side.

She said, "I like your new neighbor."

He scowled at her. "That's all Faith is. A neighbor. Nothing more."

A smug look settled over his mother's features. "Isn't that what I said?"

"What you say and what you mean are often two different things."

She patted his arm as if he were a child. "Now you sound like your father. Go and take care of your peaches. Don't worry. I will keep a close eye on your neighbor and her child. I think it's about time I got to know them better."

Chapter 13

On Sunday morning Faith entered the home of Adam Troyer, the handyman in Hope Springs. His house had been chosen for the preaching service. Kyle was at her side.

She glanced down at him. It would be a long morning for a boy who wouldn't be able to understand the Pennsylvania Dutch preaching or the readings from the German Bible. How would he handle it? In the five days that he'd been with her he seemed to be adjusting well, but this might be stressful for him.

Sitting on a bench on the women's side of the aisle, she looked Kyle in the eyes. "You must sit on that side with the men today."

"But I want to stay with you."

"You are too old to sit with the women. I'll be right here. You must be quiet and respectful as we talked about last night. Amish children do not make a fuss, even when they are bored or tired."

"But I don't want to sit by myself," he whined.

"The boy can sit with me."

Faith glanced up to see Adrian standing beside them. She couldn't control the rush of happiness that swept though her. Even Kyle's face brightened.

He said, "Hi, Adrian. I didn't know you were going to be here."

Faith nodded her appreciation for Adrian's offer to sit with Kyle. "*Danki,* Adrian."

His gaze settled on her face. Heat filled her face, and she knew she was blushing. She looked away determined to control the intense longing that took over whenever he was near.

No matter how often she told herself a match between them was impossible, her desire to spend time with Adrian grew stronger, not weaker.

Adrian placed his hand on Kyle's shoulder. "Come along. We must find our place."

He led the boy away and found a seat near the back of the room in case he had to take the boy outside. He wasn't sure how Kyle would act during the long, solemn service.

Amish children were taught from infancy to keep quiet during Sunday preaching. Amish mothers usually brought a bag of ready-to-eat cereal or snacks to help occupy the *kinder* who became restless. Adrian wished he'd thought of bringing something for Kyle.

Throughout the service, Adrian remained acutely aware of Faith across the room from him. There was a look of serenity on her face as she listened to the Word of God.

Her sweet voice blended well with the congregation when the hymns began. She sang almost as well as his cousin Sarah. Both women had received the gift of song from the Lord.

Adrian was no songbird. His wife used to joke that he couldn't carry a tune in a wooden bucket if his life depended on it. He joined the congregation for each and every hymn, but he kept his voice soft and low enough not to trouble his neighbors' ears.

To Adrian's relief, Kyle remained well behaved. During the second hymn, he stood on the bench to better view the hymnbook Adrian held. The pages contained only the words of each hymn in German. The melody itself had been passed down from generation to generation in an unchanging oral tradition that reached back hundreds of years.

During the second hour of preaching, Adrian noticed Kyle's head nodding as he struggled to stay awake. He wasn't the only one. Several of the elderly members and a few of the youngsters were having trouble, too. Adrian slipped his arm around Kyle's shoulders and pulled him against his side. Kyle soon dozed off.

From across the aisle, Faith caught Adrian's eye. Her soft smile encompassed both he and the boy. It was the kind of smile that made a man feel special. Made him want to earn more of them.

At the end of the service, Bishop Zook rose and faced the congregation. He read off the names of the young people who wished to be baptized into the faith two weeks from today. Adrian recognized all the names. He knew them and their families. He had watched them grow up. All of them were making the commitment after having experienced something of the outside world during their *rumspringa*. Like himself, most of them were ready to marry and start families of their own.

None of them had any idea of the heartaches that might await them.

Bishop Zook said, "And now I have one more matter to place before you. Our sister, Faith Martin, has come among us seeking to practice the faith of her fathers with piety and humility. She has asked to become a member of our congregation. As you know, this decision is not up to me alone. Therefore, I ask this question of all. Is there anyone who knows a just reason why this sister should not become one of us?"

Silence filled the meeting room. Adrian glanced at Faith. Her eyes were downcast as she awaited the verdict. The bishop's wife shifted in her seat but didn't stand up. No one spoke.

After a few moments, the bishop smiled broadly and said, "Come forward, Sister Faith. In the name of the Lord and the Church, I extend to you the hand of fellowship. Be ye a faithful member of our church."

Adrian relaxed. No one had spoken against her. Faith stood and walked to stand before the bishop. He took her hand, but because she was a woman, he then gave her hand to his wife who greeted her with a Holy Kiss upon her cheek.

Faith was now a member of their community and subject to all the rules of their faith. Adrian glanced at the boy sleeping against his side. She would have to raise Kyle in the ways of the faithful. It was a good life, and he was happy for the boy.

When the services came to an end a few minutes later, Adrian woke Kyle, and the two of them followed the other men outside. Kyle yawned and squinted up at Adrian. "I'm hungry."

"We'll eat soon."

Faith approached them. Happiness radiated from her face. She said, "Kyle, you were very well behaved today."

"I fell asleep," he admitted.

Her happy smile made her even prettier this morning. Adrian said, "Congratulations."

"*Danki.* Kyle, why don't you come with me now and let Adrian visit with his friends."

Other members of the church crowded around to offer their congratulations and welcome. Adrian stepped aside. It was her special day, and he was glad for her.

Because it was such a beautiful day, the meal was set up outdoors. The younger people soon had a volleyball net set up between two trees on the lawn. A dozen of the boys and girls quickly began a game. The cheering and laughter from both participants and onlookers filled the late-summer afternoon with joyous sounds. Faith sat on a blanket in the grass with Kyle beside her. They were cheering for the girls.

"She has the makings of a good mother, don't you think?"

Adrian looked over his shoulder to find his cousin Sarah observing him with interest. She'd always had an uncanny knack for knowing what he was thinking. He didn't pretend ignorance.

"She is good with the boy."

Sarah settled herself on the tailgate of the wagon beside him. "Faith tells me that you have been good for the boy, too."

"He reminds me of Gideon."

Sarah cocked her head to the side as she studied the boy. "A little maybe because of his red hair, but Kyle's hair is darker and curlier. Is she going to send him to our Amish school or to an *Englisch* one?"

"I don't know."

"You haven't asked her?"

"It's none of my business." He looked down to pretend he didn't care one way or the other.

"That's odd."

"What is?" he muttered.

"It's just that the two of you seem so close."

He slanted a glance her way. "What's that supposed to mean?"

"The two of you seem close, that's all. You've been working at her farm since the day she moved in. People notice."

"People should mind their own business."

"You know that's not going to happen. You're single. She's single. She's a member of our church district now. There's nothing wrong with courting her."

He drew back in shock. "Is that what you think I'm doing?"

"Me? No, of course not. I know you better than that."

Mollified, he said, "I should hope so."

"You're being kind, that's all."

"Exactly."

"What your mother or others think is beyond my control."

"Mother thinks I'm courting Faith? I will straighten her thinking out on the way home, today."

"Before you do that, let me ask you something. Has

your mother invited any single women to your family dinners recently?"

He thought back over the past month and realized she hadn't. "No."

"See."

"See what?" He couldn't follow her reasoning.

"Kindness brings its own reward."

"Speak plain, Sarah. What are you hinting at?"

She patted his arm. "All I'm saying is that while you are being kind to your neighbor, your mother has stopped searching high and low for someone to catch your interest."

"That's not my reason for helping Faith."

"I'm not suggesting it is. You have a kind heart, and Faith needs all the help she can get until she has her yarn business up and running well."

"That's right."

"It would be okay if you did decide to court her."

He looked into Sarah's eyes. "I don't know if I can take that chance again."

She laid a hand on his arm. "You can, otherwise you will miss out on something special. Lovina wouldn't want you to waste your life grieving for her. You know that. She is happy with God in heaven. She wants you to be happy, too."

"What if something happens to Faith or to Kyle? How could I live through such a loss again?"

"Adrian, you can do one of two things. You can blame God for your misery or you can turn to Him and draw strength from His love. He is always there for us."

"You make it sound so easy. It isn't."

"Answer me this. Were you better off before you met Faith?"

"Nee."

"If you were given one and only one chance to kiss her, would you take it?"

He would take it in a heartbeat. *"Ja."*

"Then why are you turning down the chance to love her for a lifetime?"

He had no answer for Sarah, but she didn't seem to expect one. With a pat on his arm, she left to join Faith and Kyle on their quilt.

As was his custom, Adrian left the gathering early, went home and cut flowers from his garden. On his way to the cemetery, he pondered his feelings for Faith, what they meant and what he was willing to do about them. Did he have a chance to love her for a lifetime? Was that really within his grasp? The thought excited and frightened him. What if he loved and lost her, too?

At his wife's graveside, he laid the new flowers over the dried husks of the old ones. He stared at her headstone, but he was at a loss for something to say.

Turning away, he took his usual seat and leaned forward with his elbows braced on his thighs. Suddenly, the words came pouring out. "I never meant it to happen, Lovey. I wasn't looking for someone to care about. In my whole life I never wanted to share my hopes and dreams with anyone but you."

Until now. Until Faith. He raised his face to the sky. "Is this wrong? How can it be wrong to care about such a good woman? Faith is a good woman, a strong woman, but she needs someone to take care of her and her boy."

And I need someone to care about me.

Wasn't that the truth he'd been hiding from?

Adrian closed his eyes. "I've been dead inside for a long time. Waking up is painful, Lovey. I'm not sure I can do it."

Chapter 14

Faith sat at her kitchen table with her checkbook in front of her on Thursday morning. She'd been able to pay her outstanding bills with the money she'd made at the market and she still had money left over. Her small bank account was growing at last.

In her wildest dreams she hadn't imagined doing this well so quickly. She'd sold all the yarn she'd taken with her to the market and had taken orders for several dozen additional skeins plus eight of her white baby blankets. She would have to redouble her spinning and knitting efforts to keep up.

Adrian's mother had invited Faith to join their co-op group and display her handmade wares each week on market day. With the cool days of fall not far away, yarn for warm socks, sweaters and mittens were sure to be in high demand.

Kyle came running into the room. He stopped beside Faith to grab a leftover breakfast biscuit from a plate in the center of the table. "My room is clean."

"*Danki,* Kyle."

"Is Adrian coming over today?"

She missed Adrian's presence as much as Kyle did. Maybe more. She'd gotten used to having him around. Some foolish part of her heart continued to hope that he'd come over with a new excuse to spend time with them, but it hadn't happened.

"I doubt it, dear. His work in the orchard is done. You will see him at the next preaching service."

"But that's another whole week away." Pieces of biscuit sprayed from his lips.

"Don't talk with your mouth full."

He swallowed. "I don't want to wait until church. Can't we go visit Adrian today?"

"No. Miss Watkins is coming today."

Faith hoped his sudden pout wasn't going to lead to a temper tantrum. "Why is *she* coming?" he demanded.

"It's her job to find out if you are happy here. Are you happy?"

Confusion clouded his eyes. "Can I go play with Shadow?"

A pang of disappointment stabbed her. Why couldn't he answer a simple question? "You may, but try not to get dirty."

He darted outside, letting the screen door bang shut behind him.

Was he unhappy living with her? He seemed to be adjusting well to this new way of life. She had been worried those first few nights, but he'd not had a nightmare for the past week.

Faith closed her eyes and took a deep breath. Her new life in Hope Springs was turning into a dream come true. Kyle was with her. The church community had welcomed her with open arms. Her business was off to a great start, and her share of the peach money had been an added bonus.

"Through you, Lord, all things are possible. I humbly give thanks for Your blessings."

Little more than a month ago she had arrived in Hope Springs with barely enough to support herself. Now, she had enough to support Kyle, too. An important step toward his permanent adoption. Would his social worker think it was enough? The Amish were frugal people. Faith didn't need a large sum of money to live comfortably. Could Caroline Watkins be made to understand that?

An hour later, the sound of a car pulling into the yard alerted Faith to Miss Watkins's arrival. Faith opened the door and waited as Caroline came up the steps. "Good morning, Miss Watkins. Do come in. How are you?"

Caroline said, "I'm fine. This shouldn't take long today. I'll make a quick tour of the house and then I'd like to talk to you and Kyle separately. Is that all right?"

"Certainly." Faith took a seat at the kitchen table and waited. She tried to ignore the nervous dread that started gnawing at the inside of her stomach. She knew there was nothing to fear, but she was afraid anyway. This woman had the power to remove Kyle from her home.

Ten agonizing minutes later, Caroline came back into the kitchen with smile on her lips. "Everything seems in order, Mrs. Martin. How are you getting along with Kyle?"

Faith let out the breath she'd been holding. "It's going well. He works hard and plays hard. We went to the Summer Festival in Hope Springs last week, and I think he really enjoyed himself."

"That's great to hear. Where is Kyle?"

"He's down in the barn playing with Shadow, the baby alpaca. The two of them have become fast friends. Shadow is living up to his name for he follows Kyle around whenever the boy is near. Would you like me to go get him?"

"I'd rather talk to him alone." Caroline went out the door.

Faith began her preparations for making bread. Keeping busy was better than pacing the floor and wondering what was going on between Kyle and Miss Watkins. What if Kyle told her he didn't like it here? What if he complained that he had too much work to do? A dozen unhappy scenarios ran through Faith's mind. Her stomach rolled into a tight knot.

A few minutes later, Miss Watkins returned to the house. Faith dusted the flour off her hands, set her bread dough aside and turned around. "Are you finished already?"

Her worry knot doubled in size when she saw the green speckles on Miss Watkins's clothes. Myrtle had been at it again.

"I'm so sorry. I should have warned you about Myrtle." Faith wet a kitchen towel and handed it to Caroline.

Caroline wiped her face and brushed at her blouse.

"Their spitting is a disgusting habit. I couldn't find Kyle. Where else might he be?"

"He said he was going to the barn."

"He isn't in the barn. I called but he didn't answer. He wasn't with the baby alpaca." She scrubbed at her shoulder.

"Perhaps he's in the orchard."

"Does he disappear like this often?"

"No, of course not." Faith rushed outside and began frantically calling for Kyle. She and the social worker made their way from one side of the orchard to the other without any sign of the boy.

When they arrived back at the house and saw Kyle hadn't returned, Faith said, "We should go to the neighbor's farm and see if he is there."

"Has he done that before?"

"No."

Miss Watkins pulled her cell phone from the pocket of her slacks. "Can you call them and see if he's there?"

"My neighbors are Amish. They have no phones."

Miss Watkins bit her lip, then opened her phone. "We are wasting valuable time. I'm going to notify the sheriff that we have a missing child."

Adrian lay on his back beneath his grain binder and loosened the last bolt holding the sickle blades in place. It came loose easily, and he lowered the bar to the ground. His cornfields would be ready to cut soon, and he needed to make sure his equipment was in good working order. Sharpening the sickle blades was his first priority.

"What ya doing?"

Adrian twisted his head around to see Kyle squatting beneath the equipment with him. "I'm getting my machinery ready to harvest corn. What are you doing?"

"I came to help you."

"You have, have you? Where is your *aenti* Faith?" Adrian wormed his way out from beneath his equipment with the long row of blades in hand. He looked eagerly toward the house, but he didn't see Faith anywhere.

He had stayed away from her the past few days because he knew if they came face-to-face, he wouldn't be able to hide his longing or his fears. He hadn't been ready for that. Was he ready now?

Kyle said, "She's at home with that mean social worker."

Faith wasn't here. Adrian tried not to let his disappointment show. He focused on Kyle. "You must not speak badly of others, Kyle. You must forgive them for the wrongs they do."

"Why?"

"Because that is what God commands us to do. Why do you say your social worker is mean?"

"'Cause social workers take kids away from their moms." Kyle glanced over his shoulder as if expecting to see one swooping down on him like a hawk.

"Where did you hear this?"

"Dylan and Tyrell told me."

The names weren't familiar. Adrian asked, "Who are they?"

"My friends in Texas. They were in foster care with me because a social worker took them away from their mom. They told me not to like Becky too much cause a social worker would come and take me away to a new place, and one did. Dylan and Tyrell had been in three foster homes so they knew it would happen and it did."

"Becky was your foster mother?"

Kyle nodded. "I liked her a lot."

Adrian sat on the steel tongue of his grain binder. "I'm sorry you were taken from someone you cared about, but I know that Faith loves you and she wants you to stay with her for a long time."

Kyle turned away from Adrian and patted the side of the machine. "What does this thing do?"

"This is a grain binder. It cuts cane or corn into bundles of livestock feed."

"How?"

Adrian understood Kyle's reluctance to talk about matters that troubled him. Wasn't he the same way? Didn't he avoid talking about his family because it brought the pain back sharp as ever?

He said, "The machine is powered by this gasoline engine. My team pulls it through the field while I stand up here to guide them." He indicated a small platform at the front.

"Up here?" Kyle climbed the three metal ladder rungs and stood behind the slim railing that allowed the driver to lean against it and kept him from falling while he drove his team.

The boy grinned when he realized he was now taller than Adrian. He stretched his hands out pretending to hold the reins of a frisky team. "What do I do next?"

Adrian walked around to the side of the machine. "You guide your team along the corn rows. This sickle bar cuts the thick stalks about a foot off the ground. The reel lays them evenly onto this wide canvas belt. The belt feeds the stalks into a mechanism that gathers them together into a bundle, then wraps it with twine and knots it."

"Then what?"

"You must decide. See that lever in front of you?"

"Yup." Kyle reached beneath the safety rail to grasp a metal handle.

"Pull it back and the bundle is kicked out the side of the machine where it will lay in the field until I come back and stack them into tepee-style shocks."

"Why make a tepee out of them?"

These were things Adrian would have explained to his son if Gideon has lived. It was part of being a father, teaching the children how to farm and wrest a living from the land.

Kyle wouldn't have anyone to teach him unless Faith chose to remarry.

Would she remarry for the boy's sake? The thought didn't sit well with Adrian. What if the man she chose was unkind to her or to Kyle the way her first husband had been? He knew a few Amish husbands who believed they should rule their families with an iron fist.

"Why build tepees with them?" Kyle asked again.

"Because they shed water if you put the bundles together in an upright position. As they dry and shrink, it allows more air to flow around the inside of the bundles and they dry better. I put about twenty bundles into each shock."

"What if I push this lever forward?"

"Then the machine dumps the bundles onto a trailer that is pulled behind me, and my brother stacks them together so we can haul them to the barn."

"I wish I had a brother. That would be cool."

"It is sometimes, but sometimes they can be a pain in the neck."

Kyle climbed down from his post. "Can I see Meg and Mick?"

The boy had taken a liking to Adrian's team and had begged to ride one on the way home from market. Adrian hadn't allowed it then as they were on the highway, but he saw no harm in it now.

"*Ja,* they are in the barn."

"Can I ride one of them? They are like ten times bigger than the ponies at the fair."

Adrian thought of all the work he had to finish. Put side by side with Kyle's eager face, Adrian found only one conclusion. The work could wait.

In the barn, Adrian opened the door to Meg's stall and led her out to the small paddock. He hoisted Kyle to her broad back. She was so wide that the boy's feet stuck out straight instead of being able to grip her sides.

Adrian said, "Wrap your hand in her mane."

"Won't that hurt her?"

"*Nee,* it will not, but it might keep you from falling off."

Grasping the halter, Adrian led the mare around the paddock. She walked slowly and carefully, as if aware of the precious cargo she carried.

Kyle grinned from ear to ear. "I can see all the way to Texas from up here."

"How's the weather down that way?"

Shading his eyes with one hand, Kyle said, "Sunny and hot."

After the third time around the corral, Adrian stopped Meg and held his hands up to Kyle. "Come along. I have much work to do. I must sharpen my sickle and get my binder back together and Meg wants to have a good roll in the dust."

"Okay." Kyle reluctantly left his high perch. They walked back into the barn, leaving Meg in the pen where she promptly lay down, rolled onto her back and frolicked in the dust she raised.

As they passed her stall, Kyle looked at Adrian. "Do you want me to *redd-up* her stall?"

Tickled by Kyle's use of an Amish term, Adrian knew the boy would soon fit into their Amish ways and leave his *Englisch* past behind. He stared into Kyle's eyes and saw he was dying to please.

Adrian stroked his beard. "Reckon I could use a good stable hand now and again."

Puffing out his chest, Kyle asked, "Where's your wheelbarrow and your shovel?"

"I will get them for you."

When he returned with the requested tools and gave them to Kyle, Adrian leaned on the stall gate to watch the boy work. It took him a while, but he managed to rake up the mess and push the wheelbarrow back to Adrian.

Sighing heavily, Kyle said, "Alpacas are much easier to clean up after."

"They are not as big as Meg."

"No wonder Aunt Faith raises them instead of horses."

Adrian chuckled. "No wonder."

Kyle pulled at the Band-Aid on his palm. "It came loose."

Adrian bent down to see. He removed the bandages and looked at the angry red sores. "You should have told me they were hurting you."

"They don't hurt." Kyle put his hands behind his back.

"Lying is a sin, Kyle. I know you want to please and prove that you are a good helper, but Faith will have my hide if these get infected. Come up to the house and let's get them clean."

In the kitchen, Adrian gently washed Kyle's hands and patted them dry. He applied an antiseptic cream to them and wrapped a length of gauze around each palm. "Is that better?"

Kyle flexed his fingers. *"Ja."*

"I think I may have a pair of gloves you can wear over them." He rose and led the way to Gideon's room. Opening the door, he experienced the same catch in his chest that always hit him when he stepped over this threshold. The room looked the same as the day his son had left it.

On the blue-and-green quilt that covered the bed lay a baseball glove and a carved wooden horse. Gifts meant for a birthday that had never arrived. Crossing the room, Adrian pulled open a dresser drawer and retrieved a small pair of knit gloves.

"Try these on." He turned to hand them to Kyle and froze. Kyle was on his knees by the bed galloping the toy horse across the quilt.

He grinned up at Adrian. "This looks like Meg."

Adrian held back the shout that formed in his throat. *Leave that alone. It belongs to my son.*

He knew Kyle wouldn't understand. The boy meant no harm. He was simply doing what boys did—playing with a toy as it was meant to be played with.

Is this part of Your plan, Lord? Am I to see that I'm being greedy and selfish by hanging on to these things?

Gideon would share his toys with this boy, I know he would. He had a kind heart like his mother.

Adrian forced a smile to his stiff lips. "I made it to look like Meg. I was going to make another one that looked like Mick."

"You made it? Cool beans." Kyle stared at the toy in awe.

"Would you like to have it?"

"Can I?" His eyes grew round.

"It is yours if you want it."

Kyle grinned. "Thanks. I mean, *danki.*"

"You're welcome. Now try these on." Adrian held out the gloves. They proved to be too small.

Knowing a pair of his would be much too large, Adrian said, "Try not to get dirty."

"That's what Aunt Faith tells me."

"Does it work?"

"Not so much."

Adrian smiled as he ruffled Kyle's hair and went outside to finish his work. He sharpened his blades while Kyle galloped little Meg across the workbench and jumped her over hammers and assorted tools. It felt good to have a child with him again.

He still missed his son, still wished it was Gideon with him, but he was able to enjoy Kyle's company and appreciate the boy for who he was.

Adrian was reattaching his sickle blades when the sound of a car coming up his lane drew his attention. He rose to his feet and saw the sheriff's white SUV roll to a stop in front of his house.

Adrian looked at Kyle seated on the ground beside him. "Does your aunt know you are here?"

The boy shrugged.

Adrian shook his head at his own thoughtlessness. "That is a question I should have asked an hour ago."

He held his hand out to Kyle. "Come. You have some explaining to do."

Reluctantly, Kyle rose and walked with Adrian toward the sheriff's vehicle. The passenger's door opened, and Faith rushed toward them, a look of intense relief on her face. In her hurry she stumbled and would have fallen if Adrian hadn't lunged forward to catch her.

He held her tight against his chest and breathed in the fresh scent of her hair. She fit perfectly against him. It felt so right to hold her this way. She looked up at him with wide, startled eyes. Eyes filled not with fear, but with the same breathless excitement she had awakened in him.

In that instant he knew she felt as he did. The next move was up to him. Did he dare risk his heart again?

Chapter 15

Faith rested in the safety of Adrian's embrace, relishing the strength and gentleness with which he held her. Gazing up into his face, she saw his eyes darken.

Did he feel it too, this current between them that defied her logical, sensible mind?

How had it happened? How had she fallen in love with him?

He said softly, "Kyle is okay."

"I knew he would be if he was with you," she whispered. She and Kyle would always be safe if Adrian was with them. If only it could be this way forever. It couldn't. She knew that.

Adrian was still in love with his wife. She couldn't compete with a ghost.

Besides, she had to concentrate on Kyle. Finalizing his adoption had to be her top priority. Adding Adrian to the picture would only complicate and delay things.

Reluctantly, she left the comfort of Adrian's embrace and sank awkwardly to the ground beside Kyle. She gathered him close in a tight hug. "I was so worried when I couldn't find you."

He wrapped his arms around her neck and hugged her back. Suddenly, he let go and stepped away. Faith saw he was looking at the sheriff and Miss Watkins as they approached.

Faith cupped his chin and turned his face toward her. "It's all right. You aren't in trouble."

The sheriff pushed his hat back with one finger. "Looks like the lost sheep has been found."

Miss Watkins clasped her hands together. "I am so sorry that we wasted your time, Sheriff Bradley."

"Don't be. I like a happy ending. I just wish all my calls were so easy."

Miss Watkins focused her attention on Kyle. "You frightened us very badly, Kyle. Why did you run away from home?"

"I didn't."

Faith accepted Adrian's hand as he helped her to her feet. She said, "Kyle, you must let me know when you are going to visit a friend or a neighbor."

"Okay."

Miss Watkins stepped forward with a sharp frown on her face. "What's wrong with your hands, Kyle?"

"I got some blisters. Adrian fixed me up. He gave me this horse." He held up the toy.

Glancing between the adults, Miss Watkins leaned down to Kyle's level. "How did you get blisters? Did you touch something hot?"

"No." He shrank away from her and toward Faith.

Faith said, "He got them cleaning out a stall and helping us with the peach crop."

Adrian spoke up. "He rubbed his bandages off cleaning one of my stalls. I washed his sores and re-dressed them. He'll be okay in a few days."

Holding out her hand, Miss Watkins asked, "May I see your blisters?"

Kyle buried his face in Faith's skirt and put his hands behind his back.

Turning his face up to hers, Faith smiled encouragingly at him. "Is it okay if I unwrap them?"

He held out his hands. Faith unwound the dressing from his right hand. Miss Watkins took a closer look, then said, "Okay. Kyle, why don't you go to the car with Sheriff Bradley. I bet he'll show you how the radio works."

The sheriff nodded toward his SUV. "Come on, Kyle. Would you like to turn on the flashing lights?"

Kyle glanced from Faith to Adrian. "Is it *verboten*?"

Faith exchanged an amused look with Adrian, then said, "It's not forbidden. It is okay for Amish boys to do such a thing."

Kyle followed the sheriff, but the worried expression lingered on his face.

Miss Watkins folded her arms. "I will be the first to admit that I'm not familiar with Amish ways, but to work a child of six until both his hands are covered in blisters is not acceptable."

Faith cringed before the social worker's anger. Fear stole her voice. Beside her, Adrian said, "The boy worked hard to prove that he belongs among us. We did not make him do this."

Caroline shook her head. "Be that as it may, I'm not convinced this is the best arrangement for Kyle."

"Please, don't take him away from me." Faith wanted to race to the car, grab her child and hold on to him so tightly that no one could take him from her. Adrian's hand settled on her shoulder holding her in place.

Caroline sighed heavily. "I don't want to take him away, Mrs. Martin, but I have to know that he's in a safe environment. I would be neglecting my job and Kyle's welfare if I placed him in a questionable home."

"I'll do anything you ask. Please, don't take him away," Faith pleaded.

"Ultimately that decision is up to a judge. I'm here to help make the adoption possible. I want you to re-think how much work a child of six should be doing. I'll be back to visit again next Friday. Before then, you will need to make a list of Kyle's chores. We can go over them together and see if we can agree on what's appropriate for his age."

"I can do that," Faith quickly assured her.

"Keep in mind that he's going to be in school. There will be even less time for him to do chores." She walked back to the sheriff's vehicle leaving Faith and Adrian alone.

Faith started to follow her, but Adrian caught her arm. "Faith, we need to talk."

"I can't. Not now."

His shoulders slumped in defeat. "All right. Go home and take care of your child."

She squeezed his hand. "Thank you, Adrian."

"For what?"

"For understanding." Faith left him and took a seat inside the sheriff's vehicle.

"Are you ready for your first day of school?"

Bright and early Monday morning Faith climbed into the buggy beside Kyle.

He hooked his thumbs through his new suspenders giving them a sour look. "Do I have to wear these? I look like a dork."

"You must dress plain now. All the boys will be wearing them."

"Are you sure?" He let them snap back against his chest.

"*Ja,* I'm sure. Do you like your hat?"

He raised his flat-topped straw hat with both hands and looked up at it. "It's okay. It's like the one Adrian wears."

"He wears suspenders, too."

"Yeah, he does, doesn't he?" That mollified him.

"Are you excited about school?"

He sat back and folded his arms over his chest. "No. Everyone's gonna think I'm stupid 'cause I can't speak Pennsylvania Dutch."

She folded her hands in her lap. "Kyle, you are learning our language just as the Amish children at school will be learning English. If you help them, they will help you and nobody will be stupid."

"Maybe." He didn't sound convinced.

Faith cupped his chin and raised his face so she could see his eyes. "I know this is hard for you, but school is not all bad. You will learn many good things. Do you like to play baseball?"

"Yes."

"Amish children also like baseball. When I was in school, we played it almost every day. Not in winter, of course. In the winter, we went sledding during recess."

"Really?" He looked at her with interest.

"Really."

"That sounds kinda cool."

She grinned. "It wasn't cool. It was downright cold." She poked his side making him giggle.

"Can I drive the buggy?" he asked.

"You may, but just to the end of the lane." Faith had no fear that Copper would bolt. The mare was well trained and placid. In fact, it was hard to get her into high gear anymore.

"Hold the reins like this." Faith demonstrated. Kyle was quick to copy her and soon had Copper moving down the lane. Faith sat ready to take the lines at the first sign of trouble. Thankfully, they reached the highway without incident.

"How'd I do?" he asked as he handed the reins back.

"Very well. You're a natural." She headed Copper down the road toward the schoolhouse a mile and a half away. After today Kyle would be walking, but she wanted to make sure he could find his way. Besides, the first day of school was special for any child, and she wanted to be a part of it.

When the building came into view, she said, "We're almost there."

Kyle slumped in his seat again. "Do I have to go? I feel sick."

She understood the anxiety he was feeling, but she knew he would soon make new friends. Faith had met earlier with his teacher, Leah Belier. A young Amish woman in her early twenties, Leah seemed devoted to students and to helping them learn. She had promised she would do her best to help Kyle adjust to his new surroundings.

Faith stopped the buggy on the sloping lawn of the one-room schoolhouse. Several other buggies were tied up alongside the building. Children were already at play on the swing set and the long wooden teeter-totter.

Faith sensed Kyle's interest, but he moved closer to her. Before she could convince him to get down, Leah came out of the schoolhouse door and waved to Faith.

Faith returned her greeting. Kyle buried his face in Faith's lap. "Can we go home, please?"

Leah was quick to assess the situation and approached the buggy. "You must be Kyle King. I'm so glad to meet you. I was hoping you could help me this morning."

Kyle eyed her with suspicion. "How?"

"I need a strong young boy to ring the bell for me."

Looking past her, Kyle assessed the situation. "I guess I could do that."

"Wonderful. Faith, would you like to sit in on class today?"

"I would."

After securing Copper to the hitching rail, Faith walked with Kyle to the school building where Leah waited for them. The teacher pointed to the bell rope hanging inside the doorway. "Give it a yank, Kyle. It's time to start our classes."

Gritting his teeth, Kyle pulled with all his might. The bell clanged loudly.

Leah clapped her hands. "Very good, Kyle. You're every bit as strong as you look. Now, I need someone to put pencils and papers on all the desks. Can you help with that?"

"Sure."

"*Danki*. That means thank you."

"I know."

"The papers and pencils are on the table behind my chair. The desk directly in front of mine belongs to you."

The other children began entering by twos and threes. Leah welcomed them all by their first names, asking after family members and previous students. It was clear she enjoyed her job.

Faith took a seat at the back of the room where several young mothers sat visiting with each other.

She stayed for the first hour of class, just long enough to make sure Kyle was going to be okay. Leah kept all the students well in hand as she switched back and forth between English and Pennsylvania Dutch to make sure everyone understood her instructions.

After leaving the school, Faith drove home and set to work spinning another batch of yarns. Once they were done, she would take them into town after she picked up Kyle. She had a special treat in store for him.

By early afternoon, she had several dozen skeins ready to be dropped off at Needles and Pins. She hitched up Copper again and arrived at the schoolhouse just as the main door opened and a rush of children poured out.

Kyle, grinning from ear to ear, skidded to a halt beside her and held up a piece of paper. "I drew a picture of Shadow. Did you know we're the only people in Hope Springs who have alpacas?"

She grinned at his enthusiasm. "I suspected as much."

"Anna Imhoff and her brothers want to come over and see Shadow. Can they?"

"Perhaps tomorrow. Today, we must go into town and celebrate."

"Celebrate what?"

"Your first day at school. It's a big deal and it calls for a celebration."

"What kind of celebration?"

"I'm treating you to supper at the Shoofly Pie Café."

"Can we get pizza?"

"That sounds perfect."

"*Goot.* That means good in Pennsylvania Dutch. I learned it and some more words, too."

"I'm pleased to hear your day wasn't wasted. Did you make some new friends?"

"Anna Imhoff wants to be my friend, but she's a girl."

"Girls can be friends, too."

"Her brother, Noah, started teasing me 'cause I can't talk Amish. Anna got mad and scolded him."

"Then she sounds like a very good friend to have. Did everyone play baseball at recess?"

His mood went from happy to dejected. "Yeah, but no one picked me for their team."

"You are little yet. I'm sure you'll play many games when you're older."

"Maybe if I got a glove."

Leah approached the buggy. "He did well, Faith. He needs to work on his sums and his reading, but overall he's a bright, friendly boy."

"Wonderful." It was a relief to know that Kyle was fitting in. She had worried that the language barrier would make school unhappy for him.

Leah left to speak to other parents, and Faith turned Copper toward town. Once they reached Hope Springs,

Faith dropped off her yarns at the fabric store and drove on to the Shoofly Pie Café.

She and Kyle entered the homey café and were instantly surrounded with the smell of baking bread, cinnamon and frying chicken. A young Amish girl came forward. "*Velkumm* to the Shoofly Pie café. My name is Melody. Would you like a table or a booth?"

"A booth," Kyle answered before Faith could say anything.

The waitress led them to one of the high-backed seats that lined the walls of the room. Faith slid into the nearest bench. Kyle scooted in opposite her and propped his elbows on the red Formica tabletop.

Suddenly, Kyle's eyes lit up. "It's Adrian."

The boy waved. Faith turned to see her neighbor entering the door. He raised a hand and waved back. He was carrying a small package wrapped in plain brown paper and tied with string.

He stopped beside their booth. Faith wished her heart would stop trying to gallop out of her chest each time he was near.

Kyle spoke up eagerly. "I went to school today."

Adrian grinned at him. "So I heard. How was it?"

"Pretty fun. I learned to count to ten in Amish and how to say please and thank you."

"Those are all good things to know." Adrian focused his gaze on Faith. "How have you been?"

Missing you madly. "Fine, and you?"

"Busy. I'll start cutting corn tomorrow if this nice weather holds."

She couldn't care less about the mundane details of his life. Just seeing his face brightened her day.

He asked, "May I join you?"

Surprised and delighted, she said, "Certainly."

Kyle scooted over to let him sit down. Adrian said, "I brought you a present, Kyle." He slid the package toward the boy.

"Why? It's not my birthday." Kyle tore open the wrapping to reveal a baseball mitt. It was too big for his hand, but he didn't seem to mind. "Cool. I've been wanting one like this forever."

Adrian smiled at him. "Happy first day of school."

Faith couldn't put her finger on it, but there was something different about Adrian today. He was more lighthearted, happier than she had seen him. She liked the change. She liked it a lot.

He met her gaze. "Every boy needs a good baseball glove."

She said, "You didn't need to spend money on Kyle. I could have gotten him one."

"It's an old glove I had lying around. I thought Kyle might put it to good use."

"I sure will. Now they won't pick me last." Kyle smacked his fist in the pocket.

Faith's heart warmed to see Kyle so excited and happy. She started to convey her thanks, but Adrian stopped her with a shake of his head. "It's nothing."

The look in his eyes said differently. Then it hit her. She reached across the table to lay her hand on Adrian's arm. "It was Gideon's glove, wasn't it?"

"It was, but now it is Kyle's." His glance settled on her nephew. It was easy to read the deep affection he had for the boy.

It was only when Adrian looked into her eyes that she became unsure of his feelings. He said, "I know

Kyle's adoption is your main priority right now, but when that's over, I'd like to talk about the future."

Faith pulled her hand away. The future? What was he suggesting? Did he have more plans for the farm, or was he suggesting they could have a future together? Her heart raced as her breathing quickened. "The hearing is the last day of this month."

He winced. "That is a long time to wait."

"Then perhaps you should come over this evening if it's important." She bit the inside of her lip as she waited for his reply.

"It is important to me and I hope to you. *Ja,* I will come by later."

"I'm having pizza," Kyle announced.

Adrian tweaked the boy's nose. "Sounds good to me. I like pepperoni and extra cheese."

"Me, too." Kyle looked at Faith. "What kind do you like, Aunt Faith?"

"I'll have whatever the two of you are having."

Food was the furthest thing from her mind at the moment. What was on Adrian's mind that couldn't wait? Did she dare hope he returned her feelings of affection, or was she tricking herself into imagining what wasn't there?

"You're late getting back from town," Ben said, as he finished greasing the wheels of the grain binder and wiped his blackened fingers on a piece of cloth lying on top of the machine.

"I had supper at the café. Are you done already?" Adrian checked his brother's work and found it satisfactory.

"*Ja.* When will you start cutting?"

"I took a walk through the corn this morning. I

think it will be ready by the end of the week, if it doesn't rain."

"*Dat* wants to start on our fields early tomorrow. We should be done in four or five days. When we're finished, I can come and give you a hand."

"I always appreciate your help with the farmwork." Could he trust Ben with an even more important task?

Adrian hooked his thumbs in his suspenders. He wasn't ready to reveal his intentions toward Faith to his family just yet. He wanted to know her feelings first. She had been adamant that she would not remarry. If those were her true feelings, he would respect them and never bring up the subject again.

He needed to speak to her alone, but he couldn't do that with Kyle listening in. Knowing the boy's penchant for turning up in the wrong place at the wrong time, Adrian didn't want to risk it.

The smart thing to do would have been to wait until the adoption was over or at least until the boy was in school tomorrow, but Adrian didn't want to wait another day to know if Faith cared for him as he'd grown to care for her.

Oh, he'd had every intention of waiting until the time was right…then she'd smiled at him in the café and laid her hand on his arm to comfort him. The understanding in her eyes had done something wonderful to his heart.

His carefully laid plans had flown out of his head, and he'd told her he would be over tonight.

Tonight! This was what he got for his impatience. He had to rely on his baby brother to help him secure time alone with Faith.

"Ben, I'm wondering if you could give me a hand with something this evening?"

"Sure. What do you need?"

Drawing a deep breath, Adrian forged ahead before he could change his mind. "I need someone to stay with Faith Martin's boy for an hour or so."

There was a long moment of silence, then Ben crossed his arms. "Why?"

"Because…because I need to speak to Faith, alone."

Ben grinned from ear to ear. "You're going courting."

Adrian closed his eyes. This had been another bad idea. What was wrong with him today? "I never said that."

"You don't have to say anything. It's written all over your face. The whole family has been wondering when you'd finally wise up. Wait until I tell *Mamm* she was right about you two."

"Please, don't. Not until I know how Faith feels."

Ben stepped forward and laid a hand on Adrian's shoulder. "She'd be a fool to turn you down and I don't think Faith Martin is anyone's fool."

"I pray you are right."

"Let me wash off this grease and then we can go. I won't keep you waiting to see your lady love." Ben walked away, chuckling to himself.

Adrian blew out a deep sigh of frustration. This was to be his punishment for involving his baby brother. Ben was never going to let him live this down, and he was never going to keep it a secret.

Twenty minutes later, the two men were driving toward Faith's house with Ben at the reins. Adrian's stomach churned with butterflies now that he was actually on his way. He rubbed his sweaty palms on his pant legs and tried to figure out what he was going to say.

Ben slipped his arm around Adrian's shoulder and gave him a brotherly hug. "Relax. She isn't going to bite your head off and I doubt she spits like an alpaca. You should drive her over toward the Stultz place and take the left fork just past their barn. The road winds up in a pretty little meadow beside Croft Creek."

"Where the old stone bridge has fallen down?"

Ben shot him a surprised look. "You know the place?"

"You don't think you're the first fellow to take a girl out there for a picnic, do you? *Dat* took *Mamm* there when he was courting her."

"No kidding? Our folks?" Ben looked as if he'd bitten a lemon.

It was Adrian's turn to laugh. "Love finds all sorts of people, little *bruder*. Every papa and granddad you see was once a young man with stealing a kiss on his mind."

"I reckon you're right." Ben pulled the horse to a stop in front of Faith's gate.

She and Kyle were both outside. Faith sat at her spinning wheel on the porch. Kyle was playing on the swing Adrian had built for him. The moment Kyle caught sight of them, he jumped out of the swing and ran toward them.

"Howdy, Adrian. Howdy, Ben. What are you doing here?" He slowed to a walk when he drew near the horse.

Ben hopped out of the buggy. "I've come to see your alpaca herd up close."

"I'll show them to you. We've got a new cria. His

name is Shadow and he belongs to me. Adrian gave me a baseball glove. Want to see it?"

"Sure. Maybe we can play some catch after we're done seeing your critters."

"Cool beans."

Ben gave Adrian a wave and walked toward the barn with the boy dancing beside him.

Adrian sat in the buggy as Faith came down the steps toward him. She looked so pretty this evening in a dark purple dress with an apron of the same color over it. His butterflies returned in full force. He nodded toward her. "Evening, Faith."

She paused behind her gate. "Hello again."

"It's a right nice evening, isn't it?" He tried not to fidget.

"Very nice."

"I was wondering if you might like to take a buggy ride?"

She glanced toward the barn. "I'm sure Kyle would enjoy that."

"Ben is going to stay here with Kyle until we get back."

"Oh." Her eyes widened.

Adrian held out his hand. "It will be just the two of us."

Faith hesitated. She wanted to go with him, but what was she getting herself into? This wasn't going to be a farming discussion. She had sense enough to know that. Could he really want to be alone with her because he was ready to open his heart to another woman? To her?

Was she ready for another relationship?

There was only one way to find out. She pushed open the gate and took his hand to climb in his buggy.

When she was settled beside him, he clicked his tongue and slapped the reins to set Wilbur in motion.

At the highway, he turned south toward his farm but passed by his lane without stopping. She asked, "Where are we going?"

"Some place we can talk without being interrupted."

He turned off at the first dirt road to the Stultz place and then took the left fork just past their big white barn. The little-used road wound around the side of a hill and came out into a small meadow. A white-tailed doe grazing near the trees along the creek threw up her head and then bounded away in alarm.

Adrian drew his horse to a stop. "Will it bother you to walk a little way?"

"I'll be fine."

"It isn't far." He got out and helped her down. As his strong hands grasped her waist, she realized she didn't fear his touch. It didn't matter how strong Adrian was. He was always gentle.

Together, they walked side by side into the forest and down a faint path. She could hear the sound of the water splashing over rocks. The smell of damp earth and leaves mingled with the scent of pine needles crushed underfoot. A few yards later, they came to the remnants of an old stone bridge, an arch broken in the middle and covered by leafy vines. Just below it, a wide flat slab of stone jutted out over the creek. A single boulder made a perfect seat in the center of it.

"How pretty it is in here." Faith sat on the moss-covered stone. The coolness of the forest and the rushing water brought a welcome relief from the summer heat and the heat in her cheeks.

Adrian took a seat beside her. "This was one of my wife's favorite places."

There it was, the reminder that he still loved his wife. Faith's heart sank. She looked down at her hands clasped together in her lap. How foolish she'd been to think there could be something between them. "I can see why she liked it."

Adrian said, "I'm sorry. I didn't bring you here to talk about Lovina."

"I understand if you feel the need to talk about her. You must miss her very much." If nothing else, Faith could lend a sympathetic ear. If that eased his pain even a little, then she would be glad.

"I did miss her deeply for a very long time, but lately I haven't been thinking about her as much."

"Why is that?"

"Because I've been thinking about you."

Faith raised her face to look at him. "Me?"

"You have no idea what kind of effect you have on me, do you? You and your creatures upset my solitude, played havoc with my work, forced me to take a look at the way I…wasn't living. Until you came, I was only biding my time until I died, and I didn't even know it."

"I'm sorry." She didn't understand what he was trying to say.

He smiled at her. "Don't be sorry. Don't ever be sorry, Faith Martin."

He reached out and cupped her face in his hands. "You and Kyle have brought joy to me when I never expected to have it again. I will never be able to thank God enough for bringing you here."

Before she could say anything, he bent his head and kissed her.

Startled, Faith pulled away. Adrian's hands still cupped her face. He stared into her eyes, waiting.

Waiting for her to say yes or no.

Oh, she wanted to say yes. She closed her eyes and leaned into his touch. Softly, his mouth covered hers again.

The sound of the rushing water faded away as Faith tentatively explored the texture of his lips against hers. Firm but gentle, warm and tender, his touch stirred her soul and sent the blood rushing through her veins. She had never been kissed like this. She didn't know it was possible for her heart to expand with such love and not burst.

When Adrian drew away, she kept her eyes closed, afraid she would see disappointment or regret on his face.

"Faith, look at me," he said softly.

"Nee."

"Why not?"

Old insecurities came rushing back to choke down her happiness. "You will say you're sorry. That this was a mistake."

"It was not a mistake. I will kiss you again if you need me to prove it."

Her eyes popped open. She couldn't believe this was happening.

He sat back. "I'm rushing you. That wasn't what I had in mind when I brought you here."

"Why did you bring me here?"

"To tell you that I care about you and about Kyle. To discover if you care about me. I know this is too soon, we've only known each other a short time. I know you have much on your mind and you are worried about Kyle's adoption, I know you have said you'd never marry again, but—is there a chance you could look with favor on me and allow me to court you?"

"Adrian, I don't know what to say."

"If you'd but nod, I'd take that as a *goot* sign."

She smiled at his teasing, even though she saw the seriousness in his eyes. How was it possible to feel so happy?

"*Ja,* Adrian Lapp, you may court me, but I warn you, I'm no prize."

"I will be the judge of that."

The word "judge" brought her back to earth with a thump. Would the adoption proceeding be put on hold if Miss Watkins or the agency learned of this? Would Adrian be subjected to the same scrutiny she had endured? It could take months. Now that the hearing was finally drawing near, she couldn't face another delay.

"Adrian, this must remain just between us until after Kyle's adoption is final."

"Why? Surely it could not hurt your case for the *Englisch* to know I stand ready to serve as Kyle's father."

She grasped his arm. "Perhaps not, but I can't take that chance. We must be friends until then and nothing more."

He covered her hand with his large warm one. "I will always be your friend. Do not look so worried, Faith. It is all in God's hands."

He was right. She relaxed and nodded. "I have faith in His grace. It will be fine."

* * *

Faith tried to retain her positive attitude as the week slowly rolled by. Miss Watkins's coming visit would be the last one before the official adoption hearing. Her recommendations would weigh heavily with the judge.

After supper on Thursday evening, Faith cleared the table and then sat down beside Kyle. He was coloring a page for his homework assignment. She said, "I have something important to talk about."

"What is it?" He exchanged a red crayon for a green one and began to work on the grass in his picture.

"Miss Watkins is coming tomorrow."

His small browed furrowed. "Why does she keep coming back?"

"Because she wants to make sure you have a safe place to live."

"I want to live here."

She planted a kiss on his brow. "I want you to live here, too. I love you."

He kept his mouth closed. He wasn't ready to say those words to her. Would he ever be? She went on as if nothing were wrong. "I want you to promise me that you'll stay close to the house tomorrow while Miss Watkins is here."

"Why?"

"We don't want her to think you don't like it here. That you'd rather live someplace else, do we?"

Confusion deepened his scowl. "I don't like it here a whole bunch."

Faith drew back in surprise. "You don't? I thought you were happy here. Is it school? Do you dislike your teacher, or is someone bullying you there?"

"School is okay. I don't want to talk about it." He gathered his paper and crayons and ran out of the room.

Faith stared after him in shock. Was she doing the wrong thing trying to raise him as Amish? Would he be happier in a home with *Englisch* parents? What should she do?

If only Adrian were here. She looked out the window toward his farm. What advice would he give? She hadn't seen him since he'd asked permission to court her. She wanted to believe it was God's plan for them to have a future together, but she was afraid to hope for such happiness.

It seemed as if she'd spent her entire life being afraid.

That night she went to bed but sleep proved elusive. She tossed and turned beneath the covers and prayed that she was doing the right thing.

When the morning finally came, she made breakfast and went out to do the chores. When she called Kyle down, her heart ached for him. His eyes were puffy, and he looked as if he hadn't slept any better than she had.

"Kyle, we should talk about what's bothering you."

"Nothing's bothering me. Can I have jelly on my toast?"

She set a jar of peach preserves on the table and waited until he helped himself. "Kyle, do you want to live somewhere else?"

He put down his toast without tasting it. "No."

"If you do, that's okay."

"Where else could I go?"

"I'm not sure, but there are a lot of people who would love to have a little boy like you."

"No, I can't go anywhere else. I have to stay and take care of Shadow. Shadow needs me. I'm his friend."

"All right. It's time to get ready for school. You'd better hurry. You don't want to be late."

She walked Kyle to the end of the lane and waited with him until the Imhoff children arrived. Faith bit her lip as she watched them walk down the road toward the school swinging their lunch coolers alongside.

When they were out of sight, she glanced toward Adrian's farm. She wanted to talk to him, to share her burden and her fears. Biting her thumbnail, she waged an internal war. Tell him or don't tell him? Before she could decide, she caught a glimpse of him driving his grain binder into the cornfield.

He had more than enough work to do. She didn't need to add to his troubles.

She opened her heart and began to pray. "Dear Lord, please let the social worker's visit go well. Let Kyle come to love me as I love him and to be content here among Your people. Give me the strength and wisdom to guide him throughout his life."

A car whizzed by, bringing her attention back to the present. She turned and walked toward the house. There was plenty of spinning to keep her busy until Kyle came home again. Praying while she was spinning was easy, too, and she had a lot of praying to do.

It was a few minutes before four o'clock when Miss Watkins arrived for her last visit. Faith put her spinning away and went out to greet her. After exchanging pleasantries, Miss Watkins got down to business. "Have you had a chance to make out a chore list for Kyle?"

"I have." Faith produced the paper hoping she had done as Miss Watkins wanted.

After reading it, the social worker looked at Faith. "Is he to clean stalls every day?"

"It is a chore most Amish children take care of at his age without a problem. I've limited it to just Myrtle's stall. Shadow is his animal, and he must take care of her."

"All right. That's a valid point." She reviewed the rest of Faith's paper and said, "It seems like a lot of work for one boy."

"There is much work to be done around here and I can't do it all."

Caroline glanced at her watch. "I thought you said he normally gets home from school at four o'clock. It's four fifteen."

Faith rose to look out the window. The lane was empty. "He should be here any minute."

"I'm concerned that he doesn't have enough supervision on his way to and from school."

"Amish children walk to school. He doesn't walk alone. The Imhoff children walk with him."

The two women sat together in silence until another fifteen minutes had passed. Faith rose to her feet again as worry gnawed at her insides. She opened the door and walked out onto the porch. Had Kyle gone to Adrian's instead of coming home?

A splotch of red by the barn caught her eye. Kyle's lunch pail sat beside the barn door. She turned to Miss Watkins. "He's here. That's his lunch cooler by the barn door. He must have gone to do his chores first."

Faith walked down the steps and crossed the yard with Miss Watkins right behind her. As soon as Faith opened the door, she knew something was wrong. Myrtle was calling frantically for her baby as she rushed from one side of the stall to the other. Shadow was gone.

"Oh, Kyle. What have you done now?"

Miss Watkins came up behind Faith. "What's wrong?"

"Kyle has taken Shadow. I need to find Adrian."

Faith rushed out the back door of the barn and through the orchard to the cornfield where Adrian was working. His horses plodded along with their heads down as they pulled the large grain binder. The noise of the gasoline engine running the belt almost drowned out the clatter of the mower head as it sheered off cornstalks as thick as her wrist with ease.

He was headed toward her, but he didn't see her. His attention was focused on the binder as it dumped out bundles of cornstalks and on keeping his horses traveling in a straight line. Faith hurried toward him knowing he would help her find Kyle.

She stumbled several times as she crossed the rough ground. Where could Kyle have gone? Why had he run away again?

She was within fifty yards of Adrian when movement in the cornfield caught her eye. She crouched down to see better between the stalks. Was that Kyle hiding in the corn?

A scream erupted from Faith as she realized the danger Kyle was in. Adrian didn't see him. The deadly blades of the binder would cut through a boy as easily as it did the tough corn.

She began to run, screaming at the top of her lungs to get Adrian's attention. Screaming at Kyle to get out of the way. She had to reach him. She tried to run faster, but her weak leg gave out and she fell.

Lying in the dirt, she screamed Kyle's name as tears blurred her vision.

Please, God, let them hear me. Please save my child!

Chapter 16

Adrian wiped the sweat from his brow and braced his tired body against the rail at the front of his binder. His head pounded from the constant roar of the gas engine and the exhaust fumes that drifted toward him. As much work as he'd gotten done today, he knew the hard part was still ahead of him. Gathering the bundles of corn and stacking them together was a back-breaking chore.

He kept his eyes glued to the binder reel. For some reason, it occasionally threw out a bundle that wasn't tied. He felt the tension in his reins change, and he looked toward his team. It was then he saw Faith running toward him across the stubble field.

She was shouting and waving her arms, then she fell. He didn't know what was wrong, but he knew he had to reach her quickly. He slapped the reins against his horses' rumps and urged them to a faster pace. The bundles of corn fell off the conveyor belt and broke open on the ground.

Faith waved him back. He could hear her shouts now, but he couldn't make out what she was saying. Miss Watkins was running toward him, too.

Suddenly, a black blob darted out of the cornfield directly in front of his horses. They shied, and he pulled them back into line when he realized it was Shadow. In the next instant he heard Faith yelling Kyle's name, and he saw the boy step out directly in front of him.

"God, give me strength!" Adrian hauled back on the lines to stop his horses, kicked the shutoff switch on the engine to kill it and threw the lever that stopped the mower blades. The horses reared back at his rough handling. The noise of the machine died away to silence.

He kept his eyes shut as the vision of Gideon running in front of that car played out to its horrible end.

"Not again, God. Don't let me see him die. Please, don't let me see him die."

He heard Faith's voice first. She was sobbing. He opened his eyes and blinked to focus. Kyle stood barely six inches away from the blades.

Adrian tried but couldn't catch his breath. He collapsed onto the platform with his head spinning. By this time Faith had reached Kyle. She had him in her arms, holding him close. Shadow, frightened and lost, called pitifully for his mother.

Faith carried Kyle toward Adrian. She called out, "He's fine. Praise God, he's fine."

He waved her away. He didn't have the strength to stand. "Take him home."

God had given him a chance to redeem himself. He

hadn't been able to save Gideon, but Kyle was alive. "Thank you, God."

Adrian gained his feet and turned his team toward home. He couldn't work any more today. Being afraid was part of being human, but shutting himself off from others hadn't lessened the pain of his son's loss. Like a knife left in a drawer unused, the edge stayed sharp. He vividly recalled every second of that terrible day.

Living meant using all his emotions. Living his faith meant trusting God to strengthen him in times of sorrow and of joy. He loved Faith and he loved Kyle, but was he strong enough to live each day knowing he could lose either one of them as he'd almost done today?

He wasn't sure.

Faith knocked at Adrian's door a few minutes before seven o'clock that night. She wiped away her tears as she waited for him to answer. She didn't know where to turn, so she had turned to the one constant in her life.

The door opened and Adrian stood before her, his face gray, his eyes sunken. He looked as if he'd aged ten years in one day. She probably looked worse.

His voice sounded raw when he asked, "How is he?"

She thought all her tears were done, but apparently she had more. They began to flow again. "They took him away, Adrian. The social worker thinks I can't provide a safe home for him and that his running away is proof that he's unhappy living Amish."

"Faith, I'm so sorry." He stepped out of the shadows and drew her into his arms.

"I don't know what to do," she wailed. Clinging to Adrian was like holding on to a rock in the middle of a raging river. She'd never needed anyone more than she needed him at this moment.

He led her into his kitchen and deposited her on a worn wooden chair. "Would you like some coffee?"

She missed his touch the moment he pulled away. "*Ja*. I'm sorry to come running to you with this, but I didn't know where else to go. I haven't even thanked you. Your quick reactions saved Kyle's life."

"We must thank God for little Shadow. I knew as soon as I saw him that Kyle couldn't be far away."

Adrian sat beside Faith and took her hand in his. "When I saw Kyle in danger I saw my son dying again, and I couldn't deal with that. I came home and lay on Gideon's bed. As my fright faded, I felt he was there with me. He was not. He's in a wonderful place where I can't go yet. I must remain here until God calls me. I realized my fear was part of being alive. You and Kyle have brought me back to life."

Tears choked her. Clearing her throat, Faith said, "I can't lose him, Adrian. I can't."

What she was about to say would put an end to anything between them. "If I move to town and live in an *Englisch* house with electricity and a telephone and enroll Kyle in the public school, they might let me keep him. To do that, I need money. You once told me if I couldn't manage the farm alone that you would buy it. Well, I want to sell it to you now."

The sadness in his eyes deepened. She couldn't bear to cause him pain, but if she had to choose between their happiness and Kyle, then it would be Kyle.

"Faith, do you know what you are saying? To do such things would go against the *ordnung*. It would put you outside of our faith. You would be shunned by everyone in the church. Your friends, my family. Can you really want this?"

She didn't, but what choice did she have? She was so confused and scared. "I don't know. I only know that I don't want to lose Kyle. Will you buy my farm?"

He sat back in his chair. "*Nee*. I will not. Do not turn your back on your faith at a time like this, I beg you. I did, and it was wrong. Grasp on to it, and it will become your strength. It took me long years to discover that, but I know it is true."

"You will not help me?"

"Not like this. Ask me anything, but I can not help you turn your back on God."

"You know what it is to lose a child." She couldn't believe what she was hearing. She'd been so sure she could depend on him.

"I know what it is to lose a child and I know what it is to find God."

The kettle on the stove began whistling. Faith rose to her feet. "I'm afraid I can't stay for coffee, after all. Good night, Adrian."

She had to get out of his house before she started weeping again. Tears would not fix this.

Adrian took the kettle off the stove and leaned against the counter with his mind whirling. Today, he'd finally come to realize God had already given him the strength he needed to face life's frailties and uncertainty. He'd come to believe that a single day loving Faith and Kyle was better than a lifetime of hiding from more pain.

Now, he was losing them both. Not by death, but by her choice.

He understood why, but that didn't ease his sense

of betrayal or loss. Faith had made a vow before God and men to remain true to the Amish religion their ancestors had died to preserve and to live separate from the world. God commanded them that it must be so in 2 Corinthians 6:14

"Be not yoked with unbelievers. For what do righteousness and wickedness have in common? Or what fellowship can light have with darkness?"

This was a mistake Adrian could not let Faith make. He took up his hat and headed for the door. He needed wiser counsel and he prayed Bishop Zook would be able to give it.

"Good luck in there today." Samson Carter, a white-haired man with a neatly trimmed white beard turned around in the front seat of his van to smile encouragingly at Faith.

"*Danki,* sir." She gathered courage before stepping outside.

He said, "I'll wait for you here."

"I have no idea how long this will take."

"Not to worry. I brought a book to read."

Mr. Carter ran a van service in Hope Springs. The retired railroad worker earned extra income by driving his Amish neighbors when they needed to travel farther than their buggies could comfortably carry them.

Faith got out of the vehicle in front of the county courthouse in Millersburg. She had just enough money left to pay Samson when he took her home.

Her farm was on the market, but until it sold she wouldn't have the money to rent a place in town. The extra money in her bank account had gone to pay the lawyer that was meeting her here today.

She glanced up at the courthouse. Three stories tall

and built of time-mellowed stone, the building was capped with an elaborate clock tower that rose another story higher. A long flight of steps led up to the main doors on the second story. Narrow arched windows looked out over the well-manicured grounds and a monument to Civil War veterans.

As Faith stared at the building, her anxiety mounted. Behind which window would Kyle's fate be decided?

She remembered Adrian's words about holding on to her faith. Could she do it if it meant losing Kyle?

She closed her eyes. "May Your will be done here today, Lord. Grant me the strength to face the outcome, whatever it may be. Pour Your wisdom into the heart and mind of the judge that he may rule wisely."

Did God listen to the prayers of someone about to turn her back on her faith? When it came time to tell the judge she would leave the Amish world in order to adopt Kyle, could she break her most sacred vow? She closed her eyes and saw Adrian pleading with her not to make that choice.

Why had God put this test before her? Hadn't she suffered enough?

It took her a few minutes to climb the steps. Once inside, a friendly security guard directed her to the correct courtroom.

Mr. Reid, her attorney, waited for her in a chair outside the courtroom door.

He rose to his feet. His smile was polite. "Are you ready for this?"

Was she? Did she have the courage to speak up for herself and for Kyle? A second later, she remembered Adrian's advice at her very first church meeting.

"If I were you, I'd go in with my head up and smile as if nothing were wrong."

It had been good advice that day. She would follow it again. Putting her shoulders back, she pasted a smile on her face and nodded. "It is in God's hands."

"Indeed it is. I will do most of the talking. You may answer any questions the judge directs at you. Have him repeat it if you don't understand."

"Will Kyle be here?"

"He won't be in the courtroom, but it's my understanding that he will be nearby."

"Will I be able to see him if the judge rules against me?"

"Let's cross that bridge if we come to it. Are you ready to go in?"

Fear closed her throat. All she could do was nod.

Mr. Reid held the door open. The room beyond was paneled from floor to ceiling in rich dark wood. At the front, the judge's bench stood on a raised platform. A large round seal was centered on the wall behind it. Flanking the seal were two flags, the United States flag and the Ohio State flag.

It wasn't until she took a step inside the room that she realized she wasn't alone. The few dark wooden benches were filled with Amish elders. Around the outside of the room, three deep, stood more Amish men and women waiting quietly, some with small children at their sides or in their arms.

Many of the faces she knew from her own church district, but there were many people who were unknown to her. Faith stood rooted to the spot. What were they all doing here? As she gazed about, one man stepped forward from the group and walked toward her.

Adrian.

Her heart turned over in her chest. Tears blurred her vision. When he said he wouldn't help she had been crushed. Why was he here now? Had these people come to denounce her?

She stiffened her spine. "Adrian, what are you doing here? Who are all these people?"

"These are your friends and your neighbors and the people you will do business with in the years to come. We are here to speak for you and for our way of life. The Amish way is a *goot* way for Kyle to grow up. He may have been *Englisch* when he came among us, but he is Amish in his heart and so are you. The judge must understand this. You do not have to face this alone, Faith. We stand with you."

In that moment, Faith could not have loved him more. He had done this for her, gathered together people to speak on her behalf. *"Danki."*

"You are welcome, *liebschen.*"

The heat of a blush crept up her neck. "How can you call me dearest when you know I was ready to turn my back on our faith?"

He took her hand. "Because I must speak what is in my heart. Listen to God, Faith, and then speak what your heart says is right."

Mr. Reid spoke in Faith's ear. "We should take our places. It's almost time to begin."

Letting go of Adrian's hand was one of the hardest things she'd ever done in her life. He gave her fingers one last squeeze and then went back to his place beside Elam Sutter and Eli Imhoff.

Her attorney led her to a small table just behind the railing that separated the judge's bench from the rest of the courtroom. Caroline Watkins sat at an identical table on the opposite side of the aisle. She nodded politely to Mr. Reid but didn't speak as she opened her briefcase and pulled out several files.

Faith sank gratefully onto the chair Mr. Reid held out for her but had no time to gather her thoughts. The bailiff at the side of the bench called out, "All rise for the Honorable Judge Randolph Harbin presiding."

A small man with silver hair entered from the door behind the bench. He wore a dark suit and a bright green striped tie.

He paused for a second to survey the packed room in surprise before stepping up and taking a seat behind the bench. He beckoned to the bailiff, and the two men shared a brief whispered conversation.

When the judge was ready, he spoke to the entire room. "This is a hearing on the petition of Faith Martin to adopt the minor child, Kyle King. Is Mrs. Martin here?"

Her attorney rose to his feet. "She is, Your Honor."

"Very good. Miss Watkins, I understand you represent the child for the State of Ohio."

She rose also. "I do, Your Honor."

"Good, then let us proceed." The judge leaned back in his chair and clasped his hands together. "Mrs. Martin, it is my understanding that you wish to adopt Kyle King and that you are his only living relative. Tell me a little bit about your circumstances and your wish to adopt Kyle."

Faith's pulse hammered like a drum in her ears. She expected it to leap from her chest at any second. She glanced over her shoulder and saw Adrian standing with his arms crossed over his chest, just the way he had been standing the first time she'd seen him outside her door. He nodded once and lifted his thumb. He believed she could do this. She believed because he did.

She rose to her feet and faced the judge. "Your Honor, I am Kyle's aunt. His father was my only brother. I can't tell you how much Kyle reminds me of him. Every day he says something or does something, and I see my brother all over again. I loved my brother and I love his child. I love Kyle's smile and his sense of humor. I love the feel of his hand in mine when we cross the street together. I know he loves me, too. I would do anything for him."

"I see that you are Amish, as are the many people you have brought to support you."

Faith heard a voice say, "If I may speak, Your Honor?"

She turned to see Bishop Zook rise from a seat behind her.

The judge arched an eyebrow. "And you are?"

"I am Bishop Joseph Zook. Mrs. Martin did not ask us to come today. We heard that this good woman might lose custody of her nephew because she holds to our ways. We wish only the chance to say that our ways are not simple and backward as some may think."

"I am very familiar with the Amish and their ways. My grandfather was Amish but left the church. Had he not, chances are I would be a farmer or furniture maker and not a judge. You'll have your chance to speak after I've heard from everyone else. Thank you."

The bishop resumed his seat. Judge Harbin said, "Miss Watkins, you've investigated this case. I have read your report, but would you summarize your findings for the court, please?"

She looked at Faith sadly. "No matter how much I wish I could say having Kyle stay with his aunt would be in his best interest, I simply can't do it. Kyle's father left the Amish faith and chose to raise his son in the modern world. He had money put aside for his son's college education. If Kyle were to grow up with his aunt, he would only receive an eighth grade education."

The judge turned his pen end over end. "The ability of a parent to provide higher education is not a prerequisite for adoption. Are you sure you're not letting your personal feelings on the subject influence you?"

"I don't believe I am, Your Honor. My job is to do what's best for him. Kyle has had significant difficulty adjusting to an Amish home. They live without electricity, something he's never done before. He has run away at least three times that I know of. The last time put him in great danger. I feel an Amish farm environment is simply too dangerous for this young boy who has grown up without any experience around machinery and animals. Now, if Mrs. Martin would agree to move into town and enroll Kyle in the public school, I think he would be much happier. I also think it would make his adjustment to living with his aunt much easier. I would agree to a new trial period of six months if this were the case."

"I see. Mrs. Martin, would you be agreeable to such a move?"

These were the words Faith dreaded hearing. She could keep Kyle if she gave up her faith, or she could stay true to her faith and perhaps lose the child she loved.

Please, God, let this be the right decision.

She shook her head. "*Nee,* I would not. She wishes

me to raise Kyle in an *Englisch* home with electricity so that he might have television and video games to play with. Yes, he is used to such things, but they do not make a home. A home is a place where a child is loved and raised to know and love God."

She studied the judge's face, but she could not tell what he was thinking. He began reading the documents before him, turning each page slowly. After a few minutes, he looked toward Bishop Zook. "Bishop, what is it that you would like to say to this court today?"

The bishop rose to his feet again. "I would ask that Adrian Lapp speak for us today."

Adrian came forward and stood beside the bishop. "I have come to know both Faith Martin and her nephew, Kyle. It is true that Kyle has had a hard time adjusting, but it is not because he can't watch television. It's because he is afraid to love his aunt. He's afraid God will take her away as He did his parents."

Miss Watkins spoke up. "Your Honor, this man is not a child psychologist."

"But I am a man who knows about loss and about the fear of losing someone if I allowed myself to love again. I lost my wife and then my son when he was only four years old. But I lost more than my family. I lost my faith. I no longer trusted God. I was afraid to love again just as Kyle is afraid. But God brought Kyle into my life to show me how wrong I've been."

Adrian turned to Faith. "I see now that loving someone is never wrong, be it for a little while or for a lifetime."

She bit her lip to keep from crying.

He faced Miss Watkins. "By taking Kyle away from Faith, you are proving him right. Don't take away the person he is afraid to love. Let him come to know God's goodness and mercy. Let him find the strength to love again."

The judge laid his papers aside and rubbed his chin. "You speak very eloquently, Mr. Lapp. I appreciate your insight. Miss Watkins, would you have the boy brought to my chambers?"

She objected. "Your Honor, the child is barely six years old. He's far too young to know what is in his best interest."

"That's true, but that's not what I'm going to ask him about. Mrs. Martin, will you and your attorney join me in my chambers? Mr. Lapp, I'd like you there, as well."

"Yes, Your Honor." Mr. Reid gathered his papers together and closed his briefcase.

The bailiff called out, "All rise."

When the judge left the room, Faith turned to look at her attorney. "Is this a good thing?"

"I'm not sure, but let's not keep him waiting." Mr. Reid held out his hand, indicating Faith should precede him.

Chapter 17

Together, Faith, Adrian and her attorney entered a spacious office situated just beyond the courtroom. The same dark paneling lined the walls except where floor-to-ceiling bookcases jutted out. They held hundreds of thick books bound in dark red, green and gray.

"I'll have you three sit over there." Judge Harbin indicated a group of brown leather chairs near the windows. He then proceeded to make himself comfortable on a matching leather sofa in the middle of the room. Before it sat a low coffee table. It held an elaborate chess set with figures carved from dark and light woods.

The door to the outside hallway opened, and Miss Watkins came in holding Kyle by the hand. Faith's heart contracted with joy at the sight of Kyle's face. She longed to race across the room and snatch him up in a fierce hug. She made herself sit still. When Kyle saw her, he tore away from Miss Watkins and launched himself into Faith's arms.

Tears blurred her vision. She whispered, "I have missed you terribly."

His voice shook as he said, "I'm sorry I ran away. I won't do it again."

Adrian laid a hand on Kyle's shoulder. "You are forgiven."

Faith stroked his hair. "I'm just happy you are safe."

Miss Watkins took the child by the hand and said, "Kyle, I have someone you need to meet. This is Judge Harbin and he has a few questions for you."

Faith and Kyle reluctantly released each other. She said, "Go and talk to the judge. I'll be right here."

"Promise?" There was such pleading in his eyes that it broke Faith's heart.

"I promise," she managed to whisper past the lump in her throat."

Kyle allowed Miss Watkins to lead him away. Adrian took Faith's hand and held it between his strong, warm fingers.

The judge patted the cushion beside him. "Have a seat, young man."

Kyle glanced at Faith. She nodded to tell him it was okay. The boy climbed on the sofa and propped his hands on his thighs. Miss Watkins took a seat near Faith.

The judge leaned toward Kyle. "My name is Randolph Harbin. These people have to call me Your Honor, but you can call me Randy. Kyle, do you know what a judge is?"

He pondered a second or two, then said, "A guy who sends people to jail?"

"Some judges do send people to jail, but I'm not that kind of judge. I'm the kind of judge who decides what's best for kids like you. Do you know how to play chess?"

Kyle shook his head.

"I guess you're a little young for that. How about checkers?"

The boy's eyes lit up as he nodded quickly and pointed toward the windows. "Adrian has been teaching me."

The judge swept the chess pieces from the board and set it between him and Kyle. From a drawer beneath the coffee table, he pulled out a stack of red and white disks and offered them both to the boy. "Tell me how you know Adrian."

After choosing the red pieces, Kyle began placing them on the board. "He's our neighbor. He's helping me become Amish so the boys at school will stop teasing me."

Judge Harbin slowly laid out his pieces. "Do they tease you a lot?"

"Not as much as they first did. Anna Imhoff gets mad at them if they do."

"And who is Anna?"

"She's my friend. She doesn't make fun of me because I can't speak Pennsylvania Dutch. She says her friend, Jonathan, can't speak it either and he's a grown-up. She's giving us both lessons. I can say a few things. Do you want to hear?"

"Sure."

"*Mamm* means mother. *Dat* means dad. *Gross-mammi* is grandmother. *Velkumm* is welcome."

"I'm impressed with what you've learned so far. Has your aunt been helping you?"

"Lots."

"I imagine she's a very good cook. What kind of things do you like to eat?"

"Have you ever had shoofly pie? It's the best. Aunt Faith makes it for me twice a week."

"I like mine with a tall glass of milk."

"Me, too!" Faith smiled at the amazement in Kyle's voice. She squeezed Adrian's hand.

"Do you have a pet at your aunt's house?" the judge asked.

Kyle grinned and folded his arms over his chest. "Yes, but it's not a cat and it's not a dog. I bet you can't guess what it is."

"Is it a horse or a baby calf?"

"Nope. It's a baby alpaca. I bet you never would have guessed that."

"Never in a million years."

"A baby alpaca is called a cria. Mine is black. Aunt Faith let me name him Shadow. When we sell his fleece, I get to keep *all* the money."

"You sound as if you really love your aunt."

Kyle's shoulders slumped. He glanced from the judge to Faith, then down at his feet. In a tiny voice he said, "Not too much."

Faith pressed her fingers to her lips. Her heart ached for Kyle.

The judge moved a checker. "How much would be too much?"

"I don't know." His voice got smaller.

"You don't know or you don't want to tell me?"

"I don't want to tell you."

"Why not?"

"'Cause I don't want God to hear."

"You don't want God to hear that you love your aunt?"

Kyle held a finger to his lips. "Shh! If God thinks I love her, something bad will happen."

"What makes you say that?"

"Because I told Mommy and Daddy I loved them when they left me at school and then God took them away. God wanted them in heaven instead of with me. He's very mean."

"I'm sure it must seem that way to you, but He isn't."

"He's not?"

"No. In this job, I talk to God all the time."

"You do?"

"Absolutely. I need His help to make good decisions. Sometimes those decisions are very hard, but I believe His will guides me."

"Would you ask him to bring my parents back? I really miss them."

Faith squeezed Adrian's hand. Poor Kyle. He had suffered so much. She only wanted to hold him and make the hurt go away.

The judge shook his head. "I know you miss them, but they can't come back. They are watching over you. Right this very minute. God is watching over you, too."

"That's what Aunt Faith says."

"Kyle, God has His own way of arranging our lives. Things happen that we don't like, that frighten us and make us sad, but He loves us, just as your parents loved you. Now, since I talk to God all the time, is there anything you'd like me to tell Him?"

Kyle glanced toward Faith. She read the indecision and the longing in his eyes. He turned back to the judge. "Tell God I want to stay with Aunt Faith and not to take her away to heaven."

Judge Harbin patted Kyle's head, then said, "Miss Watkins, would you take Kyle out to the courtroom and wait for me there? Counselor, you and Mrs. Martin may return to the courtroom, too."

"Yes, Your Honor."

"What does this mean?" Faith glanced at her attorney, but he simply shrugged.

Adrian helped her to her feet. "Be brave. It is in God's hands."

When everyone was assembled in the courtroom again, Judge Harbin motioned to Kyle. "Come up here, young man."

Hesitantly, Kyle walked up and stood beside the bench. Judge Harbin picked up his gavel. "Kyle, do you know what this is?"

"A hammer."

"It's called a gavel. It's a very powerful tool. If I say, 'order in the court' and bang this gavel, everyone has to be silent."

"Cool."

"It is way cool. Today, I'm going to let you use my gavel because this is a very special day. It's a day you will always remember. Today, we are going to change your name to Kyle King Martin. Do you know why?"

"Because you are going to let my aunt adopt me?"

"That's right. And when I say it, I want you to bang

that gavel so that everyone knows it's official. Are you ready?"

Kyle nodded and took the gavel in his hand. Judge Harbin looked out over the courtroom. "I do hereby grant the petition of Faith Martin to adopt the minor child, Kyle King."

Grinning from ear to ear, Kyle smacked the gavel down as hard as he could. The courtroom immediately erupted into cheers.

Late in the afternoon, Faith and Kyle got out of the van in front of her house. Samson carried Kyle's bag to the porch, congratulated Faith again and drove off. On the front steps of her home, holding Kyle's hand in hers, she raised her face to the sun and closed her eyes. Kyle was staying! Praise God for His goodness.

Kyle was hers.

The phrase echoed inside her mind in an endless refrain. She could scarcely believe it. Her prayers had been answered. She had regained her child and her faith all in one day.

When she opened her eyes, they were drawn across the fields to Adrian's farm. Much of the happiness in her heart was due to him. If Adrian had not gathered the church members together and spoken for Kyle, the day might have had a very different outcome. Love for Adrian warmed her soul.

Her thoughts were interrupted when another car came up the drive. To her surprise, she saw it was Miss Watkins. What was she doing here?

When Kyle saw the social worker get out of her car, he threw himself against Faith, wrapping his arms around her legs. "I get to stay, right? The judge said so."

Faith quickly sought to reassure him. "You will stay forever and ever."

He looked into her eyes. "Are you sure?"

"I am."

Looking to Miss Watkins and then back to Faith, he whispered, "You promise?"

She picked him up and kissed his cheek. "I promise."

Miss Watkins came forward. "I give you my word that you can live here for as long as you want, Kyle. Just promise me you won't run away again."

"I won't. Not ever. Aunt Faith, can I go tell Shadow I'm staying?"

Faith lowered him to the ground. "Go tell all the animals."

He raced away to the barn. Faith pressed her hand to her lips to hold on to the joy that filled her to overflowing. To think she'd once wondered if she could love her brother's child as much as her own.

Miss Watkins cleared her throat. "I hope you realize that I only wanted what was best for Kyle."

"I know that."

"Would you mind if I stop in to see him from time to time? He's a remarkable young man." Tears sparkled in the depths of her eyes.

Faith grasped her hand. "You will always be welcome in our home."

"Thank you." Caroline returned to her car and drove away. When the dust settled, Faith saw Adrian walking across the field toward her.

How could one heart hold all the love she felt without bursting? It truly was one of God's miracles.

On the day they'd first met, she had wondered what

it would be like to have a husband so strong and sure of his place in life. Would she have the chance to find out or had she ruined her chance at happiness by her willingness to put aside her religion?

She prayed he could forgive her.

She waited until Adrian reached her side. He took off his hat. "Faith Martin, I have something I wish to speak to you about."

He sounded so nervous. Had he to come to tell her he wanted to call off their courting? His reaction at the courthouse had given her hope that he still cared for her. She said, "I'm listening.

"You have too much work to do to get this place ready before winter. You don't even have hay put up for your animals yet and your barn needs repairs."

"That is true." A lecture on her property wasn't what she had been expecting when she'd seen him coming.

"It will take the entire fall to get things ready."

"You're right. It will."

"I have hay and I have paint."

She crossed her arms. "Is there a point to this?"

He turned his hat around and around in his hands. "Your boy needs a man to help guide him on the path of the righteous."

· "I agree. Bishop Zook has offered to help in just such a fashion."

"That is *goot*. You are not alone, Faith. There are people who will willingly help you carry your burdens."

"You mean like pruning my trees and shearing my alpacas?"

"*Ja*, those things, too."

It wasn't exactly the declaration of love she longed to

hear. Maybe he had changed his mind. Did he see her as fickle and weak? Mose always said she was weak. Had he been right?

"Adrian!" Kyle's excited shout made them look toward the barn. The boy came running toward them at full speed. Adrian dropped to one knee as the boy raced into his arms.

Wrapping his arms around Adrian's neck, Kyle said, "I get to stay here forever and ever."

"That's something I was hoping to talk to you about."

Kyle drew back to look him in the face. "What do you mean?"

Adrian glanced up at Faith. "I reckon I should ask both of you since you're a pair now."

"Ask us what?" Kyle demanded.

Adrian rose to his feet still holding Kyle. "I never thought I would love anyone the way I loved my son and my wife. But, Faith, I love Kyle as much as I loved my own son, and I love you as much as any man can love a woman."

Faith heart began pounding in her chest as it swelled with happiness. She couldn't speak.

Kyle said, "Are you gonna get mushy with my Aunt Faith? Ben said you were gonna."

Adrian grew serious as he gazed into Faith's eyes. "I must have a chat with my brother, but in this case he was right. Faith, will you marry me and live as my wife for all the days God gives to us?"

She choked back her tears of joy. "I will."

She took a step closer and cupped his face with her hands. "I didn't believe love like this was possible, but now I know it is. We are truly blessed."

Adrian lowered Kyle to the ground and took Faith in his arms. His kiss was everything and more than she'd dreamed it would be. After a long breathless moment, he drew back and tucked her head beneath his chin. "Thank you for saying yes. Thank you for showing me my way back to God."

Kyle wrinkled his nose. "Does this mean we're going to live at your place?"

Adrian smiled at him. "If that's all right with you?"

"I reckon it is. Guess I'd better go tell Shadow we're moving, after all." He took off and jogged toward the barn.

Adrian's eyes softened as he watched Kyle. "I can't believe I was so afraid of love and hid from it all this time."

"I was afraid, too, but you have shown me that a man can be kind even when he is upset. I learned to trust you, Adrian. That is something I was sure I would never do again. You've given me the one thing I need that no one else can give me."

"What is that?"

"Your love."

He smiled and pulled her close. "*Ja,* my heart holds all the love you will ever need."

She gazed into his eyes, happier than she could ever remember being.

He said, "I don't want to wait to marry you. I hope you weren't planning on a long courtship."

Unable to resist teasing him, she said, "I don't think we should rush into anything. It takes a long time to get to know a person well."

He nodded. "You're right. We should give ourselves two years."

"At least." She tried to keep a solemn face but failed. There was no way she could wait that long.

Pulling her close again, he whispered, "I'll be lucky to last a week. How soon can we get hitched?"

"With all the preparations I need to make…six months." When he was holding her close it sounded much too long to wait.

"My mother will help, and if I know her, she'll cut that time in half."

"If she can help arrange a wedding in three months, she is a worker with great talents."

"Then both of you should get along fine for you are one, too, my love."

When his lips closed over hers once more, Faith knew she'd found more than a home in Hope Springs. She'd found courage, a family and a love unlike anything she'd dreamed was possible.

* * * * *

We hope you enjoyed reading

Light the Stars

by *New York Times* bestselling author

RAEANNE THAYNE

and

The Farmer Next Door

by *USA TODAY* bestselling author

PATRICIA DAVIDS

Both were originally Harlequin® series stories!

From passionate, suspenseful and dramatic
love stories to inspirational or historical,
Harlequin offers different lines to
satisfy every romance reader.

New books in each line are available every month.

LOVE INSPIRED

INSPIRATIONAL ROMANCE

Uplifting stories of faith, forgiveness and hope.

Harlequin.com

Gabe Fisher heard the rumble of a truck approaching and
then a horn blaring. He glanced in that direction and saw
a woman walking into the roadway. Her gaze was fixed
on something in the distance. Didn't she hear the truck?
The trucker would never be able to stop in time. Gabe
dashed toward her.

The truck's brakes squealed. Gabe heard screaming
behind him. He yelled at her to get off the road. She didn't
move a step. He closed his eyes and launched himself
toward the woman, knowing they were both going to die.

He hit her and locked his arms around her as they
landed on the hard pavement. His momentum sent them
rolling to the grassy verge on the opposite side of the
road. When the vehicle flew past, he kept his eyes closed
for several seconds until he realized he was alive.

He opened his eyes and gazed at the woman beneath
him. She pressed her hands against his chest. "You saved
my life."

"Are you hurt?"

"I don't know. My head hurts."

The rush of adrenaline drained away, leaving Gabe weak and shaken. "Don't move until you're sure. Didn't you hear the truck?"

She was staring at his mouth. "I saw a moose. I wanted a closer look."

He rolled off and sat beside her. "It was almost the last thing you saw."

Her family surrounded them and helped her to her feet. They were motioning with their hands as they hugged her and checked her for injuries. It dawned on Gabe that they were using sign language. Was the woman deaf? Was that why she hadn't heard the trucker's horn or his shouts?

Jonah, pale and shaken, left his sister and came to sit beside Gabe. "You saved Esther's life. I'm the one *Daed* sent to look after her. I reckon I didn't do such a *goot* job. I just remembered something."

"What?" Gabe asked.

The child looked up. "Esther is the one *Mamm* picked for you."

Don't miss
Someone to Trust
by USA TODAY *bestselling author Patricia Davids,*
available February 2021 wherever
Love Inspired books and ebooks are sold.

LoveInspired.com

LIEXP23300

LOVE INSPIRED

INSPIRATIONAL ROMANCE

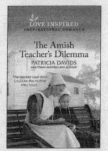

Save **$1.00**

on the purchase of ANY
Love Inspired book.

Available wherever books are sold,
including most bookstores, supermarkets,
drugstores and discount stores.

- ✂

Save **$1.00**

on the purchase of ANY Love Inspired book.

Coupon valid until March 31, 2021.
Redeemable at participating outlets in the US and Canada only.
Not redeemable at Barnes & Noble stores. Limit one coupon per customer.

Canadian Retailers: Harlequin Enterprises ULC will pay the face value of this coupon plus 10.25¢ if submitted by customer for this product only. Any other use constitutes fraud. Coupon is nonassignable. Void if taxed, prohibited or restricted by law. Consumer must pay any government taxes. Void if copied. Inmar Promotional Services ("IPS") customers submit coupons and proof of sales to Harlequin Enterprises ULC, P.O. Box 31000, Scarborough, ON M1R 0E7, Canada. Non-IPS retailer—for reimbursement submit coupons and proof of sales directly to Harlequin Enterprises ULC, Retail Marketing Department, Bay Adelaide Centre, East Tower, 22 Adelaide Street West, 40th Floor, Toronto, Ontario M5H 4E3, Canada.

52616802

U.S. Retailers: Harlequin Enterprises ULC will pay the face value of this coupon plus 8¢ if submitted by customer for this product only. Any other use constitutes fraud. Coupon is nonassignable. Void if taxed, prohibited or restricted by law. Consumer must pay any government taxes. Void if copied. For reimbursement submit coupons and proof of sales directly to Harlequin Enterprises ULC 482, NCH Marketing Services, P.O. Box 880001, El Paso, TX 88588-0001, U.S.A. Cash value 1/100 cents.

5 65373 00076 2   (8100)0 12465

BACCOUP23300

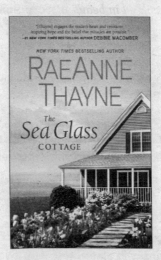